IMPLOSION

IMPLOSION

An Economic Thriller about War,
Environmental Destruction and
Corporate Greed

A Novel based on Facts

Peter Koenig

iUniverse, Inc.
New York Lincoln Shanghai

Implosion

An Economic Thriller about War, Environmental Destruction and
Corporate Greed

Copyright © 2007, 2008 by Peter Koenig

iUniverse books may be ordered through booksellers or by contacting:

iUniverse
2021 Pine Lake Road, Suite 100
Lincoln, NE 68512
www.iuniverse.com
1-800-Authors (1-800-288-4677)

Because of the dynamic nature of the Internet, any Web addresses
or links contained in this book may have changed
since publication and may no longer be valid.

ISBN: 978-0-595-45349-8 (pbk)
ISBN: 978-0-595-69391-7 (cloth)
ISBN: 978-0-595-89661-5 (ebk)

Printed in the United States of America

*   *   *   *   *

The scathing criticism of the World Bank, IMF, and similar institutions is not meant to be an accusation of the staff. Most are highly dedicated and professional individuals, whose work is devoted to distributing the world's wealth more equitably--and to reducing poverty.

Thanks to the World Bank's staff, Mr. Wolfowitz had to resign his post as President, amidst scandals of nepotism and corruption, after only two years in office. The institution's Board of Directors and representatives of its member countries closed their eyes for more than a year to Wolfowitz's deceitful, arrogant management style. They acted only under pressure of the staff and the media.

This book intends to highlight the high-level political interference and manipulation of the world's foremost economic development institutions by domineering member governments for the benefit of their corporations, their elite--and to the detriment of developing countries' populations, the very people they are supposed to help according to their UN-backed mandates.

*   *   *   *   *

Cover Design: Mónica Vega-Christie; Website: www.vega-christiestudio.com

For:

Monica

Julia　*Daniel*　*Sabrina*

CONTENTS

Glossary xi

Foreword xxi

1.   The Kidnapping.. 1

2.   The New Society University, Buenos Aires,
      Argentina 9

3.   The Base 17

4.   Europe and the Empire... 19

5.   The Guaraní Liberation Front 25

6.   The Dungeon 30

7.   The Ayacucho Connection 46

8.   The Chase.. 53

9.   The US Treasury at the International
      Monetary Fund... 59

10.   The World Bank's Secret Board Meeting...................... 67

11.   The Fight for Water, Gas and Oil 81

12.   Burning of Coca Fields, Cash Crops—and
      Children 89

13.   The Venezuela Factor 97

14.   Police State versus Democracy 101

15.   The Group of 77 Conference—Dacca,
      Bangladesh... 106

16. US Congress and CEOs—Closed Door
     Hearings 129

17. The Financial Ivory Towers of Washington..................... 140

18. The Freedom Ranch.. 149

19. World Bank Staff in Solidarity....................................... 165

20. Saving Project 'Golden Enterprise' 173

21. The Grasberg Goldmine.. 202

22. Reassignment to Sudan's Darfur Region......................... 217

23. Turning Point 226

24. The Emperor's Master Plan—the Collapsing
     Trust in the World's Main Reserve Currency 240

25. The Empire Strikes Back 246

26. The New World 262

27. The Implosion... 270

Final Chapter—Epilogue.. 284

Author's Notes 287

Glossary

'Bellavista'	Fictitious name for Peruvian partner of U.S. mining corporation exploiting the *Yanacocha* mine
CAMISEA	Huge gas and oil extraction project (consortium of some 25 transnational corporations) in the Cuzco Amazon region of Peru
ERB	'Ejército Revolucionario Boliviano' (ERB—Bolivian Revolutionary Army)—a fictitious militia organization, their *comandante* is Jaime Rodriguez
Eudemonism	Economic system based on social values and human wellbeing (based on Aristotle's concept of ethics)
Financial Ivory Towers	World Bank and IMF
'Freedom Ranch'	Headquarters of *'Save the Amazon'*, located on the outskirts of Tarapoto, at the edge of the Peruvian Amazon
FTA	Free Trade Agreement
GDP	Gross Domestic Product (economic indicator for a country's annual internal production)

'*Gold Dust*'	Fictitious name for the U.S. mining corporation exploiting the Grasberg mine in Papua, Eastern Indonesia
GLF	the Guarani Liberation Front—fictitious international activist group in defense of the '*Guarani*' aquifer', the world's largest freshwater reserve—Santiago is their chief rebel
Hydrocarbons	In this Novel are referred to as Petrol and Gas
Kilimanda	Fictitious country in East Africa
Machiguenga	Indigenous society living in the Cuzco Amazon; their livelihood and environment is being destroyed by the *CAMISEA* petrol and gas exploration project
'*Mariscal Estigarribia*'	Military Base in North-Western Paraguay
Matanga	Fictitious island country in the Indian Ocean
MDG	Millennium Development Goals—Eight major development targets to improve health and other social services, set by the United Nations (September 2000—Millennium Declaration) and to be reached by 2015
MRC	'*Movimiento para el Rescate de los Cocaleros*' (Movement to Save the Cocaleros—their *Comandante* is Lucho)—fictitious organization
'*Mujibur Rahman Center*'	Fictitious conference palace in Dacca, Bangladesh, where G-77 meeting takes place
NGO	Non-Government Organization, also referred to as 'charity', or not-for-profit agency

Petroleros Bolivar	Venezuela Oil Company—fictitious name
STA	*'Save the Amazon'*—a fictitious international socio-environmental NGO, a research center for anti-globalization activities
'Sweetwater Mining Corporation' ...	Fictitious name for U.S. mining corporation exploiting Peru's *Yanacocha* gold mine in Cajamarca, Northern Peru
TLC	Tratado de Libre Comercio
'Vision for a new World'	International workshop, organized at the *'Freedom Ranch'* by Moni Cheng, the Novel's main protagonist
'XXION Oil&Gas', *'Mercurio Oil'*, *'Chavelin Oil'*, *'UK-Petrol'*	Fictitious names for international petroleum corporations

*****

Names of Main Protagonists

Moni Cheng	Principal female character, leader of the *Save the Amazon*
PJ	Alias Paul Jordan—principal male character, a renegade World Banker
Ahmend	Alias Mokhtar, head of a non-profit health agency (AIDS), and clandestine organization for the independence of South Sudan—fictitious names
Alonso Gonazo	Fictitious name of former Bolivian President

Antonio Esteban	Peruvian Member of Parliament, Socialist Party, friend of Uncle Gustavo's—fictitious name
Aurora Jimenez	Spanish Executive Director, World Bank—fictitious name
Contessa	U.S. Secretary of State—fictitious name
Cynthia	PJ's ex-wife, living in Sevilla, Spain, mother of Primavera, their daughter
Dick Dingo	President of the World Bank—fictitious name
Eric Svensen	Executive Director of the Nordic Countries, World Bank—fictitious name
George Blandell	U.S. Secretary of the Treasury—fictitious name
Gustavo	Moni Cheng's uncle and adoptive father
Haviland Gersten	Managing Director of IMF—fictitious name
Hernan	Melissa's cousin, activist for the independence of Santa Cruz and Tarija, Bolivia—fictitious names
Jaime Rodriguez	*Comandante*—Rebel leader of the Bolivian Revolutionary Army—fictitious names
Jamal and Ramona	Leaders of activist group "*Grasberg Demise*", a socio-environmental NGO in Papua, Indonesia—fictitious names
Jim Werter	Chief Executive Officer (CEO) XXION Oil&Gas, Bolivia—fictitious names
Lucho	*Comandante*—'*Movimiento para el Rescate de los Cocaleros*'—MRC (Movement to Save the Coca Growers)

Marco Vidali	World Bank Director for Andean countries—fictitious name
Marvin Fox	CEO Mercurio Oil, Bolivia—fictitious names
Mary	Aunt Mary—Uncle Gustavo's wife
Maurice Vernier	French Executive Director, World Bank—fictitious name
Melissa	Jim Werter's Secretary (XXION Oil&Gas, Bolivia)
Mr. Moffot	CEO of '*Gold Dust*', U.S. corporation exploiting Grasberg mine in Indonesia—fictitious names
Mr. Sukarato	Mayor of *Timika*, city closest to the Grasberg mine—fictitious name
Primavera	PJ's younger daughter, living with her mother in Sevilla, Spain
Raul Sanchez	PJ's boss at the World Bank
Ron Rommel	Former U.S. Secretary of Defense—fictitious name
Rosalind	PJ's second wife, who left without a trace
Sybil	PJ's older daughter, living in Finland
Veronica and Enrique	Close friends and associates of Moni Cheng at the '*Freedom Ranch*'
Ms. Zengh	Chinese Executive Director, World Bank—fictitious name

"… I shall be telling this with a sigh; Somewhere ages and ages hence; Two roads diverged in a wood, and I, I took the one less traveled by; And that has made all the difference."

—Robert Frost

Thanks and Appreciation

Thanks go foremost to '*Radio Pacifica*', as well as to WPFW, Washington D.C.'s Jazz and Justice Radio, but specifically to Amy Goodman's '*Democracy Now*'. Amy's and her team's extraordinary daily newscasts gave me information that was nowhere else available; information hidden and at best deformed by the corporate media and more often than not ignored by other public broadcasting stations.

People who inspired me include my good friend Alfredo Sfeir-Younis, who has taught me about the collective energy in pursuit of peace; and in no order of priority, Greg Palast, BBC Investigative Journalist, whose work gave me insight into the Machiavellian world of capitalism; John Perkins, who dared to tell the world about his own experiences with corporatocracy and the primary financial institutions in his Bestsellers, '*Confessions of an Economic Hit Man*' and '*The Secret History of the American Empire*'; as well as the historians and human rights activists Howard Zinn, who reminds us of the Power of the People; Noam Chomsky, whose mastery of undistorted history has long ago projected the ascent of the neo-conservative U.S. Empire; as well as Jimmy Carter, who far beyond his Presidency is fighting for justice and peace. And there are many silent heroes, whose voices are oppressed, but who nonetheless motivated and encouraged my writing.

Not least, I would like to acknowledge Clive Hamilton, Australian political theorist, who in his 2002 "Growth Fetish", shares my ideas about a new economic model, where 'wealth' is human wellbeing, peace and social equality—*Eudemonism* ('*Eudaimonism*', Greek term coined by Aristotle to describe a concept of ethics leading to human and social happiness and wellbeing).

'*Wikipedia*', the free Internet Encyclopedia, is an extraordinary source of information and facts (despite recent corporate meddling) about all aspects of world politics, history, philosophy and life. It offered me a wealth of data and historic details, and so did specific websites—too many to name them all. I am deeply grateful to all those who contributed to these invaluable resources of knowledge.

Heartfelt thanks go to my friends and reviewers for their patience and sensible advice: Jerry (Bethesda, Maryland), Harald (Oslo), Karl and Kurt (Geneva), Cloudia (Honolulu), José (Lima), Daniel—both Daniels (Denver and Lima)—Gerhard (Frankfurt), Fernando (Turks and Caicos), Bjorn, (Vientiane, Laos), and Fadi (Washington, DC).

I am grateful to Herta for her patience, professional editing and advice. Warm thanks to my daughter, Julia, who from an insider's point of view gave me sensible pointers. And, finally, affectionate appreciation to my wife Monica, who designed the book cover, for her many invaluable ideas, but above all for her loving encouragement to persist and persevere with this 'project'.

Foreword

The world is a kaleidoscope of political, economic and fiercely violent hotspots. Sporadically, the media exposes some of them, those of primary interest of the reigning power. They flair up on the front page of newspapers and on television news like brushfire, stay in the limelight for a few days, then they disappear. They are hardly ever analyzed, let alone connected one with another. They are handled like deliberate distractions from the real world of wars, globalization and corporate greed.

We live in a *crisis society*, drowned in a cacophony of news, of which we comprehend only disparate fractions, and which keep us aloof and unaware of the Big Picture.

This novel is fiction based on facts—'*faction*'. It attempts to connect the dots between these seemingly unrelated events, through a riveting story about a young, determined Andean woman, who finds her kindred spirit in a renegade World Banker. They and a group of likeminded idealists and visionaries from around the world are fighting this unfettered capitalism and corporate greed that is engulfing the globe, with dissemination of truth information and with non-violent actions, in view of a new economic system based on social justice, equality and peace. A series of Author's Notes at the end will provide the reader with some of the true stories or facts behind those illustrated throughout the novel.

Judging from my own experience in a lifelong career in development economics, the Western approach to stamping out poverty has failed miserably. The World Bank, IMF and other so-called development institutions have loaned trillions of dollars to poor countries over the past five decades—to no avail. Instead of reducing destitution, this gigantic influx of money has increased debt and impoverishment. The average well-being of an African, for example, is stuck at the level of the early nineteen seventies. Never mind the World Bank's illustrious mission statement ... "Our Dream is a World Without Poverty"—at the entrance of its flamboyant HQs in Washington DC.

Mandated by the money lenders, the debtor countries have to cut food and energy subsidies and restructure and privatize public and social services. This has resulted in massive unemployment, higher prices for food, water and electricity. To service their debts, developing countries are forced to sell off their natural resources—mostly hydrocarbons, gold and other high-value minerals—at a pittance to typically U.S. transnationals. If this movement continues to go unchecked, most developing countries are condemned to poverty in perpetuity.

Today the two foremost financial Ivory Towers are nothing less than extensions of the U.S. Treasury. They are mere instruments of Big American Corporatocracy. These financial institutions vehemently propagate and practice a neoliberal economic model—privatization and laissez faire 'free market' theories *ad nauseam*—which has proven to be a complete and utter failure the world over.

But there is light at the end of the tunnel. Two bold premonitions of the novel have already materialized since I started writing it: The head of the World Bank, Wolfowitz, was kicked out, not so much by the institution's Board of Directors, but by its irritated, unwavering and persevering staff. And Venezuela's President Hugo Chavez has announced the creation of *Banco Sur*, a South American development bank for socioeconomic advancement of the subcontinent. The new institution is expected to gradually displace the Financial Ivory Towers and their associates.

The people of the world are waking up. Citizens revolt against the systematic, ruthless destruction of their environment and societies, against the theft of their natural resources, and against privatization of their public services. They rebel against the Anglo-Judeo-Christian Empire's unilateral annihilation of their social fabric and cultures. They revolt against the imposition of the neocon's short sighted two-dimensional capitalist growth values.

The democratic liberalization of Latin America from more than 500 years of domination and colonization and from the fangs of the '*Washington Consensus*' doctrine sends a strong message to the rest of the world. It is catching on. The power of the people is unstoppable. Informed people cannot be oppressed.

—Peter Koenig

1

The Kidnapping

Santa Cruz, Bolivia—a hot summer Saturday evening in late January 2007

The stranger, sitting at the candle-lit table in the crowded *Oro Negro* restaurant, was visibly nervous. His eyes darted from his watch, to the TV screen in the corner and to the entrance. He was obviously waiting for someone. The place was filled with the lively rhythm of a bossa nova, but sporadically interrupted by CNN's monotonous reporting of the war. He vaguely overheard something about Shiite terrorist commandos killing five U.S. soldiers, and three roadside bombs killing 90 Iraqis. The news had become so repetitive, hardly anybody in the bistro paid attention.

He felt insecure in this place, where he was the conspicuous gringo, sticking out like a sore thumb. He knew nobody in this town. Not even the person he was supposed to meet.

Suddenly the door opened and an alluring young woman entered. She wore tight jeans and a body-hugging white blouse, revealing her tanned midriff. She looked like she was in her mid to late twenties. Even the laid-back clientele turned to catch a glimpse of her. An idle waiter asked whether he could help. She muttered something, glancing at the stranger's table. The waiter smiled slyly. He accompanied her to the gringo's table.

Getting up in his well-mannered way, the stranger held out his hand to greet her. She ignored the gesture, walked around the table and kissed him on the cheeks, whispering, "We know each other; just act as if we knew each other. It's important that we do not look like strangers." He looked a bit perplexed, but nodded. They both sat down. Her eyes surveyed the room to see if anybody had paid attention, but it seemed that no one had. The brief visual commotion faded. She introduced herself, "I am Moni Cheng. I hope you haven't been waiting too long. I was held up by a police road block. The demonstrations, you know. They suspect everybody to be an insurgent, even if you don't look like one."

For a few seconds, she looked at him intently. This tall, youngish looking middle-aged man didn't appear conventional at all. His longish dark, slightly curly hair covered his ears and his mustache and broad smile put charming creases in his cheeks. He had a faintly darker-than-white complexion, but was clearly not Latino. 'Where could he be from?' she wondered.

He was immediately suspicious. Not because of her roadblock story, but because of her good looks. When his boss, Raul Sanchez, mentioned the meeting with this young woman—how did he know her anyway?—He hadn't said how strikingly beautiful she was. Could it be a plot to lure him into the hands of the enemy? Maybe she was someone else. James Bond movies came to mind, in which beautiful and sexy women seduced the good guys who were to be 'neutralized' by the enemy. His thoughts were quickly distracted, though, as he was charmed by Moni Cheng's dark sparkling eyes with a slight Asian slant, her dark, almost black, shiny hair framing her high cheekbones. She had a radiant smile showing a tiny gap in a row of otherwise impeccable teeth. Charming, he thought. He had a special liking for women who had what he though was a birthmark in their smile. Did it remind him of his long departed mother?

Noticing his stare, she gently tapped his arm, "Are you listening?"

"Oh, yes, of course. I was just wondering ..." He wanted to say, why Raul didn't warn me about your knock-out looks. But instead said, "Where's your name from? Are you of Chinese descent? And by the way, I am Paul Jordan. But everybody calls me PJ."

"Hi, PJ. I am so glad to finally meet you. Raul told me a lot about you."

Again, he was surprised. How could Raul have told her *a lot* about him? Did his boss know her that well?

"My name is not my real name. I mean, they say my real name was Pilar." She said. "My Uncle Gustavo who raised me, he and my Aunt Mary gave me this new name. He said it would remind him of his mother Monica, who died when he was only twelve. But he kept a fond memory of her."

She discretely glanced around the room. Nothing had changed. So she continued. "I grew up in Ayacucho, in the Sierra of Peru. When the police found me in the burnt-to-the ground ruins of my parents' modest house up on the hills above the city, they took me to my dad's brother, Uncle Gustavo. I was less than a year old. My parents and three siblings were killed in the fire. They said it was an assault by the *Senderos*. But maybe it was the military. We don't know for sure. They want me to believe it was the *Senderos*. I think it was the military. Whoever did it also destroyed or stole the little my parents owned. I don't really remember my parents. My uncle showed me a few photographs. That's all. The perpetrators let me live, perhaps because they didn't see me, or maybe I was too small. Even murderers could have a heart—no?" Her perfect English had a slight Latino tang, almost unnoticeable.

"I am so sorry," he said.

"Don't worry. It's been a long time. Plus, I really have no memory of my parents. Uncle Gustavo and his family just call me Moni Cheng. This was at once my first and last name. Uncle Gustavo's last name is Muñoz. Since he is my dad's brother, it would be mine too. But I never use it. I'm just Moni Cheng. Period. Like you are PJ."

She looked at his watch. A sign that she was under time pressure? But she continued anyway. "One day, my uncle explained to me this odd composite name. Not only was Monica his mother's name, but she, his mother, also told him about her favored Saint, *Santa Monica*. She was apparently a brave and gentle, but determined, woman, born in the fourth century in North Africa, and died at the age of 54 near Rome. She was married to a pagan with a hot temper. She had three sons. Her married life was far from happy, but she endured with patience and kindness and became a guiding light for other women, who suffered a similar fate in her native town."

He stared at her attentively, giving her the impression he was really interested in the Saint story. "My uncle is not religious at all. He looks at religious books, like the Bible, the Old Testament, the Koran, the writings of Buddha—as documents of history and philosophy. But Saint Monica's story really impressed him. He was and is a really loving adoptive father to me. He made me enter the University of Ayacucho, from where I later transferred to the University *'La Catolica'* in Lima. He wanted me to become like *Santa Monica*, strong and bright, with a bold mind. I remember all this because sub-consciously it must have impressed me a lot. But I am sure, I will never be a saint, or come even close to matching her sainthood." She paused with a glowing smile. "Of course, I don't want to be a saint either. I don't believe in that stuff."

Then she added, "Also, judging from artists' renditions of Santa Monica, I do not resemble her at all. The Saint didn't look like a Chinese. The *Cheng* part of my name has to do with my Asian looks. My uncle often told me, 'Asians are smart people, with a lot of perseverance. Moni Cheng, you will become an important woman in your lifetime. You will change the world'. I always laughed. I think I look more like a native Andean Indian than Asian. He was so kind to me. I miss him, haven't seen him for almost a year."

PJ was intrigued by the story and wanted to know more. But right now, this was not the reason for their meeting. He needed other information from her. He strongly hoped this was not the last meeting, that there would be plenty of opportunities to learn more about her. He said, "Sounds very interesting. Maybe later you could tell me more about your adopted family and how you became a famous Andean woman. When Jaime Rodriguez contacted me suggesting I meet with you, he said you had important information for me that would *blow my mind*—he probably meant that will surprise me."

Moni Cheng looked at him as if she were sizing him up, his trustworthiness. And then she said, "Yes, Jaime is a good man. He told me you are a little naïve but not the bad kind." She paused reflectively. Then by way of mending the possibly slight insult, she continued, "Sorry, those are his words; you don't look naïve to me. He also said if I convince you with what I have to tell you, you may help us. It may indeed be a shock for you, but you will survive it, especially if you have an open mind, as Jaime says you do."

She took a sip of the mango juice the waiter had brought and took a deep breath. Time was clearly not an issue. For PJ this was an indication of trust. He felt good.

She continued, "Here is the story. Since you worked in Bolivia, you must know that this is a very poor country. The vast majority of the people are destitute. About eighty percent of them are indigenous. They live in an economy completely different from the one that reigns in La Paz and other big cities, where the white elite lives. According to your institution, the World Bank—we also call it the G8 Bank, because it serves mainly the rich G8 countries—most of the Bolivian population earns less than a dollar a day. I don't really know how these bankers calculate this, because many of the *Aymaras* and *Quechuas* never see money, they barter and trade goods amongst themselves. Anyway, they *are* very poor. But I do not understand why their poverty should be comparable to a dollar amount."

PJ had a hard time concentrating on what the attractive woman in front of him was saying. He was totally mesmerized by her, to the point where she nodded at him with a smile, "Are you listening?"

"Yes, of course. I am here to help. Tell me how."

"The poor *Indios* have always been poor, since their independence some 200 years ago. In fact, they have not known independence for at least 1,000 years. First they served the *Incas*, then came the Spaniards. When the Spaniards eventually left under the pretext of giving the natives their independence, the white elite, the Hispanic descendents of the colons, kept dominating the indigenous populations. Times may now change. As you know, one of theirs, Evo Morales, of *Aymara* and *Quechua* descent, was recently elected President."

"So I heard," PJ interjected.

"But Bolivia is also a very rich country. Surely, you must know that too. In its ground lays a fortune of natural gas, more than $600 billion worth. The President wants to regain control over what belongs by nature and by the state's sovereignty to Bolivia. Bad tongues in the foreign media call this 'nationalizing' the production of gas, which is now dominated by foreign companies, many of them from Brazil and Argentina, but also some Americans and Europeans. In fact, what he wants is to renegotiate exploitation agreements to get a fairer deal for his people. This means breaking contracts."

His gaze was still steady. But he twirled his fingers nervously, thinking, 'What does she want me to do about these contracts?'

As if she didn't notice his emerging unease, she went on. "If he does so, your Bank has threatened to freeze all ongoing operations. Worse, your director said all outstanding loans would be called back at once. The International Monetary Fund would apply the same rule, a total of about $1.2 billion."

She stopped wondering what impact such a stark message would have on PJ, her hopefully new ally. But he gave no visible sign of shock. She continued, "Do you have any idea what this would mean? It could mean civil war, because the government would have to reduce the already low salaries of civil servants and other meager social benefits. The World Bank wants to help the foreign companies which have been looting Bolivia's gas over the last ten years, leaving only 18% of the profit in the country. We want *you* to help us. You know the insides of the Bank, you have connections."

Now PJ was indeed shocked. First, he had no idea whether this was true. Second, how could he help? He was a simple economist, working only on infrastructure projects, roads, water supply systems, and so on. This immediately brought to mind another problem, *privatization* of public utilities. Privatization of water supply in Cochabamba and El Alto were other disasters for Bolivia in which the World Bank was involved, in fact, they were the instigators. Contrary to what his smart and pretty discussion partner thought, he had no 'connections' of any significance.

But he didn't want to deceive her. He started, "Yes—but how … how could I possibly help?"

Before she could answer, Moni Cheng's smart cell phone with its salsa ring interrupted the conversation. She reached for her purse, grabbed her phone and said "Hello," which was followed by about a minute of silence. Her face grew somber, then dead serious. Finally she said, "Right now?" And then "OK."

Disconnecting her mobile, she got up and said, "I must go right away. An emergency. I'll be in touch." And then she was running out the door.

PJ didn't even have time to think 'what next,' before the door slammed open again, and three masked gunmen stormed towards PJ's table. They were dressed in black, the two in front with handguns drawn, and a third a couple of steps behind with an AK47. Two of them grabbed him under his arms, the third staying back covering the restaurant, while his colleagues dragged their hostage out of the place. His last thoughts before being pushed in the backseat of a waiting car were about these James Bond movies.

*   *   *   *   *

2

THE NEW SOCIETY UNIVERSITY, BUENOS AIRES, ARGENTINA

A few days later ...

At four o'clock in the afternoon, the building of the 'Sciencias Economicas' of the New Society University of Buenos Aires at Avenida Cordoba was abuzz with people. At least a thousand students and visitors were crowded into the main aula. Two adjacent halls were full with its overflow. The event was a presentation by a Peruvian woman on the state of globalization, corporate greed, and imperialism.

The occasion was to mark Argentina's intermediate but remarkable success in reducing its poverty rate from more than two-thirds of the population in early 2002, right after the economic collapse, to less than one-third in March 2006.

Through a back door a stunning looking young bronze-skinned woman, in a lofty white summer dress and a red silk scarf, stepped onto the small podium, walking towards the microphone. A moderator greeted and embraced her, then presented her to the public as Moni Cheng, a recent PHD graduate in socio-economics from the university *'La Catolica'*, in Lima, Peru, where until recently she had been teaching international trade and development. In her capacity as an academic, she had unsuccessfully argued with a Peruvian congressional trade commission, against the Free Trade Agreement (FTA, or *TLC—Tratado de Libre Comercio*) between Peru and the United States. The commission promoted the FTA against all odds.

The presenter went on explaining that about two years ago with two like-minded international friends she created "*Save the Amazon*," a non-profit organization with an agenda reaching far beyond the environment. She was inspired by the social and environmental calamities emanating from the FTAs and 'globalization,' the shiny trend word encompassing everything from corporate expansion to increased poverty. Moni Cheng had become an activist in the fight for environmental protection, moderation in the use of natural resources and for lessening the plight of the poor.

The audience gave her a standing ovation, yelling welcome wishes, slogans of sympathy and indicating their consent, before even listening to what she had to say. The young lady was standing tall behind the mike with a disarming smile, sparkling eyes and a face framed by a long, dark, flowing mane. She bowed lightly a couple of times towards the full aula, then lifted her arms, in a thank-you gesture and asked for quiet.

"It is an honor to be here this evening to share some experiences and ideas with you, my friends and fellow-students; one never ceases to be a student, because the universe of knowledge is infinite. I would like this conference to be as interactive as possible. So, you are welcome to interrupt me if you have a burning question." She glanced at the moderator for approval.

"Let me begin with an anecdote, in fact, a devastating experience I had a couple of weeks ago, when I visited *Yanacocha* (*see Author's Note 1*) in the high pampas of the Andes, in the northern part of the *Cajamarca* Region of Peru. *Yanacocha* is one of the world's biggest and most profitable goldmines. Up to now it has produced more than 100 tons of gold at a value of more than $7 billion. It is an open pit mine, stretching over 250 square kilometers. It straddles a large watershed.

"It is so profitable that the World Bank's private financing arm has lent it $150 million and taken a 5 percent equity share in it. The mine is run by the world's largest gold mining firm, the US Sweetwater Mining Corporation. A partner and lesser shareholder is the Peruvian company Bellavista.

The audience was quiet.

"The mine is also beset, as you may imagine, by far reaching corruption, involving Peruvian and foreign government officials during the reign of President Fujimori. Government officials were paid to push legislation through Peru's Congress that would exempt Sweetwater from paying taxes, allowing them to fully expatriate their profits and closing an eye to environmental misconduct by the company. In addition, Sweetwater paid the local police extra money to protect the mine from local *campesinos* who may claim their abrogated rights."

Some stirring and murmurs came from the audience. But Moni Cheng went right on. "This is a completely illegal practice, but can be found almost everywhere, when U.S. corporations have a large stake in 'exploiting'—in most cases this is an euphemism for 'stealing'—another country's valuable resource. Authorities usually close their eyes. They are paid to do so."

Voices could now be heard. An angry young man yelled, "This is sheer disrespect of environmental and social protection standards! A few years ago, a large amount of Mercury was spilt by a truck, contaminating the area of *Choropampa*. Some thousand people were poisoned. They have not yet received any compensation."

In the front row, a young woman with dark-rimmed glasses and short brown hair stood up, waving for attention. "I am Peruvian and know first hand how these people couldn't care less about the damage they cause. All they are interested in is profits. My father has been working there until recently, when cyanide was discharged into waterways and underground water reserves. The company didn't warn the population about the accident until about 20 people got poisoned and had to be hospitalized. My dad was one of them. He barely survived. Now he can hardly breathe and can no longer work. He was such an active man. Now he is just lying on the sofa and is embarrassed that he doesn't even have the energy to help my mom in the house. It is so sad

… to see him. He was such a strong man, caring for his family.…" The woman started sobbing.

Moni Cheng explained, "To separate the gold from the rock, the company uses large quantities of this highly poisonous substance. Instead of safely disposing of the toxin, the corporation simply releases it into the wilderness, killing fish, fauna and flora, including medicinal plants used by the indigenous population. People and their livestock have become ill. A council of victims launched a law suit against the company in Peru—to no avail. They then took the case to a court in the U.S. and are now awaiting the result—hoping at least to be compensated for lost income from the destroyed and contaminated soil and water."

Moni Cheng's eyes darted across the audience for other comments. There were none. She continued. "The company is relentless in its drive to maximize profits. People recently took to the streets, when they learned about Sweetwater's plans to expand the mine into a new area, called "*Cerro Quilish*," a mountain believed to harbor billions of dollars worth in gold, but a mountain also rich in water resources. For the local farmers *Quilish* is a sacred mountain. They fiercely distrust Sweetwater, perhaps remembering the story of *Atahualpa*, the Inca Emperor, who promised his Spanish captors a room full of gold to buy his freedom. The Spanish took the gold but killed him anyway."

Hesitant laughter and sympathetic voices went through the conference hall. Moni Cheng continued. "The *campesinos* know that foreigners steal their resources and destroy their habitat. *CAMISEA* (*Note 2*) the oil and gas company in the Amazon region is another typical case of environmental destruction. As for the gold mine, thousands of protesters in the town square of Cajamarca have forced the company to cancel its expansion plans—for now …"

She lifted her head in a questioning manner. "But for how long?— According to the latest reports, the company is now promising all sorts of comparatively trivial 'presents' to the population, like schools and health centers, a road which would mostly serve the mine's own interests. All this with no firm commitments to a timeline. They may find a thousand reasons to delay delivery of these goods. What's worse, the government has, in principle, already acquiesced to these 'gestures.' Pressure may be strong for the local populations to go along with it and give the company free reign to also invade and pollute their holy mountain."

Another male voice from the audience: "To make things worse, most of these companies have been exempt from paying taxes. In other words, they take the entire profit from mines and oil fields out of the country, leaving misery and poverty behind. Even people who work in these mines are still poor. They have nothing that would perhaps one day improve their standard of living."

The tone of his voice increased. He waved his left fist. "They get poorer and poorer, with life expectancies falling because of the contaminated land and water; and because of the increase in human misery. And institutions like the World Bank—in fact a UN agency—condone this behavior by becoming a shareholder of the company. This is an outrageous shame!"

The man made his point. He got cheers. The audience was ready to rise in a sympathy protest wave of applause. But Moni Cheng, with a calming hand quieted them down. "Any questions?"

A young man with a *Che Guevara* tee-shirt wanted to know what happened with the lawsuit in the U.S. courts.

Moni Cheng answered, "Sweetwater was able to delay it for more than three years. No settlement is in sight yet. And if and when it comes, it is too late for many and not enough for those who must survive and go on with life in *Yanacocha*."

What was supposed to be a little anecdote for starters had already become a major discussion topic. It looked promising for the rest of the seminar. Lack of interaction was not to be feared. Nevertheless, now she had to move on.

She said, "This is but a vivid example of corporate greed, an invasion helped by so-called 'globalization' and imperial power, ruthlessly supported by the US military killing machine. I will step back in time and talk from the perspective of history and attempt to analyze where we stand today, why and how events—like the downfall of Argentina, the economy of one of Latin America's richest countries—was made possible, and why there is literally no end in sight. Actually, if we, the citizens of the world at large, look on without a consolidated ... without united and strong actions to stop this brutal invasion of land and property by our North American neighbor, their subjugation and torture of our citizens, we may all live in poverty and under a cruel dictatorship in less than a generation.

"Don't forget, over the last 40 years, and after hundreds of billions—trillions in fact!—of so-called development investments by the World Bank, the International Monetary Fund—IMF (*Note 3*), the Inter-American Development Bank (IDB) and the like, the proportion of rich and poor in Latin America has not changed. If anything the gap between the haves and have-nots has grown wider. This is even reflected in one of the World Bank's own reports."

Moni Cheng took a sip of water, paused a moment and smiled at the audience with alert eyes. She continued. "Let me remind you of a little bit of history which will lead into today's globalization ..." she hesitated, and then went on, "and tomorrow's downfall. The quest for global dominance is not new. It is almost as old as mankind and stretches from way before the Mesopotamian, Egyptian and Greco-Roman Empires to the more modern ones of the Mores, the Ottomans, Spain, Portugal, Italy, the United Kingdom, and France. They all attempted to take over the world's riches for the enjoyment of their elite. Dominance meant subjugating conquered lands and people and whatever they owned. Until the emergence of the more recent Western European Empires 'natural resources' were largely limited to land and people and their potential to work the land and soil.

"These empires have eventually collapsed, caved in by peoples' uprisings or been defeated by other emerging empires. With the Industrial Revolution in the middle of the 18th Century in Britain...."

Moni Cheng halted as shouts became audible from the corridors of the university. But ignoring them, the guy in the *Che* shirt rose again. "The world had the good fortune of Marx and Engels. This enormous social injustice was fertile ground for their philosophies. But mind you, principals of socialism or communism were practiced already in different forms and shapes by ancient cultures, some of them right in our Hemisphere, like the Mayas and Incas. Many of today's isolated tribal cultures, from the Amazon to Africa to the jungles of Sumatra, are practicing some kind of socialism."

The noises from outside the auditorium became stronger and now also caught the attention of the audience. Moni Cheng said, "Something is going on out there ..."

A fairly corpulent blond female student, her hair in a bun, and with a freckled distraught face, interjected, "What does all this have to do with 'globalization' or the downfall of Argentina's economy? We are being side-tracked here. This is not a forum for leftist propaganda. It is a university. We are here to learn about Argentina's disastrous economy, about our corrupt rulers who brought this calamity upon us and then try to blame foreigners, about the unpaid debt ..."

She couldn't finish her sentence. Almost simultaneously the two side doors to the conference hall swung open and a bunch of rowdies stormed in throwing firecrackers at the audience. Screaming chaos ensued. The police barged in from the entrance back-stage, subdued the intruders and dragged them out. All that happened in the span of a couple of minutes and left the conference in disarray. People started leaving the *sala*.

Moni Cheng shouted to be heard. "Please, please—don't go away! We are not going to be displaced by a bunch of hecklers. Let us reassemble and decide how to continue...." Her voice trailed off in thin air. Most people scrambled to leave the aula. Only a few hardcore types stayed behind, silently waiting this out.

To herself, Moni Cheng reflected whether there may have been a connection between the last intervening blond and the intrusion of the trouble makers. Was she giving them a signal? Was this all planned …

* * * * *

3

THE BASE

Meanwhile in Paraguay ...

At the U.S. Military Base in *Mariscal Estigarribia*, an American Army Colonel was shouting at General Valdez, "Your government signed an agreement six months ago with my government allowing the establishment of a U.S. base here. We are bringing in 1,000 men to train your own people for the next three years! Otherwise you are helpless when the social unrest spills over from Bolivia."

A red-faced Valdez replied, "Yes, I know of the agreement. But it says 300 men and not 1,000. Besides, there is no conflict. Bolivia is our neighbor and friend. I order you to withdraw at least 700 men within a week."

In a room next door, a BBC news bulletin was reporting that twelve U.S. soldiers were missing in Iraq. The foreign press suspected that they defected. But a spokesman for the Pentagon insisted that they were abducted and the perpetrators would be brought to justice.

Mariscal Estigarribia is a town of about 50,000 in the sparsely populated, desert-like *Chaco Boreal* region of northwestern Paraguay. In 1945 it was a military outpost, known as *López de Filippis* and was later renamed to honor the general whose strategy allowed Paraguay to take control of the region during the *Chaco War* (1932-35), a territorial dispute between Bolivia and Paraguay. Bolivia attempted unsuccessfully to gain better access to the Paraguay River, which would have given the landlocked country access to the Atlantic.

The sparsely populated area is ideal for military maneuvers. It is also strategically located to strike the southeastern provinces of Bolivia, where huge gas extraction investments of international petroleum companies are located, including large U.S. corporations.

Mariscal Estigarribia also happens to be sitting on top of the *Guaraní*, arguably the world's largest fresh water aquifer system. It is shared between Argentina, Brazil, Paraguay and Uruguay. It extends over an area of about 1.2 million square kilometers, has an estimated volume of about 40,000 cubic kilometers and could supply the world population for 150 to 200 years with 100 liters per person and per day. It is an enormous resource to capture, as the world's fresh water pools are receding. U.S. and European water supply corporations have long been eyeing this aquifer, as water may soon become a highly valued commodity, perhaps exceeding petrol.

Before the gringo colonel could respond, General Valdez' cell phone rang. His face remained stern, emotionless, as he listened to the message. When he finished his conversation, in which his only response was "Yes sir," he told the U.S. colonel, "OK, we will discuss this tomorrow with the Minister of Defense." Without saluting, the colonel turned on his heel and left the room.

Valdez sat reflectively on the chair behind his desk. Why had the Defense Minister changed his mind? Wasn't he the one who told Valdez before that the Americans were exaggerating again and that no way would they be allowed to break their agreement and bring in 700 men more than had been agreed earlier?—As he was pondering these thoughts, he heard explosions and gun fire in the distance. It must be coming from the city. He jumped to his feet, ran out the door and raced off in his Land Rover toward town.

*   *   *   *   *

4

Europe and the Empire

At the New Society University in Buenos Aires ... continued

The unrest was cleared up. Of the thousand plus attendees to the conference celebrating the success of the Argentinean economic recovery, only a couple of dozen were left after the melee. Moni Cheng led them through a back door of the big hall to a small conference room on the third floor, away from the main thoroughfare of the University. Two rows of folding chairs were arranged in a circular formation. Moni Cheng was seated among the guests.

Her white dress bore some sooty stains and streaks, traces of the clash. The red scarf was now mesh-like, decorating her ponytail. She was in her full element and appeared totally undisturbed by the recent events. She opened the gathering lifting a small plastic bottle of water as a toast. "*Salud!* And thank you friends for persevering. We will not be outdone by some hooligans who were probably paid by an obscure group of people interested in keeping the truth about the dark decade of Argentina under wraps—or to stop the truth from being spread to the public."

The group returned the toast with the bottles they collected from the University cafeteria on the way to their new venue. From the second row across from Moni Cheng, came the determined voice of a young man with a beard and glasses, a truly intellectual frown on his face. Moni Cheng had not noticed him before.

He said, "The few of us left here, we all know what happened to Argentina. Let's not rehash it. Anyway, the same or similar attempts of subjugating South American countries is going on as we speak, I think of Ecuador, whose currency, the *Sucre*, was converted to the dollar in 2000, of course, under pressure of the usual villains, the World Bank and IMF. They acted on behalf of the U.S. Government which is interested in dollarizing all economies harboring resources that are of interest to them. They then can be more easily manipulated. The same is happening to Peru. They officially maintain the *Sol* as their legal tender, but over the past ten to fifteen years, the economy has gradually adopted the dollar for all major transactions, like real estate deals, motor vehicle purchases and most large construction contracts. By volume, some 70 to 80 percent of all money transactions are already carried out in dollars. Both Peru and Ecuador have huge hydrocarbon reserves … must I say more?"

There was no direct reaction as his eyes circled the room. He seemed distracted. "What I really wanted to suggest is to talk about the role Europe should have in world affairs. They seem to linger on the sidelines, while the American Empire is taking over the world." He pensively stroked his beard and continued, "This sad dollarization just reminds me of my home country, Honduras, where you can practically no longer find menus in restaurants with prices printed in *Lempiras*. They are all in dollars. What's worse, people just accept it."

The man was visibly unhappy. To help move him back on track, Moni Cheng asked, "You would like us to discuss the role of Europe?—That would certainly be an interesting debate. What is Europe doing to stem this trend? Where is Europe entering this equation? Europe has a history, is supposed to have dignity and common sense after a long experience in warfare. Is there any plausible explanation why they sit on the sidelines while all these devious, deceitful, corrupt, Machiavellian American shenaniganisms are taking place?" She didn't hide her anger and was sure it also reflected the opinion of the

Honduran friend and probably of most, if not all, the students in the room.

Moni Cheng continued. "Let me step back in history and try to find an answer. Yes, where does Europe stand in all this?" Her face appeared somber. "During the last two centuries, Europe internalized the blows from the fall of its empires and from two World Wars. Only in the last 50 years, has it started to come to grips with its own identity. It is not there yet. In the process of working towards that goal, and instead of building up a weapons arsenal that might compete with the U.S., Europe has built a system of social protection, unparalleled elsewhere in the world. It is a combination of industrialized capitalism and the socialist ideas of equality through social safety in health, education, unemployment and old age. Much of the added value from production was channeled into this social safety net for all—largely at the cost of tangible economic growth and militarization."

A dark voice almost next to Moni Cheng said, "I am Hans from Germany." He was a tall guy. He wore heavy boots and had a big dark mustache, from behind which a broad smile opened up like the sun appearing from behind a cloud. He continued, "I have been living in South America for the last three years. I am amazed and delighted at the political developments that have taken place here. After all, as of now about 80 percent of the southern subcontinent's population live in left or left of center democracies. And I mean Democracies with a big D, because their leaders have all been democratically elected. Nothing to compare with the manipulated, obfuscated and treacherous elections that are taking place in the United States. This new scenario is already opening up to new markets, to Europe, away from the northern dominance, to which Latin America has been subjected since its independence."

He realized he hadn't made his point yet about Europe, so he added, "What I mean is that in part, thanks to the South American countries' bold move away from North America and towards Europe—and even Asia, Europe is slowly awakening to the reality of having been bulldozed and left behind by the steadily rising Judeo-Anglosaxon, U.S.-led imperial power and that new alliances are possible. European countries don't need America for their economies to survive. For example, for Argentina, the European Union is the first partner in cooperation, investments and trade. Some European countries may still be inclined to stay the course of the Empire, but not the people. You find at least three quarters of Europeans who are opposed to U.S. politics around the world, especially their wars and violence, and who increasingly dislike American omnipotence.

A flamboyant redhead with dark-rimmed glasses in the front row shook her head. She stood and said to her German colleague, "How dare you say, Europe is waking up? When your own people recently elected a rightwing government, when France just moved to the right? This is the first time in the Fifth Republic, if my memory serves me, that the French have elected a right-wing government, including the parliament. Previous governments were either left of center or right of center, often with a 'co-habitation' status, when the President had to choose a Prime Minister from the opposition. And what about the eleven new EU members? They were all recently freed from the dominance of the former Soviet Union. They are happy to be in the EU for the subsidies they now will get and because of the proximity to the European market. But politically they are more aligned with the U.S. neocon, free-for-all politics than with Europe's traditional social-democracies ..."

She sounded utterly disgusted and was almost out of breath. But she wasn't quite done. "Sorry to say, no awakening yet! From their honorable high grounds in the 1950s and 60s, European governments have become a spineless lot of political wimps, dancing to the beat of the American Empire. Examples abound: their position of buckling under to the pressure of the U.S. during the Israeli-American 2006 aggression against Lebanon; and what are they doing to stop the American supported Israeli genocide in Palestine?—They cave in and follow the

U.S.'s deadly sanctions on a freely and democratically-elected *Hamas* Government."

Although this promised to become an interesting debate, Moni Cheng felt that there was little direction to it. Why not convert the discussion into a constructive workshop on Europe's role in the world theatre. She intervened, gesturing with her water bottle towards the woman who just spoke, "What's your name?"

"I am Gabriela from Paraguay."

Moni Cheng now pointed the bottle to Hans and then to the Honduran friend who said he was Anastasio and asked them, "How would you like to lead three working groups for the rest of the day—and if needed tomorrow too—all discussing Europe, its future role in the global circus? And maybe you can even think of a new world economic system, based on equality. We all have noticed the present one does not work for most of the people. It is not sustainable. If you all agree, I propose that we discuss what we, *we* the people, can do to engage European governments to stand up to their world responsibilities, to become an effective counterweight to the U.S. corporate empire."

The group nodded in agreement, one guy yelled, "Yes, right on!"

"Before we embark on our working group tasks," Moni Cheng declared, "Let me invite you to an international brainstorming forum, '*Vision for a new World*', that shall take place a few weeks from now at *Save The Amazon's* Freedom Ranch in *Tarapoto*, Peru. I will get you the precise dates after consulting with my colleagues."

Gabriela smiled. She was proud to have contributed to this debate, and to being considered a member of this activist organization. She stepped towards Moni Cheng to embrace her, when a massive thud shook the building, small pieces of cement and dust raining down from the ceiling.

*   *   *   *   *

5

THE GUARANÍ LIBERATION FRONT

A few days later ...

Just after nightfall at a hidden camp, some 30 km east of *Mariscal Estigarribia*, Santiago was sitting with his back against the front wall of his hut. From inside the house came the sounds of a television reporting on the war in Iraq. Another two hundred Iraqis killed. An employee of a U.S. contractor was kidnapped and beheaded. An American helicopter was shot down. All five U.S. solders aboard were feared dead.

Santiago was addressing about three dozen of his comrades of the *'Guaraní Liberation Front'* (GLF), who were assembled in a half-moon around him.

"Comrades," he exclaimed, "the explosion and subsequent shots you heard this afternoon from the city center have nothing to do with us, although the mayor blames us for it. That is what the news media broadcast throughout the country. They need a scapegoat and we are ideally suited for this role. We don't like the establishment of *Bacal* in our city, or the rumors that they may take over the city's water supply system, and we have said so. Peacefully. This looks more like U.S. instigated violence. The CIA may have paid off a group of rightwing radicals to spread unrest, so that the police and military can interfere—and to justify the large American presence on our soil."

The GLF was an activist group that came into being a few years earlier as an environmental non-governmental organization—NGO for short—to protect the huge *Guaraní* aquifer. In the meantime, the group had become a political organization to defend this enormous underground freshwater reserve against foreign interests. They became alarmed when the Bacal Company established an office on the outskirts of *M. Estigarribia* about six months earlier. Bacal is a California-based service and management giant, a formidable U.S. government contractor. They are also connected with *Halbatar*, a Texas-based oil exploration and service company. Together they own a sizable minority share in *Danube-Water*, an international water supply and sanitation corporation with headquarters in Vienna, Austria.

Santiago continued, "But what are we going to do, if Bacal does take over our city's water supply system? It is only a small step from managing water to exploiting our *Guaraní*." He glanced around to make sure everyone was listening.

A short-haired brunette in blue jean shorts joined in, "You remember the case of El Alto and Cochabamba in Bolivia, where a popular uprising had to kick out *Danube-Water* after they tripled tariffs and people's water supply was cut off when they couldn't afford to pay. Several people were killed in the fight with police?"

"You are right, Cintia," answered Santiago. "We cannot just stand by and watch. But let's try peaceful means, before we use force. The mayor has agreed to meet with me tomorrow afternoon. I would like two or three of you to come with me. Why don't you join me, Cintia—and you, Roberto and Gonzalo, may also want to come along." He noted his colleagues' signal of agreement.

"OK, let's meet here at noon tomorrow. In the meantime, maybe you, Gonzalo, can find out who was behind the riots this afternoon."

* * *

The following afternoon, the four literally stormed out of townhall, where they'd had a completely frustrating meeting with the mayor. As they were walking to their rickety '74 Chevy, Santiago fumed, "I am sure the mayor was paid off. That's why he didn't even want to listen. Besides, Gabriela, his secretary told me in confidence that the mayor was called this morning to a secret meeting with the Minister of Defense."

Gabriela was a clandestine member of the GLF. For obvious reasons she couldn't attend GLF meetings, but had a close relationship with Santiago. She had also just returned from attending a conference on 'Globalization' in Buenos Aires. She'd taken a couple of days off from work, disguised as sick leave.

The group piled into the Chevy and drove towards the outskirts of town, when Gonzalo said, "About the riots yesterday, the demonstrators were no right-wingers. They are workers of the municipal water company. A friend who works there told me that a day before they were contacted by two well-spoken guys. They said they represented a socialist movement with branches in labor unions throughout Latin America and they wanted to support them against privatization of their water company. They gave them booby traps, loudspeakers and apparently lots of money."

Santiago thought this sounded suspicious. He didn't know of a leftist movement that incorporated all of Latin America. He said, "I don't believe this story. I've never heard of such a movement. There is something fishy here. We'd better find out more about these two 'brotherly sympathizers'. Gonzalo, through your friend at the water company, could you investigate who these guys are, where they can be reached. This is not over yet. We have to prepare employees. Fortunately, there was nobody killed yesterday. But the harm was done. This is probably enough justification for the thousand U.S. troops to stay in the country."

The road leaving the city was still cluttered with cars and motorbikes in the late afternoon traffic. Santiago was at the wheel, when his phone rang. He answered and listened in silence, then said 'thank you' and hung up.

He shook his head. "What did I tell you, amigos? Gabriela says the mayor met this morning with the Defense Minister ... and, and with General Valdez, the commander of *Fort Estigarribia*—and—believe it or not, the U.S. colonel, the commander of the U.S. contingent at the Fort." He paused for effect and continued, "The topic was short and sweet. Yesterday's riots. The Minister cannot afford risking Bacal's safety, lest the country risk the ire of the U.S. Government and with it the annual $ 300 million USAID package. Or so he was told by the U.S. Ambassador, who called him immediately after the riots. In other words, the thousand American soldiers will stay. We are lucky, if they don't increase the number."

That evening, Santiago went to Gabriela's apartment. He usually waited until nightfall and parked a few blocks away. He always made sure he wasn't being followed, because he didn't want to jeopardize Gabriela's job and life, and also his relationship with her. In addition to providing him with valuable information, she was also a wonderful, smart woman, and a great lover. He wished he could see more of her and more openly. The only time they'd been able to freely walk the streets and act like a couple was about a year ago when they went to Mar del Plata for a ten day vacation. Even then, they didn't travel together, but met at the hotel.

Gabriela must have been waiting. As soon as he knocked at the door, she opened and pulled him in. They kissed passionately, stumbling to the bedroom. Santiago loved this ritual. They passionately pulled each others' clothes off. Then, with a sudden change of pace, when they stood naked, embracing, she gently kissed him all over, starting with his face, slowly working her way down. Eventually they would drop to the floor and make love, leaving the neatly made bed intact.

Later, at a candle-lit dinner table, she took his hand and looked him in the eye, "There is more to the story than I could tell you over the phone. I saw a secret document, or something like a plan. Later this year, Bacal plans to take over our municipal water company with the help of a World Bank loan. Most important, under their 30-year concession contract they will have unlimited access to the waters of the *Guaraní.*" She eyed him earnestly. She had his full attention. "In exchange, the U.S. government plans to give Paraguay a present of sorts—$300 million of aid per year for the next three years. Just imagine how much they must estimate the value of this fresh water source to be! Of course, that's peanuts compared to the real value of this tremendous underground pool. The document was signed three days ago between the U.S. Ambassador and our President."

The following morning, Santiago left Gabriela's bed early. Usually he stayed until she got up, had breakfast with her and then left. But this time, after a sleepless night, he rose and dressed at five, wrote on a piece of paper, "Sorry, had to leave early. Let's plan a vacation. How about the Amazon region of Peru? I have never been there." He had no idea that Gabriela had just been invited to a '*Vision for a New World*' forum in Tarapoto.

He had very warm feelings for Gabriela, but could never get himself to tell her that he loved her. Instead, he drew a rose and signed 'Santiago.' Probably Gabriela would not know whether this was his way of telling her he loved her, or whether he was just leaving her with the symbol of the socialist movement.

*   *   *   *   *

6

THE DUNGEON

When PJ woke up, he opened his eyes to pitch black surroundings. He had no idea where he was or how long he'd been unconscious. He felt thirsty, then he noticed a steady, slow dripping noise and a foul mildew smell. He figured that the oppressive air must mean he was in a small room, perhaps an underground bunker.

His last memory was of the three men dragging him out of the restaurant in Santa Cruz. They must have drugged him. His bones ached. Besides his voracious thirst, he felt okay. He had no notion of time. Hours or days could have passed since he was captured. They'd left him in a sitting position. When he wanted to move his limbs, he couldn't. Then he realized he was tied to a chair.

He wondered what they wanted from him. What they planned to do to him. Hours went by before a door opened. The narrow stream of light revealed a black silhouette. A flashlight hit his eyes.

"Are you finally awake, Mr. Jordan?—I hope you had sweet dreams." These words came from a male voice in perfect American English.

"Where am I? What the hell is this all about? What do you want from me?" PJ demanded in a petulant voice.

"Hey, not so fast. One thing at a time. First, we can't tell you where you are; second, Mike will ask you a few questions and if we are happy with the answers, we'll let you go."

PJ noted the name, but it didn't mean anything to him. "At least stop shining that damn light in my eyes."

The man didn't answer, nor did he shift the flashlight. Instead, he approached PJ, and PJ saw that he had a gun in his other hand and that he was masked. Was he one of the kidnappers? Difficult to say. The one with the flashlight called to his buddy, "Hey Mike, come here. We've got some work to do."

Another silhouette appeared in the opening, his face also covered by a black ski mask. He carried a big knife. The blade scared PJ more than the gun. But the knife, for now, only served to cut him loose from the chair. They yanked him up, and PJ noticed how weak he was. His knees felt wobbly as he they pushed him forward into a brightly lit room. His eyes squinted from the sudden light, and once they adjusted, he looked around the bare room. Just a couple of chairs and a little table in the middle of a room. A light bulb hung from the ceiling. A spotlight from one of the corners painted a round white circle on one of the chairs in the center. They pushed him to sit down on it.

PJ tried, but he had no idea what this was all about. He'd seen scenes like this in movies and had read about them in spy books. Why him? It had to be related to Moni Cheng, he thought. But what? "Who are you? What do you want from me?" he said.

Before he could take a breath for the next question, the guy called Mike slapped him in the face. "We ask the questions, not you, understand?"

PJ gave him a blank look and said nothing. In the next instant, Mike hit him again. "Understand, I asked."

"Yes."

"Who sent you to Santa Cruz?"

"My boss and colleague, Raul Sanchez."

"Where is he?"

"No idea."

He was struck again. This time by Mike's right hand, the one with the gun. PJ's left eyelid split open, blood ran down his face profusely.

Afraid of being hit again, PJ ventured an answer. "Last time I saw him, he was in the World Bank's Lima Office."

"When did you last talk with him?"

"He called me three days ago and asked me to go and meet a young lady in that restaurant in Santa Cruz." As he spoke, he realized he didn't tell them the entire truth. In fact, Raul only told him to meet Jaime Rodriguez. Jaime would arrange a meeting for him with an important woman. He also felt like he'd just betrayed Moni Cheng. What if they didn't know about her? But this doubt was erased in the next instant.

"Where did Moni Cheng go when she left the restaurant?"

"I don't know. I'd hardly started speaking with her, when she received a phone call and ran out of the restaurant. Less than a minute later, you, or three men like you, busted in and kidnapped me. That's all I know." He was afraid, he would be hit again. But so be it. That's all he knew. That time nobody slapped him.

Mike asked, "How do you know Jaime Rodriguez?"

PJ was surprised. Why did they know about Jaime Rodriguez, the *Aymara* rebel leader from Potosi? In fact, he didn't really know him. He only saw him once and that was because of Raul. So he'd driven from La Paz through Potosi on his way to Santa Cruz. The truth was he didn't really know why he'd met him. The only thing that came out of their brief meeting was the directive to meet Moni Cheng in Santa Cruz. Raul had confirmed this, when PJ called him after his encounter with Jaime. This is what he told his captors.

"And what did Rodriguez tell you?" Mike said.

"That I should go to this particular restaurant and wait for a young woman. She would tell me more. He didn't even mention her name. I suspected it had something to do with gas wells, but I am not really sure. As of now, I don't know, because Moni Cheng never really got to speak to me." This wasn't quite true either. But they wouldn't know.

The two hooded men glanced at each other, and then abruptly left the room. PJ was left alone for a couple of hours, the spotlight on his head. After a while, he felt a burning sensation on his skull. He grew exhausted, closed his eyes and tried to sleep, but couldn't. He was nervous. Who were these men? They must be Americans. Where was the third one?

When they returned, Mike spoke, "Okay, we'll let you go. Just make sure you stay on the right side."

"What is the right side?"

"You'll know, as soon as you transgress."

They grabbed him by the arms, put a hood over his head, pulled him up some stairs, out into the cool fresh air, and then pushed him in the back seat of a car. They drove for hours over curvy, bumpy roads, before getting to what seemed to be a more even highway. The car radio was on an English speaking station; pop music, every so often, was interrupted by a news bulletin. The news kept repeating itself: In Afghanistan, allied forces bombed a wedding, killing 120 local civilians, including 37 children. NATO forces claimed they were terrorists, although ground searches did not reveal any such links.

Then the vehicle stopped. The door opened and two pairs of hands pulled him out and dropped him by the side of the road. Doors slammed and the car sped off. His legs were free, but his hands were bound. He struggled to his feet and managed to pull off the hood. It was daylight, probably early morning, and very cold. He had no idea where he was. He walked towards a group of houses in the distance. They'd taken everything away from him. He had no phone, no money, no ID.

A farmer tending to a few llamas in a small corral told him that he was near the town of *Sicuani*, in the Peruvian Sierra, about an hour's drive away from *Cuzco*. The man cut off the ropes around his wrists and invited him in to have some breakfast, which consisted of boiled potatoes, *Habas*, salty fresh cheese and a pot of hot tea. PJ felt energized from the hefty meal.

He was surprised that the farmer didn't ask him any questions. It occurred to him that strangers suddenly appearing in handcuffs and with bruised faces must not be uncommon in this region. Scary. But he didn't give it any more thought. He just wanted to move on. He had to get to Lima as fast as possible and talk to his boss.

After breakfast, the peasant accompanied him to the road, stopped a truck loaded with vegetables and asked the driver to give his guest a ride to Cuzco.

* * *

PJ stood in front of the monumental cathedral in the central plaza of Cuzco, where the truck driver had dropped him off. Before he moved on, PJ sold him his watch, the only thing of some value the kidnappers didn't take. For the 50 Soles he got, he could at least make a phone call to Lima.

It was early February. The mid-summer sun was pleasantly warm, but almost never hot in this historic Inca capital, 3,400 m above sea level. Cuzco had a population of about 800,000. It was a city established in the 11th century by the Inca *Manco Capac*, who enjoyed a god-like stature in the Inca Empire and was said to be a direct descendent of the Sun, their God. Legend had it that *Manco Capac* and his wife and sister *Mama Ocllo* were borne from the waters of *Lake Titikaka*. They settled in the fertile Cuzco plains. Cuzco means 'naval' in Quechua, the language still spoken by the indigenous population. The Incas were known for their extraordinary architecture and mortar less stonework. The temple of the Sun, *Coricancha*, as well as the fortress, *Sacsahuaman*, built to protect the capital city, were typical for this building style of finely cut and perfectly fitting stones. Cuzco's inner-city was based on Inca-constructed foundations up to the first floor, on which Spaniards later added one or two additional stories.

Life under Inca rule was generally more pleasant and peaceful than under the Spaniards. The Incas followed a feudal-socialist economic system, in which everything belonged to the Emperor, but he assured that every one of his subjects had what they needed to live a decent life. But the Inca Empire was also known as the *'Empire of Blood and Gold,'* because of its cruelty toward other tribes which they dominated. The *Inka*, as the Incas called their Emperor *Atahualpa*, was killed in 1533 by *Francisco Pizarro*, who led the Spaniards from Cajamarca to Cuzco to take over, plunder and destroy the city.

Pizarro was then unopposed by local forces. He appointed *Manco Capac II*, a half-brother of the assassinated Emperor, as a puppet ruler of the Inca Empire. Under Spanish rule, Cuzco became an art center with the well-known *Cuzqueño* School of Painting, whose main purpose was to overshadow the Inca culture with their own Catholic painting. Today, Cuzco is Peru's third largest city and one of South America's foremost tourist attractions.

In a restaurant by the *Plaza de Armas* over a cup of coffee, PJ was trying to sort out his thoughts. Strange things happened. Why did Moni Cheng leave the restaurant just seconds before the kidnappers charged in? Did she know all along that this was going to happen and she was warned by them moments before they stormed it? Why did the kidnappers not ask him what he was doing in Santa Cruz?

They must have known that he didn't just come to meet with this pretty young lady, that he'd come to discuss investment possibilities for the World Bank with the oil companies to expand their gas extraction infrastructure. Maybe they figured, with the arrival of Evo Morales, there was a slim chance that any foreign investments would be made to support the oil and gas industry in Bolivia. He needed to talk to Raul. And then he had to—or wanted to—find Moni Cheng, to finish the conversation that had ended so abruptly.

PJ went to a phone booth in the rear of the restaurant. The switch-board operator at the World Bank's Lima office said that Raul Sanchez was not in. She didn't know where he was. He hadn't come in this morning. But she gave him his home phone number. Raul answered on the third ring, Samba music in the background. He listened to PJ's story without comments. At the end he said, "We have to talk face to face. I will call LAN Airlines. They will issue a ticket for you. There is a flight leaving at four this afternoon. My driver will pick you up at the airport in Lima. I expect you for dinner, and you don't need a hotel. You have my address."

"Yes I do." And before PJ could ask any more questions, his boss hung up.

It was shortly before two. There was enough money left for a taxi to the airport. He had no luggage so it should be possible to make the four o'clock flight.

There was also enough time to catch up on some of the latest news. He grabbed the *Andean Herald*, an English newspaper, from a nearby table. On the front page was a photograph depicting a large building, badly damaged on a corner, smoke, debris, a car wreck, running people caught in motion, police cars … the caption said, "Car bomb ripped off portion of Buenos Aires' New Society University's Entrance."

He wondered why. But as he continued reading, blood rose to his cheeks. He read the story of Moni Cheng's presentation, about which, of course, he knew nothing. Police were investigating who could have been behind this hideous attack. They had no suspects. The hecklers they arrested earlier, when they raided the conference aula, had alibis and said they knew nothing about the car bomb. According to them, they were just a bunch of kids who said they were tired of all these for-eigners coming to Argentina to spread communism.

The paper also said the conference was held in celebration of the favorable data of Argentina's economic recovery. They printed a brief synopsis of the events since 1991.

Argentina's economic collapse was the result of 'Globalization'. Under pressure of the U.S. and the International Monetary Fund, the government agreed to carry out a set of harsh economic reforms, including, in 1991, the convertibility of the Peso on a one-to-one ratio to the dollar. The latter under the pretext of reducing Argentina's astronomical rate of inflation. As a result, inflation was reduced and imports initially became cheap. Bankruptcies of domestic industries increased, generating a flight of national capital. Argentina's infrastructure gradually deteriorated. Foreign borrowing rapidly increased and debt could no longer be paid back. The World Bank and IMF kept generously delaying repayment dates and further lending to the country. By doing so, they encouraged other lenders, mostly North American private banks, to add to Argentina's debt burden. The onslaught of US corporate takeovers of local manufacturing and service industries, exacerbated large-scale expatriation of profits and massive unemployment.

The crisis peaked when in 2001 the government froze all bank accounts. People took to the streets, protesting by banging pots and pans—also known as 'cazerolazo'. Demonstrating citizens' clashing with the police became a common sight in Buenos Aires. On December 21, 2001, the violence caused several deaths, bringing down the Government of Fernando de la Rúa. The interim Government of Adolfo Rodríguez Saá was incapable of dealing with the debt and resigned within a week. His successor, Eduardo Duhalde, nominated by Congress, effectively ended the dollar-peso one-to-one convertibility which was the origin of a ten year economic disaster.

About at the same time, in the early nineties, the same instigators, IMF and World Bank, driven by the profit-hungry U.S. corporatocracy inflicted a similar calamity on Russia, by forcing massive privatization of state enterprises. The last ten years of the 20th Century produced the worst economic tragedies in modern history.

Back in Argentina, in May 2003 Duhalde called elections which Néstor Kirchner won. With a number of savvy economic measures, Argentina took back control of its economy: an aggressive tax collection plan, encouragement of import substitution by facilitating access to credits for local businesses, the rebuilding of a social safety net and tough negotiations with international creditors to discount its debt. The Government managed to stabilize the economy. In 2003, the country made a drastic turnaround. From a GDP loss of more than 10 percent in 2002, it jumped to a more than 8 percent growth. GDP increases have hovered between 8 percent and 9 percent through 2006. The benefits of this recovery are reflected in the remarkable reduction of poverty which in five years was reduced from more than two-thirds of the population to less than one-third today.

PJ remembered well, where he was and what he did, when the media lauded the Argentinean Government in 1991 for having taken this drastic step, which would reduce Argentina's hyper-inflation and salvage their faltering economy. The announcement had one of those impacts on him that one remembers for the rest of the life, like the time and place when he'd learned about President Kennedy's assassination. Then, already, he thought it would become a disaster for the Argentineans. How could a government in its right mind adopt the currency, the economic parameter of another country for their own economy? The script was on the wall. But the World Bank showcased Argentina as an excellent example of economic discipline.

He paid, took the newspaper with him, walked out into the bright sun of the *Plaza de Armas* and waved down one of the countless taxis.

* * *

Raul's driver was at the airport in Lima holding a huge cardboard plaque with PJ's name painted on it. That wasn't necessary, because PJ recognized the chauffeur as one of the two office drivers. The ride to Raul's *Miraflores* apartment was slow. Evening rush hour.

Raul lived in a superb apartment on the 7th floor of a brand new 18-story tower on the *Paseo de la Reserva*, just behind the Marriott, with a panoramic view of the Pacific. This was especially attractive during the short summer months, when Lima was under a cloudless blue sky; pleasantly warm, but not too hot, because there was always a little breeze along the Pacific coast.

Raul opened the door himself. "Hi, good to see you intact. Do you need medical attention?" PJ shook his head to indicate he was alright.

Raul led him to a surprise. Moni Cheng was sitting on the balcony at a little cocktail table, greeting him with a lovely smile and a hug. She joyfully said, "I am glad to see you again. We have to finish our conversation. I am sorry for what happened to you. Raul told me your story. But you have to give me more details."

PJ just nodded. He was fascinated by what he saw, like the first time: this most attractive, self-assured young woman. He couldn't call her 'girl', because her personality gave her the stature of an adult, yet, an adult with a twist, one with a girlish, seductive charm. He was wondering what she was doing at his boss's place. He didn't know she had such a personal connection to him. He was almost jealous. Clearly, he had to see her again, and see her alone.—A second train of thought though was more down to earth: *'Why had she so suddenly rushed out of the restaurant, leaving him to his torturers?'*

What first came to his mind was the newspaper article about the car bomb. He shoved the paper across the table, pointing to the front photograph, "I am glad to see you in good health. I had no idea you were also into the university-circuit."

She gave him a sly smile, "Yes, you have no idea about the sort of things I am into," and left him wondering.

In the meantime, Raul brought three *Pisco Sours* from the kitchen. For a moment they admired the sunset in the warm breeze. PJ didn't want to bring up the car bomb. Raul probably didn't even know about it.

"Now tell us what happened from the beginning," said Moni Cheng, addressing PJ, "and we will together try to make sense of it."

When PJ was finished, they looked at each other in silence for a moment. Raul suggested, "The kidnappers must be part of the rebel movement. You know, Jaime Rodriguez and his crowd. They hate the World Bank, any foreign or potential foreign investor. They would like to nationalize the gas and oil companies." Reflecting a couple of seconds, Raul added, "In a way this is understandable. The poor *Indios* have never had anything, and now that the country's underground treasures have been discovered, they still get nothing. They see the oil companies and the elite in La Paz take all the profit and they are left empty handed." As if seeking her approval, he glanced at Moni Cheng.

She didn't respond. Instead she said with a forlorn look, "What is going on in my country, Peru, is not much different from the resource looting in Bolivia. Just look at *CAMISEA* gas fields. At today's prices the value of this treasure could easily surpass $300 billion. This is being tapped by foreign companies in the Amazon. They are leaving behind less than ten percent in royalties and taxes. In addition, they destroy valuable rain forest, displace indigenous people, killing them if they resist."

Now she looked both her partners in the eyes and continued, "They have built a pipeline, gas liquefaction plant and sea outlet at the fringes of the large *Paracas* Nature Reserve, just a three hour bus ride south of Lima. Two-thirds of the reserve are in the pristine *Paracas* Bay, home to the *Ballestas* Islands with more than 230 species of birds, penguins and sea lions. All of this is at risk of being destroyed by oil and gas leaks. 'Why is the pipeline in this protected location?' you may ask. Simple: because an outlet further north, in a less precarious zone, would have cost several million dollars more."

With audible anger, her voice raised, she said, "The corporations' profit economics have certainly no consideration for social and environmental values!"

PJ could not stop himself from interjecting, "And your government approved."

Moni Cheng nodded, "They've all been bought." She continued, her fury rising by several notches, "In the Amazon, according to the Native Federation of the *Corriente* River, every barrel of oil extracted produces nine barrels of toxic water pollutants. This has been confirmed by my Ministry of Health. They say the water contains high concentrations of hydrocarbons and heavy metals, like lead, cadmium, mercury and arsenic, not only poisoning the *Achuar* people, who live on the river's banks, but also destroying the basin's ecosystem, their livelihood. The Health Ministry further reports that two-thirds of *Achuar* children have excess levels of lead in their blood, and in practically all of the *Achuars* the level of Cadmium surpasses safety standards.—Yes, this is known. But does the government take serious actions against the criminal polluters?—No, of course not, as you can imagine. These figures are not even widely published."

PJ felt even more attracted to Moni Cheng, as he saw the woman's anger rise. He felt her commitment to *her* people, the natives of the Andes, of all of South America. He would have liked to give her verbal support, but he didn't say anything.

Moni Cheng was visibly agitated. She continued: "Since the loading terminal's two years of existence, according to environmental non-government organizations, several leaks have already done considerable harm.

"In addition, the petrol tankers, five to ten per week, come loaded with several hundred thousand tons of water from other seas for stability. When replaced with petrol or liquid gas, these waters mix with the rich biodiversity of the *Paracas* Bay, destroying the reserve's delicate bio-balance. A second liquefaction plant and terminal are planned, the location of which is still under dispute. Environmentalists say resolving the conflict is only a question of time to negotiate a *backshish* (a pay-off) acceptable to all parties. They also predict that if this ruthless exploitation is not stopped, the ocean reserve will be gone in less than twenty years—in about half the time of the negotiated concession."

She paused to let the message sink in. "For once, your Bank is not directly involved, but the Inter-American Development Bank is. Little difference."

Raul scratched his head. He didn't like this conversation. "Mind you," he said, "this was largely arranged by your wonderful former President and his national security and spy chief. He was giving away your country, rather than stopping the corporations from stealing the resources. And I imagine he got paid well for it."

"How dare you put it in this one-sided, biased perspective?" Moni Cheng answered furiously. "Granted, they are thugs, not leaders. But there was enormous pressure by the U.S. government with promises of foreign aid and a Free Trade Agreement, plus pressure from the International Monetary Fund and the World Bank, under the pretext of stimulating economic growth—growth which by the way goes practically all to the elite and not to the needy poor."

Her sweeping hand gesture describing how the elite takes all, knocked two Pisco Sour glasses off the table and sent them crashing onto the floor. She heeded no attention to this, but instead shouted, "Plus these corporations offer heaps of cash to the corrupt decision makers to pass secret legislation to let them literally get away with murder. Yes murder!" She underlined emphatically. "They are killing hundreds of indigenous people in the remote Amazon, poisoning them with toxic waste and shooting them when they demonstrate against the pollution of their lifeline—the *Urubamba* River and adjacent soil. Pollution has killed thousands of fish and rendered their *chacras*, their plots of land, infertile."

Raul felt himself in a delicate position. He was aware of what she was saying. "I agree. But first we should discuss how we can help Bolivia to get more of their riches. How to convince Jaime Rodriguez, that the World Bank's involvement is good for him and his people. If it is not us, it may be someone else. Perhaps our competitor, the Inter-American Development Bank. Or worse, a consortium of private banks. They will have no respect for the natives, nor for the environment."

Moni Cheng shook her head incredulously, "Don't play naïve. Your World Bank is not one iota better. Jaime is not a fool. As you already know, my idea is simple—just leave them alone! They can take care of themselves. And even if they don't use their resources today, they are theirs. They are in *their* ground for their children and future generations' use, whenever they are ready. There is no need to sell them for a pittance just to satisfy the greed of U.S. consumers and the oil companies' shareholders, and, of course, to pay off the debt that your institution so readily inflicts on these countries."

Raul couldn't let go. "Well, in my opinion, it's still better if the World Bank comes to a reasonable agreement, than if the angry oil companies call for help and the U.S. military invades the country, or worse, if their secret forces assassinate Evo Morales."

"Is that a threat?" Moni Cheng's eyes flashed across the table. PJ observed with some satisfaction that the relationship between the two was deteriorating fast.

Raul dove into his little memory trove of recent Latin-American terrorist history, trying to use it to deflect the listeners from his real opinions. "No, but it has happened before in Latin America and other parts of the world. Remember, when *Jaime Roldós*, the democratically elected President of Ecuador in 1979, died in May 1981 in an airplane crash, after the Ecuadorian Congress passed a new hydrocarbon law that reduced the powers of U.S. oil companies? And coincidentally, two months later in July 1981, *Omar Torrijos*, the Panamanian President, was also killed, presumably by U.S. interests, when they planted a bomb in his plane, because he was negotiating with the Japanese for the construction of a new, enlarged canal rather than with U.S. corporations? These are not threats. These are realities. The World Bank can sometimes play an intermediary role."

She stared at him intently and said nothing for a while. Then, "OK, I take note."

Raul continued, "See, let's go and meet Rodriguez together. Maybe with you present we can talk sense to him."

"You mean, I should betray him, so he may better understand what's at stake?"—After a pause, she went on, "let me think about it.— It's getting late. I have to go."

Somewhat surprised, he asked, "You don't want to stay over night?"

"No, I can't. I still have to see some friends tonight, and tomorrow morning early, I want to visit my parents, I mean my uncle and aunt, in Ayacucho, remember?"

She smiled at PJ. "Good bye—see you around. Too bad we couldn't resolve the world's problems tonight. But I am glad you are alright." Then she got up, bent over to give PJ a kiss on the cheek. As she did, she pressed her hand in his shirt pocket, depositing something, and walked through the glass door. Raul followed her to the entrance. PJ could make out their silhouette in the half-light. He heard Raul say, "Sorry, if I upset you. I just wanted to be realistic."

He kissed her on the mouth. In PJ's view much too long. Were they lovers? Then, like last words, "Please call to let me know what you think about a joint trip to Bolivia." She nodded and slipped out the door.

Raul slowly shuffled back out to the balcony. "Let's go for a bite to eat. There is this nice little 'bodeguita' around the corner. Excellent food and not too expensive."

Later that night, PJ sat on the bed in Raul's guest room, reading a local newspaper he'd grabbed from Raul's living room. The paper reported on anti-war demonstrations on several California university campuses, how the police on horseback were crushing them, literally trampling them to the ground, and spraying them with tear gas. Two students were killed in the melee; many had to be rushed to hospitals for emergency treatment.

Kent State University, the precursor to the end of the Vietnam War, came to mind. May 1970, a peaceful antiwar demonstration. Without provocation, National Guardsmen opened fire, killing four young people and wounding many more. What about freedom of expression? he thought. Violation of the fundamental First Amendment of the American Constitution isn't new; it's been practiced for decades. All in the quest for power, political and corporate power and greed, all for the rich, the elite. He continued this line of thinking and felt that the fall of the Berlin Wall had only exacerbated such actions using 'preventive' invasions of resource-rich countries as an excuse. The only questions were: where will the Empire strike next and how can it be stopped?

Then he remembered Moni Cheng's hand slipping into his shirt pocket. He took out a half-crumpled piece of paper. There was a number scribbled on it. Starting with a '9', it must be Moni Cheng's cell phone umber. He was suddenly elated. He felt his life was about to take a turn, a change for the better. That night he slept very well.

He also suddenly remembered that he'd forgotten to ask her about the phone call that made her abruptly leave the restaurant in Santa Cruz. He'd call her tomorrow. And another funny feeling in the back of his mind bothered him—Raul's behavior was strange. Was he just playing the devil's advocate in this little confrontation he'd had with Moni Cheng, or was it something else?—Would he have known about the kidnapping, before it happened? Where did he really stand when it came to the question of supporting the natives, fighting poverty, versus representing the interests of the corporatocracy?

*   *   *   *   *

7

The Ayacucho Connection

Moni Cheng was disappointed, although she'd suspected for a while where Raul stood. Why had it come out so clearly tonight? Had she been more perceptive because of PJ's presence? Clearly, PJ was interested in her. The way he looked at her gave her a rather pleasant feeling. Tonight she'd finally realized the time had come to end her relationship with Raul.

This on-and-off love affair with Raul hadn't satisfied her in a while. It had been all right when he was in Peru and they'd met in all sorts of odd places, although she'd often had the feeling they weren't quite matched intellectually, that they weren't on the same wavelength. Tonight had proved that. Then he'd disappear for weeks. He never said where. But she suspected back to Washington, where he was officially based, and where his family lived. She didn't like that.

And she definitely had no plans to visit Jaime Rodriguez with him. Now way would she betray Jaime. He was a friend and ally in the struggle for the local people's rights. She walked to the corner and grabbed a taxi. With some luck, she could still make the ten-thirty flight to Ayacucho. She was really looking forward to seeing Uncle Gustavo and his family—her family, again.

On the plane, before she dozed off, she was thinking of the gas and oil extraction in her country; about the *CAMISEA* destruction of the pristine Amazon biodiversity and the native peoples' livelihoods, about which Raul clearly didn't want to speak. How could she and *Save The Amazon* help Peru, and especially the poor *Selva* and *Sierra Indios*, to get a fair share of the wealth pumped out by these foreign companies; and what could be done to protect the rainforest? The indigenous people's source of life—the bio-treasure for generations to come?

* * *

In the taxi, even from afar, Moni Cheng could see the lit windows of Uncle Gustavo's house. She'd called them as soon as she arrived at Ayacucho airport. Her uncle had sounded happy to hear her voice, but he also sounded worried. When she asked whether something was wrong, he just said, "No—we'll talk when you get here."

Now she was concerned. Her uncle came to the door as soon as the car stopped in front of the house, gave her a big hug and carried the only bag she had. They entered the kitchen, where Aunt Mary and Joni, a cousin from a neighboring village, were sitting at the table with cups of *Mate de Coca* made from coca leaves grown in the Andes. After the warm welcome, she noticed the house to be unusually messy. Despite their humble possessions, everything was always clean and nicely put in place.

"What's wrong?" Moni Cheng asked.

The three looked at each other and then Uncle Gustavo said, "We had unexpected visitors. They broke into the house and turned everything upside down. It must have happened this afternoon. Fortunately, we couldn't find anything missing. They messed up your room especially badly. You will have to check it out for yourself. We have cleaned up a bit, but much remains to be done. This will be for tomorrow. We thought you might have a hunch what this is all about. We don't know much about what you are doing, other than that you are working for this *Save the Amazon* organization in Tarapoto. We called you. They didn't even know where you were." He paused. Moni Cheng could hear the reproachful undertone in his voice.

She said, "You can use my mobile number and reach me almost anytime you want. Look, I am so sorry for what happened to your house, and I am sure it has to do with me. I have no idea who could be behind the break-in, but will do everything possible to find out."

Of course she suspected that whoever had done this was connected to the same people who'd kidnapped PJ. "I am going to see whether anything is missing from my room. I'll be right back."

She glanced around at the mess, which was much worse than the rest of the house. Her first priority was to check her desk, where she kept her papers, maps, notes, photographs. The folder with photographs of STA headquarters was missing. It contained some aerial views of their offices at the outskirts of Tarapoto, but mostly of her with friends and colleagues in their offices and the patio, where they ate lunch when it was not raining, and where they had occasional meetings. Why would they steal her photos? Nothing else seemed to be missing, not even her jewelry. Among the mostly inexpensive pieces she owned, was a ruby gold ring which presumably used to belong to her mother. She quickly decided not to mention the missing pictures. No use alarming them.

Back in the kitchen, she said, "Everything seems okay. Nothing seems to be missing."

"The question then is, what were they looking for?" asked Gustavo, worriedly.

She was tired, wanted to sleep. They could talk more tomorrow, then she'd feel more clear-headed. She would stay all day tomorrow and then fly to Tarapoto on Tuesday. As she kissed everybody good-night, she heard a beep from her cell phone, the kind that announces a text message. On the way to her room she read the note. It was from her friend Santiago, from Paraguay. "Need to talk, call you tomorrow at 9."

After breakfast, she went to the market to buy food for her family. She took the motor scooter, so she didn't have to carry the bags. It also allowed her to just greet people she knew instead of stopping and chatting. On the way back she got two phone calls.

The first was from PJ. He wanted to know who'd called her that night in the restaurant in La Paz, just before she left so abruptly. She told him it had been Jaime who warned her of the attackers. Jaime had thought they were only after her and would leave PJ alone.

"How did he know?" PJ asked.

"From a policeman in Santa Cruz, a friend of Jaime's. He has friends all over the country," she said, adding, "the kidnappers asked whether a girl fitting my description was in the restaurant."

"They didn't even ask about me?"

"No, apparently not. Strange ... makes me think they must have known that you were there if I was there."

"Right. Asking for you was only a disguise for finding out or actually confirming, that I was there. Who told them? And who are they anyway? I have a suspicion."

"What?" she asked.

"Let me do some more research. I'll call you back later today, if you don't mind."

"No, no, of course not," she said, quietly pleased that he would.

"I'd like to see you again. Alone. I'm confused about what's happened in the last few days," PJ said. "Also, I thought Raul's reaction yesterday was strange. I feel like I'm playing a role, maybe unwittingly, but what is it?"

"There is a lot going on that you are not aware of, PJ. I appreciate the fact that you are interested," she said. "Maybe you can play a role for us, rather than for them. If you like and you are free, and without telling anybody where you are going, I suggest you come and meet me at the resort in Tarapoto, perhaps in a few days. You don't have to decide now."

"What do you mean by 'resort'?"

"Well, we sometimes call it our resort. It's actually a big ranch nestled outside the city at the fringes of the jungle. We have numerous bungalows for guests. It is our center, the headquarters of '*Save the Amazon*'. Quite interesting. You will see when you get there. It is too complex to elaborate now on the phone."

She added, "Oh, and by the way, we—me and my colleagues at STA—are organizing within the next few weeks a workshop-like forum '*Vision for a new World*' at our retreat in Tarapoto. I'll let you know when the dates are set. In any case, you'll most likely arrive before then. It'd be great to have you participate. I hope it will help us analyze how the destructive course of 'globalization' can be stopped or at least altered, and, how to engage the Europeans in the process."

"Yes, I like the idea," PJ said enthusiastically. "I'll let you know when I can make it. Ciao, talk to you later." He hung up.

The second call was from Santiago. She was surprised by it.

"I haven't heard from you or seen you for a long time, Moni Cheng," he said. "You must be aware of the recent events in Bolivia, a people's uprising with the election of Evo Morales. The *Aymaras* and *Quechuas* believe they can take back their gas and cancel the contracts with the foreign corporations."

"Yes, so I have heard." She said.

"It's not that simple," he continued, sounding almost professorial. "What you may not know is that in an agreement with the President of Paraguay, the U.S. Armed Forces have brought 1,000 men to our military base, *Mariscal Estigarribia*, practically turning it into their base. For training purposes! How ridiculous!" he said, his voice rising in anger. "It's close to the Bolivian border, to be more exact, close to the provinces of *Tarija* and *Santa Cruz,* where the U.S. gas fields are. You get my point?"

Moni Cheng worried that her cell battery was low and that the call would be dropped. She wanted to ask him why his government allowed the stationing of 1,000 U.S. soldiers on Paraguayan territory, but she knew he'd tell her what he could.

He went on, "The other official reason for the gringo presence is to protect 'Bacal', the California-based water giant, who is about to take over the water supply system of *Mariscal Estigarribia*. There were already riots; probably 'enemy'-induced, in anticipation of this take-over."

She could imagine his mischievous smile, when he said "enemy-induced," meaning that the Americans had a hand in it, either through the CIA or their henchmen. He continued, "My immediate concern is Bolivia. You know, the results of the recent referendum on the autonomy of Santa Cruz and Tarija Provinces ask overwhelmingly for independence. The Central Government objects, of course, because that is where the nation's resources lie. This may lead to nationalization of oil fields exploited by U.S. corporations—and those of *petroleros* from other countries, of course. But only the U.S. corporations benefit from their national army to defend their interests, no matter how unreasonable they are. The build-up of the *Mariscal Estigarribia* base is just logical. This could lead to a bloody confrontation. I suggest coming to see you and our international friends and comrades at STA headquarters to strategize. What do you say?"

Wow, what a story she thought. The timing was perfect. She could introduce him to PJ. "Perfect," she said. "In a few weeks we are planning a brainstorming workshop—*'Vision for a New World*'—at the Ranch. Please make sure you will be able to stay through this happening. I'll get you the precise dates later. Someone from the World Bank will also be there. I just met him. He seems to be an ally, or at least a potential ally. We will find out."

After a slight pause he asked, "Are you sure you want to share our talks with a representative of the World Bank?"

"Trust me, he is alright."

Hesitantly he said, "OK, if you say so. But maybe we should test him before giving away our secrets. By the way, I'll bring Gabriela, my girlfriend, if you don't mind."

"Of course not. She is already invited. I met her a few days ago in Buenos Aires, at the New Society University, where we held a seminar on ways to prevent corporations from taking over the world. Gabriela was a very active participant. We immediately became friends. Didn't she tell you about it?"

The phone went dead. She didn't hear his answer anymore, if indeed there was an answer. Finally some pieces of the puzzle started to show, she thought. The meeting in Tarapoto could be a meaningful step in a new direction. But, we're not there yet, she reflected.

*   *   *   *   *

8

THE CHASE

In Lima, PJ slept late. When he woke up—at about 8:30 AM   he immediately called Moni Cheng from Raul's apartment. Later he found a sticky note on the kitchen table. Raul reminded him to take it easy, to come to the office at his convenience and that they would discuss next steps.

PJ wasn't hungry. He only needed coffee and a piece of bread in his stomach. Other than what he wore, he had nothing. Not even a shirt to change into. Getting new clothes, a cell phone, a laptop, were his priorities for the day. Then he had to figure out how to get away for a few days, to Tarapoto, without Raul finding out where he was going. That may be tricky. But he could always say he needed a few days to rest after this kidnapping.

By 10 he was in the World Bank's Lima office. It was a sunny day, still warm. Today, there was no early morning fog in the air. When he entered the office, he could see Raul on the phone behind the closed glass door of his cubicle. He seemed to be concentrating on the conversation that he didn't notice PJ, who went straight to the visitor's office next door. There he thought he would wait until Raul finished. Nobody else was in the room.

The visitor's office was a large room with a dozen computers to accommodate visiting missions. In a corner it had a round table for discussions and a telephone with headphones and mouth piece. The wall separating this room from Raul's office wasn't totally soundproof and PJ could hear Raul's muffled voice. As he listened more carefully, he overheard some of the conversation. His name and last night's meeting came up. Then he heard something which took him by surprise. "They let him go too soon ... right, he may become a nuisance; we can't let anything interfere with *Golden Enterprise* ..." PJ carefully put the headphones over his ears, pressed the 'mute' button and then gently the red one, the only lit outside line.

On the other end of the line, probably someone in Washington, came a familiar voice—"... because of his vulnerability for beautiful women, his tendency to lean toward the underdog, we asked them to keep him for at least a week incommunicado, to be nasty with him, to say it kindly, in short, to instill fear in him, so he would not stray in the future and follow our instructions."

Raul asked, "Why use him at all?"

"Because we also recognize his strong characteristics. He has a strong logical mind. He's good at convincing people with his arguments, when he wants to. But now we have to take him off the scene for a while. Give him some paid vacation to recuperate after this ordeal. He will buy it. I will talk to the State Department so we don't lose track of him. He may become suspicious. Call me later." The line went dead.

PJ was sure he'd heard the voice of Marco Vidali, the Chilean, Chicago-educated, World Bank Director for the Andean Countries. The guy was a known ultra-right winger, and PJ suspected he might be an adherent of Opus Dei. But he had no idea to what extent the U.S. machinery had taken over the Bank.

He had to disappear now, before Raul could have him followed. But how could he pass by Raul's office without being seen? Jumping from the window was impossible. The office was on the sixth floor. He first peeked out of the visitor's room. Raul was scribbling some notes. PJ stepped quietly into the corridor towards the entrance, when Raul called, "Hey PJ, you're here already. Thought you needed some more sleep. Let's talk about our next moves."

PJ quickly answered, "OK, I'll be right back. I need to use the bathroom, must have eaten something that didn't agree with my stomach."

Raul waved him on. PJ headed straight for the exit and down the elevator. Outside, he flagged down one of the hundreds of taxis roaming the streets of Lima. He asked to be driven to the *Larco Mar* shopping mall and requested that the driver wait a few minutes for him. He ran through the downstairs galleries of shops until he found an ATM and got some cash. Then he left the mall on the other side, where he hailed another cab. About a half hour passed between the times he'd left Raul's office and arrived at the bus station, *28 de Julio,* in the center of Lima.

His plan jelled as he approached the station: He would take a bus to *Huaraz*, where he would buy some clothes and a cell phone, so he could communicate with Moni Cheng. Then he would take a taxi to *Chimbote* and from there another cab or bus to Tarapoto. But leaving Lima now was his first order of business.

On leaving the city behind, PJ began to relax, and he reflected on his past. His life had been too rocky and unstable for too long. He welcomed a change. Although he realized that the life one leads is an inherent part of one's character and doesn't change simply because of escaping a physical environment and tormenting circumstances. In the days and weeks to come, he hoped to take some time to analyze his life and how he got to where he is today. Vidali had a point when he commented that he had a vulnerability vis-à-vis beautiful women, and that he had an inclination for the underdog, but Vidali's last point, the logical mind, was his next and most important challenge for his immediate survival—and to overcome these perceived 'weaknesses' which he actually enjoyed, but, admittedly, which also had placed him into trouble more than once.

He grew up in the rural south of France, the son of a of a Parisian journalist and a North African immigrant who'd worked his way through night school to become an architect. He was eleven when his parents separated, and a year later they divorced. Although they both loved him, he felt pulled back and forth between them, and guilty towards the one he wasn't with. His mother was very demanding. He felt he could never do anything right. His dad was more relaxed, but seemed to give in too often to his mother. In the end he wasn't sure how far he could trust him. He tried desperately to fulfill his mother's wishes, though he never succeeded. Frustrated by his incapacity to meet these demands and by his father's weak personality, he felt the need to put physical distance between himself and his parents as soon as he hit college age. A year later his parents reunited in an attempt to give it another try. But they had no such chance. Shortly thereafter they died in a car accident.

He moved to Paris then, and registered with *Science Po* and studied Economics and International Relations. There were always plenty of girls he liked, girls from all over the planet. He was never alone for long, but wasn't able to hang on to the same girl for long either.

About six months before finishing his Masters he met Cynthia, a student from Seville, who did a year abroad at the faculty of Beaux Arts at the Sorbonne in Paris. She was a painter and thought Paris was the place to gain experience and exposure. She didn't realize that Paris was full of such people, who all sought recognition, that competition was extremely tough—and unless she knew somebody who knew somebody who knew somebody, chances to make a career were slim. Of course there was always the unlikely possibility of being brilliant, or being at the right time at the right expo, when an exquisite or eccentric rich art connoisseur might also be there, taken by the artist's painting—or her looks. Although that wasn't Cynthia's case. She persevered, teamed up with a couple of other artists, made it to a tertiary, later secondary gallery circle and sold a few pictures. Not bad for a student from Andalusia.

Shortly after their graduation they got married. He accepted a job from a U.S. paper company in South Carolina. They moved to

Charleston. A year later they had a daughter, and called her Primavera, because she was born on a sunny day in spring. But Cynthia felt out of place in the U.S., which made him unhappy, because he couldn't resolve her unhappiness, at least not immediately. At the same time, his job, marketing paper products, didn't meet his expectation. He saw the environmental and social failures linked to the industry. The disposal of untreated effluent from pulp manufacturing into the Cooper River, the unchecked logging in the Appalachian Mountains which supplied much of the company's raw material—and then the miserable conditions of the workers, many of whom were black and illegal immigrants, with little education, easily exploitable. They had to work 12-hour shifts a day to make a living.

He'd needed to look for another job. He wanted to contribute something positive to humanity and thought the World Bank would be the place. After all, when he visited them for an interview in Washington—there, at the main entrance of the Bank was this large inscription "*Our Dream is a World Free of Poverty*" He couldn't go wrong, he thought. Today he often thinks the sentence should have been completed: "*... And we make sure it will just remain a dream.*"

The marriage with Cynthia didn't work, but they didn't divorce for Primavera's sake until she was 10. A few years later, Cynthia and Preemie moved back to Spain. Since then he had seen his daughter only sporadically.

His work at the World Bank wasn't what he hoped for, perhaps because of his naïve way of seeing economic development as an honest effort of working for greater equality in the world. Now, at 53, he was wondering how he could ever have been tricked into such beliefs. He wanted to escape it. He also wanted to strengthen his relationship with Primavera. She was 18. He saw her about once or twice a year, during his vacation in Europe. The only occasion he spent some time with her on his 'turf,' was last year, when she came to visit for four weeks over summer break. They traveled through the West Coast and the Rockies and enjoyed the 'quality time' with each other.

He smiled. Preemie often referred to the time they spent together as 'quality time.' He missed her badly. It was part of his agenda now to analyze what he must do differently to get more out of life, to live happier than in the past. His later marriage to Rosalind was also short-lived. Another sad, failed story. He didn't want to think about it. As he watched the yellow-reddish desert pass by his bus window, his thoughts drifted off and he fell asleep.

* * *

When PJ didn't appear after 10 or 15 minutes, Raul started wondering what had happened. He hadn't looked that sick. He went and knocked on the bathroom door. "Everything OK?" he asked. There was no answer. He knocked again, and then gently opened the door. It was not locked. The toilet was dark and empty. His mental wheels started to turn. Had PJ perhaps overheard his conversation and fled? Where could he have gone? He hoped his trail hadn't already gone cold. He asked the secretary at the reception whether she'd seen PJ. She hadn't and after a few phone calls within the office, it was clear that PJ had left. Raul had to call Vidali immediately. The chase had started. It could derail the entire "Golden Enterprise" project.

*　　*　　*　　*　　*

9

The US Treasury at the International Monetary Fund

The lush, mahogany and leather office of the International Monetary Fund's Managing Director was bathed in late afternoon sunlight. On a sofa and chair, separated by a stylish wooden coffee table, the U.S. Secretary of the Treasury, George Blandell, leaned confidentially toward his international counterpart, Haviland Gersten, the IMF's Managing Director. He was Dutch. A gentleman's agreement between the United States and the European Governments, the strongholds of the World Bank and the IMF, divided the helms of these UN-aligned world bodies, also called Bretton Woods Institutions. The President of the World Bank has always been a U.S. citizen; the IMF's Managing Director is usually European.

The American Treasurer had called the meeting. It was urgent and had to be kept secret. Blandell thanked the Director for his willingness to meet him on such short notice. "As you can imagine," he said, "the issue at hand is a matter of great importance. It will require many more meetings and a strategy, a concerted effort by the principle Fund members, or shall we call them 'Fund owners'?" he mused.

"Let's make this informal. The discussions will flow more easily," Blandell suggested. "May I call you Haviland?"

"Havi is what my friends call me," said Gersten.

"OK then, Havi. As you know the U.S. economy has been under tremendous pressure over the past six years. We are spending far more than we take in from taxes. Never mind the tax cuts. Some people say they stimulate the economy and more tax money will flow into the treasury. Be that as it may. It hasn't happened yet. Since we are the most powerful nation in the world, we print as much money as we need and want. Nobody controls us.

For example, as you may know, we shipped cargo planes full with billions of freshly printed greenbacks in cash to Iraq. Some 12 billion. Officially to back up the 'new' Iraqi Central Bank. About 9 billion got 'lost'—the money is securely stashed away in places around the country, where it is used freely to buy off politicians and other movers and shakers.

Havi was stupefied, but didn't show it. Instead he simply said, "Yeah, it just adds to the U.S. debt which is spread around the world and owned by foreign treasuries."

Blandell ignored him. "We currently have about $10 to 12 trillion cash in circulation throughout the world. Ten years ago, there was only one trillion.

"What I am concerned about," he continued, "is that our accumulation of public debt is unsustainable. It stands close to $10 trillion today. And let me just add, the huge cost of the wars and conflicts we are engaged in around the globe, contributes significantly to this national burden. But, as long as we can keep printing new money, and as long as consumption grows, which makes the economy grow, the rest of the world trusts in the dollar. National coffers around the world are filled with our dollars as their chief reserve currency. And, let's not forget, these countries also absorb the dollar's inflation. This, of course, is good for us. It spreads the risk around the globe. Nobody is interested in a falling dollar. About half of the public debt is held by treasuries abroad. China and Japan combined, own more than $2 trillion. The rest of the world, predominantly OPEC and the European Union are holding at least another $2 trillion.

"I see," Havi acknowledged. "And you are afraid this cannot go on forever. Well, you are quite right."

It was true that the U.S. had a huge trade deficit, which was growing by the day. If his memory served him, it was currently at a cumulative total of $ 6 or 7 trillion, feeding pretty mightily into the nation's total debt, the sum of which—public and private combined—was about $48 trillion at the beginning of 2007. The total Gross Domestic Product was only $13.5 trillion. To pay back the debt, the U.S. would have to work about three and a half years without spending a penny. Back in 1957, the debt had only been about one and a half times larger than the country's economic output.

Havi, a burly man, with unusually long slender fingers for someone of his build, realized that he'd caught the treasurer's attention. He wanted to cash in on the momentum and continued, slightly raising his hand. "Your liability grows at a rate of more than $1.5 billion per day; indeed, an alarming situation. It surely has to do with indiscriminately printing money, as you say. This can hardly be called 'monetary discipline'. Your economy is not exactly a trust booster. Your big creditors, China, Japan, the oil-producing Gulf States and even Europe, are already diversifying their reserves, selling off dollars for Euros—or maybe, who knows, even gold. In times of crisis people have traditionally reverted to gold."

He paused to let what he thought was a brilliant conclusion sink in. Blandell's smile seemed to concur with what he'd been saying, and so Gersten continued, "Well, you may argue that thanks to this deficit your economy grows. You are importing lots of goods from abroad to be consumed at home—cars, TV sets, cell phones. A lot comes from China and Japan which helps their economies to do well. So, you have here a clear mutual interest, a symbiotic relationship of the bad kind. Since these countries also hold your debt, they don't want to see their dollar reserves collapsing; gradually shrinking—yes, as they fill up their coffers with other hard currencies. Plus, another factor you should not forget, my friend: A good portion of the merchandise you import from abroad to feed this absurd debt-ridden consumerism, is made by U.S. companies, who migrated to cheap labor countries, like China, India and South Korea. If the dollar falls, these companies and, for that matter, many other foreign-based companies, will no longer be able to produce competitively for the U.S. market. It is a good idea to have foresight, George. I hope it's not too late. But surely, you must have reasons to worry now more than, say, a year or two ago."

Havi was wondering what the point of Blandell's visit was, but didn't ask. He didn't want to show his eagerness to find out the reason behind this out of the ordinary meeting. Instead, he let now Blandell talk. It was obvious, he wanted to go through the full background before making his point. He had talked enough for now. He could already sense Blandell didn't like his tone one bit, even though he might agree with him.

In Blandell's mind, the IMF's lynchpin was far exceeding his authority. Instead of showing his disdain for Havi's arrogance, Blandell said: "Our intelligence reports indicate indeed, as you mention a slow but steady divesture of dollars into other currencies, Euros, Asian currencies by China and Japan—and most importantly the oil producers. The House of Saud's wealth is known to nobody, not even to our President, although his family has an intimate relationship with the Saudi Family. Yet we have become aware that Saudi Arabia keeps a minimum of their oil money in dollars. Most of it is immediately converted into Euros and a few other hard currencies like the British Pound, the Yuan and Yen. And it is of course, no secret that oil producers, especially Iran and Venezuela, have talked about pricing their black gold in Euros instead of dollars.

Havi, trying to score another point, interjected: "And Saddam was about to do so, when the first Gulf War and the subsequent embargo should have prevented him from going this route. In fact, for the limited amount of oil he was allowed to sell under the 'Oil for Food Program,' administered by the United Nations, he did convert the receipts into a Euro account. Naturally, your Administration immediately converted the account back to dollars after the 2003 invasion."

Blandell was eager to stop him right there. But Havi felt bold. He wanted to finish his point. "In fact, many believe, the 2003 invasion had a lot to do with Saddam's threat to sell oil in Euros after the embargo. Your country could never allow an oil producer to set a precedent, lest you risked a collapse of your currency—and your economy. By the way, you must be aware of the IOB project, the 'Iranian Oil Bourse'—an oil exchange to be set up in Teheran. At the IOB eventually everybody may sell and buy hydrocarbons in Euros. Sometimes I wonder, whether this is not the hidden, but real concern when your government talks about attacking Iran, rather than the alleged nuclear threat. Of course, the claim that Iran has or is about to produce weapons of mass destruction is about as phony as when we were made to believe they existed in Iraq. Likewise, Iran's role in Iraq is insignificant. At best it's provoked by your own people. To find a reason to attack. We older guys remember what the U.S. did in Vietnam to have a pretext to start a war. Of course, striking Iran would not only erase the IOB project, but would also allow your country to take possession of Iran's hydrocarbon treasures, by some accounts the second largest in the world."

Blandell's grin was now gone. He looked rather annoyed. He must have thought, *'How dare this gnome, who is nothing more than a peon for our Treasury, come out with remarks he has no substantiation for.'* Instead he merely said, "Yes, we know that the oil producers are weary of the dollar."

The head of the IMF couldn't help observing, "You mean sooner or later the wobbling bicycle, the U.S. economy that is, will hit a wall, at which point more than the dollar, the entire capitalist system might collapse. So, what is your solution?"

Now he couldn't hold it anymore. "What would you like the IMF to do?"

The U.S. Treasurer seemed content. He overlooked the gnome's snide remarks. He finally got to the point of his visit: "The Gold Standard!" he exclaimed without hesitation. "We would like you to re-introduce the Gold Standard.

"Remember, in the olden days," Blandell was now very frank, almost exuberant in bragging to the head of the IMF how the U.S. had screwed the world economy. "We had to balance our liquidity with gold. That made for sound accounting. But then, the Vietnam War and the increasing debt changed all that. Ever since Nixon abandoned the Gold Standard in 1971, when we needed more money than our tax revenues produced, we just printed it. And the world kept buying our Treasury bills. Never mind that in economic terms our money is hardly worth the paper it is printed on. We have nothing to back it up."

Then, as an afterthought, he added with a cunning grin, "Except of course for the oil wells we run around the world. They are worth trillions. And since we also control, *de facto,* the currency in which the oil is sold and through our corporations the world market price, one could safely say—we are safe."

Blandell pressed on. "It is trust that counts. Our creditors trust in the world's largest economy. In God we Trust …" he added with an obnoxious smile. His openness sounded like a confession which of course it wasn't. He just felt very secure in the confines of the International Monetary Fund, which of course he, the representative of the U.S. Treasury, controlled. "Our economic growth is an empty balloon. Almost one-fifth of our growth is accounted for by out-of-proportion medical costs; our 'high-stakes' legal industry accounts for another fifth."

And on he pressed, putting his cards openly on the table. "A big portion of our GDP stems from weapons manufacturing and sales for the wars we fight—and for the wars others fight on our behalf, those civil wars and disturbances in Africa, for instance. Though when you subtract the destruction of our environment at home and the long-term value of exploiting non-renewable resources, our real growth might well be negative. One day the world may wake up and react. The wobbling bike, as you call it, will find its abyss. Some are already awake. And if we don't have something solid, durable, and sustainable to back up our greenback, our economy may collapse, pulling down the rest of the world.—You wouldn't want that to happen, would you?"

Wow, this guy's sudden frankness is almost gory. I don't like it at all, Havi thought. But he said, "And how are you planning to amass ten trillion dollars worth of gold, before the world wakes up?"

"We don't need 100 percent equivalency in gold, as the system required in the past. A ten or twenty to one ratio will do just fine. Trust and our huge oil reserves around the world will make up for the difference. But what we do need is the re-introduction of the gold standard. All the other industrialized nations and oil producers alike have to adhere to it too." Blandell looked at him pointedly. "That's where you come in. I am aware that you are representing an international organization. You will need some consensus among the members. Let us take care of the G8 clan. You work on the rest of the world."

Havi was thinking hard for a few moments. Then he smiled, with a mischievous idea of his own. He didn't like this unchecked American supremacy. "The idea is not bad. But you and the other G8 members need time to acquire the gold at low cost, before everybody gets the hint. Where do you buy the heaps of gold, before anybody notices?"

Blandell's response was quick. "Forget the G8. They'll play along, as they usually do. We will make arrangements. They don't need to know right away. But, how are we doing it? Well, we are already doing it. Clandestinely. Almost unnoticed by the world. We basically own the *Grasberg* mine in *Irian Jaya,* now called *Papua,* in Eastern Indonesia, just across the boarder from New Guinea; and we also control *Yanaco-cha* in Peru. They are said to have the world's largest gold reserves. Grasberg has proven reserves of 46 million ounces of gold, perhaps much more. At today's market price of about 750 dollars per ounce (1 Troy Ounce = 31.1 grams), and maybe higher, if we wish it to be higher, the proven deposits are worth some $35 billion. The Colorado-based gold extraction company, Sweetwater, has operations in five continents, including *Yanacocha*, which is estimated to harbor the largest gold deposits in South America. Sweetwater's exploitation is at very low-cost, including special tax-free arrangements granted by the Peruvian government. We have also quietly started buying gold in bulk, so to speak, already ten to fifteen years ago from South Africa and Russia."

Blandell was proud of himself. He had made his presentation and was ready to go. "One more thing, "he said, "Naturally, there must be a fixed price to control the Gold Standard, not the market price. That would be too easy for speculators to abuse.—I'll let you think about it. We'll be in touch, in a few weeks."

Havi stayed silent. With furrowed brows, he followed Blandell's retreat out the door. He didn't like one bit what he was hearing from the Treasurer of the United States. But he also knew that reintroducing the gold standard could only work as long as there was trust in the U.S. economy. 'Trust' is the word, as Blandell said. But this trust was already faltering throughout the world. Rather sooner than later, Havi reflected, another economic system had to emerge, one in which values of material growth would be replaced by values of human wellbeing, social equity and advancement towards World Peace.

*   *   *   *   *

10

The World Bank's Secret Board Meeting

... A few days later ...

Literally 'in the house next door' to the International Monetary Fund, on the 13th floor of the World Bank building, a secret meeting took place in the President's private conference room. The President had invited with a '*Confidential and Important*' note the Executive Directors (EDs—the representatives of the member governments) of the G8 members (Canada, France, Germany, Italy, Japan, Russia, UK and the United States), as well as those of Australia, the Nordic countries, the Netherlands, Spain and Switzerland.

They sat around an oval conference table in Dick Dingo's rather Spartan looking office. Dingo, the President of the World Bank, was an appointee of the President of the United States and had a long history as a neo-conservative in various high-level positions in the U.S. Administration, dating back to the 1980s. He also was a key architect of the wars in Iraq and Afghanistan, and was one of the main authors of the *Project for a New America in the 21st Century*, formerly '*Pax Americana*'. Plus, he was one of the presidential team of advisers which arrogantly called itself the '*Vulcans*,' after the Roman God of Fire.

He had a reputation of being rude and single-minded, and having little knowledge of development economics. He reputedly used the World Bank to carry out the U.S. Government's agenda.

Never before had a group of Board members received a secret invitation, like the one today. They looked at one another in uneasy silence, an odd smile here or there, wondering what this 'selected' group was all about.

When Dingo walked through the door, he opened the meeting at once. "I would like to talk to you about the World Bank's new agenda over the next five years. This institution needs to make some rather significant changes in its orientation. It has to adapt to modern times. If you'll look at the agenda, you'll see the three topics I would like to discuss."

The participants did as they were told, and read along as Dingo listed the agenda items. "First," he said, "is privatization of inefficient public services; second, budget support and programmatic lending, mostly through 'Poverty Reduction Strategy' credits and loans, which, as you know, are mere transfers to our clients' treasuries to bail out their bankrupt economies; and," and here he paused, "third, is reconstruction of Afghanistan and Iraq."

His eyes darted around the room for approval. Instead, he encountered stony faces, serious, some with strained eyebrows. "OK then, to the first point, *privatization*: After two years in office and several trips to Africa, East and South Asia, as well as Latin America, it has become clear to me that in most of these countries the public sector doesn't function as it should. Let's face it, public services don't work well in developed countries either. That's why many of our governments have initiated radical reforms, including the privatization, full or partial, of these defunct sectors. The World Bank is investing billions of dollars in infrastructure projects, water supply, energy production and distribution, communication systems, transportation. Most of the time these sectors are run by public enterprises with abysmal efficiency records and with high degrees of corruption."

So far he had the attention of all attendees, though he could detect a frown here and there. But, as he had them all listening, he also wanted to make an even less popular point. "By the way, this largely applies also to the health and education sectors which do not provide the services people deserve. I therefore strongly urge you to go along with my proposed policy change. Future infrastructure projects are to be closely linked to privatization, or at least to a private sector participation or partnership, with the idea that the government's share will be gradually phased out. This is part of a reform process necessary in the developing world, if these countries are ever to emerge from poverty. Governments who disagree may be deprived from World Bank funding."

An uneasy rustle went through the room, whispering voices, particularly among the European Executive Directors. The U.S. representative sat quietly, waiting for the next blow, while the eyes of the British ED darted nervously around the room.

"Mr. President, I am very concerned about this shift away from what I would call a reasonable approach," said the flustered French representative, Mr. Vernier. "The World Bank's management has been rather aggressive in seeking to convince governments to be more receptive to the private sector. Often countries are not ready for political or institutional reasons. We have to respect their sovereignty. In fact, I have more than once been approached by African Finance Ministers, complaining that they are being pressured to privatize. One even used the word 'blackmail'. He was blackmailed to privatize his country's water supply, or else the World Bank would no longer support the sector. I reserve my approval of this radical policy change until the full forum of Executive Directors has had a chance to reflect and comment on this." He paused.

Dingo stepped in and spoke before Vernier could resume. "I have no intention of presenting this to the full house. But let me move on to the next point."

But this time, before Dingo could start, the representative for the Nordics, Eric Svensen, who had a reputation of being a straight shooter, raised his hand and started talking, "I fully support the position of my French colleague. Many of the Bank's client countries, particularly the poorest ones, are not ready for the private sector to take over, nor do they see the advantage of such a move. And frankly, I do not either. One cannot indiscriminately privatize, as you propose. Each case is different and has to be assessed individually. Developing countries also complain—and from my experience in many cases rightly so—that foreign corporations just come in to take out profit of an enterprise; profit that would otherwise stay in the country. They also tell me that many corporations, and those are apparently mostly large U.S. corporations, come into a country under the pretext of privatizing an inefficient utility. But once they are in, they find ways of getting their hands on to natural resources, which they then shamelessly exploit, and often this is accomplished with the encouragement of the World Bank."

A roar of indignation over this practice went through the room.

Dingo was outraged and wanted to interrupt this man for his shameless interference with his own policy presentation. As he hammered his little gavel on the table to signal that he requested quiet, Svenson lifted his hand and just continued. "Most of our client countries do not have the legal system to control and monitor private enterprises, the way we do. Besides, look at Europe. Most of our public services are run by public enterprises. This applies certainly for the bulk of the sectors you mentioned. Water supply and sanitation services are particularly precarious. We have witnessed disastrous results, *Buenos Aires (Note 4)*; *El Alto* and *Cochabamba (Note 5)* in Bolivia, Manila and many more in Africa. If you wish, I will present you with a list of unsuccessful privatization efforts with World Bank involvement. In Europe, most water supply and sanitation services are managed by municipal public enterprises."

He glanced around the room and saw no disapproval among his European colleagues. In fact, he could tell they agreed with what he was saying. He went on, "And that is the case even in France and Spain, where privatization of water has made the biggest inroads. These public enterprises may function according to commercial principles. But they are not private. Perhaps the Bank should pay more attention to well-functioning public enterprises and promote this much less controversial model."

Svenson was keen on presenting an idea that had been successfully applied with development assistance from his own government. The idea involved partnering two public utilities from countries with similar backgrounds for training and learning purposes. He continued, "It may take a bigger effort, associating a well-functioning public company in one country with a less well functioning one in another country, but this has been done in many cases at reduced cost and with far better, more equitable and longer lasting results, than those of profit seeking private companies. After all, this is what our development institution is all about. I do not believe we should veer from that model just to bow to private interests ..." he paused, "and to a culture of blanket privatization."

This time louder supportive comments came from those in the room, with the notable exception of the U.S. and UK representatives.

Dingo didn't even give Stevenson the courtesy of responding. He moved on, virtually ignoring the ED's comment. "My next point," he said, his brow furrowed, "is budget support and programmatic lending. We need to do more of this, especially in poor countries, where we have 'Poverty Reduction Plans' in place. In order to implement them, countries need a massive influx of funds. They need help with their national budgets through loans. The World Bank can simply finance a slice of a country's budget. Otherwise most of the countries would never have the necessary resources to make a significant dent in reducing their poverty."

Suddenly the door swung open, and a female assistant of Dingo's rushed in. She seemed worried and headed straight to Dingo, putting a note on the table in front of him. Faint noise could be heard through the open entrance from the outside of the building. Barely reading the note, he looked at her angrily, yelling, "What is this all about?"

The woman looked embarrassed for being scolded in front of the Board members. Yet her message was urgent. A vice-president had asked her to convey the message to Dingo. "Mr. President," she started with a timid, worried voice, "Ethiopians are demonstrating in front of the Bank. They've come in large numbers; much larger than expected. They are demanding that the Bank stop lending to their country, which they say is led by a corrupt President and his clan of thugs and thieves. They are carrying banners claiming that the World Bank's representative in Addis Ababa is cozy with this fraudulent bunch."

She paused, hoping to get a reaction, but Dingo said nothing. He appeared uneasy. He didn't know what to say. He realized his bad temper didn't improve his image with the Board of Directors.

The noise that had been faint now grew louder and everyone in the room recognized it as unrest from the streets. They heard megaphones demanding something or other, rhythmic shouts and yelling from what seemed to be hundreds of people, mixed with police sirens.

She had a job to do and continued. "Mr. President, this is more serious than the traditional demonstrations. It's threatening to become violent. They are preparing to break into the front door. They want to see you. They are calling for you to come out and talk to them ... your anti-corruption propaganda ... they seem to be wanting to take you up on it ..." She ran out of words, lowered her head in embarrassment, turned around and rushed out the door.

Before the door slammed shut, Dingo shouted behind her, "Let the police take care of them. That's why we have police!"

Dingo, ignoring this little incident, glanced at his pile of notes. Without much attention to his guests, and how they may have reacted to this interlude, he pressed on, "In addition to the previous points I made, our checks-and-balances procedures are too complex and time consuming, and they delay implementation of almost every project. On a number of occasions I have heard these complaints from finance ministers, especially in Africa. Budget transfers would take care of it."

This time, the EDs restlessness was clearly visible. Ms. Zengh, the Chinese representative—slim, tall, with a silk scarf decorating her neck, and attention-catching black-rimmed glasses—was obviously upset. She exclaimed, "Mr. President, already today, almost half of the World Bank's annual lending is handed out as 'blank checks,' so to speak; precisely the type of budget transfers you were talking about. Many of us believe this proportion is far too high. These loans do not stimulate economic or social growth. Incidentally, this was confirmed by a recent analysis of the World Bank's internal evaluation department which senior management seems to ignore. These transfers just add to the foreign debt of poor countries. Many of them have had difficulties repaying their debt for years. In fact, many of the poorest countries which receive such 'blank checks' are also in this dubious league of 'debt forgiveness', the club of *Highly Indebted Poor Countries* (HIPC). While on the one hand, the G8 graciously cancels the debt of the HIPCs, the World Bank turns around and thrashes more debt down their throat. More unproductive money that one day will have to be paid back ... or forgiven."

Dingo wanted to interrupt, "Lets discuss this in another forum ..."

But the Chinese representative, now angrier than before, stopped him in his tracks. "Mr. President, I am not finished and I beg you the courtesy to let me finish. Your predecessor, and now you, are putting the fight against corruption on top of the World Bank's agenda. These no-strings-attached operations are mere invitations for corruption."

Dingo again attempted to interrupt, but Ms. Zengh stood up abruptly and raised her hand. "Mr. President, we all know that corruption is rampant in almost all of the World Bank's client countries, especially in Africa. And by the way, your own country, the U.S., does not provide the world with a good anti-corruption example ..."

Dingo yelled, "I request that you keep such ridiculous views to yourself!"

"Sorry, Mr. President, this remark, albeit true, may not have been appropriate. But let me go on. These countries have no legal system to effectively monitor how funds are spent. They have no institutional know-how to help prevent financial fraud. As a matter of fact, what little legal and institutional capacity exists is controlled by the ruling elite and their cronies and, therefore, is useless."

The representatives of Spain, Italy and Russia at once said— "Agreed."

Zengh was so furious, she left the conference. Everyone knew the Chinese were the only ones with enough backbone to counter Dingo. They didn't need the World Bank, but profoundly disagreed with the ways the American Administration was using the institution for its own purposes. Lacking the outspokenness of other dissenters in the European camp, China had become the most ardent opponent of the World Bank's neo-conservative economic reform theories being spread around the world.

During the debacle between Dingo and Ms. Zengh, Giovanni Rossi, Italy's delegate, had an idea. He called his assistant on the cell phone. A few minutes later she discreetly entered the room and without a word put an envelope in front of Rossi.

The Italian representative, who'd been quiet until now, rose, adjusted his glasses and said, "Mr. President, since you do not seem to listen to reason and insist on totally non-productive budget support operations, I want to show you and my colleagues something that should shock you."

He held up the envelope and said, "This is a short video, covertly filmed with a cell phone. The faces of the people were blurred so as not to disclose their identities, nor, of course, shall I disclose that of the person who made the film. It is about a meeting that took place a couple of months ago in the private office of a Finance Minister of one of the Andean countries—and I shall of course not divulge which one. An official of one of Washington's financial institutions—and, again, its identity shall remain secret—intends to engage the Minister of Finance in …" But, see for yourself.

Dingo hammered his ridiculous little gavel again and yelled, "This is not the place, nor the occasion for this type of presentation. I will not allow it!"

Several EDs rose in protest, including Mr. Rothschield, the delegate of the United States. He said, "We would like to see it. It is indeed important to know what is going on. After all we are talking about possible corruption. Right?"

He glanced at Giovanni Rossi, who nodded and said, "See for yourself." Rossi was of two minds about whether the American was really sincere in seeing the potentially damaging evidence, or whether he just made believe for the benefit of his colleagues and out of political correctness.

Dingo was overruled. He didn't like it, but he had to swallow it. He went to his desk, pushed a button, and a retractable screen descended from the ceiling.

Rossi proceeded to insert the DVD into the projector. After some initial flickering, two blurry black and white figures appeared on the screen. One was seated behind what appeared to be a heavy desk. His face was even more blurred, certainly beyond recognition. The flag behind his chair was also made unrecognizable. In front of the desk, from a rear angle another seated person was visible. He was leaning forward. His features were more in focus, but the head was also fuzzed out. Of more importance was the dialogue. The clip started in the middle of it.

The Finance Minister asked, "You are telling me, we should not renegotiate the hydrocarbon contracts? Do you know what this means?" He paused a few seconds, as if for rhetorical impact. "This would mean that for the next 20 to 30 years, as long as these exploitation concessions last, we would continue to receive these tiny miserable royalties of ... percent. The amount was beeped out, so as not to reveal the originator of this video clip. According to him, it would be life threatening.

The Minister continued, "I cannot do this to my people. We are a poor country, rich in resources from which the vast majority of our people have not benefited up to now."

The person whose back was to the camera replied with a male voice, though it too had been distorted by the editor of the film to prevent recognition: "You really don't need the money from the sale of your gas and petrol. Our bank will lend your country any amount of money that you wish and need to fulfill the President's campaign promises. We have several lending instruments for these loans. They could consist of straight budget support operations, in which case we would transfer a certain amount of money in several phases. In your case it could be anywhere from $500 million and $1 billion. We would simply agree on a number of priority sectors in which you plan to reach certain investment and reform achievements. But this is very flexible. We know that circumstances can change for many reasons and your government may not be able to achieve the goals. This would not be a reason to stop disbursing the loan."

He paused, waiting for a reaction. But the Finance Minister stayed quiet, looked his interlocutor straight in the face and said, "And what else?"

The distorted voice continued, "Well, there are so-called 'DPLs'— Development Policy Loans. Here too, we would agree on a number of sectors in which your government would introduce certain policy reforms ..."

"Like what?" Interrupted the host.

"For example, privatizing certain inefficient public sectors, like maybe water and electricity, and even health and education could be considered." He hastened, "But again, not to worry, we know that some of these steps are highly political and cannot be carried out overnight. If necessary, we could agree on targets that have already been fulfilled, on say, reform measures which your government has already implemented. This would be easy. If so, no 'performance monitoring' would be necessary. In any case, like before, we would not stop the loan, if the time-table of targets could not be adhered to."

The disguised voice stopped again. This time his discussion partner didn't respond. So the voice continued. "We have also what we call a SWAP ... no this has nothing to do with the stock exchange type Swaps. It is what we call a 'Sector Wide Approach Project'. Here we would agree on a sector for which the loan would be designated, say, 'education'. You may use the funds for the country's education development plan. Again, we realize that priorities may change. If nothing else, it would look good in the media, *'... (name of country bleeped out) borrows ... millions (amount bleep out) to move forward with education for all'.*"

Now the figure with the fuzzy voice leans back as if waiting. "What do you say?"

Then the Minister said, "But these are loans. They would have to be paid back—and with interest," he added. "Yes, they would have to be paid back. But only after ... years (number bleeped out) of grace, and over ... years (number bleeped out). By the time repayment comes around your government will have long been succeeded by another one. But in the meantime, you and your government could have benefited from the loan ... ehh, I mean politically benefited from it."

After a few seconds, the Minister asks, "What if I don't go along with your proposal?"

The bank representative reflected for a while. He stroked his moustache. He had an answer ready, one that was destined to test the Minister's limits. He leaned forward again. His disguised voice became now softer and darker. "Your Excellency, of course, the decision is yours. But I would strongly advise against renegotiating the hydrocarbon contracts. This could have ..."

Before he could explain, the Minister shot forward: "What?"

"Let me explain," said the banker. "The international community might not see this favorably. The media would accuse your government of 'nationalizing' foreign investments. As a consequence, your

Government's credit rating may drop critically. Besides, your personal safety and that of your President ... you know ..."

The Minister became now visibly and audibly angry. "Are you threatening me?—Has it ever occurred to you development kings, a better term would be 'sharks'—have you ever thought that we really do not need to borrow a penny from your institutions? With all the resources we have in the ground, our economies could flourish ..." His voice trailed off, meditatively. But he recovered quickly. "All we need is the management skills to exploit and use these resources for the benefits of our people, and a legal system strong enough to prevent these ridiculously corrupt concession contracts from being signed."

He got up from his chair and addressed the man in front of him with a rather stern voice. "Thank you Mr..... (name bleeped out). That's enough for today. You will hear from us." With that he pressed a button under his desk. The side door opened instantly. An aide entered, ostensibly to guide the visitor out. The screen flickered again.

After a brief silence, an unruly rustle went through the room. The Russian delegate yelled, "This is outrageous! I propose a motion to have the World Bank eliminate these 'blank check' operations immediately from its portfolio. I don't want to see any of them in the next fiscal year."

This protest motion met with the approval of everyone in the room, except the U.S. representative and Dingo. They quickly exchanged looks, which others interpreted as meaning 'we have to consult with the boss.'

Indeed the boss, or the Emperor, as he surely would like to be perceived, would not like such a decision one bit. And since he is just a stooge for the real Emperor, 'Big Oil,' he himself would have to consult with his cronies. No way could America let the rest of the world decide World Bank policies that may be against the interests of American corporations.

This was also reflected in Dingo's thoughts. He did not like to be told what to do, and he didn't like what he was hearing. Especially now. He wanted to press on with the last point of his important agenda. The purpose of this meeting was not to change policies, but to *inform* the alleged allies. How did this Italian Mafiosi dare to interfere with his plan!

In the end it was almost irrelevant whether the EDs agreed. The U.S. was the largest shareholder in this institution, as well as in the International Monetary Fund. They could basically push through whatever policy they wanted. Granted, in the past, most of the policy decisions were made by consensus. But this could change. After all, the United States had veto power, set by the World Bank's Constitution. Major decisions needed at least an 85 percent consensus. The U.S. with almost 17 percent of total shares could block any motion it didn't like. This peculiarity was a remnant from the creation of the two sister institutions in 1945, when the United States was by far the largest contributor and demanded to have special rights.

Options for dissenters were few. The Europeans could quit the World Bank and work through their independent European Bank for Reconstruction and Development (EBRD). This probably would be welcomed by most developing countries, many of them tired of U.S. policies imposed through these institutions. But would the Europeans want to risk the ire of the Emperor? Dingo didn't think so. There was too much at stake.

Showing his displeasure with the way the meeting went, he moved on. "Gentlemen, I want to talk about the third and last item of this afternoon's agenda, funding for the reconstruction of Iraq. My country has taken on the gigantic task of removing a world-hated tyrant. We have moved into this war practically alone."

Some baffled looks, an uproar of distain and disagreement went through the room. The Dutch representative jumped to his feet and shouted, "Enough! We have heard enough of this nonsense." He grabbed his pad and rushed out the door. The others followed suit. Only Dingo and Rothshield stayed behind.

*   *   *   *   *

11

The Fight for Water, Gas and Oil

Moni Cheng had just returned from the market, when her Uncle Gustavo appeared in the door of their modest house. "You heard?" he said, "Tens of thousands of people are taking to the streets in *Tarija* and *Santa Cruz* claiming their autonomy, after they won the referendum. That could mean trouble. They want to run their oil and gas industry on their own, perhaps nationalizing, and perhaps renegotiating contracts."

Gustavo went on: "They are running way ahead of Evo. I don't know how the Argentineans and Brazilians will react, but certainly the gringos won't like it. A couple of weeks ago the Paraguayan President signed a treaty with the U.S. to let them station 300 troops at their *Mariscal Estigarribia* base, close to the border of Tarija. The Americans have already tripled their contingent and are amassing some 1,000 soldiers close to the frontier. They clearly anticipated the outcome of the referendum."

What next? Moni Cheng thought. She had an idea. She had to call Santiago. He answered after the third ring. She could hear an agitated ambience. His caller-ID told him who was calling. He said, "Moni, U.S. troops are taking up position at the Paraguayan—Bolivian border. If *Santa Cruz* and *Tarija* become autonomous, the U.S. oil companies fear nationalization, and are ready to ask the U.S. military to intervene.

Our government has given them the green light to do whatever they want in this country. This morning, the Mayor of *Mariscal Estigarribia* announced that the city's water supply and sanitation system will sign a 30-year concession contract with Bacal. You know what this means?"

He paused to take a breath. "If that happens, our *Guaraní* aquifer is being *'globalized'*, gone to the Empire. We have to prevent this by all means. This is our priority. Although I wish I could also help the Bolivians, I am afraid our group is not large enough to divide forces. And maybe I won't be able to come to Tarapoto either in the next few days."

Moni Cheng was surprised at the speed of evolving events. She replied, "Don't worry. We will postpone our meeting by as long as it takes to deflect these threats by the super-power. Here is an idea I want to discuss with you. The Bolivian Revolutionary Army, the ERB, is led by a friend of mine, Jaime Rodriguez. He is based around Potosi. Nobody knows exactly where his headquarters are and where he lives, probably he sleeps at a different place every night. But I know how to reach him."

There was a crackling on the line. She asked, "Are you still there?" The reply came as a grunt.

She continued, "As they do in my country, Peru, the U.S. Army has under a special agreement with the Bolivian Government, several hundred so-called 'advisers' in the country. They are supposed to train local military and police in the fight against coca growers, the 'Cocaleros.' In fact, the gringos are doing much of the fighting, or rather, destroying of coca plantations, themselves. The American soldiers' real purpose, though, is protecting American petroleum giants. I am sure Jaime will be glad to give the U.S. troops some resistance."

There was a pause. She could tell that Santiago was preoccupied with his own problems. He finally answered, "Sounds great. I just hope nobody will get hurt. I have to run. Let's stay in touch. *Un abrazo!*"

* * *

During the next 72 hours events developed fast, faster and unlike anyone might have expected. It was the momentum of dynamics playing out. After talking with Santiago, Moni Cheng tried to call PJ to explain to him that their meeting in Tarapoto had to be delayed. But his cell phone stopped ringing after five sounds. She made several attempts before it occurred to her that he may no longer have a cell phone. The jerks who'd kidnapped him, probably had taken it, in which case she was endangering herself by calling. If they held on to it, they could trace her. She just had to wait for him to call.

She then talked to Jaime Rodriguez in Potosi, who immediately and happily concurred with her proposal to confront the U.S. troops deployed around the oil fields. His enthusiastic agreement sounded like a long-held desire for vengeance on those who'd destroyed the livelihoods of his friends and comrade farmers. He and his warrior friends would occupy strategic sites of the XXION Oil&Gas and Mercurio Oil gas fields which are certainly already protected by Bolivian troops and the U.S. 'advisers'. The appearance of Jaime and his ERB could trigger a clash with them and precipitate the intervention of American soldiers stationed across the border, in Paraguay.

Jaime, as well as Evo Morales, his country's new President, always held the opinion that if the West had drug problems in their cities, that's where they should place their efforts, not here in their country. Ending the demand for cocaine and coca production would return life to what it was for thousands of years, when coca was used as medicine by local populations and provided a decent living for the farmers. But it had become increasingly obvious that those who appeared to fight coca at its source had a myriad of other, neo-liberal interests. The official coca war assured that the price for coca extract and cocaine remained high in drug-consuming countries for the benefit of the coca mafia, including members of the U.S. agencies pretending to fight it.

Implosion

This apparent battle against coca was also a cover for a creeping U.S. military infiltration into Andean countries to gradually control and take over their natural resources—oil, gas, gold, and fresh water.

* * *

This same evening, when the overwhelming vote for autonomy of *Santa Cruz* and *Tarija* was being broadcast around the world, the Governors of the two provinces jointly announced on TV that they would now actively participate in the negotiations of the gas fields with the oil companies and that nationalization was not excluded. Nervous and excited managers of the two U.S. oil corporations called on the local police force to take up positions around the gas fields. They had paid millions of dollars over the past three years to ensure this kind of support. The police complied, that same night.

* * *

Jaime also assembled his troops, about 700 well-armed guerrilla fighters. They had shoulder-held rocket launchers, AK-47s, hand grenades, as well as knives and pistols for close-range, one-on-one fighting. They were equipped with body armor and could move noiselessly in the jungle. It would take them the whole night to drive from the Potosi highlands to the tropical low lands of *Santa Cruz* and *Tarija*. He selected the 300 best trained guerrillas, divided them into two groups of 150 each. He would lead one team to head south to the *Tarija* gas fields; his deputy and close friend, Roberto, piloted the other team north-east to the *Santa Cruz* exploitation platforms. The remaining 400 guerillas were divided equally and ordered to take up support positions in the areas of *Villa Montes* and *Charagua*, just distant enough from the installations not to be immediately noticed.

In the wee-hours, just before sunrise, the first squads moved into position around the key platforms, their vehicles hidden in the forest. In the early morning twilight, shrouded in tropical mist, Jaime could see dozens of American military vehicles—jeeps, trucks, armored amphibious vans—in front of the extraction installations. But all was quiet. Not a soul was visible.

* * *

During the same night, in Paraguay, Santiago and his *Frente de Liberacion del Gurani* rebel team moved from the outskirts of *Mariscal Estigarribia*, by car, bicycle and on foot, to the western part of the city, where the municipal water supply headquarters were located. By dawn they were all in place. Just before eight, when the first employees and workers were expected to arrive, they took to the streets with posters and placards, reading, *"No a la privatización"* (no to privatization), *"El Guaraní es nuestro"* (The Guaraní is ours). They chanted "BACAL go home" and *"No Dejamos que Roben Nuestra Agua."* They prevented the staff from entering the compounds.

Soon the police arrived in full riot gear with teargas containers and high-pressure water houses. The two sides clashed. A tumultuous melee ensued. The demonstrators were driven into side streets with streams of water and teargas grenades. Clouds of the eye-burning gas hung in the air. But Santiago's troops reassembled, divided into three groups and surrounded the police.

At this time, three military convoys arrived with at least 50 armed soldiers. Spurts of machine-gun fire cut through the early morning hours. They were warning shots. The demonstrators turned around, preparing to run for cover, when the gunfire was directed at them. The streets filled with screams and cries for help. In less than ten minutes all was over. The shooting stopped. The streets were littered with injured people. The moaning of the injured mixed with the whining sirens of approaching ambulances. Several people were dead.

* * *

The evening news, broadcast around the world, announced that the riots resulted in 12 dead and about 30 injured. The cause for the upheaval was reported differently by the U.S. media, BBC and other European channels. In the words of CNN, for consumption of the North-American public, the demonstrators tried to interfere with a legitimate contract signed between the Mayor of *Mariscal Estigarribia* and 'Bacal', the U.S. water giant. The rebels were throwing rocks, and then started shooting at the police, which triggered the machine gun fire by the police. The report was in stark contradiction with the video clip which clearly showed a bunch of unarmed demonstrators. Paraguayan and U.S. military intervention was not mentioned at all.

The French TV5, BBC and other reports were closer to the truth. Gunfire was unprovoked and started by arriving Paraguayan military, intermingled with U.S. troops, who had been stationed in the country a few weeks before, under a new contract between the Uruguayan and U.S. Governments. The pretext for this agreement was to train Paraguayan soldiers and to carry out joint maneuvers. However, the real purpose was suspected to be for the protection of 'Bacal', as well as trouble anticipated between the protesters and the Oil companies across the border in Bolivia. There was also a fleeting mention of the *Guaraní* aquifer, exploitation of which would fall in the hands of a U.S. corporation, if the local public water supply company would be privatized.

The following day, under pressure of a worldwide media outcry—except in the United States—the President of Paraguay went on television to apologize to the victims and their families. He assured his citizens that he, single-handedly, had canceled the contract between the city of *Mariscal Estigarribia* and Bacal; that Bacal would close its office in Paraguay and move out of the country within two weeks.

* * *

On the day of the Bacal announcement, about 3,000 *Machiguenga* Indians from the *Urubamba* Basin Amazon region were protesting in Lima about the environmental disasters caused by Mercurio Oil. The main reason was the recent spill of about 6,000 barrels of liquid gas in the pristine tropical rainforest, the *Machiguenga* Communal Reserve. The contamination killed thousands of fish and devastated wildlife. Earlier in the year, hundreds of the *Machiguenga* Indians had blocked the river and effectively paralyzed construction of the second phase of the *CAMISEA* project. After a Special Commission ruled that Mercurio Oil had to pay some minor compensation—completely unsatisfactory and unrelated to the extent of the damage—the Indians decided to take their case to Lima. They brought along a truckload of dead fish from the *Urubamba* River which they were now spreading out on the plaza in front of the *Palacio del Gobierno*, the Presidential Palace.

What a sight! The demonstrators were joined by at least as many onlookers, who applauded, laughed and chanted, *"Fuera los Ladrones de Petroleo!"* ('Out with the Oil Thieves). Exacerbated by the summer heat, a horrendous stench of rotten fish was engulfing the entire city center area of Lima. The police arrived in gas masks and tried to push back the indigenous demonstrators and the onlookers. But the law enforcement troops did not touch the fish. Every office and government building—a large part of the government apparatus was located in the area—was getting a disgusting whiff. Eventually the street cleaning crews came, all dressed in yellow, their noses covered with white kerchiefs. They shoveled the stinking fish into an open truck and drove it to an out-of-town landfill. Eventually the fire brigade washed the plaza clean with high-pressure hoses. But the smell of fish in the plaza stuck for weeks.

* * *

That evening, the new President, who recently ascended to power under a contentious election, declared on television that Mercurio Oil had to immediately stop working on *CAMISEA II*, that the second phase required full compensation to the indigenous populations for the ecological and social damage caused during the last two years, estimated at about $200 million, and a thorough and independent environmental assessment which would set forth strict guidelines for future work.

*   *   *   *   *

12

BURNING OF COCA FIELDS, CASH CROPS— AND CHILDREN

The *Cocaleros* in the *Ceja-Selva* (term for mid-elevations on the eastern slopes of the *Cordilleras de los Andes*, in between the *Sierra*, or highlands, and the *Selva*, the lowlands in the Amazon basin, best suited for coca plantation) of Ayacucho have a small secret army to defend themselves against the U.S. military. It is called *Movimiento para el Rescate de los Cocaleros* (MRC). Their *Comandante's* name is Lucho.

Some 50 km southeast of Tarapoto, in a steamy clearing surrounded by thatched huts, Lucho was assembling his guerilla army, the MRC. Small American supplied planes had again sprayed coca fields with a strong herbicidal-type chemical, burning the coca crops. More than that, the substance also destroyed other staples, such as maize, rice and plantains. Even worse, the poison had a devastating effect on human beings. On direct contact it burned the skin on children and adults, or at best, caused severe skin rashes. This was an infraction of the agreement the farmers had entered into with *Devida*, the Peruvian agency behind the coca eradication program, financed by the United States. The contract called for a year of truce, during which the farmers could convert to alternative crops. But *Devida* and their U.S. sponsor did not adhere to the agreement. This contract breaching had to stop.

The gathering of Lucho's troops was called to organize the next steps. An earlier march on Cuzco, Tarapoto and other major cities in the *Ceja-Selva*, where coca is grown, requesting the Regional Governments to heed the terms of the treaty, was unsuccessful. Now they had to call for more decisive actions.

About 150 camouflaged natives were waiting for instructions from Lucho. The guerillas were well-armed, funded by the coca growers, but also by sponsors for wildlife and national parks, who were weary of seeing pristine rain forests destroyed by foreign oil companies. They faced an uphill battle on two fronts: preventing the U.S.-led effort of destroying their livelihood and fighting advancing neo-liberals in the form of multinational corporations, who were not only devastating the Amazon, their living quarters and source of income, but also stealing their treasures in the ground.

The MRC would first fight the spraying in two prominent coca growing areas. They would take up positions in the early morning hours and as soon as the planes started their flyovers, releasing the poisonous chemical mist, they would use their shoulder-held grenade launchers to bring them down. Most likely, these planes were equipped with machine guns and back-up troops. The ensuing battle could well result in casualties. But without resistance their existence was doomed.

Lucho and his army had close links to Moni Cheng's *Save The Amazon* and its nearby headquarters, the 'Freedom Ranch'. He always consulted with her before embarking on any drastic action. In this case he called to inform her. She told him about the demonstration in Lima by the *Machiguenga* Indians. Her only advice was to avoid casualties, so as to keep criticism low. She wished him luck and invited him to the get-together she was planning at the retreat in Tarapoto, but didn't quite know yet when it would take place. Events were running away with her agenda.

* * *

Fully equipped with the essentials, including a new cell phone and computer, relaxed clothing for the tropics, PJ boarded a bus in *Huaras* and was now on his way to Tarapoto via *Trujillo*, where he would take a plane. The road to Tarapoto was murderous. So, he decided to take the plane from Trujillo. The plan was risky. Airline passenger lists could be easily checked. He would try to travel under a false name.

At the airport in the early afternoon, he was confronted with a chaotic crowd. People sitting on suitcases, hauling bags from one line behind a counter to another; others pushing their way through to an agent, gesturing emotionally, pointing to the clock at the wall, others were yelling at each other or over the heads of people to one another. It was difficult to make out what was happening. Obviously, planes weren't leaving—but why?

He saw a calm elderly man sitting on the floor, his back against the wall, smoking a cigarette and watching the commotion. PJ charted his way through the crowds, approached him, asking "What's happening?"

The man, wiggling his shoulders, "They are shooting down planes near Tarapoto."

PJ was flabbergasted, "Why? Who?"

The old man said, "The rebels, the army of the *Cocaleros*, they're defending their *chacras* against the American planes, which are fire-spraying their coca plantations, and everything else that grows in the vicinity. While the rebels shoot at the planes, the sky is closed for air traffic."

PJ was shocked. "Did they shoot down a plane? Were people killed?"

The man said, "Earlier, on the public information system, they mentioned that one plane was downed, that several people were killed, and now Peruvian and American soldiers are fighting back. Must be like guerilla warfare."

It occurred to him that he should talk to Moni Cheng. She may be waiting, though surely she must know what was going on in her neighborhood. He got the crumpled piece of paper with her phone number form his pocket. She answered immediately, "PJ, where are you? I tried to call you, then realized you probably didn't have your cell phone."

"I am in Trujillo at the airport waiting for a plane to fly to Tarapoto, to your Ranch," he said. "But the flights are grounded, because there is shooting in your area. What do you know about it?"

"First," she said, "I am still in *Ayacucho*. A lot is going on. I wanted to call to tell you that our meeting will slip by a few days, maybe a week."

She told him about the demonstration of the *Machiguenga* Indians in Lima, the killer riots in *Mariscal Estigarribia*, and about Jaime Rodriguez Revolutionary Army's positioning around the gas wells in Boliva. This could trigger more civil unrest, depending on the Bolivian President and the governors' of *Santa Cruz* and *Tarija* decision on nationalizing the oil and gas infrastructure. And now the *Cocaleros* battle near Tarapoto. Although concerned about all the bloodshed these recent events caused, her voice sounded content; proud of the resistance movement's progress.

"And what about the shooting at planes in the Tarapoto area?" he asked.

Her voice came across rather sad. "The resistance fighters, actually Lucho's MRC, have downed two small U.S. spray planes, each with two people aboard; all killed. Now the fighting is on the ground between the MRC and contingents of the Peruvian and U.S. Army. It's quite fierce. Several deaths were reported. That's all I know."

Seemingly as an afterthought, "By the way, does Raul know where you are and what you are doing?"

Of course, she didn't know yet what happened, which side Raul was on. So he told her the story in minute detail. She should know what kind of jerk she was involved with. Jealousy was playing only a small role, he told himself.

After a long pause and a sigh, she said, "This is happening at the right time. I've been suspecting for a while that he wasn't trustworthy. But the fact that all this may be orchestrated by the World Bank's Washington Office, with the State Department, does come as a surprise. Be careful. You must know you're probably being followed."

He explained what he'd done to escape by cab and bus. Trying to take a plane was a calculated risk he was willing to take, because he was planning to travel under a false identity. But now he was stranded. Nobody knew for how long. At least for a day. With all the people waiting, it would take several aircraft to ferry the airport full of people off to their respective destinations.

Moni Cheng thought for a minute, and then said, "Yes, you are better off just spending the night in Trujillo. Tomorrow, when the mess at the airport clears up, you should fly to Tarapoto and meet my friends at the STA Ranch. They will lodge and feed you and give you some challenging conversation. You will learn about our activities, our worldwide operations, that we are actually monitoring an international network of environmental and social movements. I take it you are done with the World Bank and would rather team up with us?"

Instead of answering her last question, he asked, "When are you coming?" Then he added, "Of course, I am done with them. They would kill me if they found me."

He felt proud that she would let him into her circles of friends and activities. Plus, as he listened to her voice, his attraction for her grew. He told himself not be too obvious about it. Fortunately, she couldn't see his face, his glowing eyes.

She gave him a telephone number of the Ranch, of Enrique, her closest associate. She would call him about PJ's impending visit. He, PJ, should also call him, once his flight plans were confirmed. And, of course, she would always be happy to talk to him. These final words made his day. Although he tried hard not to let it show. He said, "OK, I'll see you then in a few days or so?" She acknowledged him and hung up.

The next morning the airport was almost back to normal, except for a long and extremely slow security line. He had checked in with his invented name and false ID, so far without problem. He was a bit nervous as he inched slowly towards the security check point. Just ahead of him was a tiny Japanese tourist. She was dressed in bulky safari shorts and blouse with a huge bush knife on her belt. With her short cropped black mop and dark sunglasses covering half of her face, camera hanging from her neck, she looked like the perfect Asian traveler.

'What is this woman thinking, trying to take this dagger on the plane?' PJ thought. She reached the electronic security gate and acted as if she would march right through, when an officer stepped to the fore and stopped her, pointing at her machete, "Madam, you are not allowed to take this knife on board."

But she was not easily convinced of separating herself from the blade. She retorted deadpan, "Sir, I'm going to jungle. People say big black panther in wilderness. This," she put her little hand around the knife's shaft, "to kill panther when he attack."

The security officer didn't know what to say. Visibly oppressing a big laugh, he looked around him. But nobody was paying much attention. PJ just smiled at him. The officer now collected his senses, bent over to talk gently to this lady who barely reached his chest. "Madam, since there are no dangerous animals on the plane, you will not need the knife. I have to ask you to please give it to me. I will nicely wrap it up in paper and plastic and put it on the plane with the luggage. When you arrive in Tarapoto, you will get your machete back along with your suitcase."

She looked at him incredulously, shook her head, slowly unbuckled the belt and handed knife and strap to the guard. She walked unperturbed, neck high, through the gate—which now had no reason to beep.

After this little incident, PJ smiled at the officer and walked straight through. Nobody even looked at his ticket, let alone his fake ID. And off he flew to Tarapoto.

* * *

The battle ensuing from the illegal coca plantation spraying of the American supported program, resulted in 18 dead, the four occupants of the plane, one American, two Peruvian soldiers; all the others were from the MRC, *Cocaleros* Movement. There were also about a dozen people injured. Many of them had to be hospitalized. In addition, the Peruvian-American forces took five rebel members captive. Nobody knew where they took them. They confiscated the land, burned the farmers' houses, the school and health center. The village population was left with nothing. Not even food, because it was poisoned by the chemical spray.

The incidence was the main caption of the international media that day. It caused furor throughout Latin America. The teachers' association and transportation trade union members took to the streets in Lima, Cuzco and Arequipa. They paralyzed the cities for a full day. The President of Peru launched an official protest with the U.S. Embassy. In an unusual step for one of the last American allies in Latin America, he also went on national television to denounce what he called barbaric acts of the U.S. military. They were here to help train the Peruvian army, so they could control drug trafficking, not kill people and destroy the livelihood of villagers.

When Lucho heard this news on television, he shook his head. This incendiary statement against the Americans was nothing but a planned charade. The gringos allowed this verbal condemnation in order to strengthen the Peruvian puppet among his people.

Down in the valley near Tarapoto, Lucho regrouped his people and strategized on how to get their colleague prisoners back, and about what to do next. They swore vengeance and agreed on a plot which, if carried out successfully, would again make world headlines. They had to strike back, or else the armed forces would take over other coca fields.

* * *

In Lima, Raul was in a state of frenzy, calling the Minister of Interior's Office, the CIA delegate of the U.S. Embassy, as well as his director, Marco Vidali in Washington, to report PJ's disappearance. Vidali suggested that he could have defected to the enemy and divulged many secret World Bank activities, though he didn't precisely know to which secrets PJ could be privy. A massive manhunt should be launched; airports alerted in the event that he left the country. Raul obliged, visiting the U.S. Embassy.

*   *   *   *   *

13

THE VENEZUELA FACTOR

The election of Evo Morales as the first native President of Bolivia, gave rise to big celebrations in the streets of Caracas and other cities throughout Venezuela. The swearing-in ceremony at the Bolivian Congress in La Paz was attended by Hugo Chavez, the President of Venezuela, and other leaders from around the world. Chavez pledged his support to the newly elected President and his country.

Morales promised his people to renegotiate the contracts with the foreign oil and gas industries. He declared the current contracts illegal, because they'd been signed by the corrupt former president, who he noted was now comfortably residing in the United States. Morales wanted the Bolivian riches to benefit its own people, especially the indigenous people, who made up 80 percent of the population and were desperately poor. They lacked most forms of physical infrastructure, such as drinking water, sanitation and decent roads, as well as schools and health services.

This was a tough promise to keep, because delegates of the U.S. State Department were visiting Morales shortly before and after the elections, warning him of the consequences nationalization could have. They were nasty. Chavez was aware of it. The Bolivian leader and Chavez had privately agreed on a fall-back position. Venezuela would buy out those foreign companies, who were unwilling to accept the reversal of the current royalty deal. The new arrangement would give 82 percent of the profits to the Bolivian government and 18 percent to the foreign oil firms. This was the opposite of the deal signed by the previous government: 82 percent for the corporations and 18 percent for Bolivia. It concerned mostly the U.S. oil companies. Brazil, Argentina and Spain had not officially accepted the proposal yet, but they were ready to negotiate. XXION Oil&Gas and Mercurio Oil knew they had army backing, so they didn't need to budge. But they were not prepared for the Chavez initiative.

After the *Santa Cruz/Tarija* referenda it was time to act. Chavez held an international press conference in which he declared that Venezuela's national oil company, *Petroleros Bolivar*, would buy out all foreign oil companies in Bolivia which didn't agree to the new contract conditions. In addition, Chavez said, his government and Cuba would assist Bolivia with a program to rapidly expand education and health services for the indigenous population in the *Altiplano, the Sierra* and the *Selva*.

The news hit the world like a bomb shell. There was factually, or even legally, nothing wrong with Chavez' proposal. The media blitz was a virtual stampede. BBC, CNN, France1, Canal-5, the Italian RAI stations, as well as the regional non-corporate media, the South American TeleSur, the Middle Eastern Al Jazeera, and the Asian AsiaLink-TV—to name just a few—were all shouting questions at the same time.

Chavez simply said, "No, the oil companies were not previously informed. The only agreement so far is that with the new Bolivian President, his advisors and the Minister of Finance. The accord needs to be ratified by Bolivia's Congress, as well as Venezuela's. On our side we do not foresee any problems, as informal consultations have taken place before this announcement. In Bolivia it will depend on the composition of Congress. But given Morales' landslide win, it's fair to assume passage of the deal."

As soon as Hugo Chavez stopped talking a storm of flashing cameras and shouted questions engulfed the scene. Chavez just lifted his hand and the noise ebbed. "One more thing—we, the democratically elected governments of South America want to stop the enslavement of our people by the neoliberal capitalist bulldozer of the north. We are intent on remaining autonomous, fully capable of managing our natural resources for the benefit of our people, not the profit of a few."

Reporters were ready to ask questions, but Chavez went on: "We ask the U.S. to withdraw their military from our countries—Ecuador, Peru, Bolivia, Paraguay—whose guise is to fight coca traffic, but we are no fools. It is clear to all of us that this creeping invasion of U.S. troops is aiming gradually at taking over our natural resources. In Ecuador, U.S. oil companies pay hefty sums, millions of dollars, to the local army, and to private companies, which act as proxies for American armed forces, for the petroleum corporations' protection. We still have a vivid and acrid memory of the attempted CIA-backed coup in 2002 in my country. But the voices and uprising of the people was stronger. This will, from now on, be the case throughout South America."

He waved to the crowds, "Thank you! Thank you all for coming. Good night."

Chavez backed away from the mike and disappeared in a crowd of advisors and bodyguards, before the eager journalists could ask any questions.

* * *

The AirCondor plane arrived in Tarapoto at about 10 at night. Enrique came to pick up PJ. On the way to the Ranch, he told PJ of Chavez' extraordinary plan. Veronica, another friend and associate of Moni Cheng's at the Freedom Ranch, welcomed them with *Pisco*

Sours. She led them to the veranda, where a midnight party was in process. Some hundred people, mostly young and energetic, were dancing to samba, singing, laughing and chatting.

PJ wondered what they were celebrating. Or maybe this joyful socializing was simply part of the *Selva* culture. PJ met with people from all over the world. They seemed to work at the Ranch. He started understanding that he had become a participant in a socio-environmental training ground for intellectual activists.

In the course of the following days, PJ made many new friends from all over the world, most of them working for organizations and NGOs whose goal it was in one way or another to improve social conditions of the poor and to fight for environmental protection. They were all invited by Moni Cheng to attend the *'Vision for a New World'* workshop. Many of them would probably stay on for a while longer to get a better grasp on the global implications of the fast advancing nefarious neo-liberalism ...

PJ was suddenly reminded of Moni Cheng's absence. He missed her, even though, he had hardly met her. But he had that ardent feeling of connivance not just because of likeminded spirits, but of a physical attraction which he felt was mutual. This *'Vision for a New World'* event would bring them closer in all ways. He just knew it. He remembered her last words when he spoke with her at the Trujillo airport that she would always be happy to talk to him. He smiled to himself, sitting on the veranda in the midst of his new friends. Their talking blurred away under his growing imagination of a romantic union with Moni Cheng.

* * * * *

14

POLICE STATE VERSUS DEMOCRACY

When Moni Cheng learned about the casualties at the coca plantations near *Freedom Ranch* she was both furious and sad. Eighteen dead! Most of them were her friends, and defenders of the peasants' meager livelihood and rights. Five MRC fighters were captured. Her main concern was for the kidnapped friends. Who knew what the Americans were doing to them. They probably tortured them, then let them smolder in misery until they die. Their practices were known around the world. Abu Ghraib and Guantanamo were just the two most publicized torture prisons. There were hundreds more around the globe, all defying human rights and the Geneva Conventions. She decided to bring the case before the Peruvian Chief of Police, and if need be, before Parliament.

In Lima, the office of Ladislaw Molotov, the police chief, didn't take well to her request to see the head of national law enforcement. She got a demeaning look from Molotov's sexy female assistant, when she told her about the purpose of her meeting. Molotov was of Russian descent with a reputation as a strongman. Moni Cheng smiled, thinking how appropriate his name was, if indeed he was the brute as which the local media portrayed him.

He was not available, she was told. "*Quizás mañana*" but nothing was sure. He was busy escorting and briefing the new President. She thought—this 'new' President ... an old one in new clothes. Naked, he was not going to be different than the corrupt thief, who emptied Peru's coffers during the eighties, then fled the country with his loot, just to return shortly before the elections, when his crimes were erased by the country's strange legal system for politicians, and worse, from the memory of the people, who voted him back into office.

This new–old President, other than the American puppet leader of Colombia, happened to be the only South American ally of the northern Empire. He would hardly endanger his relationship with the U.S. for the disappearance of five rebels, whose actions had caused the death of American soldiers. Never mind his official denunciation of the American atrocities that led to the coca battle near Tarapoto. Moni Cheng realized at once her attempt to free them through this official channel would be futile.

She thought of Antonio Esteban, a friend of her Uncle Gustavo's and a long time member of Parliament. He had salt-and-pepper hair with a bald spot in the center and thick eyebrows, and was an avid socialist. His rimless glasses gave him a distinguished look. He was a 50-year-old confirmed bachelor. Politics was his family.

Moni Cheng met him a number of times when he visited her uncle's house. He usually came for dinner, and afterward stayed until long past midnight to debate politics with her uncle. They often thought alike. When she was in high school she sometimes participated in the debates. She liked his world views, his commitment to human rights, to the rights of peasants and indigenous people, although he was more white than Indio. His integrity kept him in Parliament; nonetheless he was frustrated by the failures of this legislative body to achieve what he considered equality and basic rights of the people. Yet, he stayed the course. He was of good standing and his colleagues liked him. Maybe he would have an idea.

She called his office to get an appointment. He asked her to visit him without delay. She would never abuse their acquaintanceship. And indeed, her case was serious. The response from Molotov's office didn't surprise him. He had enough friends in the Assembly to call an international press conference. The presence of foreign journalists was essential. He would introduce Moni Cheng, who would present the case of repeated poison spraying, the human injuries, and damage to animals and food crops caused by it, in as much detail as necessary.

* * *

The press conference was called for the next day. It took place in a meeting room of the Parliament building. The President was not consulted. According to the rights under the separation of powers, the President had only to be informed. He was not happy, but could not prevent the event. Many members of Parliament, who normally would have sided with him, took a position favoring their popular colleague, Antonio Esteban. After all, he was an ardent defender of the working class and the natives, and there had been enough controversy about U.S. companies' environmental disasters. The *CAMISEA* project was a case study in the pollution of the Urubamba River, the destruction of pristine rain forest and massive fish killing. Who would have forgotten the mountain of dead fish in front of the *Palacio del Gobierno* and the accompanying atrocious stench?

Antonio and about a dozen other senators were present. The subject was *Abuse of Power by the U.S. Military*. The subject was interesting enough to attract a wide range of *periodistas* (reporters), not only from the major written media, representing all of the Americas and Europe, but also major U.S. and European TV channels were interested in the gripes this new ally of the United States had to present so publicly.

Moni Cheng, somewhat nervously pinching her nose, began explaining the background. The pretext for U.S. forces in the country—training Peruvian anti-drug agents, to help abate the drug trade—

and the real reason—the stealth infiltration of U.S. forces into resources rich Andean countries to defend U.S. corporate interests. She then progressed to the main topic, the systematic and premature destruction of coca fields, contrary to signed agreements, the spraying of poisonous chemicals, eliminating food crops and injuring people, mostly children, and animals. She illustrated last week's event, when the militia, *Movimiento para el Rescate de los Cocaleros*, had seen enough misery and devastation of poor peoples' livelihoods and brought resistance to this unilateral destruction inflicted by the U.S. troops and their extended arm *Devida*.

She was in the midst of describing the event, when the shrill sound of sirens interrupted her. Uneasy, she peered out a window, but couldn't see anything. The noise became louder, a battery of police cars suddenly stopped in front of the Parliament building. She went to the window. To her horror she saw about ten police cars in half-moon formation circling the entrance to Congress. Using a megaphone, someone started shouting: "This press meeting is illegal. You must all come out at once. You have three minutes. Then we will storm the building."

They had no choice if this event was to end peacefully. Antonio Esteban motioned the media representatives to pack up, waved the other congressmen out of the room, and took Moni Cheng by the arm. The crowd quietly left the building. When the journalists stepped out of the main gate, they were apprehended by the police, all media equipment was confiscated, and the reporters were searched and brutally pushed into two waiting vans. Antonio and Moni Cheng were handcuffed and driven away in a police car. They were brought to a prison at the outskirts of Lima, stripped of their belongings and locked into separate cells.

Peru had a long history of corrupt dictators, despots and military rulers. This violent behavior must still be embedded in the people's blood, she thought, despite the onset of a democratic government. Obviously, what just happened had little to do with democracy. It was the harsh force of a new ruler, whether dictator or not, who was eager to demonstrate to his northern ally that dissent would not be tolerated.

In fact, this was a rather stupid move. The following day, the media, foreign TV and newspapers in particular, had the event illustrated on front pages and reported on 'Breaking News' throughout the Americas and Europe. As usual, the U.S. media painted a different picture from the news seen in the rest of the world. The image of Peru, its new President, and free speech were all tarnished. The country was now more vulnerable to world attention—and so too were the clandestine incursions of American Armed Forces in Latin America and their cruel deeds.

The next morning, after the onslaught of the media, the Parliamentarian and his young protégé were set free without questioning. They went to a café and strategized on how best to capitalize on Peru being in the world's limelight. As with other events this attention would fade soon. The momentum was now. It had to be utilized quickly.

*   *   *   *   *

15

THE GROUP OF 77 CONFERENCE—DACCA, BANGLADESH

Shortly after the police crack down on the media in Peru ...

The weeklong G-77 Conference was held at the *Mujibur Rahman Center*, in Dacca, Bangladesh. The conference center was named after the founder and first President of Bangladesh. He was assassinated, along with most of his family members, in a military coup in 1975. The conference was taking place under the auspices of the United Nations.

The original membership of this forum comprised 77 unaligned, mostly developing countries. It had since grown to 133 members, but maintained its original name, G-77 *(Note 6)*.

The main topics of discussion of these periodic conferences included trade issues, labor movements and exchange of technologies. This time, though, the Conference Secretariat received a last minute request from a Peruvian Parliamentarian, Antonio Esteban. He filed a petition, signed by about 50 Peruvian congressmen, to discuss the recent case of U.S. military atrocities in Peru, the story that made the headlines a few weeks earlier. It was an unusual request that didn't fit well with the rest of the agenda. Nevertheless, it was posted by one of the member countries and could not be ignored.

A couple of weeks before the Conference started, the Executive Committee met to discuss the items on the agenda, before they were tabled at the plenary. When the U.S. military case in Peru came up, the few dissenting voices—Costa Rica, Panama, Colombia and—the Philippines, of all places—were easily crushed by this year's Chairman, the President of Brazil. He explained that this case was a subject of principle and concerned many Latin American countries, especially, but not exclusively, the resource-rich Andean countries. He mentioned Paraguay, which had just signed a treaty with the Pentagon to receive some 300 U.S. military 'advisors,' trainers of the Paraguayan Armed Forces, but the Americans sent a thousand instead. They were occupying the northern border with Bolivia, ready to defend the U.S. corporations' hydrocarbon interests in the Bolivian provinces of *Santa Cruz* and *Tarija*. Once the gringo's military were in a country, it was extremely difficult to get rid of them.

It didn't take much to convince the opposing voices. The motion was accepted. The question now was, who would present it—and how?

* * *

Bangladesh is one of the poorest countries in Asia, with half of its 140 million people living on less than a dollar a day. A dollar may be meaningless for people who have never seen money, let alone, who know what a dollar is. But that's the measuring stick for poverty used by the World Bank and the IMF, and adopted as standards around the capitalist world.—There were other equally meaningless parameters, all based on quantifiable values. They included Gross National Product (GDP), Gross National Income (GNI), and Purchasing Power Parity (PPP). The latter may bring the figures somewhat closer to reality. For example, total GDP of Latin America is estimated at $2.3 trillion, measured by official exchange rates. According to the PPP factor which measures purchasing power, the figure is about $ 4.5 trillion, almost double.

That means, the same basket of goods that would cost $200 in the United States, could be bought for $100 in South America. But it still doesn't say anything about income distribution. That's where the 'Gini' coefficient comes in. It is also just a flat, two-dimensional approach, looking at what percentiles of a country's population owns what proportion of its income. If every man and woman of a country owned exactly the same, the Gini 'factor' would be '0'. If one person owned everything and the rest nothing, the Gini coefficient would be 100. The higher the factor, the more uneven is income distribution. For example, in Latin America the Gini factor varies between 40 and 60 (Brazil about 57; Argentina and Mexico 52; Peru 47; Bolivia 42), as compared to the United States, about 42 and Europe as a whole between 25 and 34 (Germany and the Nordic countries 27; the others about 32).

These indicators, used by the world's two leading financial institutions, the World Bank and the International Monetary Fund, have become the foremost measures of wealth and wealth distribution for the western world and by the UN system at large. They appraise poverty, riches, as well as a country's creditworthiness. For the latter, a nation's GDP growth rate is crucial, no matter the extent of income disparity. The extent of mineral resources a country possesses is usually not important. This may mask the fact that these resources are gradually being gobbled up by the U.S. corporatocracy.

Quality of life, environmental protection or degradation, crime rate, food deficiency or sufficiency (calories per person per day), social segregation, level of education and general health, these more intangible values are irrelevant in the capitalist system's assessment of a peoples' or country's wealth and wellbeing. The economic yardsticks are easy two-dimensional figures that can be chalked up on a board room's flip chart, while dignified onlookers in dark suits and ties, sip their organic coffee and orange juice.

Bangladesh has also been plunged into a national crisis as a result of ongoing feuds and mistrust between the country's two major parties.

The continuous unrest is literally crippling the country, cutting transport routes from Dacca to the rest of the country. Textile industries, the leading export sector, on which some 4 to 5 million direct and indirect jobs depend, are spiraling towards oblivion. Competition is fierce in Asia. This will drive poverty figures—human misery—even higher.

Never mind these Third World calamities, from which the rest of the world, especially the industrialized west, is neatly shielded. U.S. corporate media are hardly interested in sheer human desolation, at least as long as it cannot be chalked up to the triumphs of wars waged by the almighty western Empire.

By holding this conference in Dacca, the G-77 organizers hoped to put Bangladesh on the map, so to speak, to bring its plight to the attention of the world, however brief this moment may be. Bangladesh was a proxy for many other member countries, whose destitution was comparable.

The Conference hall could easily accommodate 10,000 people. Another 100,000 to 150,000 were demonstrating in the streets. The building was almost circular with a straight wall that cut off about a quarter of the ring. On the inside, in the center of the wall was a large multi-purpose podium with a half-moon seating arrangement around the podium. The building was bright, had a cupola ceiling decked out with large triangular glass panes to let the light shine through. However, ventilation was insufficient, especially with Dacca's hot and humid climate. And with a full house, the air was pretty stuffy. G-77 attendees were sweating. Those who arrived in formal or semi-formal attire soon took their coats and ties off. But overall, the ambiance was relaxed and jovial.

Among the dignitaries were Hugo Chavez, President of Venezuela, the newly elected President of Ecuador, Rafael Correa, as well as the President *en-exilio* of Mexico, Manuel López Obrador, whose leadership, according to many international observers, had been stolen by a right-winger during a contentious and highly disputed election. It was widely said, that the vote had been fraudulent. The outcome more than pleased Mexico's northern neighbor. It was a great relief for the neocons, their *Walmartisized*, low-end, but hugely lucrative economy, and a victory for the further privatization of the poor people's meager assets and their powerful labor.

The keynote speaker of the Conference was the new President of Ecuador. He introduced the UN Secretary General and other dignitaries, leaders of countries. He said this was a special conference. In addition to addressing the Group's usual concerns with trade, globalization, and migration, the time had come to bring the world's attention to specific events and calamities afflicting the globe ... wars, conflicts, torture, human rights abuses, looting of natural resources, destruction of the environment. Others would address these topics. He himself would use the opportunity to tell this global audience about the new era that was dawning in his country, that he was allying his country with Venezuela and Bolivia, and, on an even larger scale, with Brazil and Argentina.

President Correa in shirt-sleeves and without a tie, started his formal speech. "Friends from around the world, let me tell you, first, that I am humbled by the overwhelming confidence the people of Ecuador have given me during these recent elections, that they have withstood the lies and manipulations of my opponent, whose campaign was driven and funded by the United States; second, that I will not let them down. I will do whatever it takes to improve the plight of the vast majority of our people."

He looked around the aula and continued. "The majority of our citizens are poor. Many of them have no health services and no access to schools. Yet, Ecuador is a very rich country. We have natural resources which are being looted by American oil corporations. I want to change this by renegotiating contracts with these companies, so that our wealth is distributed to our indigenous and native inhabitants, whose livelihoods have been destroyed by these same companies. I also want to hold them responsible for protecting the environment, the pristine rivers and biodiversity of the Amazon region."

Pausing to take a breath, Correa looked around the stadium, as a storm of applause rose from the 10,000-some audience. He graciously waved and continued.

He was working up a steam. Excitement rose through his voice. "We also want to break loose from the fangs of the World Bank and the International Monetary Fund. These agencies, which serve corporate America, have tried to dictate to us that in return for loans, so-called structural adjustment loans, we must allow the oil companies to take 90 percent of their profits out of the country and leave a mere 10 percent behind, hardly enough to pay the debt service on these international loans, let alone improving the human conditions of our poor. In reality, these loans are huge blank checks that fatten the wallets of the rich, they serve no development at all. Can you believe such an atrocity?"

A growl of disbelief went through the aula.

"Yes, you heard correctly," Correa asserted. "It is because of the popular uprising that my predecessor was ousted, that we were able to stop this 'legalized' theft. He was ready to sign these criminal contracts. What do we need these institutions for? Once we take charge of our own country, our wealth, revenues from oil will allow us to pay back our debts to these institutions, as well as other creditors, and we will create our own development policies, choose our own priorities, not those imposed by the *Washington Consensus (Note 7)*, represented by the World Bank and the IMF."

"Further," he went on, "we will not renew the lease for the U.S. Military Base at *Manta (Note 8)*. As many of you know, this base operates under the pretense—as they all do—of helping the Ecuadorian people, helping the government fight drug trafficking. The truth is that the American military is protecting U.S. oil companies from the wrath of indigenous inhabitants. They are part of the so-called '*creeping invasion*' of U.S. forces into Latin America. From *Manta* they also infiltrate our neighbor, Colombia, to support right-wing guerilla groups and activities under *Plan Colombia*, the State Department's multi-billion dollar program that claims to eradicate coca and fight drug trafficking. Again, the real purpose is to secure U.S. corporations' petrol and gas extractions."

The audience grew visibly and audibly agitated at hearing about these American injustices. Gaining full confidence, Correa continued, "Ladies and Gentlemen, how in the world could the cocaine trade have flourished in the last four years under the just re-elected President of Colombia, if the billions of dollars under *Plan Colombia* would have truly been dedicated to eradicating coca?—Why do I talk about Colombia?—Because Colombia is an example of what may have become of Ecuador, if my opponent had been elected. I know that the danger is still there. The enemy doesn't just give up and go away. There is too much at stake: billions of dollars worth of petrol under our land!

"There have been political assassinations before in my country. I am fully conscious of Jaime Roldós death in an airplane crash in May 1981. Shortly before his death he passed legislation—environmental rules, higher royalties—which would have made life more difficult for American hydrocarbon extractors. His American puppet successor reversed these laws.

"Ladies and Gentlemen, and foremost my fellow Ecuadorians, under our democracy, health services and education will not become merchandise, consumables through privatization. Thank you." He received a standing ovation, and bowed to his audience before stepping down from the podium.

There was a sudden commotion at one of the entrance gates. Police wrestled with a handful of demonstrators, or what appeared to be intruders. The uniformed lawmen prevailed in subduing them. The incident was hardly noticed by the audience. But it did not escape Moni Cheng's eyes. She was sitting in the front row, among the conference speakers.

Later in the night, in her hotel room, she learned from a local TV reporter that the apprehended demonstrators were in fact Latinos who attempted to capture one of Peru's representatives, "a young lady by the name of Moni Cheng." They'd infiltrated the building to watch her moves and capture her in the melee as she exited the Conference Hall. The police received an anonymous hint. She was terrified and at the same time determined to get to the bottom of this alleged kidnapping scheme. It would give her even more vigor to stand in front of the plenum and make her case.

* * *

In the morning, before the Meeting started, Moni Cheng and Antonio Esteban went to the Dacca Police Headquarters. They were immediately received by the police chief. He introduced himself simply as Ali. His muscles bulged out of the too tight uniform. He had a dark half moon of short hair around his bald scalp and a broad smile on his face. His demeanor was simpatico. He had suspected that they would show up. He asked them to make themselves comfortable and showed them a sofa and two fauteuils in his spacious office, while he was rummaging for a file in his mahogany desk drawer.

He eventually found the dossier. "Here are the transcripts of the interrogations. Three young men, ages 18 to 21. They were armed with pistols. According to their passports, one was Peruvian, the other two Colombians. We questioned them individually. Their stories matched. They seemed to be fairly inexperienced in what they were supposed to do."

He waited for comments. But the two guests were eager to get the full story. "They said they were students at the Pacifica University of Lima. Three men approached them in the street, asking them whether they wanted to earn some good and quick money. Of course, that's how it always works. Some threats in case of non-performance, and they were bought. They were suspiciously loitering in front of the main entrance to the Conference Hall, waiting to kidnap the young lady, when she would emerge in the crowds after the meeting. We received an anonymous call. That's how we discovered them." He nodded towards Moni Cheng, "She was to be silenced for the duration of the conference. It didn't appear that they wanted to harm her. They seemed to have been unaware of Mr. Senator's presence."

The police chief looked at Antonio in deference, wondering whether he was indeed a congressman from Peru. He added, "They said they were paid $ 10,000 a head and a round-trip ticket to Dacca. One of them complained that it wasn't even a business class ticket."

"Who were the men who bought them off for this deal?" Esteban asked.

"They said they didn't know, but one of them hesitated before emphatically insisting he didn't know. That's how we figured that they have an idea who gave them the orders."

"And you didn't press the point?" The Senator asked incredulously.

"Don't worry," Ali quipped, "they are behind bars. They will talk sooner or later. The conditions of our prisons are so bad," he raised his eyebrows "dirty, stinking, full of rats and thieves, street gang thugs ... they will talk soon, the 'fine' young men," he said, with an ironic smile. "They won't stand it for long. I told them they can go, if they talk. They are each in a different cell. One will break sooner or later.—You are welcome to talk with them. Maybe you have more tools to convince them...." He said with a cunning twinkle.

Without hesitation, Esteban asked, "Where is the prison? I want to see them—now, if that's possible. The sooner we know who is behind this, the better. We are only in the second day of the conference, and who knows what else may happen. There are other speakers who may be at risk. I would like to ask you to guard the *Mujibur Rahman Center* with your best men; to watch out and apprehend any suspects. I will also ensure that there is consistent media coverage—international media—not just the first and last days. This may also detract potential perpetrators.—Now, may I see the prisoners?"

Without answering, the Police Chief got up, went to the door and called a stray policeman. "Take these people to the Zhia Prison. They want to see the three Latinos we arrested yesterday."

"No, I am going alone," said the Senator, and looking at Moni Cheng, he added, "You better stay here under police protection until I am back."

Moni Cheng was ready to protest, she wanted to return to the Conference, she didn't want to miss the Venezuelan President. But she relented; realizing she would never succeed in convincing Antonio. Being such a close friend of her uncle's, he would not allow anything to happen to his friend's adopted daughter. She knew that he had a lot of admiration for her, for what she did and stood for.

And now addressing Ali, Antonio said "Is it far, the prison, I mean?—And how long do you think it will take before I am back?"

Ali grinned again. "No it's not far. Just a few blocks from here, but it could easily take an hour to get there, fighting traffic jams. Now, how long will it take you to be back?—that depends entirely on your sales skills, if you know what I mean."

"I know perfectly what you mean."

He gave Moni Cheng a hug and assured her that he would return soon. He stormed out of the Chief's office, the policeman in tow.

* * *

It was mid-afternoon, when he came back. Moni Cheng was sitting on a wooden bench, in the hall of the police office, along with a myriad of people of all shapes and appearances. The run-down place reeked of curry and sweat, a wonderful combination that would bring most westerners to the brink of puking. But Moni Cheng didn't even seem to notice it. She was reading the *International Herald Tribune*.

"How did you get this paper?"

"A nice police officer, who saw me bored and felt sorry, brought it to me. He must have picked it up in a hotel lobby.—What's new? Did they talk?"

Antonio was thinking, how best to tell her, without making her even more worried. He adjusted his rimless glasses, as he always did, when he was reflective. "Yes and no, they talked. At the beginning all three of them refused to even meet with me. They were so terrified of losing their lives. Apparently their 'masters' back in Lima warned them against divulging anything ... or else ..."

He cleared his throat. "Eventually two of them agreed to meet. I met with them individually. They corroborated each other's stories. The third one refused, even at the risk of being incarcerated indefinitely."

He took a breath and again touched his glasses. "Here is what I make of it. The two prisoners repeated what they already told Ali, that they were approached by three men. It seems that one of them spoke Spanish with a Peruvian accent. He told them they were from the Peruvian Secret Service. This could have been the truth, or simply a trick to buy them off easier, because they assumed it was an honor for anybody to work for the Secret Service. Apparently the conversation between the Secret Service people and our perpetrators was brief. The former didn't give them time to reflect on the proposal. That's how it usually works. With threats and pressure, they normally get what they want."

Now he shook his head before he continued, "Look, I believe they don't know who is really behind it all. The third guy was so scared he wouldn't even talk when I promised him freedom and that nobody in Peru would ever find out."

He continued, "The three students were apparently bought with three heavy, padded envelopes that each contained $10,000 in $100 bills, a roundtrip ticket, as well as a small handgun. José, one of the two students who spoke to me, said they were perplexed, so much money and the tickets were already issued with their names printed on them. 'Really scary!' he said. Then, before the brief encounter was over, the secret service guy who spoke the least, in a heavy English accent wished them farewell, saying, 'if anybody knows about this, you better say good-bye to your friends'. That was it."

As an afterthought, Antonio added, "Oh yes, the entire ten minute event took place in the very popular bistro '*Aruba*' by the *Ovalo Gutierrez* in Lima's lush San Isidro district. Knowing this may help the investigation."

Moni Cheng said, "Maybe we can find out more back in Lima. I don't think this attempt of shutting us up is over yet."

Antonio didn't want to frighten her and suggested, "You better stay out of this. Let me take care of it. I know some people who could probably find out. If our illustrious President himself is behind it all, I promise all the Peruvians will know about his methods to defend 'democracy and free speech'."

"And now what?" she asked.

"I tell Ali to let them go. I promised them. The third one too. He isn't worse than the others. He just fears for his life. Maybe more so than the others."

With these words he opened the door to Ali's office. "They talked. They told me as much as they knew. Please let them go. They are too scared to do any more harm."

Ali wanted to know, "So who were these 'evil-doers' in your country?"

"The truth is," the Senator said, "I don't know exactly. But I will find out. And when I do, I will let you know—as a thank-you for your cooperation. We really appreciate your help."

Ali smiled awkwardly, scratching his jaw, "You are welcome." He telephoned his assistant, "Let the three Latinos go".

* * *

Back at the Conference Center ...

That evening, the Bangladeshi Foreign Ministry hosted a banquet for the G-77 Conference participants at the Sheraton near the *Mujibur Rahman Center*. The UN Secretary General attended the dinner, and so did a number of conference observers from European countries—Spain, Germany, France, the UK, Switzerland—as well as from Japan and Australia. The United States was conspicuously absent. Moni Cheng and Senator Esteban sat at the table with the delegates from Ecuador, Venezuela, Bolivia, Mexico and Sudan. Moni Cheng wondered how the Sudanese representative came to be seated at the table with them. She would soon find out. In anticipation of what the G-77 attendants were going to learn tonight—he obviously was already informed—he wanted to sit with the Latinos, whom he thought capable of making revolution.

All attention was on a huge TV screen.

There was Ron Rommel, the infamous U.S. Secretary of Defense, addressing a NATO conference, somewhere in the capital of an oil-rich former Soviet Republic. It was like a farewell speech to the international troops. Rommel used his last opportunities before stepping down under pressure to hammer back his notorious defense strategy. His policies were always the same, envisaging how to bring the world to the knees of the Empire's reign. He would never hesitate to use aggression.

Rommel would soon be succeeded by another man with blood on his hands. This one is a former CIA Director, who directed clandestine killer operations in Central America, while arming Iran. This happened at the same time that Rommel courted the then President of Iraq, selling him poisonous chemicals and other weapons of mass destruction with which the eight-year (1980-88) Iran-Iraq war was fought, leaving more than a million civilians dead. The two pronged approach of supporting both armies, Iran and Iraq, was found necessary by the United States, nurturing and extending the war as long as possible. It was in America's interest to weaken both countries to the point where they could easily be taken over, their huge hydrocarbon reserves be appropriated by American oil giants. This is precisely what is in the process of happening today. The strategy being implemented these days was already in the making in the 1980s.

Transmitted via satellite TV, Rommel praised NATO for the great job they did in liberating Kosovo from Serbian oppression (never mind the 5,000 civilian deaths, caused by the U.S dominated NATO bombings in the ten-week war in 1999). He welcomed the new Eastern European NATO members; stressed the need to persevere in Afghanistan, to increase allied troop levels so that they could defeat the *Taliban* (meaning 'student') and *al-Qaeda* (meaning 'the foundation').

The U.S. Defense Chief also talked about the lingering civil wars in Sudan and neighboring countries, South Sudan, Darfur, Chad and into the Central African Republic. He raised fear that the huge petroleum resources could go to the 'enemy', the rebels, who then would sell it to the Chinese and buy the most sophisticated weapons with the oil revenues, making them a threat to the entire central and North African region.

Expressing his disdain for the UN, Rommel said that in the light of the United Nations' inability to bring peace to the region, consultations were going on, as he was speaking, to extend NATO forces to Sudan and Chad. Then the reporter of AsiaLink-TV came on, closing this news clip with a curt and cynical comment: "World brace yourself against the fangs of the unstoppable beast, lest your last resort is a desolate country, whose only natural resources are abject poverty, famine and disease."

The AsiaLink-TV reporter then switched to another topic. "Now some Breaking News from the region, coinciding with Mr. Rommel's NATO summit. In Afghanistan, NATO Officers rebel against the U.S. NATO General in Brussels. They claim their troop strength cannot withstand Taliban pressure and that if this trend is allowed to continue, the Taliban will take back their country within a few months. They also complained of massive desertion. NATO soldiers disappear in uncharted mountain terrain. Of the 12,000-strong peacekeeping army, at least 1,500 have already deserted."

The anchorman switched the program to another Breaking News story: In Sudan, *'The UK New Business Journal'* reports on the U.S. channeling hundreds of millions of dollars into Southern Sudan through its aid agency under the guise of rebuilding war-torn infrastructure and housing. In reality these funds are largely used for propaganda against the South Sudanese Government, to keep the smoldering unrest alive.

With that remark, he showed a film clip depicting South Sudan's wealth of oil reserves by means of a rig manned by Chinese workers. A local commentator said that most of the oil, about two-thirds, was currently being extracted by China. The U.S. was eager to pave the way for American oil giants, who have been shunned so far, to grab at least a piece of the pie and eventually to push the Chinese out.

The Sudanese representative at the Latin-American table was from South Sudan. He introduced himself as 'Mokhtar'. He was tall, slim, brown-skinned with more Berber than typically Arab features. He got up, raised his fist and yelled: "These animals, they are fomenting a civil war in Southern Sudan. The highly publicized, so-called Comprehensive Peace Agreement signed in January 2005 between the Government in Khartoum and our Southern Province, was broken almost the moment it went into effect. The massive influx of dollars into the

South is helping arm guerrilla factions and provoking a lingering civil war!"

Much of the dining room's attention shifted to the Latino table. Mokhtar hadn't finished. "Everybody knows that war-stricken destitute people first have to fend for daily survival. They leave their country and their resources vulnerable to the vultures. That's what's happening to us!"

People from the neighboring table applauded.

Someone from a corner of the restaurant shouted: "There should be another Nuremberg, where all these war criminals would be brought to justice!"

Another round of applause and cheers followed.

The applause almost drowned out the approaching police sirens— but not quite. The dinner guests wondered what was going on, looked nervously around the huge gathering to see signs of trouble. There were none. Yet, the shrill sounds of alarm continued. The almost deafening sirens were probably mounted on police cars which were stationary, surrounding the Sheraton.

A loudspeaker shouted suddenly: "Attention please! The hotel management has received an anonymous warning. There is apparently a dangerous terrorist among the guests. Nobody is to leave the dining room. It has been sealed it off. The police will now carry out a search. We ask everybody to please cooperate."

As soon as the announcement stopped, the four doors slammed open and armed police in riot gear stormed in. Two guards remained at each door, to prevent the suspect from fleeing. The police had a photograph of the presumed terrorist. They went from table to table, looking into the people's faces. When a team of policemen approached Moni Cheng's table, Mokhtar became nervous. He dropped a napkin on the floor and was now trying to retrieve it, his head disappearing under the table. To no avail. A policeman lifted him up, held his head straight, another one shone a flashlight into his face and yelled, "That's him. We found him."

They dragged him out of the room and asked the other occupants of the table, including Moni Cheng and the Senator, to follow them. Mokhtar and the others were put in separate cars. They sped off in the direction of Ali's office.

Ali was waiting at the door. "Hi there. I didn't think to see you so soon again." He greeted Moni Cheng and her companion.

"Neither did we," said Moni Cheng. "What's going on?" He didn't answer, but directed them instead into a waiting room, where the delegates from Ecuador, Venezuela, Bolivia and Mexico were already seated. They were restless, wondering what might happen to them. A policewoman entered, saying that they would all be interrogated momentarily.

After a few minutes, Ali's stately figure appeared in the door frame. He called, "Ms. Moni Cheng and Senator Esteban, please come with me."

The two exchanged a questioning glance. But they said nothing. They followed Ali through the door. Once outside and a safe distance from the others, Ali said, "I don't think you have any links to the suspect. You may go."

But Antonio wasn't satisfied with this curt dismissal. "Could you please tell us what the story is? What is Mokhtar accused of? Except for his emotional outbreak at the table when he saw the film clip about oil exploitation in his country, he behaved like a very nice guy. Could you please elaborate?"

Ali said, "Please come with me." He led them into his office. "Please sit down." He moved behind his desk and plumped down into his chair and continued. "This man, Mokhtar, is from South Sudan. He is a member of what they call in Khartoum a terrorist group. In fact, they are a small group of rebels fighting for total independence of South Sudan from Khartoum. They are disguised as a health NGO, supporting AIDS victims. He also goes by several other names, depending on the circumstances. In international circuits he is often known as Ahmed."

"So he wasn't really representing his country at the G-77 summit." Moni Cheng asked rhetorically. "That explains why he sat at the Latino table."

"Correct," said the Police Chief. "He came to 'observe' the delegate from Khartoum. But there is no evidence that he wanted to do any harm. In any case, the man is unarmed. Other than rebelling against the news about the exploitation of their petrol and the gringos' interference in their Sudanese internal affairs, he hasn't done anything wrong. He will probably go free before the night is over."

"Who denounced him?" The Senator wanted to know.

"We don't really know." A weary Ali replied, "For all I know, it could be the Americans who want this Independence Movement stopped. They are seeking access to the hydrocarbon resources of South Sudan. With the help of Khartoum, they might even be able to kick the Chinese out. But the Independence Movement is a nuisance."

Antonio got up. "Thanks, Ali. Who knows when we'll meet next." He said this half jokingly. At this rate ..." And he left it there. Instead, he asked, "May we leave?"

"Of course. Enjoy your stay in Dacca!" He accompanied them to the door.

* * *

When they got back to the Sheraton, the dining room was deserted. In fact the entire hotel looked empty. So much for an aborted evening. They took a moto-taxi to their hotel which was a small three-star inn, called *Saidpur*, named after a small city in northwestern Bangladesh in the *Rajshahi Division*. The name of the guest house reflects the nostalgia of the couple who owns it. The place was located just behind the Mujibur Rahman Center.

A large-screen TV was on in the corner of the lobby's tiny seating area. On display was a close-up of the stern-faced U.S. Secretary of State, Ms. Contessa. She sported her usual frown between her darting eyes. Antonio and Moni Cheng couldn't help stopping to watch what was going on.

The scene played in Tel Aviv, where Ms. Contessa was holding a press conference with the Israeli Prime Minister. According to the commentator, the President of Palestine refused to see her, and the people of Gaza barricaded the main road which entered their bombed-out patch of land, so she could not enter their territory.

The screen showed Contessa praising Israel for their adherence to the ceasefire with Lebanon, for their efforts to re-establish peaceful relations with their northern neighbor. No mention was made of the almost complete destruction of Southern Lebanon's housing and infrastructure by the massive blanket bombardment of the Israeli Air Force, the thousands of landmines Israeli soldiers left behind, daily killing and maiming children, the nuclear-spiked American supplied bunker-busters that left land, water and vegetation in Southern Lebanon dangerously contaminated with poisonous uranium residues for who-knew how many years to come.

When a reporter asked why she was not welcome in Gaza and couldn't meet the Palestinian President, she was not without an answer. "There can be no peace, if there is no talk. And there can be no talk with a people led by terrorists ..."

This sounded absurd, but interesting enough for Moni Cheng and the Senator to sit down and watch the unfolding of this intriguing scene. They exchanged looks but said nothing. They were leaning forward as if this would allow them to better absorb the story being presented.

On the screen, an irate reporter shouted from the floor: "You call them terrorists! They have been democratically elected. A Nobel-prize winning former President of yours led a team of international election observers and reported that the results were proper and indisputable. How can you come to our region and call us terrorists!"

Contessa looked at the Prime Minister, who shook his head, meaning 'don't answer; move on to the next question'. Her eyes darted around the room, purposefully avoiding the two Al-Jazeera journalists, who eagerly attempted to get her attention. Instead she called on a woman in the back in a black dress and black head scarf.

The lady got up, revealing a long black T-shirt with white inscription: 'War crimes committed by the United States of America', followed by a long list of countries, all the way down to below her knees. The young woman asked, "Could you please explain why your country unilaterally helps Israel to commit crimes against its neighbors, to kill Palestinian and Lebanese children and women, to destroy our houses, to steal our land, to starve the Gaza population into misery, to …"

Before she could finish her sentence, two Israeli policemen subdued her on the floor, hand-cuffed her and dragged her from the room. But she turned around once more and shouted, "You want Apartheid like in South Africa …" Then the door slammed shut behind her.

Contessa looked speechless, embarrassed—nodded at the Prime Minister, who took the microphone and said: "Ladies and gentlemen, that's it for today. Thank you." And the pair hurried out through the back door.

The anchorman came back: "This is AsiaLink-TV. In other news today…."

* * *

The following morning....

After the mid-morning break, the conference saw Moni Cheng on the podium. In jeans, purple jacket and red bandana around her neck, she looked attractive and unlike the rest of the delegates. Many of the male delegates thought her a pleasant sight. The hall fell silent. The Bangladeshi Minister of Foreign Affairs introduced her as a Peruvian environmental activist and freedom fighter, who had a special message to bring to the forum, a message that was of importance for all the G-77 members. "The floor is yours, Ms. Cheng."

Moni Cheng adjusted her scarf, took a sip of water and began: "Ladies and gentlemen, what happened in Peru, I am sure, happens in many countries, Latin America and elsewhere."

She recounted the events at the coca plantation near *Tarapoto*, the breach of contract by the U.S.-led Peruvian forces, the spraying of toxic chemicals, poisoning of children and animals, destruction of peasants' livelihoods, contamination of water—and finally the *Cocaleros* liberation movement that launched an attack against the gringo-led perpetrators, resulting in downed spray-planes, 18 people killed and five resistance fighters abducted by American forces.

She took a sip of water. She had the audience's full attention and continued telling them the story of the Peruvian Police Chief's refusal to see her and the Peruvian Senator, "Who, by the way is here with me." She bowed slightly and motioned towards Antonio Esteban. "He will speak later on another matter of concern to us, Peruvians—international trade—but, I am sure, it preoccupies many other governments too."

She went on, explaining how the Senator had organized the press conference in Congress, to bring the occurrence to the world's attention, how the media event was shut down by a raiding police squad under orders of the U.S.-backed new Peruvian President.

She concluded, "Friends and colleagues, many of us here represent fledgling democracies, but democracies we have chosen." Smiling she added, "Even sometimes with leaders we don't like, but still a social system in which by definition we must have freedom of speech and expression. Of course, disagreement with the United States is part of freedom of expression. It is our right. But they, the Americans, don't like it. They will do everything to oppress our opposition, even kill our leaders, if they object to their intruding policies.

"Then they bring back dictators and despots who bow to their wishes." She looked around the huge hall, "Remember President Allende, Chile, 1973, the CIA-backed military coup that killed him? They installed Pinochet, a murderer and torturer, who also ransacked the country neocon-style for the benefit of the elite. In his 17-year reign, he killed 20,000 Chileans, tortured 60,000 and drove a million into exile—an armed puppet of the United States."

She looked around the huge conference aula. "Friends, we must resist this! We must not fear them. We are strong. We can unite. We, in Latin America, have 550 million people; almost double the population of the United States. Let us not forget, united we are strong! Thank you."

She bowed to the public who gave her a standing ovation, cheering and clapping, as if to ask her to come back and tell them more. She thought it was reminiscent of the time she stood in front of a much smaller audience at the New Society University in Buenos Aires. Then she waved and stepped down.

She was hardly at the bottom of the stairs of the podium, when her mobile rang. She answered smiling; expecting a congratulatory call, but her face froze. "OK, I will be on the next plane to Indonesia ... yes, by tomorrow night I hope to be in *Okaba, Irian Jaya.*" She looked nervously for the Senator, she needed to leave immediately. He was already on the podium. Waving him good luck with a smile was all she could do. She would leave him a note in the hotel.

Other highlights of the conference included the speeches of the Mexican President *in-Exile*, who would speak about NAFTA's devastating effects on the Mexican farmers; Senator Esteban would address the subject of Free Trade Agreements (FTA), especially the case of

Peru. President Bongo of *Kilimanda*, a landlocked East African country, tricked his way into the conference. The despot and dictator intended to improve his image by addressing the meeting talking about the trillion dollar arms trade, responsible for killing millions of innocent victims, an arms trade which this hypocrite encouraged. He was booed out, when he tried to force his way onto the podium. He left in a hurry, disappeared without bodyguard into the street masses of Dacca.

Closing remarks were made by the President of Brazil.

* * * * *

16

US Congress and CEOs—Closed Door Hearings

Simultaneous to the G77 Conference....

Once a month, the CEOs or their deputies of the 30 most important US corporations meet in a secret place in Washington to discuss 'lobbying strategies' with Congress, to agree on the amounts of money that were to be paid by corporations so as to push through specific legislation in their benefit. The meetings' monthly agenda usually amasses hundreds of thousands, sometimes millions of dollars from sponsoring corporations. No wonder, U.S. corporations have a large advantage in doing business around the world, as compared to transnationals of other nationalities (*Note 9*).

Due to the secret nature of this event, no records are kept during the meeting. However, this one meeting was clandestinely filmed by a Congressman from Ohio with his cell phone. The Congressman's name shall, of course, not be revealed. He was so disgusted by the maneuverings of the event, that he leaked the tape to the British weekly magazine *The New Citizen* in London. The paper produced a transcript-style editorial. Here are excerpts.

> The secret meetings are usually hosted by the special congressional Commission on American World Dominance (CAWD). The covertly taped session took place in a secluded, little known conference room on Capitol Hill. In addition to the largest and most

powerful U.S. corporations, also present were the major players of highly influential Congressional Committees, among them Ways and Means, the Defense Committee, the Senate's Intelligence Committee, the Judiciary Committee, the Trade Commission— and, by special invitation, the National Rifle Association (NRA). Blatantly absent was the Black Caucus. But also present were Dick Dingo, President of the World Bank, Haviland Gersten, Managing Director of the International Monetary Fund, as well as the French Director General of the World Trade Organization (WTO). The latter three, constituted the notorious key actors in the circus of international finance and globalization. There was also Ms. Contessa, Secretary of State, the token African American in this all-out WASP Republican Administration. The global financial and trade organizations had to dance to the tune of the various congressional committees, which were fully aligned with the corporate and Congressional decision-makers.

The topic was "How to appease the American people by selling them the American Way of Life in Perpetuity." Many citizens are getting increasingly weary, even upset by their tax dollars being spent on wars abroad, mostly Iraq and Afghanistan, and other battles around the world fueled by U.S. corporate interests. These armed conflicts absorb an enormous amount of resources—close to a trillion dollars in 2007—while at home social institutions like the health systems and general education are crumbling for lack of money.

Worldwide, according to WHO and UNICEF, more than a billion people have no access to drinking water and about 2.6 billion lack basic safe sanitation, annually killing more than 1.5 million children under the age of 5 from intestinal diseases. Investments in this vital infrastructure, costing less than half the U.S yearly war budget, could wipe out this world calamity.

On that day's secret meeting agenda were domestic and foreign policy items. The most burning domestic issues were (1) the cost of health care, (2) the deterioration of public education, and, to some extent, (3) agricultural subsidies in the face of Free Trade Agreements, which the United States peddles around the globe, with emphasis on its Latin American neighbors.

On the international front, priorities included (1) the high cost of the war in Iraq, juxtaposed with the high profits of the war and oil industries, (2) the necessary advancement of globalization, especially in taking over the world's hot spots of vital natural resources required to maintain the 'American Way of Life' and, finally, (3) the highly inflated and debt-ridden U.S. economy.

According to the chairman, once the extent of the huge debt and the empty American economy is discovered by the rest of the world, trust in the U.S. dollar will likely falter. A sudden collapse of the U.S. currency is, however, unlikely, because too many dollars in the form of treasury bills are filling the reserve coffers of countries around the world. Nonetheless, decisive forward looking actions are required now, and they need to be kept secret from the rest of the world. Otherwise, world economic chaos could destroy the wealth of the rich and eventually bring down the well-being of the populace at large, which could lead to public unrest or even civil wars in the G8 countries.

The Chairman of CAWD referred to the recent events in Latin America and elsewhere in the world, where leftwing leaders are taking over former allies. He said, "I wanted to call on you to discuss and forge a new strategy that will allow us to maintain 'The American Way of Life', no matter what. It will lead us further in our quest for world dominance."

His main concerns were how to resolve a few issues at home and abroad, all in the way of helping U.S. corporations take better and more efficient control of crucial sectors.

"On the domestic front," he said, "we face the staggering cost of health care, and a possible revolution of close to 50 million people without health coverage. In 2004, we spent almost two trillion dollars, about 16 percent of our GDP on health. In other words, the cost of health for every American was about 6,300—and rising.

This is about twice the average of other OECD countries. Yet, we are the only rich country that does not guarantee universal health coverage. Fundamental revisions are necessary. Congress has allocated over half a trillion dollars for the next ten years to salvage the Medicare system. Yet, the States' bureaucracies are gobbling up the money without any signs of the schemes' improvement. More responsibility will have to be given to the private sector, the private medical service providers and the pharma-industry. The public sector has utterly failed."

A member from the ranks of the Democrats dared to raise his voice, "Mr. Chairman, these billions of dollars, including the Medicare package, are mere subsidies for the bloated pharmaceutical and health care corporations. They bring no benefits to the public at large. The poor and destitute are worse off today than they were before this huge budget transfer. In fact, Congress approved a cut in Medicare benefits of 22 billion dollars over the next ten years, leaving millions of elderly without access to affordable medication. This disastrous health care package will rapidly swell the number of uninsured Americans towards the 20 percent mark of the population."

The last words were drowned out by increasingly raucous protest, an indication that not all were tuned in to the voice of protest.

The Chairman sounded his gavel, "Ladies and gentlemen—this is precisely why we have to complement these measures, which we found were insufficient. We need to introduce additional steps, like the idea of 'Health Savings Accounts', the so-called HSAs. Individuals could make monthly deposits, a tax-deductible amount, into personal HSAs, up to a maximum of, say, US$ 5,000 per year."

Another dissenting voice questioned the chairman: "How could poor people, families of four whose annual income does not exceed $ 25,000, afford deposits of $ 5,000—This is outright ridiculous. It is obvious that you, Republicans, have no idea how the majority of Americans live."

The speaker also referred to the deductible, which could be as high as $2,000 to $ 5,000 per family per year, and to the insurance premium, which could amount to several thousand dollars per family per year, under the proposed scheme. He called it "another bonanza for the rich."

The Chairman had no answer, other than stuttering that he believed this was the only way less privileged families could get a more equitable and affordable share of health care. He said, the details needed to be worked out, and that, of course, the new system would rely on the virtues of the private sector. The proposal would be submitted to Congress later in the year.

No more objections were heard, because all those who didn't agree must have thought it was a lost cause to debate the issue in this forum. Or perhaps they simply felt no serious concern, since they and their families would not be affected by the new system.

They also knew, as long as the public at large buys the new system—the brainwashing influence of the administration's public relations apparatus works wonders—a potential civil uprising may be appeased.

The Chairman was eager to move to the national education structure which he considered was in shambles.

He said, "Primary and secondary school performance nationwide—with some notable exceptions—is on the decline. This is unacceptable for the U.S., the richest nation with the destiny to lead the world to a higher plane."

He tried to impress on the audience that the country could no longer afford putting tax dollars into a defunct public education system. Instead, he proposed a system in which education would gradually be privatized. New Orleans after Hurricane Katrina, he said, was a case study for chartered schools. Students from poor families would receive vouchers to pay a portion of their tuition fees. And he referred to private sponsorships to play an increasingly important role in the country's future education system. Our children's education. Tongue in cheek he added: "Along similar lines as you, ladies and gentlemen, already do," nodding at the ranks of CEOs, in reference to the huge corporate endowments to Ivy League and other major universities.

The Chairman recognized, however, that the conversion of the current public education system to a private system could not happen overnight. "But it is not too early to start now. We cannot afford to lose more of our most precious wealth—the human capital to produce the leadership this country needs to assume its mandate in the world."

Not everybody agreed. Somebody in the back, it appeared, probably a Democrat, shouted: "This is again going to favor the privileged classes. The low-income people will not be able to afford private schools, no matter whether they receive some voucher in primary school or not."

He also mentioned private college tuitions, which were climbing rapidly towards the 50,000 dollar level. "With more than half of U.S. households earning less than that, how can they afford a decent education for their kids?" he asked.

Another daring voice rose from the rear area, where most Democrats seem to have chosen their seating. "Yes, and teaching will be oriented towards corporate needs and the whims of other influential interest groups, including religious factions. Where is our genuine, unbiased education going?—This is unacceptable."

The murmur grew to an angry outburst. Interestingly though, the anger did not appear to be aimed at the neo-liberal proposal, but against those who dared to object.

According to the Congressman's accompanying note, the ensuing rage was at the point of evolving into a melee. Armed security officers appeared at the different entrances, prominently holding riot sticks, dissuading angry politicians from breaking out of control.

However, their intervention was not necessary. The noise ebbed to a near whisper, as the Chairman caught his breath, indicating with his gavel that he wanted quiet, and calmly said, "Ladies and gentlemen, there is no need for worry. You all know, our fine institution, the Military. They have for decades offered free education to students who could otherwise not afford it. All they have to do is register with the Armed Services and they will be taken care of. And you also know that we do need soldiers for many years to come. The Global War on Terror will be with us indefinitely, possibly for generations. In addition, we have to succeed in our mission to bring democracy and freedom to the world. So—colleagues and friends, there is no reason for concern. Nobody who is willing to learn and study will be denied the opportunity, regardless whether poor or rich. In addition to free education, the Armed Services will also provide free health care. We are entering a new World Order with equality for all."

The Chairman emphasized the last sentence with three strikes of his gavel, which at the same time signaled that no more discussion would be tolerated.

No one contradicted the Chairman. Why?—Because they all thought it would be useless. They also saw the policemen. And, after all, they themselves had enough money to send their kids to respectable, high quality private colleges.

The Chairman seemed in his element: "Let us now move to the last domestic issue—which is also an international topic—protection of our farmers in light of the rapidly proliferating Free Trade Agreements. We all know that our wheat, rice and cotton production is the finest in the world. To remain so, requires research, technology and the lifelong dedication of our farmers. However, farmers in other countries also produce wheat, rice and cotton. Through the FTAs, we are opening their borders for our goods, but we also open our frontiers for some of their agricultural produce.

So that our farmers can remain competitive, we must not only require our FTA partners through unilateral conditions to produce less wheat, rice and cotton, but we also must keep our farmers competitive by paying them higher subsidies."

A swell of angry protest rose from the Left and the Right. They expressed their disagreement with FTAs in general and with subsidies in particular, because billions of dollars of tax money is channeled into the farm community, rather than into needed infrastructure projects—roads, dams, and telecommunication.

A dare-devil from the Left lost his patience. He let his conscience speak. With raised fist he stepped into the alley. "Mr. Chairman, we are not subsidizing farmers. We subsidize huge agro-corporations, some of the most profitable ones in the world!—Plus, we are not playing fair game with our trading partners, whom we force to reduce cultivation of specific crops which are in our export interest. We are destroying the livelihood of many small farmers in developing countries by flooding their markets with our subsidized produce. We should not support such unethical commercial practices."

This was the strong voice of a Senator from Massachusetts, whom nobody interrupted. His pronouncement was followed by silence.

The policemen at the entrances flexed their sticks. Their faces suggested that they considered being engaged in a brawl with members of Congress the perfect story to carry home or to the neighborhood bar. But to their disappointment, the situation stayed calm.

Once more, the Chairman rose to the occasion, "Mr. Senator, we are damaging and eliminating our small family farms if we don't support them financially. Do you want to carry that burden on your conscience?"

"Mr. Chairman, you and I know, as well as many of our colleagues in this room, it is the large agro-complexes that crush the small farming business, not the lack of subsidies."

An acquiescing murmur could be heard throughout the room. But the Chairman was unmoved. He continued, "Well, ladies and gentlemen, this is not the final word. You will have an opportunity to debate this and other issues we discussed this afternoon in full congressional sessions in the coming weeks. The purpose of this meeting is merely to inform you in advance of the Administration's major items on the domestic and foreign agendas."

The Chairman went on, "There is more work ahead for today: we have to talk about the foreign policy agenda which will affect us all domestically. Let me just introduce this debate by saying whatever we do abroad will have a direct impact at home. To maintain our way of life, which is necessary for the world to see us as leaders, during the next generations we may face shortages of energy, fresh water and possibly certain minerals, like gold. Since our economy functions on high debt, which is unlikely to change in the near future, it may, sooner or later, be challenged by our trading partners around the world."

He continued, "This should not worry us. Today we are in possession of the most modern technologies in satellite imagery. It allows us to identify major and, in some cases, even minor resources, deposits of all kinds, oil, for example, around the globe. We also have the military strength and weapons capacity to support friendly nations' internal struggles for freedom and democracy. We will need allies, and we have the means to make allies. The many conquests we are currently involved in and plan to embark on in the near future will come at a high cost. We will need to ask some of our closer allies, the other G8 nations, to participate with a larger share in some of these expenditures. Since they will benefit from our conquests, they should do this voluntarily, though, I realize, in some cases they may have to be coerced, uhh, I mean diplomatically encouraged."

"Before we take a break, let me remind you why we are assembled in this special meeting. Obviously, this plan requires the close cooperation of all of our powerful international corporations, and primarily 'our' International Financial Institutions, the World Bank and the International Monetary Fund, as well as, of course, the Inter-American Development Bank."

He said 'our,' knowing full well that most parties present had disdain for the UN system. And for sure, these three UN organizations were effectively controlled by the U.S., and he didn't hesitate saying so. Deliberately he didn't mention WTO, knowing quite well that this trade organization included the EU, a mighty trading block which was more often an adversary than an ally. There was more to be gained from bilateral Free Trade Agreements than by dealing through WTO.

As an obvious afterthought, he emphasized: "We are lucky; these institutions are practically under our control."

"Let me end this debate on a positive and reassuring note." He smiled towards the CEOs. "I have invited you here, ladies and gentlemen, ambassadors of our global and powerful corporations, as a sign of gratitude for the good work you are doing abroad in perpetuating American values—and we Americans are proud to see your presence all over the world ..."

The Senator from Massachusetts, who was still visibly agitated, got up, shook his head in disbelief and started walking towards one of the exits. In his mind he must have seen all the red Coca-Cola signs, the yellow MacDonald's arches and the green Starbucks emblems in countries and cities where they were anathema to the local cultures, where they stuck out like sore thumbs. He didn't dare think of Wal-Mart, lest he begin to yell again, risking being escorted out by the guardians of order. What a farce, he must have thought, as he left the conference room.

The Chairman watched the incident with a smile, but continued unperturbed. "As I said, we are proud to see our symbols of success all around the globe and we are adamant that your success and achievements persevere for years to come. For this reason, let me also assure you, that our military will stand ready to defend your interests—your interests are the interests of our nation, in fact, of the entire 'Free World' ..."—He was now so excited at his own words that he almost tripped over them in search of superlatives.

"Whenever the security of your staff abroad and your investments are challenged, be assured that our institutions, our security system, will be there to defend you."

"And finally," he continued, "I do not need to remind you, this debate is taking place behind closed doors, not accessible to the media, and we expect the full cooperation of all those who are participating, regardless of reaching consensus on all measures under discussion. After the break we will continue with our international agenda. For transparency vis-à-vis our people and the rest of the world, the President will make a televised announcement, when the strategic steps are defined and worked out in detail."

As an editorial addendum to the publication, *The New Citizen* wrote, "Mr. Haviland Gersten, Managing Director of the International Monetary Fund, was visibly displeased by the course of events and the arrogance of the Chairman. He shook his head and was the first one to jump out of his seat (literally) to take the coffee break."

*　　*　　*　　*　　*

17

THE FINANCIAL IVORY TOWERS OF WASHINGTON

The Washington Monument is a pale obelisk built of granite, marble and sandstone. It was erected for George Washington, first President of the United States, as a symbol of respect by the citizens of this country. It was designed by architect Robert Mills. Construction started in 1848, was interrupted by the American Civil War, and finally completed in 1884. Standing 169 meters tall, it was the world's highest structure at the time, but was surpassed five years later by the Eiffel Tower in Paris. Today it is still the tallest edifice in Washington.

Since these more honorable times, Washington D.C., the Capital of the Free World, the self-anointed term coined by the inner Beltway crowd, has become a temple of power, so to speak. Political, financial and military powers are all united in this space of 177 square kilometers. The city is home to all three branches of the Federal Government, and headquarters the world's two major financial institutions, the World Bank and the International Monetary Fund. Although, they are physically shorter than the revered Washington Monument, their financial influence peddled around the world, has become a massive and unequivocal instrument for the U.S. Government and its Big Corporatocracy.

These institutions help bring countries to their knees, making their public services and natural resources vulnerable for privatization and appropriation.

The amalgamation of Washingtonian power casts these organizations as Financial Ivory Towers. Even though their capital base is much weaker than that of many large private banking institutions *(Note10)*, the power they wield is inflated by political influence. The disproportionate strength manifests itself mostly by leveraging additional resources from private banks and other multi- and bilateral lending institutions. Loans from the World Bank and the IMF to a country are a nod for others to do likewise. It conveys 'creditworthiness,' according to a set of 'good behavior' conditions defined by the *Washington Consensus* and approved by the two UN organizations.

Almost from their inception, the two agencies have primarily served U.S. corporate interests. It is perhaps fair to say that until the mid-nineties, the World Bank's agenda included a token concept of *'poverty alleviation.'* Albeit with mixed results, a portion of its lending portfolio was dedicated to rural development and social sectors. When after 1995 the Republicans took over Congress, the blanket flew off, and neo-liberal policies came to the fore. Gradually, so-called project lending was substituted by 'structural adjustments.' When countries started protesting against such operations, the World Bank invented new names for the same old trade, 'development policy lending' and 'budget support operations'—and a SWAP is a loan for a *sector-wide* approach. These are all euphemisms for 'blank checks,' transfers from the World Bank to the treasuries of client countries, with hardly any accountability required. The amounts are in the billions.

Today, project lending for 'poverty alleviation' type operations— rural water supply and sanitation, small scale irrigation, rural development, health and education—are but a veneer around a rotten column of a culture of devastatingly ruthless indebting of countries without generating socio-economic development.

Justifications for these lending practices are mere 'statements of intentions' or lists of priority sectors, handed by the governments to the World Bank. These no-questions-asked operations do not follow the rather rigorous procurement rules applied to development projects. Oversight by the World Bank on how funds are spent is minimal. Fiduciary accountability of most developing countries is largely absent. So, these operations are sheer invitations for fraud and corruption.

In 2002, structural adjustment-type lending amounted to almost two-thirds of all lending, with virtually no detectable economic gains for the developing countries; to the contrary, their debt burden rose. The beneficiaries are the elite and graft-takers. But the debt becomes a national liability, to be repaid by the sweat of the workers.

The World Bank and IMF are, hence, paving the way for transnational corporations to enter a country and suck it dry of its resources, leaving at best meager royalties behind which may just help service the nation's financial liabilities. Defaulting on World Bank and IMF loans is an international crime, to be punished with the loss of 'creditworthiness' in international financial markets, a stigma that keeps investors and private lenders away.

So—the circle of misery continues. No end is in sight for the poor and destitute.

After lively debates in the World Bank's Board, the proportion of adjustment operations decreased, hovering between 35 percent and 40 percent in the last few years.

The United States-imposed President of the World Bank, Dingo, is adamant in implementing the neo-conservative agenda of the Empire. This means, privatizing what is left of social services and safety nets in developing countries, essentially transferring public assets, accumulated over years by the labor of their people, into the claws of private for-profit corporations. Countries that refuse to play the game will face the ire of the Ivory Towers, threats of being cut off their lending and by implication, their creditworthiness in the financial world.

* * *

... *a few days after the Closed Door Hearings*

In the Board Room of the World Bank, this time with all delegates assembled, President Dingo knew that the topic he was about to raise was a contentious one—replenishment of the International Development Association (IDA). The G8 and other rich nations every three years make grant contributions to this lending agency, the soft lending arm of the World Bank. IDA makes loans to the poorest countries, interest free, repayable over 40 years, including a ten-year grace period. The IDA functions like a revolving fund. Repaid credits go back into IDA's accounts to be loaned again. The periodic restocking of the IDA fund serves to increase the lending potential of the agency.

"Today we have an important item on the agenda", Dingo began, "the ... replenishment of IDA. Our target is to obtain 18 billion dollars for the next three-year phase."

Uneasiness could be felt in the room; soft voices were heard, nothing comprehensible, though. Dingo didn't pay any attention and continued. "I would like to make the round, asking each of you, who are traditional contributors to IDA, to confirm the amounts we may expect. Let me start with the European Union members ..."

Now the voices grew louder. It was obvious, Dingo's attempt to replenish IDA wasn't welcome, much less popular, and his method of proceeding even less so. He knew it. He also knew the reasons, but never bothered to discuss them, or to enter into a dialogue with the Board members about the issues they had with the World Bank's and IDA's lending instruments. The sense of superiority he conveyed, made his acceptance by the Board members, especially by those representing G8's and other wealthy countries, even more unlikely.

But it wasn't a European who spoke first. Ms. Zengh, the Chinese representative, raised her arm and stood up, "Mr. President, I think it doesn't come as news to you that many of us do not agree with the ways the World Bank lends money ..."

Dingo attempted to interrupt, "this is not a topic for discussion this afternoon. I would like to remind you ..."

But Ms. Zengh wouldn't let him finish. She was angry. "Mr. President, I ask you the courtesy to let me finish. I know it is not the subject for discussion today. But you have refused so far to discuss lending instruments with the Board. Many of us—actually the majority of us ..." and she looked around ... "have strong views about the World Bank's ... misuse of resources."

Now there was growing dissent in the room; voices could be understood, most of them supportive of the Chinese ED. Except for the U.S. representative. Mr. Rothshield shouted: "Colleagues, order please! We are not running the Bank, the President and his management team are, and today ..." His voice was drowned out by Aurora Jimenez, the Spanish representative, an attractive lady, in a long reddish flowery dress. She looked like she came straight out of a Flamenco theatre.

She spoke majestically, "We do not agree with the American position, or for that matter, that of the World Bank's President. Today I speak for the core members of the European Union, except for the United Kingdom, whose representative has not come forward with a clear opinion. But as far as 'Old Europe' is concerned," she looked with a devious smile to her European colleagues, "we will not discuss IDA replenishment, before other questions are resolved. Our main concerns are, as you very well know, structural adjustment type loans, or whatever euphemism you may use to circumvent the problem, as well as privatization."

The others agreed with her, silencing Dingo.

The Spanish ED continued. "'Matanga', this beautiful, peaceful island country in the Indian Ocean, though extremely poor, qualifies as a 'Highly Indebted Poor Country'. Matanga has benefited from the generosity of the G8. They have received about 400 million dollars worth of debt relief. However, instead of pursuing a strict socioeconomic development policy for future lending, the World Bank, or in this case IDA, has resorted to a 'poverty alleviation' program, consisting merely of budget support transfers. Over a four-year period, the country is to receive about $500 million in 'blank checks', so to speak. The only justification is a shallow list of priority sectors in which these funds are to be spent."

Her dark eyes flashed around the conference table. She continued, "By looking a bit closer, it becomes clear that the President of *Matanga*, or family members of his, have a business interest in these so-called priority sectors. There is no accountability on how the money is actually spent. Even if there were, the country has no institutional or physical capacity to absorb these funds in ways beneficial to the people. Despite all this knowledge, about which your highly educated and highly paid economists must be aware, and despite your highly publicized fight against corruption, the World Bank, actually IDA, goes ahead to push a half billion dollars of debt down that poor country's throat. And this, after just having canceled $400 million of debt, which the Bank and the G8 considered *Matanga* could not pay pack without going through extra hardship."

"What's more," she continued, "according to a staff member, whose name I shall not disclose, a senior government official commented to him, 'why in the world are you giving my government blank checks? We have no idea what happened with the first *tranche* of ..." she hesitated a moment and then divulged the amount, "... 110 million, transferred a year ago. We, the people collectively, and our children, will eventually have to pay it back'."

She pressed her final point. "Is it by sheer coincidence that petrol has recently been discovered off the southern coast of *Matanga*? And XXION Oil&Gas is currently drilling for their fortune?"

Furious, Dingo ignored her last statement and yelled, "So, we have whistleblowers among the staff!—I'll find out, who these traitors are."

Ms. Jimenez hadn't finished. "I truly hope, Mr. President, you will not go this route. The distrust in management that besets the staff since you took over the institution's Presidency is beyond anything one could hope for in an efficient UN organization. The World Bank had the reputation of being the best of the lot.

"Let me just add to your concept of 'traitors'. Your representative in *Matanga* recently gave an interview to a world-renowned financial newspaper. Granted, he may have been a bit dozed by whisky at the time. He commented to the reporter about the extent of corruption going on in the upper circles of *Matanga's* Government. Are you having him arrested as a traitor?"

Dingo was speechless for a moment. His authority seemed to be broken. Although his relationship with the Board has never been like a Saturday evening outing, now it seems to have reached a new low.

One more time he tried to rescue the discussion of IDA replenishment. "Fine. You have a valid point, but we must discuss these issues separately. Let's get back now to IDA …"

Again he was interrupted. This time by Maurice Vernier, the French delegate. "Sir, with due respect," he said, though his facial expression suggested Dingo did not deserve his respect, "we are not ready to talk about IDA, without first reaching a consensus on the institution's future lending practices. I would like to bring to your attention another point. This one on 'privatization'. It was reported to me not by a staff, but by a government official of the *Cocoa Coast* in West Africa. The World Bank is financing rehabilitation of various urban water supply systems. Privatization is always on the table when the World Bank gets involved with water supply systems. As the *Cocoas* dared to voice their reluctance to lease their utilities to a foreign company, the World Bank official in charge threatened to halt future support to the sector. This, in simple terms, is blackmail and not acceptable, not to the *Cocoa Coast*, and not to the Board."

The room was silent. Dingo must have realized there was nothing he could do to bring the discussion back to IDA replenishment.

Vernier hadn't finished yet. "Many of us had the impression that the World Bank changed gears. After so many failures around the world—more than the best known cases of Argentina, Bolivia, and the Philippines—it would seem to be a time to retreat, to take stock and invent a new approach. Your managers may publicly say that's what they are doing, but behind the scene they are pushing the old model.—Why?—It's good for their careers. These are easy projects, almost as easy as structural adjustments. You hire a contractor, give him a concession and the money to implement the changes, and then it is up to him to perform. You can do three of these types of projects with the resources for one of the more complex ones, where your staff actually has to design, supervise and make corrections, if the design wasn't quite right in the first place. Your staff is gaining 'brownie' points with the neo-conservative management for privatizing the public sector. Your incentive system, Mr. President, is skewed; it judges quantity over quality."

Now an uproar went through the conference room. Dingo was visibly nervous. He scratched his head. "Quiet please." He pounded the table with his ridiculous little gavel. "These are important topics, but ..."

The Board was making a racket. Before Dingo could finish his sentence, Eric Svensen, the Nordic countries' representative barged in. "Sorry, Mr. President. We will not discuss IDA today. In light of the just released report of the World Bank's Evaluation Department, fundamentally saying that this institution has bitterly failed to lift poor countries out of poverty, it is more important to analyze and correct the failure rather than simply pouring more money after the same unsuccessful efforts. There are indeed countries, like Brazil which have been wary about following the World Bank's advice. They have consistently done better. They have not just strived for economic growth—the one and only dogma that the World Bank and the IMF touts around the world—but rather for better income distribution. I suggest you set a time on the Board agenda, to debate these vital points to get to the bottom of the problem. I also suggest you invite staff and hands-on managers to this meeting."

He didn't stop: "Mr. President we know and you know that 'privatization' is but a modern word for 'colonialism'. We do not want an institution that supports colonization of poor countries—of any country!"

With these words, he got up and walked out of the room. Others followed. To the chagrin of Dingo, gradually all of the Board members left the conference room. The last lingering characters staying behind were the representatives of the United States and the U.K. It was not clear whether out of sympathy for Dingo, or because they wanted to separate themselves from the rest of their colleagues, so as not to be seen stepping out of line. The Board became a scene of chaos and rupture between the World Bank's President and the majority of its shareholders.

*   *   *   *   *

18

THE FREEDOM RANCH

Some 7,000 km south of Washington....

Living at the Freedom Ranch (*El Rancho de la Libertad*) headquarters of *Save the Amazon* gave PJ some distance to recent events. Now, after several weeks, he could step back and observe what was happening in Peru and the other Andean countries he had worked for (or had he actually worked *against* them?) as an official of the World Bank. Thanks to the many other foreigners, representatives of environmental and peace organizations from around the globe, who were working and studying at the *Save the Amazon* laboratory of social innovation, he was able to see a pattern developing throughout the world. It was not a pretty one. It was a relentless advancement of American corporate super power, sustained and supported by the U.S. armed forces, and the institution he used to work for.

The Ranch was equipped with the most sophisticated communication gear, hidden away in a secluded bunker with powerful antennas camouflaged in tree tops. This was also the emergency rescue place, where several hundred Save the Amazon, or STA members could temporarily be housed in case of an emergency.

At any given time, people from all over the world, representing their organization, were doing specific investigation work at the Ranch. They usually were invited for periods from 6 to 18 months, during which they were working on programs of special concern to their countries or of their organizations particular cause. Many also came for shorter periods, training courses and seminars. They had weekly meetings to brief each other on their activities. In potential political or other emergencies, the STA center would act as an advisory body, providing legal and strategic advice and in some cases even financial assistance. The STA received funding from its associated members all over the world, but most of the resources came from the *coca* farmers (*not* the drug intermediaries) of the Andean countries.

The Ranch, on the edge of the tropical rain forest, consisted of a wooden main complex, decked out with a wrap-around veranda and containing different conference halls, a cafeteria, an adjacent coffee shop and a health center, outfitted with the latest technologically-advanced equipment. From this central building, about a dozen smaller buildings spread out forming a crescent that covered an area of about 20 hectares, compliments of the Municipality of Tarapoto. These bungalows also contained smaller conference rooms and work areas, but served mostly as dormitories for the steady flow of guests from all over the world.

The multicolored palette of tropical flowers, birds, talking parrots of all hues and shades, panthers, snakes, fist-size spiders, scorpions and giant ants—as well as the famous *Ayahuasca* (a hallucigenous liana, used by Shamans as main ingredient in a concoction that is ceremonially ingested to 'travel' to unknown dream places and to explore one's innermost self, but foremost to treat drug addicts), formed the background to the farm. The entire campus of this laboratory of peace research also had wireless internet access. In short, this special hacienda offered a uniquely warm, friendly and pleasant ambiance which inspired thinking about and working on solutions to combat the ferocious consequences of 'globalization' and help stop the rapid decline of the world's wellbeing.

One afternoon PJ was sitting on the ample porch of the Freedom Ranch with Ahmed, from the southern Sudan Health agency, fighting the rapidly growing HIV/AIDS calamity in Sothern Sudan. Ahmed just arrived in the morning from Dacca, where he attended the G77

Conference. He was still jet-lagged. They were sipping *Masato* (a typical drink from the Amazon Region made of fermented maize), enjoying the peaceful tropical humming and occasional bird cry of the tropics. Ahmed told PJ that he met Moni Cheng, actually shared a table with her and other Latin American colleagues, during a recent G-77 summit in Dacca. She invited him to the impending workshop *Vision for a New World*. Again, PJ was surprised at Moni Cheng's active life. She seemed to be everywhere. But he didn't ask any questions, hoping that soon he would be able to receive the answers directly from her lovely lips.

He trailed off dreaming, when he heard Ahmed mention Dacca police. PJ asked out of the blue, "What happened that you needed the police?"

Ahmed recounted the fake terrorist story, and also divulged his other name, Mokhtar. He felt there was no need to hide it at this Ranch full with like-minded comrades and freedom fighters.

PJ said rhetorically, "So your HIV/AIDS organization is a mere cover for your Independence Movement? Cool. You are working on two fronts. And where do you get the funds from?"

"The oil companies. They don't want to be taken over by Khartoum, that is, the Americans. They'd rather be independent."

Ahmed grew animated talking about the plight of the Sudanese people, particularly in the South and in the Darfur region (*Note 11*), both of which harbor huge oil reserves and where civil wars are being waged. He described in horrific detail—only possible from someone who had vivid memories of such experiences—how women and girls returning from distant markets, or from fetching water, were systematically raped and their possessions stolen. Often they were killed. Spreading insecurity and fear among people is a common strategy of domineering powers. It's a bonanza for weapons producers and traders, a trillion dollar business, two-thirds of it dominated by the U.S.

Ahmed also described his amazement about Freedom Ranch, how his colleagues who arrived a few weeks earlier, were startled when they realized that *Save the Amazon* was far more than the name would suggest. It was an international research center for environmental and human rights issues with links to associations, organizations and activist groups throughout the world. In fact, the STA Ranch was effectively the coordination hub for these topics within the G-77.

Suddenly Lucho, the *Comandante* of the '*Movimiento para el Rescate de los Cocaleros*' (MRC) burst onto the terrace, "Friends"—with a smile flashing an ironic glance heavenwards—"our Lady, Moni Cheng, was just on TV. She was talking at the G-77 Conference in Dacca about the fight we had with the Americans and their *Devida* puppets. But mostly she talked about the press conference at the Peruvian Congress, where she and a Senator were prepared to make the government's killer alliance with the Americans public, and to describe how the news conference was promptly aborted by a police squad. She wanted the world to be aware that Peru was not unique, that U.S. military invasions penetrate borders throughout Latin America. The practice was particularly prevalent in the Andean hydrocarbon rich countries."

He added with a somber voice, "Moni Cheng apparently was almost abducted by some CIA-hired guys at the G-77 Conference, to silence her before her speech. Knowing her, she will not just abandon this one."

PJ was shocked to his soul, when he heard the abduction story. But he refrained from asking any questions, lest he reveal his feelings for her.

As he guided the two into the cafeteria, Lucho told them, "But now, friends, the Senator, Peru's unofficial representative at the Conference, who also accompanied Moni Cheng, is on the podium. We still have some brave men in our country, people who are not afraid to speak out, despite our new government's apparent embrace of the Gringo Doctrine. His words are being beamed around the world, certainly to the displeasure of his country's President." They rushed through the open glass doors to grab a seat in front of the huge TV screen.

The transmission came via satellite from AsiaLink-TV. The anchor-man was at the end of his introduction, when the camera focused on the speaker on the podium.

At first blurry, then moving into focus, Antonio Esteban, Senator from Peru, stood at the podium. "Friends, my colleague Moni Cheng made a compelling call to all of us to hold human rights and personal freedom in the highest regard, to resist other countries' interference, and to defend our sovereignty. These same principles apply to trade.

"The United States is peddling bilateral, so-called Free Trade Agreements around the world, especially in Latin America, and more so, where there are natural resources. These FTAs—or as we call them *TLCs*, for *Tratado de Libre Comercio*—are a clever move by the Americans to circumvent the slightly stricter rules of the World Trade Organization (WTO), or to deal with larger trade blocks, like *MercoSur*. Bilateral agreements with the U.S. are always a David and Goliath issue. The FTA's objectives are to open the borders of developing countries for highly subsidized American agricultural goods. They are abrogating poor countries' rights to use generic medication so that U.S. pharma-giants may infiltrate the developing countries' markets not only with expensive, but also often out-dated, medicine. So far FTAs were vigorously rejected by all of South America's countries, except for Colombia. Peru is now another exception, where the government—not the people—has already approved it."

"I will give you a few examples of how the FTA would affect us, Peruvians—I say 'would', because Congress may still undo the treaty which would not come into effect until next year. There is hope that this mistake can be corrected. I will fight for it."

"In *Agriculture* the TLC would facilitate exports of high value Peruvian crops, like exotic fruits and vegetables, paprika, asparagus, artichokes and the like, to the United States. This would increase foreign exchange earnings for Peru. But the income would not be distributed equitably. Since small holding farmers, who make up the vast majority of our agricultural force, do not have the capital to invest in the equipment needed to produce the high quality crops required by the United States, their fate is sealed. They either sell their land or enter into long-term leases—which is about the same as selling—with big agricultural firms. If they are lucky these firm will employ them for a while as cheap labor."

He paused, looked around cramped conference hall and took a sip of water before he continued. "Therefore, the main beneficiaries would be large Peruvian companies, many of them in the hands of large U.S. corporations. They would fix the prices for the farmers who have been bold enough not to cave in selling or leasing their land, and control the markets.

"A downside of maybe even greater dimensions—Peru would have to reduce considerably the cultivation of traditional crops, like rice, maize, cotton and others to make space for these products to be imported from the United States. Small peasant farmers would be especially hurt. They planted these crops for generations. They would be forced to sell their '*chacras*' (Quechua for plot of land). This would require compensation and training to convert to other products or to find new jobs and a new way of life. The social cost would be tremendous.

"Many of the farmers who would have to abandon their *chacras* would migrate to already overcrowded cities, creating more shanty towns, more destitution. This gigantic social burden has hardly been discounted from the potential benefits of the FTA. The U.S., G8 and other rich countries subsidize their farmers so that they will not leave their fields."

Esteban paused again to sip some water. From the floor came boos and chants '*unacceptable*'—'*will not be tolerated*'—'*no FTA's for G-77's*'—'*lets boycott gringo goods*'. The Senator raised his hand, asking for quiet. He continued:

"*Intellectual property*—under this heading Peruvians will be forbidden to import or use generic medication. Instead, they would have to import brand name pharmaceuticals. Most affected would be the poor, children and the elderly. The socio-economic cost to our people, especially the poor, is unfathomable. People would no longer have access to cheap drugs, health indicators would decline, children's learning capacity would be eroded by frequent school absenteeism, and untreated illnesses would reduce family incomes. The overall standard of living and well-being of the population would be compromised for the gains of North American pharmaceutical corporations."

Now the outrage was even greater. Delegates got to their feet. The Vietnamese representative was shouting, "Let us establish separate trade agreements. The U.S. has lured us into WTO (*Note 3*), which is dominated by the G8. This usually means profits for the elite and declining income for the poor of our countries. The G8 will continue their farm subsidies, while prying open our borders for their subsidized goods. Let us create an alternative to WTO!"

The huge screens in the cafeteria, all transmitting the G-77 summit, flickered at once. The commotion at the conference was suddenly heightened by the scream of a hooded male voice: "*Down with the subversives!*" Then from four different angles of the aula: "*Kill the G-77!*" and Molotov cocktails were thrown towards the podium. The place erupted with shrieks of fear. People were running in all directions. Patches of carpet and some seats were on fire. Police stormed the stadium from the three entrances, but the five hoodlums escaped in the mêlée. Emergency firefighters rapidly extinguished the flames.

The AsiaLink-TV reporter was aghast. "Never has anything like this happened at a U.N.-sponsored meeting ..."

True, PJ thought, he couldn't remember a similar boldness of right-wingers, of violently disrupting an ongoing UN event. But there were other U.S. interferences in the U.N. processes. Take the period leading up to the Iraq invasion, when the Americans wanted to know who was for and against them, tapping the phones, mostly of developing country delegates, so they could blackmail them into changing their opinions and voting for the United States. Then the constant badgering of any U.N. motion or activity by the fascist-like bully, the

U.S. Ambassador to the U.N., who eventually had to resign, since he would not have gotten the nod for renewal of his mandate even by the conservative U.S. Congress.

There were other remarkable U.N. moments the correspondent must have forgotten. For example, in 1960, when Khrushchev interrupted British Prime Minister Harold MacMillan at the U.N. General Assembly, by pounding his shoe on the pulpit; or more recently at the U.N. General Assembly in 2006, when Hugo Chavez brandished Noam Chomsky's *'Hegemony or Survival'* and referred to the President of the United States as the 'devil who came yesterday and was leaving behind a smell of sulfur'.

"But fortunately," the reporter continued, "nobody has been reported hurt. Order is being reinstated. It is not clear when and how the Conference will continue. We will keep you informed. In the meantime, let's switch to another hair-raising event."

A newscaster from Jakarta reported, "In Indonesia's eastern most province of *Papua* (formerly *Irian Jaya*), where the infamous *Grasberg* gold mine is located, a small ship disguised as a fishing boat was hijacked in the *Arafura Sea* off the southern port of *Okaba*. Apparently, on board was more than a billion dollars worth of gold bullion. The ship was sailing to a small port in Sumatra, where the gold was to be transferred to a United States Marine vessel, destination U.S.A. It is not yet clear who the hijackers may be. But speculations are that the environmental activist group, *Grasberg Demise*, was involved. Their leaders, Jamal and Ramona, a soft-spoken pair of pacifists"—two portraits flashed across the screen—"have long advocated sabotaging the mine, which is also the world's second largest producer of copper, because of the environmental disaster caused by the 700,000 tons per day of *'tailings'*—highly toxic waste material that results from extracting the minerals. This waste seeps into the ground, polluting one of the last unspoiled rainforests in the world and the pristine *Aikwa River,* which is life sustaining for thousands of settlers along its banks. We will continue bringing you the latest news on Grasberg and the missing cargo."

In the meantime, the crowd in the cafeteria grew. All eyes glued to the TV screens around the walls. After all, this was precisely the type of news they would learn from and use in the upcoming '*Vision*' workshop.

AsiaLink-TV was obviously waiting to receive word from the G-77 Conference on its status. In the meantime, the news 'fillers' were exciting enough. The reporter said, "And also from Indonesia—in *Banda, Aceh Province*, the region which suffered tremendous destruction and death from the Tsunami in December 2004, indigenous insurgents have been struggling for independence for years. Now they continue fighting. But their recent uprising is aimed at expelling the U.S. hydrocarbon thieves, as they refer to them. They also decry the American-supported Indonesian military, which defends the oil companies. Today a miracle seems to have happened. The demonstrators and the military have united. Together, at least a hundred thousand strong, they were dancing in the streets, asking for an immediate halt to U.S. corporate exploitation. This unlikely alliance between the people and the military is extraordinary. A military spokesperson said that the soldiers realized their fate was the same as that of the citizens of *Aceh*, that they were also being robbed of the black treasure under their ground, because they were as Indonesian and as poor as the bulk of civilians."

Lucho, PJ and Ahmed, in the meantime, joined Veronica's table in the cafeteria. Veronica is a member of Freedom Ranch's core team and close friend of Moni Cheng's. They couldn't believe their eyes and ears. Unheard of! Finally, the soldiers realized that they were as common as the commons, that so far they were helping the foreign companies stealing Indonesians natural resources, which they can no longer accept doing.

"Imagine," said Lucho, "if such awareness were to catch on around the world, we would soon see different scenes from those that give the capitalists the upper hand because of their military might."

They nodded in agreement as the AsiaLink-TV reporter came on again, commenting on the quick progress made at cleaning up the mess at the G-77 Conference, and that the meeting would continue.

The Chairman of the Conference, the President of Brazil, appeared and declared that the perpetrators of this heinous event had been caught and would be duly prosecuted in a court of law. "The Conference will not be interrupted ... and those who are behind this attack, as well as those behind the earlier attempt of kidnapping Moni Cheng—plus those who pay the gangsters to carry out these crimes—will be held accountable. Their acts which, they tried to keep secret and disguised will be made public around the world." He reintroduced Senator Esteban from Peru, who would make a concluding statement.

The Senator stepped up to the podium to a wave of applause and friendly cheers. He smiled to the crowd and continued as if nothing had happened.

"We were talking about FTAs. Well, let me add a little known caveat embedded in these infamous treaties. FTAs in Andean resource rich countries include a widely overlooked condition, which on the surface seems to have hardly anything to do with trade. It is an *Interdiction to pursue Americans (soldiers) in international criminal courts*. It sneaks into every one of the FTA proposals by the United States to its Latin American partners. The reason is simple. Under the anti-drug program, the so-called fight against coca, the U.S. government imposes a local police and military training program under which several hundred American armed forces are brought into the country. As we have heard from Moni Cheng, in the rich agrarian fields near Tarapoto, the American military is fighting alongside or on behalf of the local forces. Given the U.S. Army's torture and war crimes records around the world, it is not too far fetched to assume that further crimes against humanity could be committed, criminal offenses that eventually might end up before an international tribunal, or the International Court of Justice (ICJ) in The Hague."

Voices of protest could be heard throughout the stadium. The Senator went on, "With this covenant, the U.S. seeks to protect itself and its soldiers against such prosecution. As the Argentinean Peace Prize Laureate said: 'Once American troops are in a country, it is very difficult to get rid of them.' The real purpose of this creeping infiltration of American troops into Latin America, as well as elsewhere in the world, is to assist American corporations to eventually take over the countries' natural resources. In the case of the Andean nations, the underground assets are mostly oil and gas. It is not by coincidence that in Colombia the U.S. armed forces are the largest American military contingent on foreign soil, except for Iraq. For good reason, the new President of Bolivia has declared an end to the United States-backed coca eradication program.

"As conceived today, the FTA would benefit only the few rich and be detrimental for the vast majority of Peruvians. And this scenario is certainly not different in other countries where FTAs are propagated."

Senator Esteban paused to let the voices of discontent ebb, and then added "As an alternative to bilateral FTAs, the President of Brazil proposes to the Andean countries to join the *MercoSur* which would give them a stronger vote in negotiations. At present, it looks like only Bolivia and maybe Ecuador, with the newly elected President, may join."

His fist raised, Esteban exclaimed, "Our strongest tool, ladies and gentlemen, is information—information and the power of the people. We have to take back our media and use them to inform, inform and inform, to spread the truth. We, the people, have to be aware at every moment what the imperial forces are up to, clandestine and distorted as they are. How they want to subdue us and control our resources. Full awareness is our weapon to fight for our rights and independence. Thank you."

He smiled and stepped down under waves of applause.

The group of people who in the meantime had assembled in the cafeteria of the Freedom Ranch echoed the Dacca applause.

At a neighboring table in the cafeteria, Harald Nuñez, the President of Mexico's United Farm Workers, the strongest union movement South of the Border, spoke up, "The case of Mexico is a flagrant example of damage done by so-called Free Trade Agreements with the United States."

The attention of what had become a parallel gathering to the G-77 Summit at the Freedom Ranch cafeteria, turned now to Nuñez' table. He was also invited by Moni Cheng to attend the international workshop, *Vision for a new World*.

He seized the opportunity, explaining how during the recent Presidential Elections in Mexico, the front runner, Manuel López Obrador, was defeated by a right-wing, business-friendly candidate. Harald expressed his strong belief that the elections were fraudulent, an effort supported by Big Business, farm business that is, of Mexico's northern neighbor.

López Obrador was seen as a threat to NAFTA. Therefore, the United States supported the outgoing Mexican President with huge amounts of money to be used in anti-Obrador propaganda and advisors to help manipulate the elections, not only promoting their favored candidate, a business-oriented neo-conservative, but making sure he would win. López Obrador, supported by millions of Mexican laborers and peasant farmers formed a parallel government in opposition. He was invited by the G-77 organizers as a special guest. He was the next speaker at the G-77 Dacca Conference, capturing the attention of the group in the Ranch's cafeteria.

López Obrador entered, his voice strong. "The World Trade Organization and the various U.S.-led bilateral Free Trade Agreements are enslaving developing countries. The North American Free Trade Agreement, NAFTA, between the United States, Canada and Mexico, requires our Government to reduce production of our main staple, maize, and to open our borders so that the United States may export its highly subsidized maize, of which they have an overproduction. In turn, with cheap labor we may manufacture consumer goods, from textiles to electronic equipment, all to be purchased at low prices by American multinational corporations."

He paused merely to take a sip of water, and then he asked rhetorically, "Did you know that total farm subsidies of OECD (*Note 3*) countries amounted in 2006 to more than $400 billion, with the US and EU accounting for more than two thirds?

"This, my friends, is the big picture. My colleague from Peru has just talked about the plight of the small farmers who end up in the rapidly growing *pueblos jovenes,* shantytowns, favelas, slums, all euphemisms for the rich to describe abject poverty."

López Obrador was adamant in wanting to illustrate the case of Mexico. "Now let me tell you what NAFTA, the North American Free Trade Agreement, did for—or rather against—the Mexican farmers. Maize is an important crop in Mexico's culture and economy. When NAFTA was signed in December 1992, the three million corn growing Mexican farmers were promised, a 15-year phase-out period of corn subsidies, along with strict import quotas. This would ensure a gradual transition to competition with more developed and highly subsidized U.S. producers. The United States produces about eleven times the corn output at triple the subsidies of Mexico's and at a cost of less than half of Mexico's.

"Instead of the gradual phase-out, farmers faced a different reality. Under the pretext of basic grain shortages, the Mexican government increased imports over NAFTA quotas, but declined to collect import tariffs. These foregone fiscal revenues cost the government more than $2 billion and at least another $2 billion to the Mexican corn farmers. The decision to abrogate the NAFTA agreement reflected the growing power of agribusiness interests, mostly in the hands of U.S. corporations, and corruption within Mexico. Instead of a long-term adjustment to competition with U.S. farmers, Mexican corn growers faced the near-impossible challenge of fully liberalized trade just three years into NAFTA. Imports doubled and the price of corn fell by nearly 50 percent."

The Dacca auditorium was quiet. The group of spectators at the Ranch didn't talk either. They only shook their heads in rueful understanding.

López Obrador's topic was not yet exhausted. He said, "Entering the last phase of NAFTA, Mexico's poultry industry is now also at peril. Mexican chicken farmers cannot keep up with the highly subsidized chicken farmers of its northern neighbor. They will have to abandon their farms, and many of them may become *wetbacks*, cheap, illegal farm workers in the southwestern United States, living under the constant threat of being forcefully deported back into Mexico, where they are confronted with unemployment—and yes—abject poverty."

He received a round of sympathetic applause. He continued, opening his following remarks with a sweeping movement of outstretched arms. "This calamity of forced unemployment into perpetual misery affects other countries too. For example, the 25,000 American cotton farmers receive almost $4 billion per year in subsidies, engendering rock-bottom cotton prices, costing African farmers about $300 million a year. In Mali, where about a third of the population, three million farmers, depend on cotton, cultivators of cotton lost $43 million in 2001, because of U.S. cotton subsidies. Mind you, 43 million have a completely different meaning in poor Mali, than it would have, say in the U.S. or another G8 country."

He concluded, "Global overproduction has been fed by rising productivity in industrial agriculture and the neoliberal mantra to export, export, export. For many developing countries, policies of the World Bank and the IMF have mandated a deepening dependency on a few commodities and a movement away from the diversification that characterized Latin American development strategies in the 1960s and 70s. This dependency makes countries particularly vulnerable when commodity prices fall.

"The notion that 'free trade' is fair and just, is a lie, a myth at best. Even trade free of subsidies favors those with comparative advantages, which for the most part are large agro-corporations with strong commercial backing from the U.S. and, in some cases, the European Union. Few developing countries, perhaps Argentina, Brazil, India and China, have the necessary agro-business potential. The farmers of most developing countries, especially in Africa, are too poor to compete, even if all OECD countries abolished their farm subsidies. Farmers in poor countries need massive support, as received by those of rich nations for decades, to build up their agricultural potential to an internationally competitive level. Unfortunately poor farmers have nobody to defend their case, and their governments are too poor to pay subsidies, notwithstanding the constant pressure from the rich G8, that 'globalization' means opening borders and abandoning trade barriers."

"What a charade this is!" Obrador exclaimed.

López Obrador bowed to his audience. He received a standing ovation. His final words: "Ladies and gentlemen. I could go on for much longer, as this is an almost inexhaustible theme. But there are others with equally important messages." He stepped down from the podium, waving to the audience.

The camera focused in on colleagues, friends and other prominent G-77 attendees who congratulated and embraced him. Strangely, Moni Cheng was not to be seen. PJ wondered why.

* * *

... In major cities of Peru....

Moni Cheng's speech at the G-77 Summit, beamed around the world, was also received in Peru, where it exacerbated the public anger, caused by the *CAMISEA* incidence and the mini coca war near Tarapota that killed several people, including rebel fighters. People took to the streets of Lima and other big cities, Cuzco, Arequipa, Trujillo, Piura, and

Chimbote. Hundreds of thousands of marchers blocked roads and railways, occupied government buildings and even the main radio and TV stations. The country came to a total standstill for three days. During this period, the air waves under the people's movement control broadcast anti-FTA programs, accusing the government of corruption.

On the morning of the fourth day of unrest, the President went on TV and declared in a solemn tone that the FTA was dead for now, that Congress would review the possibility of a renegotiated FTA, which would bring real benefits to the peasant society. He asked the people to clear the roads and please return to work.

Although trust in his words ran about as low as his approval ratings in most of the country outside of Lima, the strikers obeyed. Many knew that the government had lied before and may well lie again. At least for now, the populace's anger was appeased. Many of the protesters and intellectuals celebrated this government defeat as their victory. They felt invigorated to stand up against future authoritative decisions that defied the interests of the people.

*   *   *   *   *

19

World Bank Staff in Solidarity

... *In the Streets of Washington D.C* ...

At the Freedom Ranch in Tarapoto, PJ usually woke up early. He'd been there now for over a week. Moni Cheng had been delaying her arrival almost daily. There was the trouble with *CAMISEA*. After the *Machiguenga* Indians left the truckload full of dead fish in front of the Government Palace, tension among other Peruvians rose. They began to recognize the devastation in the Amazon region. Not only were foreign companies plundering the Peruvians' natural resources, they were also destroying the invaluable biodiversity and the habitat of the people living in their previously untouched environment.

PJ and a group of his new friends sat in the cafeteria furnished with three huge TV screens located on three walls of the restaurant. A kaleidoscope of around-the-clock world news, captured from different satellites, flashed across the monitors.

The current attention-catcher was a breaking news story on the World Bank in Washington. Apparently confidential information concerning one of the poorest places on earth, *Matanga*, an island state in the Indian Ocean, had been leaked to the Board. Dingo, the infuriated Bank President, had ordered a lie-detector test for all professionals and consultants who'd ever set foot on the island. This insane initiative had resulted in a rare move from the staff; they'd taken to the streets and gone on strike. The Staff Association declared that the work stoppage would last as long as it took to receive an apology from Dingo, and for a withdrawal of his ridiculous and demeaning request. What the World Bank's employees really hoped for was to exert enough pressure to get a resignation from the unpopular President.

Street skirmishes started peacefully, but escalated as word came from the President that those who refused to return to their offices immediately would face disciplinary actions and could even lose their jobs. Nobody returned. In fact, the staff was joined by management, first lower- and mid-level supervisors, but as the day progressed, Vice-Presidents also joined. Reporters saw that even a few Executive Directors mingled with staff.

Chanting was heard—"Dingo must go! No war criminals in the World Bank!" This was a reference to Dingo's role as one of the masterminds in the disastrous and criminal Iraq war waged by the United States. "No bloodsucking development!" was a reference to the privatization of natural resources. There was no way the staff would back off now. Employees sensed this opportunity and solidarity made them strong. Their usual fear and concern for their own welfare was gone. They were standing up against a bully and felt the real potential for victory. They stood on principle, refusing to succumb, no matter what.

Never before in the World Bank's 60-plus years of history had anything as dramatic happened. Normally, World Bank staff tended to be polite, well-educated yes-men (and women); they were subdued and rarely departed from Management's mainstream of thinking. No wonder. About two-thirds of the staff, representing about 140 nationalities, was held captive by special visas, which allowed them to stay in the U.S. only as long as they were employed by the World Bank. Though most of those from developing countries came from elite families, they understood quite well what poverty meant. They were usually not keen on losing their careers by standing up for their beliefs. This time it was different.

* * *

As PJ watched these events unfold at his ex-employer's headquarters, he contemplated his own experiences at the World Bank, the integrity of his colleagues, but also their often fearful characters and demeanors. A warm feeling grew as a result of this memory. When Veronica told him how impressed she was with the solidarity they'd just witnessed on the screen, he recalled a story of one of his colleagues several years back. It said a lot about the constant dread of political incorrectness and about the fear of being viewed as stepping out of line.

He told her about his colleague. "Joshua had been my friend and colleague for many years, when we worked together in Africa and beyond. He was Australian. Then he became sick. He was often absent and didn't want to talk about his illness. We saw each other less and less. We practically didn't talk any more. Then one day in the World Bank's cafeteria, I saw him from a distance. You could tell he wasn't well. But even if it wouldn't have been so visible, I knew."

Reflecting on this period, PJ scratched his nose. "One damp evening, years ago, on a restaurant terrace, which stood on stilts at a beach near Cotonou, in Benin, Joshua told me that his days were numbered. While he never mentioned the disease, it was pretty clear to me that he had the virus, the deadly virus that devours you from inside out. As in other situations, when confronted with an irrefutable truth, I didn't know what to say. I sat quiet, sipped my beer for want of anything better to do. Looking past Joshua's dark and piercing eyes, I must have muttered something like, 'sad, sad story, my friend. I wish I could help you.'

"Joshua's response was soft, conciliatory, but also direct, 'No worries, mate, you can't help, nor do you wish you could, because that would mean getting involved in fighting the virus. Quite an engagement. Not many people are willing or prepared to take that path. Don't feel bad. You couldn't just help me, or any one person.'

"Of course, the social disease he was referring to was AIDS and HIV," PJ said. "At the time, the pandemic was already affecting between 40 and 45 million people, a country the size of Spain. More than 25 million had died since 1981. More than a quarter of the afflicted live in Africa, about 12 million. He made me realize that those of us who worked in Africa were more exposed, more vulnerable. He rattled statistics off, as if he was updated on a daily basis. 'Our illness calls for a collective cure,' Joshua had insisted."

PJ watched Veronica, wondering whether she had anything to say. But she stayed silent. PJ continued, "I was taken aback by this piece of truth from Joshua, which indeed was a certainty. We started a conversation about work, always a nice deviation when a topic becomes unbearably hot. Work is neutral. You can always find a common denominator.

"I felt an enormous pity, when I saw this emaciated creature sitting alone at a World Bank cafeteria table, in a corner, trying to escape onlookers. He was like a skeleton. His clothes hung from his bones. His face was hardly recognizable. With his skinny fingers he was shuffling soup into this opening which was once a mouth, an attractive mouth, with lips that liked to kiss, to please women ... I wondered, with some envy, about the colorful history those dying lips must have lived. Now, they could hardly close. Soup was dripping from both ends."

Veronica seemed absorbed by this story.

PJ continued, "Joshua must still have had many friends and colleagues, or maybe only ex-colleagues. After all he'd spent most of his professional life in this institution. People looked at him, embarrassed eyes glanced fleetingly at his crushed body. Nobody wanted to walk up and talk to him. What to say? Perhaps they were sorry for him. Or maybe they were happy that their own lives had been spared. Had they deserved it and he didn't? Had they been less exposed, lesser risk-takers? Joshua was a sick man who wouldn't last much longer. He resembled an outcast in this lush cafeteria. He didn't look up, just stared at his plate. His appearance made him ashamed. Yet, he also belonged to this place. The healthy didn't have a monopoly."

Veronica shook her head. "Did you talk to him? After all, you were a friend."

"Well, I also sat alone. In earlier days, I would have just walked up to him and sat with him. 'Should I do that now,' I thought, 'walk up to him, shake his hand, careful not to break the brittle bones—'*Hi! Remember me—our times in Africa?*'—Simply ignore the ravaging disease that so obviously was closing in on his life, this still young man?—Or would that be construed as an insult?—What should I say? Ask him how he felt? What he was doing here, could I sit down? Then what?

"I hesitated, but then walked the dozen paces to the corner table, tapped Joshua cheerfully on the back, 'Hi mate, how have you been?' Without waiting for an answer, 'Remember, ten years ago, West Africa, Ouagadougou, the dusty streets, all the pretty girls smiling and waving at us on their roaring *'motocyclettes*?'"

PJ paused contemplatively, "Joshua slowly turned his head, looking straight into my face, the spoon dropping to the floor. He couldn't speak. His eyes suddenly filled with water and tears were streaming down his cheeks. He got up and walked away. I was speechless and suddenly in the limelight. All our colleagues looked at me in disgust, as if to say, '*what atrocity must he have committed upon this poor friend*'—while justifying to themselves that they hadn't shown more sympathy for their dying colleague."

PJ concluded, "It is not the first time that I was the victim of my own blunder. But there was nothing I could do. I just walked away, out of sight for the '*politically correct*', who'd rather avoid a possible gaffe, than showing a sign of compassion. My world, I thought then and I think now, 'often does not match the one of my peers. I feel like an outsider, now, of course, more than ever."

PJ fell silent. He waited for Veronica's reaction.

She again shook her head in astonishment. "What a story! What surprises me the most, though is that there is still this taboo in the

World Bank about people with HIV-AIDS. And that these people still stay in the closet. After all, there must be quite a few in international organizations where the risk factors are high. Talking openly about their affliction may help their colleagues, making them aware of the potential danger they are facing, depending on their lifestyles. Why is that?"

"You are raising an interesting point and you are also absolutely right," said PJ. "The World Bank's culture has always been one of fear. Staff is generally afraid to divulge their personal lives. They distrust management immensely. Mind you, this is not unjustified. There have been untold cases of discrimination, expulsions, reprisals—you name it, for all kinds of reasons. Imagine, someone with the deadly AIDS virus ... there are some who have come out of hiding and talked about it openly. Bu those are few and far between. Being afflicted with a deadly disease, even cancer—is like a stigma. This fits the pattern of a highly competitive environment which exists in the World Bank. It is easy to be sidestepped or outright discriminated against. Of course there is always another pretext for not being promoted, or dismissed. For the same reason, people are normally scared to speak out. Belonging to groups and having opinions outside of those sanctioned by the mainstream's doctrines is dangerous.

"All of that," PJ closes his little sermon, "has become, of course, much more acute since Dingo took the reigns of the organization. He not only doesn't like 'nay-sayers,' but also shrouds the place in secrecy. The World Bank has never been a transparent institution, which creates much of the distrust in management. Under Dingo's leadership, which actually portrays pretty much the management style of the current U.S. Administration, daily life has for many become close to unbearable."

"More power to the staff, then!" cheers Veronica. "Look how they have changed. They now dare speak out, marching in the streets, clearly expressing their discontent, even their demands for leadership change. That's laudable!"

"Yes, it is. It makes me feel proud to be part of this crowd. Except, of course," he hastened to say, "that I have already separated myself from it. Now, I believe, they would understand."

"In fact, let me say this," PJ added almost as an afterthought, "the World Bank is a funny institution. With its highly professional and dedicated people—the institution's only true asset—it would have the potential to change the economic balance in favor of the poor. These are people who work on the '*veneer*' type projects, those that are aiming for socioeconomic development, as opposed to the '*blank check operations*' which amount to almost half of the Bank's portfolio. Unfortunately, it is not this devoted staff that makes the World Bank's policy. It is the Treasury of the United States, in connivance with the other G8, that dictate the World Bank's policies through a bunch of neocon directors and Vice-Presidents which were carefully selected, screened and put in place by the Bank's President, alias the U.S. Administration. These 'gnomes' decided which countries should receive how much money, what political behavior they have to display in order to benefit from the World Bank's loans. Among these favorable behaviors is demonstrated willingness to 'reform' their economies, privatize the public sector, and establish legislation allowing long-term concessions for public services and exploitation of natural resources."

Then he added, "Most of my former colleagues are young and eager—eager to please the policy-makers for their advancements and careers. Most of them might not even realize that they are used by a thin layer of neoliberal economists as an instrument to pursue the usurping goals of the Western elite's agenda."

Suddenly the cafeteria's attention swung again to the widescreens. Other breaking news. An internal International Monetary Fund document had been leaked to the press. It talked about an imminent return to the Gold Standard. Although immediate denials were issued by IMF's Managing Director, first reactions had the financial world in total upheaval.

In another shocking story, the European Parliament had decided for now to withdraw its support to the World Bank's soft lending arm, IDA. Instead more resources would be poured into the European Bank for Reconstruction and Development (EBRD). In other words, resources that would have gone to replenishing the International Development Association, were now likely going to stock up the capital of the Europeans' own institution. They had also discussed the possible restructuring of the EBRD to increase their scope to a global level. Their current focus is on Eastern Europe and some Middle Eastern countries. The European Bank's resources would overwhelmingly be designated for social sector development.

Another blow to the World Bank ... stay tuned....

*   *   *   *   *

20

SAVING PROJECT 'GOLDEN ENTERPRISE'

At the same time, high in the Andes....

The U.S. Embassy in Lima was alarmed by Raul's news about PJ's disappearance. There was no way he should be in a position to jeopardize *Project Golden Enterprise* in Bolivia, nor to interfere in strategic advances through the military in other parts of Latin America. A *'hunt to capture or kill'* advisory was immediately issued and communicated to the CIA agents in the country, as well as in Washington. They, in turn, would inform their counterparts in the Peruvian Defense Department. In a quickly arranged video conference between the World Bank's Lima Office and the Andean Country Director at the bank's Washington HQ, Marco Vidali, they agreed that PJ needed to be replaced immediately.

The momentum of *Project Golden Enterprise* must not be lost. Vidali's position was not to increase risk by putting a new person on the job. Instead, Raul should assume PJ's responsibilities, travel to Bolivia immediately and establish communications with the rebel leader, Jaime Rodriguez.

Raul wasn't pleased at all. He liked to direct and manipulate his people from a safe distance for these risky affairs. Now he had to jump into the frying pan. And most likely he could not count on help from Moni Cheng. He had a strong sense that she had become suspicious and had either disappeared or would sabotage his plans. But he had no choice. Either he jumped ship, as well, which would endanger his life, or he'd continue playing the game, hoping that in the end he might be rewarded. He decided on the latter, went home to change, packed a small suitcase and called the office to inform his secretary about his impending trip and caught the next plane to La Paz.

* * *

In the early morning hours, hardly adjusted to the 4,000 meter elevation, with a most horrible headache from *soroche* (altitude sickness), Raul and a driver from the World Bank's La Paz Office—his name was Valdo—took to the road to Potosi for a meeting with Jaime Rodriguez.

They navigated their way through the narrow cobblestone streets of Potosi and asked a peasant vendor for Jaime's house. When they stopped their four-wheel drive in front of a traditional adobe home, Jaime opened the front door and invited them in with a broad smile. They walked into the kitchen where a large round table was fully decked with a *Pachamanca*, a typical Andean meal, including chicken, pork, llama meat, as well as *cuyes* (*cuy* is an Andean rodent often served as a delicacy for guests), accompanied by potatoes, yucca, maize, cooked bananas, mountain cheese made from llama milk, and all decorated with delicious spices and sauces.

But what interested Raul the most was a huge pot of *Mate de Coca* in the center. His headache had not gone away. *Mate de Coca* was said to help alleviate *soroche* and related ailments. He needed a clear head to negotiate with Jaime. From the looks of it, this was Jaime's family home. Jaime's appearance was that of a typical *Aymara indio*, except that he was tall and muscular. He spoke perfect Spanish and good English. He was clearly educated. "What brings you here? And where is PJ?"

"As for the second part of your question, I'd hoped you could help. He disappeared sometime around his meeting with Moni Cheng in Santa Cruz."

Jaime saw his suspicion confirmed. "Well, this is not entirely true. We know he was kidnapped by the Americans, but then I also know, that he met with you and Moni Cheng in Lima just a few days ago. So, you must know were he is better than I do."

Raul realized, he may get caught in a web of lies. Better to be honest, where it didn't matter. "Yes, you are right, he emerged after the kidnapping. We spent an evening at my home in Lima. The following morning he disappeared. I have no idea whether he was kidnapped again, or what happened to him."

"OK, then, let's talk straight. I have no clue where he is. But what exactly brings you here?—By the way, this is typical Andean food which my wife and daughter prepared. It's also a traditional welcome to Potosi. You better eat something. You'll need the energy. I mean, until you adjust to the altitude, you tend to be tired, unless you eat some invigorating food. Here is *Mate de Coca*. I believe you are in the midst of a *soroche* and could use the soothing healing power of the coca leaves."

They all started eating. The rear door opened and a young man with a bandana around his head and woman entered. Jaime introduced them as his friend and associate in the ERB, Roberto, and his sister Conchita, who was also a member of the *Ejército Revolucionario Boliviano*. They gave the visitors a friendly nod and sat down at the table.

Raul realized that he and his chauffeur were invited to a family lunch, an honor usually not granted to the enemy. He felt more at ease than when he arrived and said, "The purpose of my visit is to discuss with you Evo Morales's proposal to nationalize the oil companies. We, at the World Bank, believe this is not the way to go. You will need foreign companies, investors for Bolivia's development. You need the capital to generate growth. And, foremost, Bolivians need to be seen by the rest of the world as serious and viable trading partners. A move towards nationalization would be seen as expropriating foreign capital. It would sow distrust among your friends and neighbors."

He stopped for a moment to measure the reaction around the table. But nobody spoke, nor blinked an eye. "We realize that you need immediate cash to embark on some of the social programs your new President announced, like improving health and education services for indigenous people, providing them with vital infrastructure, such as water supply and sanitation, electricity, rural roads to facilitate access to local markets.

"The World Bank stands ready to help. We have an instrument called Budget Support Credits, which basically amount to transfers of funds into your treasury. The World Bank and your government simply agree on a so-called Poverty Reduction Program, during which you would achieve certain objectives and—bingo, the resources are transferred. Yes, the World Bank would help implement the program with technical assistance, if so desired by the Bolivian authorities. But we also realize that unforeseen events could interfere with the execution of such programs and despite best intentions, predicted results can not be achieved. We are flexible. The program can be adjusted."

He paused again, but still got no reaction. "What I am saying is nationalization of oil resources is not necessary. There are other ways of funding the admittedly much needed social programs.—What do you say?"

After more silence, during which the four Bolivians, including the driver, exchanged quick glances, Jaime said, "First, why do you speak to me rather than to the *Presidente* directly?—Second, We are not planning to simply 'nationalize' the companies. To the contrary. We are all intent on negotiating what we believe would be a fair deal, namely a reversal of profit sharing. Now the oil diggers take out 82 percent of the benefits and leave a mere 18 percent behind. We would like to turn this around: 82 percent for us, 18 percent for them."

Jaime was now energized. "The gas under our land belongs to Bolivia. This is according to our Constitution and is the case today.

The extracted gas would be taxed at 82 percent of its market value, instead of the ridiculous 'royalty' of less than 20 percent that would stay in the country under the current arrangements. Your proposal says nothing about a fairer, more equitable distribution of revenues."

He paused, but no reaction came from Raul.

"The vast majority of our people have lived under the most strenuous hardships for hundreds, maybe thousands, of years. The vast deposits of resources under their soil, resources coveted by the rest of the world, finally offer an opportunity to help our poor majority to a better life. That's all. Nationalization which you put at par with expropriation is not our first choice; it is only a remedy of last resort. So far, negotiations with the Brazilians, Argentineans and the Spaniards are still on-going; we do not know the outcome yet. The only ones who have refused to negotiate are the Americans. In case we do not achieve the proposed profit sharing arrangement, the President of Venezuela has already agreed to buy out those companies who refuse to negotiate. If this were the case, Petroleros Bolivar, acting on behalf of the Venezuelan government, would generously buy out the companies who do not agree to the proposed deal. By generous we mean 'according to international standards'. The arrangement with Venezuela is, I believe, quite flexible in term of length of contract. You see, there is no need for budget support. All we want is a fair deal for our natural resources. But perhaps you should talk to the President about your proposal."

Raul was surprised at how well Jaime was informed. "You know, of course," he said, "the American companies have military protection. The U.S. army is already in the country for the drug eradication program. A few weeks ago, the United States signed an agreement with Paraguay under which several hundred U.S. soldiers will be stationed in the country, for 'training' and so-called 'joint maneuvers' with the Paraguayan army. Most likely these troops are already at the border, ready to cross at a moment's notice. Wouldn't it be advantageous to avoid such a confrontation?"

"I urge you to talk to President Morales. My position is clear. If it comes to armed encounter, we will fight on behalf of our people," Jaime said.

"I haven't talked to your President, because I thought you had a good reading on where the President stands and would be able to convey my message to him if you thought he might consider it."

"Sorry, Raul. There is no chance that he would budge on his promise to the people, to share the gas riches with them. They voted for him. They are counting on him. Besides, what we are asking for is nothing but fair. Tell your boss in Washington to rethink his, or if you prefer, the World Bank's position. Be with us, for once, rather than the corporate world. After all, aren't you supposed to fight poverty and defend policies that may lead to a more equitable income distribution, a more just world?"

Raul had no answer. "Well, I tried to avoid a potential conflict. I guess it didn't work." And to his driver, "Let's go Valdo."

Then he turned again to Jaime and his family. "Nice meeting you guys."

He slightly bowed his head, "And thanks for the excellent lunch. I do hope we will get together again on another occasion."

They drove off in the direction of *Santa Cruz*, where Raul wanted to face the managers of XXION Oil&Gas and Mercurio Oil. Valdo remained silent. Just looking straight forward at the dusty road ahead.

* * *

Bungled Negotiations ...

Raul and Valdo arrived in *Santa Cruz* after nightfall in the midst of a tropical thunderstorm. Sheets of rain were slashing the car's windshield. Raul asked Valdo to stop the car on the side of the road, because visibility was just about zero. After less than 10 minutes, the downpour eased. *Santa Cruz* harbored the headquarters of most foreign oil companies. Raul asked the driver to take him to the compound shared by XXION Oil&Gas and Mercurio Oil. The place was fenced in and heavily guarded. Although the buildings were still brightly lit, the gate was locked. Rather than finding an oil executive at this time of night, Raul decided to come in the early morning to try his luck. After all, Vidali had only announced the approximate date of his arrival.

Raul didn't like his boss very much. Hardly anybody liked him. He was arrogant and obnoxious, treating people who didn't share his views with disdain. In addition, Vidali studied economics at the ultra-conservative Chicago School of Economics, which is based on Milton Friedman's free market fundamentalism that laid the ground for the World Bank's and IMF's disastrous 'structural adjustment' and privatization policies which prevail up to this date. The school, by the way, supplied many of the policy-making directors and Vice-Presidents of the World Bank, as well as Dingo, who was also a disciple of Leo Strauss' Philosophy of deception which is based on the belief that the elite should use lies and deceit to control the ignorant masses. Strauss also taught at the Chicago School of Economics. Vidali, with his *Opus Dei* background, was just about one of the worst right-wingers the World Bank could have put in charge of the Andean countries. They had little choice but to accept his often demeaning conceit and economic dictates if they wanted to continue receiving money from the World Bank. Except, of course, for Venezuela's President, who had no patience for the World Bank and its neoliberal approach to development.

Ecuador might now choose a similar route, as did Bolivia. They were forming a strong anti-imperialist alliance. Unfortunately, the puppet governments of Colombia and that of the recently elected Peruvian President were interrupting the string of opposition to America's hegemony and were likely to bend to the World Bank's pressures and to those of the United States.

Among Vidali's better known blunders was his open praise for *CAMISEA*, despite the project's continuous human and environmental disasters in Cuzco's *Urubamba* region—the literal destruction of an indigenous culture, the decimation of entire *Machiguengas* communities. Numerous oil spills over the last two years had largely killed off the river's fish population, from which the natives derived three-quarters of their daily protein. Today *Machiguengas* were threatened by starvation. Up to this point, *CAMISEA* and the international corporate shareholders had escaped any compensation payment or clean-up effort. Vidali called this a highly successful venture, adding at least 1 percent to Peru's annual GDP for the next 40 years, never acknowledging human loss and socio-environmental degradation.

Raul had no idea how Vidali had introduced his visit to the oil giants. He sure didn't like this mission, nor did he like the role he was suddenly given, thanks to PJ's disappearance. It was quite different to sit in the Lima office and to remote-control his peons, bringing them into situations he personally never wanted to be in, and more importantly, having them carry out a highly unpopular capitalist agendas, he himself started having increasing doubts about. Yet, he was very ambitious. His career depended on the success or failure of *Project Golden Enterprise*. Hence, he had no choice.

Raul and his driver checked into the *Hotel Alameda* and agreed to meet at seven in the morning for breakfast.

At 8:30 a.m. sharp, they drove through the high-security gate of the U.S. oil company complex. It looked like Vidali had his visit well prepared. They sailed right through the various security check points. At a quarter to nine Raul was sitting in the lush private conference room of the CEO of XXION Oil&Gas, Bolivia. A lovely young woman offered coffee and *mate de coca* with cookies and informed Raul that both CEOs from XXION Oil&Gas and Mercurio Oil would be with him shortly.

Raul felt uneasy, especially not knowing what kind of expectations Vidali had raised with the execs. His strategy was to get them to the negotiating table with the government, away from the current intransigence of sticking to contracts signed during corrupt preceding governments. But what room did he have to maneuver?

As he pondered this thought, the door opened and two relaxed looking trim North Americans in shirt sleeves without ties entered the room and presented themselves as Jim Werter, XXION Oil&Gas, and Marvin Fox from Mercurio Oil.

"How was your trip?" asked Werter. "We understand you had a rough journey last night, and that you met with Jaime Rodriguez, the rebel leader. I am sure you'll tell us all about it. But first, what brings you here, to this remote corner of the world?"

Raul was confused. Hadn't they already talked with Vidali and knew the reason for his visit? Were they playing games with him? "Well, I think you know the reason for my trip to *Santa Cruz* and my visit to your offices. Marco Vidali, or one of his associates must have explained all this to you. I wouldn't dare drop in on you, out of the blue, so to speak, to disturb important people like you."

The two managers exchanged quick glances before Werter continued, "Yes, your boss told us that by the time you'd meet with us, you'd have convinced the rebel chief in Potosi and perhaps even the new 'Chief Indio' that it would be wise not to touch signed contracts, but to honor them. So, we strongly hope this will be your message. Isn't that so, Marvin?" He grinned at his counterpart from Mercurio Oil.

Raul felt uncomfortable. "My meeting with Jaime Rodriguez was cordial. But he was firm. All contracts need to be renegotiated. That doesn't seem to be a problem with the Spaniards and the Brazilians. I did suggest that there were other ways of increasing the country's treasury so that vital social programs could be addressed. The World Bank would be willing to make resources available quickly as budget support transfers. But according to Rodriguez, this doesn't seem to interest the government. 'Why would they borrow money, when they have their own resources in the ground that they can just convert into cash?' was his answer."

Repeating Jaime's question was more than rhetorical. Raul wanted to see the oil men's reactions. But there was none. So he continued: "In a way, this actually makes a lot of sense. Jaime Rodriguez suggested I should talk directly with the President. But I believe this would not make any difference. So, I thought, we could perhaps discuss the matter. I believe, sitting at a negotiating table, would actually be a good strategy. It would show your willingness and flexibility to listen to the government's concerns. What do you think?"

Again the two oil chiefs made rapid eye contact. This time Marvin spoke. "There is nothing to re-negotiate. We have signed contracts from previous governments. International law requires that they be honored, irrespective of government changes. Frankly, we believed the World Bank would have more leverage. If this is not so, we do not need your institution's assistance. We will not renegotiate. We are prepared to defend our contracts. The U.S. military which is already in the country will defend our installations if need be. In addition, our armed forces are also ready just across the Paraguayan border. You may know we have a base in *Mariscal Estigarribia*, where about a thousand soldiers stand ready to defend U.S. interests if necessary. You may convey this message to your bosses. I think that's all. I have nothing more to say. Would you like to add something, Jim?"

"No, that is precisely my position, too. We are not here to be manipulated by left-wing governments, who do not intend to honor their contractual obligations. I believe this concludes our meeting, Mr. Sanchez."

Raul grew even more uncomfortable. What was he going to tell Vidali? He felt like a loser. But he was also convinced that there was nothing more he could do at this time. Maybe PJ was right in disappearing. Maybe he'd smelled a rat. PJ was always wary of Vidali. He figured the recent kidnapping had done the rest. Probably PJ had overheard some of the phone conversation he'd had with Vidali, just before he vanished.

"One more point, if I may" Raul uttered sheepishly.

"And what would that be?" mused Werter.

"Well, sir, you must have heard of the offer made by the President of Venezuela ... he is ready to buy you out. You or any of the oil companies which are not willing to negotiate. And he offered a fair price, covering investments and compensation for losses. Wouldn't that be more embarrassing than settling any disagreement peacefully with the Bolivians? As I said earlier, we at the World Bank stand ready to help however we can."

"You must be kidding!" Werter exclaimed. "You truly believe we would be intimidated by this bloody dictator, an ally of Castro's? No way. As I said earlier, we have military backing, if it comes down to the wire. We must now resume our daily work. It was a pleasure to meet you, Mr. Sanchez. I am sure we will be in touch."

Raul shook their hands, nodded, picked up his briefcase and was about to walk through the door which had just opened. He passed the charming secretary who brought in a tray with *maté de coca*. She looked surprised, didn't say a word, put the tray on the coffee table and left the conference room behind PJ.

Outside she said, "It looks like the meeting didn't go well, Mr. Sanchez."

"That's right," Raul almost whispered, lost in is thoughts. "But that's OK. You win some and you lose some. Today it was the latter."

"By the way, I am Melissa. Are you going to stay for a while in *Santa Cruz*? It's an interesting place. If you have time tonight, I show you some of the fun sides of this 'hot-hot' city. I know you are a very busy man. All World Bankers are. Just let me know. I have a car and I'd pick you up at the Hotel Alameda if you are free."

Wow! He thought. What a come-on. Melissa had a Madonna-look. She spoke in perfect, charmingly Spanish-accented English. He had planned to go straight back to La Paz and if possible arrange for a meeting early in the morning, if not with Evo Morales, the President, then with his Finance Minister. He wanted to get the Government's reaction, before talking to Vidali. But this could be arranged by telephone. Why not spend an extra night in La Paz. Who knew what he might get out of it. Besides, Melissa was very easy on the eye.

"Delighted," he replied. "How does eight o'clock sound?"

"Perfect. See you later—in the lobby," she said.

The ride back to the hotel was quiet. Valdo noticed that things didn't go as Raul expected, but thought it better not to ask. They arrived at the hotel before noon. Raul simply told Valdo, "We are going to stay here over night. I will leave on the first flight back to La Paz. I suggest you take the road back to the capital also as early as possible in the morning. Don't worry about me. I'll take a cab to the airport."

They shook hands and Valdo said, "See you in La Paz." Then he turned around and presumably went to park the car.

In his room, Raul called the World Bank's La Paz office, asking the Resident Representative's assistant to try to make an early morning appointment, if possible with the President, or alternatively with the Minister of Finance. It was extremely important. Would he want the Resident Representative to accompany him, she asked. Actually, no, he preferred to go alone. He didn't want surveillance during this meeting. Government officials, especially high-level ones, were often more forthcoming with information in one-on-one meetings, no witnesses. Would she please confirm the meeting, time and venue either by phone or e-mail?

Then he took a shower, the second in only a few hours. Cold water rushing over his body had an inspirational effect on him. He needed to think inventively. He needed a strategy. Actually, he needed two strategies, one to talk to the Government, the other to approach Vidali. He was sure his boss had already been called about the aborted meeting by Werter or Fox. In turn, Vidali had probably briefed the State Department and discussed next steps. If he, Raul, only knew what these 'next steps' were. It would make his discussions tomorrow easier.

After the shower, he ordered a sandwich from room service, and then laid down for reflection. Instead, he fell asleep.

* * *

He suspected that Melissa might be an agent for the State Department, and that she was working with the oil companies. Her plan would be to seduce him to get information about him, about the World Bank. They went to the same restaurant where PJ had been kidnapped. He was scared that any moment she would leave and a couple of black-hooded gunmen would appear and drag him away. But Melissa didn't leave. She was constantly talking, smiling at him with her big dark brown eyes. Her lips were moving fast. At times, they were very close to his face, and then she whispered and smiled. He didn't understand a word. But she kept chatting on and on, completely oblivious to his absentmindedness. He was too nervous to concentrate on her words, and only fleetingly did he notice her provocative décolleté. Any moment she might get up and he would be surrounded by gun-toting soldiers or rebels.

But still Melissa didn't get up. He felt edgier with every moment. He wanted to run, but couldn't. Now he felt her hand on his hand, her voice getting softer, her lips closer to his ears. She was so close now, he felt the firm mound of her breast pressing against his arm. She was almost whispering. He had no clue what she was talking about. His sense of danger became extreme. He looked around the restaurant, as if he was haunted. She seemed to be unaware of his anxiety, moved ever closer to his side. Her hair was tickling his face. Cold sweat was running down his spine. He felt like screaming, but couldn't utter a sound. Melissa kept talking. Then, suddenly it sounded as if someone rapped the table next door. He didn't dare to look. Then followed another even harder blow. He awoke. Totally wet. There was the same knock again. Someone tapped at his door. He didn't want to talk to anybody now. He heard the scratching noise of paper being slipped under the door, then steps walking away.

The note was curt. '*Call Vidali in Washington immediately*'. Why hadn't they put him through? Then he realized that his phone was on 'do not disturb' mode. If he called, it was entirely possible that Vidali would make him return to Washington immediately. He would have to explain about his planned, though not yet confirmed, meeting with the Bolivian leadership. Vidali could stop him. But he really wanted to talk to the horse's mouth, so to speak, to get their end of the story. It would be best not to call Vidali back. After all, messages can get lost in Bolivia. As he decided that this would be his course of action, vis-à-vis his manager, he gradually recovered from his nightmare and started looking forward to seeing Melissa tonight. He had an open mind. It would be interesting just to find out whether or not she had a hidden agenda.

At eight sharp he was in the lobby. She was nowhere in sight. Probably the usual, "*hora Latina*," with which he had become so familiar over the course of working in South America. Although of Colombian parents, he was born and raised in the United States with the Anglo-Saxon values of punctuality. His dad taught him that being on time was a virtue that earned respect, especially in the business world. His grandfather was closely linked to Columbia's oil industry. His father followed in the same footsteps. He migrated to the U.S., to Houston, where he landed a job with Chavelin Oil, worked himself up the ladder and eventually became an executive in their planning department. He made enough money to send his only son to Yale. The little memory he had of his mother was that she was a sweet and warm woman who loved and cared for him. God bless her. She passed away when he was only eight. An aggressive breast cancer.

Two years later his dad married a gringa who was almost 20 years his dad's junior. Raul's relationship with her was a roller coaster, love-hate affair. At times she imposed authority, showing him that she was the new woman in the house, the one who had to be obeyed. He hated it, but didn't know what to do about it. His dad was often away, and when he did manage to talk to him about his misgivings towards his stepmother, his dad just laughed and said, don't take her seriously. She is just a kid. But that was easier said than done. He had to live with her on a daily basis. At other times, she tried very hard, being nice to him, spoiling him, fulfilling his every wish, which in turn made him suspicious. It felt so false. Over time, as he grew up and she became wiser, a degree of mutual understanding set in. She became less authoritarian and he more tolerant.

While pondering these thoughts, he realized how much he had in common with the Latino culture. He lived largely in denial, feeling better than those from South of the Border, because of his upbringing, his accent-free English pronunciation—and a Yale education. Secretly, however, he admired the laid-back way they lived. Yet, when defending a cause, they were extremely serious and committed. That's what attracted him so much to Moni Cheng. He was afraid, she was now gone. They had had too little in common. In political terms they were opposites. She was a revolutionary, a non-conformist. He aspired for the power of the rich. She constantly broke with conventional wisdom. He tended to follow the party line. Although lately he didn't always agree with the World Bank's and the IMF's policies, especially with those that interfered with other countries' internal affairs. For example, it didn't feel right to him that the World Bank sided with the oil corporations, when the government offered *renegotiating* the contracts, not *nationalizing* them. But in the end, his career was more important. And he did as told by the World Bank's management.

Moni Cheng kept creeping back into his mind. If truth be told, he realized that she was too valuable to 'just' be an overseas girl friend. After all, he had his family in Washington; a wife from whom he had become increasingly estranged, which he attributed mostly to his traveling job and two lovely daughters whom he missed terribly. He would never give up his family for Moni Cheng. She clearly deserved better.

He sat in a sofa chair in the hotel lobby, sunk deeply in his thoughts, face buried in his hands, when he felt a light tap on his shoulder. He turned his head up and stared straight into Melissa's distraught and frightened eyes.

Raul was alarmed. "What's wrong?"

"Quick, let's get out of here. I believe I'm being followed. I came in through the back door. I couldn't bring the car. We should leave through a side entrance and grab a cab." She wore jeans, high-heeled red shoes and a red blouse. Despite the circumstances, her attractiveness flashed through Raul's head. He was always amazed how gracefully Latinas strode across cobble stones in their high heels.

Though confused, he followed her. She seemed to know her way around. She led him through the kitchen, smiled at the surprised staff, "Just wanted to show this important customer the friendly chefs who prepare his meals." She was steering him towards an open door that gave way to a courtyard. From there they escaped through an archway to a narrow alley which led to a dimly lit street. She ran to the corner, peeked around it, and then waved to Raul. She pointed out a car conspicuously parked across the main entrance to the hotel. Two men were leaning on the hood, chatting, but simultaneously glancing at the hotel doorway.

"See those guys?" she asked. "They were following me from the moment I left my house. I think they are planning to intercept or even abduct me. I'll tell you more later. Now we have to get away. Let's walk in the opposite direction, with our backs to them, embracing as if we were lovers, if you don't mind."

Of course he didn't mind. How could he! She slung her arm around his hips and pulled him along in a casual pace, so as not to attract attention.

He asked, "Do you know the two guys? Have you seen them before?"

She shook her head.

"How do you know that they were after you?"

"They were sitting in the car parked across the street from my apartment. Not very strategically, because as soon as I stepped out, I saw the two front doors of the car swing open and two men jumped out, rushing in my direction. That was the first time I saw them. They were unmistakably after me. I turned around, entered the building again and left by a back door."

Raul was satisfied with the explanation. The remaining doubts he attributed to his ever anxious, searching, suspicious mind. He nodded and left it there. Once they reached a busier street, she flagged down a taxi, gave the driver an address in rapid Spanish, describing how to get there, and then sighed with a giggle, "What a first date!"

The ride seemed to be taking them to the outskirts of town. She settled down in her corner of the backseat, looked Raul in the face. "I believe Werter or Fox overheard my suggestion to meet you tonight. Maybe my office is bugged. Or maybe the mail boy, who was emptying the tray on my desk, told them. They are, of course, scared I might tell you their secrets. And that's precisely why I wanted to see you. But let's talk when we are at Hernan's. I don't think a restaurant, bar, or even another hotel would be safe tonight. Hernan is a cousin of mine. The quiet type, but a strong supporter of the independence of *Santa Cruz*. He feels strongly that the gas and oil belongs to us, not even to the Government of Bolivia, but certainly not to foreigners. Hernan will give us the space to talk. I know you may not agree with him, because you came here to prod the U.S. corporations to renegotiate their contracts. But at least you don't seem to directly and unequivocally support their cause. Well, this was my impression. Am I wrong?"

Raul felt uneasy, again. Sweat ran down his neck and his back. He remembered the dream. He felt the awkwardness of the situation. He was taken for someone he was not. The purpose of his being here was actually to avoid social upheaval, not to question the corporations' rights regarding their contractual agreements. Though he must admit, being smack in the middle of this indigenous ambiance, the strong vibes for independence, for finally controlling not only their own resources, but more so their own destiny—this spirit was undeniably having an impact on his views.

For now, he decided to play along, as she repeated her question, "Am I wrong?"

"No, of course not. I wanted to convince them to sit with the government at the negotiating table. But to no avail. Tomorrow morning I am meeting with the President or his Finance Minister to tell them about my meeting with the Americans and listen to their views." He suddenly remembered that his meeting was not yet confirmed. He needed to get access to the internet somewhere to check his e-mail. Would he ever get back to the hotel tonight? What about his belongings in the hotel room if he couldn't? The first flight to La Paz was leaving at seven in the morning. He had to catch it in order to be able to attend this important meeting, in case it was confirmed.

"I need to check my e-mail. Could we maybe quickly stop at an Internet Café?"

"No need," Meslissa said. "Hernan is fully equipped with communications gear. You may use it."

He again felt nervous. What if the taxi driver was listening and reported their conversation back to the oil giants? Like a bored kid on a Sunday excursion with his parents, he asked, "How much longer?"

"Relax. Hernan knows we are coming. I managed to call him on my run to the hotel. We'll be there soon." The same non-committal answer he got from his parents in the old days. It was better not to talk anymore before they reached their destination.

He contemplated his companion with a smile of embarrassment. What if she was a counterintelligence agent, like those beautiful women in spy movies. You never knew whether you could trust them. And most of the time, when you thought you could, you were actually wrong. So he had better be on his guard. He couldn't avoid thinking of the nightmare he had this afternoon. Was his dream possibly a sign of bad things to come? What if this was actually a kidnapping and Melissa's cousin was a rebel chief, already calculating the ransom they could get for him? Would the World Bank pay to release him? He doubted it. They would follow the Americans hard line: no concessions. 'We are not negotiating for hostages.'

In any case, it was too late now. There was nothing he could do, other than play along and bolster Melissa's impression that he was on her side. But what if Melissa worked for the CIA, or as a secret agent for the oil companies? His mind was swinging from one contradiction to the next. He suddenly felt tired, very tired. But there was no way he could show his sleepiness now.

Through the din of his thoughts, he heard Melissa giving instructions to the cabbie. It looked like they'd arrived. The taxi turned into an ample driveway. The light over the entrance door lit up and out stepped a man who looked in his forties, short, but strong-shouldered. He received them with a broad smile, "*Bienvenidos amigos!*—You must be hungry. Come in. Dinner is ready."

After the customary introductions, they sat at a round table. Just the three of them. It looked like Hernan's family had already eaten. A woman, who Hernan introduced as his wife, opened the kitchen door, saying "I will serve you right away." She was a charming lady, a '*chola*' (an indigenous woman) with sparkling eyes. Clearly she wasn't just the cook at home, but may also be involved in her husband's activism. For now she served them some kind of a mushroom soup, brought two pitchers with wine and water. Then she left the room.

Hernan was obviously anxious to know what was going on. Melissa told the story starting with the morning meeting, the chase to the hotel; finally the escape, and now they were here to probe his, Hernan's, views.

She continued with an intriguing somber voice, "The reason I wanted to see you, Raul, is not just because I like your company," flashing a smile across the table, "but because I wanted to warn you, so in turn you could warn our new President."

Raul interrupted, "But you didn't even know I was going to meet him, in fact I still don't know whether I will meet with him, which reminds me, I have to check my e-mail."

She said, "I knew that you would find a way to convey a message to him, a message of this tantamount importance." Since Raul did not contradict her, she continued. "A few days ago, I overheard a telephone conversation between Werter and a guy from the State Department. They were talking about 'neutralizing' the President, if he would go ahead with the nationalization of the gas and oil fields. They were hoping that a visit of a World Bank representative—must be you—could avert this predicament. They hoped you might be able to talk 'sense' to our government and convince the leadership to honor the signed contracts. They did not even mention 'renegotiations.' It was an all-or-nothing kind of situation. I think Werter suspects that I know about this. Hence, his efforts to prevent me from seeing you." She looked at Raul, then Hernan and paused for effect. Her flashing looks from one to the other met with silence.

Raul was more than shocked. He was floored by the weight of expectations and responsibilities he abruptly felt on his shoulders and on his mind. He had no words. He just knew he had to meet with President Morales or his Finance Minister, come hell or high water. To gain time to reflect before answering, he asked, "Hernan, may I use your computer to check my e-mail. I am expecting an important message linked to Melissa's point."

Hernan showed him to a room next door, pointed to a desktop computer and returned to the dining room. Alone with Melissa he said, "Do you trust this guy? I am not sure where he stands. I never trusted the World Bank. They are in bed with Big Capital. Everywhere they go they support the corporate world, the U.S. corporate world that is."

"You are right about the World Bank. But trust me. I am sure he would feel guilty not conveying this message. In addition, he doesn't impress me as the cold-blooded G8 banker you normally find in other globalization operations, like *CAMISEA* in Peru. Besides, he is also a Latino, even though he acts like a gringo most of the time, surely he has a sense of solidarity left."

"Who says he wasn't involved in *CAMISEA*? But I hope you are right, *mi primita* (my cousin). This may be a good test. If he manages to warn our President … well, how would we ever know?"

The door opened and Raul came back. He smiled. "The meeting is set for 10 tomorrow morning. I am going to meet not only with *El Presidente*, but also with his Finance Minister. I am excited, but also awed at this responsibility. What if they don't believe me? What if they do believe me, but don't do anything to avoid the worst? What if it's already too late?"

Poor Raul's generally anxious mind was spiraling down into what appeared to be a deep hole of irretrievable pessimism.

Hernan tried to utter some encouragement, "Don't worry, as long as you convey the message, you have fulfilled your duty. It is then up to them to act in whatever way they can to avoid an assassin's bullet. That doesn't mean nationalization, or renegotiation is off the table, or that they should give in to the unreasonable request of the Americans. He could simply make it public that his life had been threatened unless he capitulated. The Venezuelan President does it all the time, and so far he has been successful."

Changing the subject, Melissa asked, "How is the autonomy movement coming along?" She was referring to the quest for independence of Santa Cruz and Tarija.

Hernan said at once, "We will first see what the government will do with the contracts of the oil companies. If they are able to renegotiate them to an 18/82 agreement that would already be a good thing. The next step will then depend on the redistribution arrangements the central and provincial governments will be able to reach. Since the treasure is below our territory, we expect to receive a larger share than the other provinces. For now we'll wait and see how our new government evolves."

"That's a good strategy," Melissa agreed.

Raul realized that this little tidbit of information was destined especially for him. This may have been the main reason for dragging him to Hernan's. Melissa thought it was important that he, as a representative of the World Bank, was up-to-date on the rumors of separation or independence of the two Bolivian provinces. In fact, there had never been talk of 'partition,' but rather of more autonomy for the two provinces, the *de facto* owners of the country's wealth. But privatization freaks like the dramatized version, so they could use more extreme force against what they perceived to be extreme positions, jeopardizing even more foreign control over the gas and oil resources.

The impending meeting the following day, for which he really had not yet prepared himself, and all the implications and expectations of this encounter, seemed to knock Raul's anxious character out of whack. He was sleepy and asked to be excused. He also wondered whether it would be safe to go back to the hotel, so that he could take his luggage along on the flight to La Paz, but Hernan advised against it. Instead he suggested he sleep in the spare room. He would wake him up at five and take him to the airport in time to catch the 7 o'clock flight. He showed Raul to the modest guest room with two twin beds. Raul fell asleep almost immediately and just woke once, when he heard the door open and somebody climb into the other bed. Later he found out that he'd shared the room with Melissa.

* * *

In La Paz, Raul went first to meet with the World Bank's Country Representative to discuss his impending meeting with Bolivia's President. To his pleasant surprise, Raul realized that the Representative himself found it was strategically better for him not to accompany Raul to meet the President. The meeting would be more informal. Thoughts could be expressed more freely than with another set of eyes and ears present. The Representative lent him a coat and tie, because he had left his better clothes at the hotel in Santa Cruz. Hernan promised to pick them up and forward the suitcase with the evening plane to La Paz.

At the Presidential Palace, where Raul was expected, he was quickly guided through the security formalities into the President's ante-room. A charming young lady, which the country seemed to be full of, welcomed him to the President's Office, escorting him through a thick leather-padded door into a comfortable though not luxurious office. Evo Morales and Fernando Gonzalez, his Finance Minister, were seated on a leather sofa and a chair. Raul greeted them, thanking them for meeting on such short notice and approached the remaining chair.

After brief formalities, the President leaned back in his fauteuil and broke the ice. "I understand you are here to mediate between the oil giants and the government. Is that right?" Raul nodded and before he could speak, Evo Morales continued, "There is no need for the World Bank's intervention. Our decision is clear. We are not planning to expropriate foreign investments of the gas and oil industry, but we want to renegotiate the contracts that were signed under a previous corrupt government. Your Bank President, Mr. Dingo, should understand this. He claims to fight corruption. If he is serious, he should support the undoing of fraudulent deals.

"We are seeking a fair arrangement. That's all. As you are aware, we are requesting the opposite percentages of the current contracts. We are also offering to sit down with our partners to negotiate the details. All of them, except the Americans have agreed to this. We are aware of the threats, directly and indirectly, the Americans have launched at us. They still have troops in our country, and there are U.S. soldiers along the border, just waiting for the signal to attack. We are not going to be intimidated."

Raul hadn't had a chance to say a word yet. He was hoping to say something, but the President continued his lecture, "Before we discuss your ideas, whatever they may be, I would like you to be aware of the historic background our people have endured and are still enduring. We *Aymaras* have been living in the Andes for at least 2,000 years. We had a highly advanced civilization, centered around *Tiawanaku*, not far from La Paz. It was only in the 15th Century, when the Incas under *Huayna Capac* conquered us. But even under Inca rule, we maintained some degree of autonomy. We were in many ways the brain of the Incas. Our culture and architectural designs can still be seen in the Inca ruins. When the Spaniards arrived late in the 16th Century we became their slaves. Even after Bolivar's independence movement under which Bolivia and Peru became independent in 1825, we remain to this day the oppressed indigenous *'indios'* of the *'Altiplano'*, the Highlands of the Andes."

He gave no sign of having finished. "We have lived a life of miserable subjugation for the last 400 years. All the promises made by successive governments to give us more power resulted in lies stretched over centuries. Today's pep talk of inclusion, a term highly revered by the World Bank, is a farce. There is no inclusion. In fact, all development efforts are geared toward further exclusion, oppression and exploitation of our people. Together with the *Quechua indios* which have had a similar history, we constitute some eighty percent of Bolivia's population, though collectively we own less than ten percent of Bolivia's wealth. Most of our people live on less than $2 a day. Although I don't know what this means in a society whose economy is still largely based on barter, but those are the indicators used by your respected organization.

Raul didn't even dream of interrupting the President.

The President furtively glanced at his Minister, who just smiled. He seemed to be used to the monologues of his President, who continued, "In the 17th Century the Spaniards discovered that we were rich. They exploited our silver and other mineral resources. You may have heard of a mine at *Cerro Rico*, founded in 1546. Under Spanish rule, Potosi became the largest city in the Americas, except for Mexico City. Potosi had more than 200,000 inhabitants. The Cerro Rico has been stripped inside-out of silver, gold, copper and finally tin, plus some other minerals, to the point that today the mountain is referred to by many as the Swiss Cheese, because it is full of holes and tunnels—empty, depleted and unusable. Even for tourists it is too dangerous to visit. But the *Aymara* have not benefited from these riches. To the contrary, they have been used as slaves, working under the most miserable and deadly conditions one could imagine. Many have died from mercury poisoning, countless accidents and diseases. Even today, with the little mining that is still going on in Potosi, working conditions have hardly improved. Average life expectancy is about 33 years.

The President sounded like a professor. Interesting, Raul thought, as he let Morales finish his point. "In the mid-1990s, we discovered gas reserves of some 4 trillion cubic feet and some petrol, most of it in Tarija. After further explorations, the reserves were estimated in 2002 at more than 52 trillion cubic feet, the second largest in Latin America, after Venezuela. In 2003, my predecessor, Alonso Gonazo, signed a contract with a consortium called Pacific LNG (Liquified Natural Gas), ignoring the protests of the population, which left several dead. Today we refer to this brave insurrection by our people as the Gas War.

The President took a white kerchief from his pocket and wiped his face. It wasn't even hot in the room. Telling the story must have triggered his emotions.

He went on. "The Pacific LNG conglomerate consists of several European and South American oil companies—Spain's Repsol YPF, The BP Group, Petrobras from Brazil are the biggest partners of the consortium. Brazil and Argentina are Bolivia's largest customers. Brazil alone buys more than two-thirds of our gas. Today there are some 25 oil companies in the country whose contractual agreements, signed by Gonazo, a friend of your Presidnet's, lets them literally loot the country. Under the contract, Bolivia may retain a mere 18 percent of the *petroleros* profits. XXION Oil&Gas is a relatively small fish in the lot. But they have the military backing of their country.

El Presidente now turned to his Finance Minister, not to let him speak, but rather to seek his acknowledgement to what he was saying. "We, the *Aymara* have been cheated. It is time to turn the wheel. Therefore we have decided that the gains should be reasonably shared between the oil corporations and the country. For the big exporters—those that extract more than 10 million cubic feet per day—the tax should be 82 percent. By the way, this is not an arbitrary figure. As you may have noticed," and now he looked again at his visitor from the World Bank, "it is what the hydrocarbon thieves are taking out of the country under the present contract provisions. We want to turn it around. We have therefore invited all companies to renegotiate their contracts within six months. Those who defy this request will be asked to leave Bolivia. We believe this is a fair arrangement. We think some of the companies may actually agree. This is not nationalization, and far from expropriating, as the foreign media likes to infer. Nationalizing would mean appropriating all the profits, which is not our intention. This is a business-like process. Besides, what's wrong with a country taking more control of its own resources? Saudi Arabia nationalized its oil wells decades ago, and so has Russia. Besides, do you know of any foreign company that is allowed to extract and sell for practically tax-free profit any of the United States' hydrocarbons, or other natural resources?"

After a short silence, he added "And, as you know, if everything fails, we still have Hugo Chavez' offer to buy out those who are unwilling to negotiate. You see, nobody would go without compensation, even if we don't agree on a new contract."

El Presidente paused and looked at Raul, waiting for a comment. Raul was speechless. What could he say? The President had already said everything. Raul had wanted to suggest negotiations instead of confrontation, to avoid social unrest and bloodshed.

As Raul responded with silence, the President smiled and said, "Let me add a little philosophical note. Our foreign currency reserves have increased eight fold to close to $4 billion since I took office. This is the parameter by which the western world is judging us. And we have to play along. We are cast into this growth ideology whether we want it or not. But we don't have to sell all our resources today to satisfy the consumer greed of the industrialized world. We will sell what we need to finally allow our indigenous people a decent living. The rest we keep in our grounds for our children, grandchildren and their children. Indigenous people are living by different standards. They are not a culture of greed, consumption and death. They are perhaps what the humanity is lacking: they are the moral reserve of the world."

Raul was flabbergasted. He uttered, "I have nothing to add. You said it all. I congratulate you for these healthy beliefs. As to your proposal to renegotiate the contracts—my idea was similar. You are doing the right thing. But is there any flexibility on those percentages?"

Morales finally laughed. "On the flexibility we'll see. Important is the mutual willingness to sit at the same table to talk reason. I find it hilarious; the World Bank tells me I am doing the right thing! Thank you. In the meantime, you will understand, we have to shield the gas fields from possible sabotage, at least until an accord, in principle, has been reached."

Raul suddenly remembered that he had an important message to deliver, one of life or death. How to broach the matter? "Mr. President" he said, "I would like to change the subject slightly, if I may."

El Presidente nodded, "Go ahead."

"While in Santa Cruz, I learned from a reliable source that your life might be in danger. The State Department has plans to 'neutralize' you, in case you do not respect ongoing contracts. Somebody overheard a conversation and told me about it. I just wanted you to be aware of this, so you may take precautionary measures."

"I am not surprised", Morales replied. "I actually suspected as much. But this doesn't distract me from our decision to discuss contractual arrangements. Nor does it prevent me from sending troops to the gas and oil fields to protect them."

The Finance Minister hadn't talked until now. "We appreciate your warning, Mr. Sanchez. We really do. This is quite a departure from the World Bank's usual mission ... promoting and forcing privatization of our water supply in Cochabamba and El Alto. In both cases, thanks to a public uprising—which again has unnecessarily cost several lives—we have taken the water services back. It is a crime to privatize vital public services for profit, like water supply which is a human right. I hope your institution will learn a lesson, not just for Bolivia, but for the rest of Latin America," he paused to reflect, "and the world, indeed."

It was clear to Raul; Gonzales wanted to make a little point on his own, since his remarks didn't fit into the preceding conversation at all.

Raul said, "Although I cannot speak for the World Bank in general, I believe such ventures are hardly on the table in Bolivia for the near future."

On that note, Raul intended to close the meeting. "Thank you, Mr. President, Mr. Minister, for your time. It was extremely useful for me, to hear firsthand what the Bolivian position is on the gas deal. I have full appreciation for your position."

Raul stood, wanting to shake the Finance Minister's hand to say goodbye, when suddenly the door flew open and the President's assistant appeared in the doorway. She was flustered, rushing towards the President, whispering in his ear, yet speaking loudly enough for everyone to hear, "I just got a phone call from a certain Hernan—he is an activist for *Santa Cruz's* autonomy—he said, Melissa, the secretary of XXION Oil &Gas's CEO, was found dead, murdered in a back alley close to her home. Shot in the back of the head. Close range. This is horrible!" The young woman had tears in her eyes.

The President immediately took the phone, called the commander of the secret police and ordered an urgent investigation.

Raul was shocked. He'd shared a room with her last night. What a tragedy! Thanks to her, he was able to warn the President. He told Morales, she was the one who had overheard a conversation between Werter and the U.S. State Department. Was this the price she had to pay? Or was it another warning that the U.S. was not kidding around? He also reminded Morales that there were some thousand American troops stationed at *Mariscal Estigarribia*, in Paraguay—that they moved right at the border and were ready to fight at the drop of a hat.

*   *   *   *   *

21

THE GRASBERG GOLDMINE

*H*alfway *around the world ...*

The *Grasberg Demise* helicopter, a four-seater, was circling above the jungle of *Papua* (known as *Irian Jaya* until 2001), the eastern-most province of Indonesia (*Note 12*). The region is the western part of the island of Papua New Guinea. Moni Cheng was peering through the window with binoculars to better assess the magnitude of the crater, the extent of the environmental damage caused by the *Grasberg Mine* (*Note 13*), the world's largest gold and copper mine. She was accompanied by Jamal and Ramona, the couple who put new emphasis on socio-environmental activism and created the non-profit organization *Grasberg Demise*, an off-spring of the earlier movement for independence of Papua. The group was a response to increasing environmental and social degradation because of the early 1990s gold rush.

Grasberg Demise, the brainchild of Jamal and Ramona, focused on the plight of indigenous people brought on by the giant U.S. mining transnational Gold Dust. It committed horrendous social and environmental infractions, dumping hundreds of millions of tons of mining waste into an untouched rain forest, one of the world's richest remaining areas of biodiversity. They were fighting, simultaneously, the American mining conglomerate and the Indonesian government for allowing the company to flagrantly disrespect Indonesia's environmental laws and giving in to outrageous corruption.

Grasberg Demise gained rapidly local support. It had about 1,500 active adherents, a fleet of trucks and four-wheel drives, three helicopters and a Learjet. The funding originally came from the mother organization, the independence movement. Later, local populations and indigenous tribes contributed to the environmental agency from their meager incomes from agriculture and fish trade. They saw Grasberg Demise as the only hope to salvage their environment and livelihood. Lately, revenues were augmented by hijacking small gold shipments. In monetary terms they represented sums that were insignificant for the giant mining corporation, not worth reporting so as to keep the mine secret and its filthy operations quiet. This latest hijacking of a fishing trawler with more than a billion dollars worth of gold bullion was an exception. It would not only bring Gold Dust's dirty operations into the world's limelight, but it would also give due recognition to the work of Grasberg Demise.

The helicopter was hovering just a few meters above the crowns of the remaining trees and underbrush of what once was a lush, rich plane of wetlands. Trees were dying and broken-off; an orange trail of poisonous wastewaters, at least 10 km long, meandered through the remaining brushwood, its acidity slowly burning away what was left of trees and marine life. Moni Cheng discovered an area of devastation which she realized was at least equal or even worse than the environmental wreckage caused by *CAMISEA* in the Peruvian Amazon.

Wherever globalization had brought multinational behemoths into the resource rich countries—most of them North American corporations that benefited in one way or another from the United States money power and defense system—there were also environmental disasters and social oppression. These were symptoms of the boundless greed of the capitalist system, now accentuated by the acute aggression of neo-liberal doctrines.

"Tell me, Ramona, how many people are affected by the Grasberg disaster, and how can this be stopped?" Moni Cheng asked.

"As many as 500,000 to a million people of the total Papuan population of about 2.8 million people may be touched directly or indirectly by this ongoing socio-environmental catastrophe. The toxic tailings kill fish and other marine life; pollute underground and surface waterways and eventually Papua's southern coastal areas of the *Arafura Sea* which abounds in fish."

Jamal added, "So far about 230 square kilometers of once abundant wetlands have been buried under mine waste and some 130 square kilometers of rain forest were destroyed. The mine produces about 700,000 tons of toxic tailings (mine waste) per day; the ore milling process uses 120,000 cubic meters of fresh water per day, all of which is dumped into *Lake Wanagon* and the *Ajkawa River*, and as Ramona said, it's seeping into the ground. The United Nations has given this pristine rainforest a special status; but to no avail, its destruction is imminent."

The helicopter was now ascending to higher altitudes, approaching a number of glacier-clad mountain peaks. Moni Cheng commented, "This is very unusual, glaciers in the midst of the equatorial tropics."

"These glaciers are threatened by the mine," Ramona observed. "They are rare equatorial mountain glaciers serving as indicators of climate change in the region. The systematic removal of vegetation and the heavy tropical rain causes killer landslides. In the last 18 months, at least 50 miners were killed, buried alive under the mud. The mine is destroying a precious, rare ecosystem that can never be recovered—or at least not in hundreds of thousands of years."

The copter was swerving around towards the southern coast line. "How about the people, the employees?" asked Moni Cheng.

"The company has about 18,000 employees," said Jamal, "with a foreign management core of about two percent. A quarter of the workers are of indigenous origins, the rest come from other parts of Indonesia. What's worse, most of the least paid employees work hundreds of meters below ground and under the most inhumane conditions. They have life expectancies not exceeding 35 years. There are reports by victims and witnesses about torture and other kinds of human rights abuses by company police and the Indonesian military in response to protests by the miners. About 200 people have been killed in recent years by the Indonesian military."

Jamal was full of information he wanted to share. "According to a prime U.S. newspaper, Gold Dust paid Indonesian military police and generals about $5 million over three years to protect the mine from journalists and environmental activists, such as us, the Grasberg Demise. Never mind that this is against Indonesian law. But other than benign protests by an acquiescent government, nothing is done against it. They have managed to shroud one of the country's richest assets and mineral resources in secrecy, away from the public eye."

As the helicopter approached the port city of *Merauke*, a plume of reddish-purple effluent, or rather mine waste, formed a half-moon of several kilometers in diameter into the *Arafura Sea*.

"I can see what you mean with the annihilation of sea life," Moni Cheng said.

The flight followed the coast line towards *Okaba*, a couple of hundred kilometers west of *Merauke*, from where the reports of the disappeared trawler originated. They landed outside of town in a small compound of a half dozen bungalows, the Headquarters of the Grasberg Demise. Hundreds of people were squeezing their faces through the iron bars of the gates to the agency's complex. Laughing and cheering they were welcoming the occupants of the helicopter, waving signs *"Power to the people"*—*"Down with Grasberg"*—*"Let them drown in their own mud."*

An elderly woman in rags, with a dirty red bandana holding her hair, yelled "They killed our fish and destroyed our shelter. They expelled us from our villages along the *Ajkawa River*. They said it was unsafe. They said we must go. At night they came with bulldozers and smashed our modest houses. We have nowhere to go—we need help!"

Jamal approached the gate, opened it, so as not to separate himself from the people. He raised his arms in a signal for quiet. "We will give you shelter and food. We have already asked the mayor to build temporary tents to house you at our cost. You can be assured this will be done within the coming few days."

His demeanor expressed confidence. He made a sweeping gesture with his right hand and said, "As to the rest of your concerns, they are our concerns too. We believe we have reached a turning point. This young lady here," and he pointed to Moni Cheng, "is the head of an international organization called *Save the Amazon*, located in the Amazon area of Peru. She is here to help us, to help us get world attention.

"There are countless organizations like ours around the world, fighting for the rights of people, people like you, people exploited and mistreated by major corporations, by so-called *globalization*, people who have had enough and are ready to stand up. We will solidify our efforts, consolidate our work and in solidarity we will prevail. The power of the people is stronger than that of any government, of any corporation, no matter how much greed and armament they display— if we, the billions of us around the world who have been deprived of our rights, of a fair income, stick together, we will overcome—we will overcome the oppressive powers of greed."

He stopped. At once he was applauded by the crowd. In a more quiet voice, he said, "Please go home now and watch the news. Starting tomorrow, every evening at six, our *Okaba* TV station agreed to air special reports from Grasberg Demise, keeping you informed of progress and of daily events. You may also contact us by phone or e-mail through our website. None of your preoccupations will go unheard."

The crowds slowly dissipated. Moni Cheng exclaimed, "Wow! You sure do have the power of speech, the might of the word, the ..."

He interrupted her, "What we mainly have is the trust of the people. They have known about our fight over the last 15 years. They know we are for them and not against them. They have seen us bail out protesters from jail, hiring lawyers on behalf of political prisoners, and suing Gold Dust, as well as the government, for human rights abuses. They have seen our actions vis-à-vis the central government, especially our interference last year, when our steady appeal through the media and demonstrations helped bringing down a corrupt police general. The bribery involved money from USAID, channeled through the Indonesian military. This was prompted by 'Queen' Contessa's visit, the U.S. Foreign Secretary, who decided to reestablish support to the controversial military. Of course, the general may have been replaced by another corrupt crony. That remains to be seen. But what is important is our relentless struggle for justice and human rights taken away by the kings of globalization, by the greedy corporate tentacles of the American Empire. The people know we are with them. That's where the trust comes from. My words alone would otherwise not carry weight."

She didn't say it this time, but she thought, 'This guy sure knows his beat. I will ask Jamal and Ramona to join us at the Freedom Ranch, especially for the workshop, *Vision for a New World*. There they will meet others who fight similar fights, exchange ideas and forge the solidarity he is so fervently talking about. Their input will be a terrific boost to our common cause.'

'Amazing!' Moni Cheng thought. She said. "It shows, you have gained the trust of people and never betrayed it. I would like you and Ramona to join me at 'STA' Headquarters, the Freedom Ranch at Tarapoto. As we speak, there is a large gathering building up for a brainstorming workshop *Vision for a New World*. Activists and freedom fighters, representatives of non-government agencies from all over the world, with a social and environmental thrust, will participate, exchanging ideas, strategies and visions. The objective of this big meeting is precisely what you want to achieve—amalgamating a worldwide solidarity for the cause of the people. And we also hope to come up with ideas to replace our current economic system in which we swim, rudderless and driven by the interests of a few, with a more equitable socio-economy, where nobody goes hungry, and for which the chief incentive would be achieving societal wellbeing."

Jamal glanced at Ramona, who responded with a smile. "Well, Moni Cheng," said Jamal, "Ramona and I will be delighted to accept your invitation. But, first, let us find out what happened to the fishing boat, where it is—and more importantly—where the loot is. And I am not referring to 'our' loot, but the Gold Dust's loot which we took from them to give back to the people and to the environment."

With a wave, he motioned his two companions towards the main building of the compound, which, not unlike the Freedom Ranch, though smaller, had a wide veranda, decked out with tables and chairs.

Inside he went straight to the office of his Chief of Operations, "Harun, meet my friend Moni Cheng from Peru ..." and before he could continue, Harun jumped to his feet, stretched out his arms to embrace Moni Cheng, "I heard you speak at the G-77 Conference in Dacca. I was very impressed. I can't believe that you are here now. The world is really a tiny nutshell."

"I see no further introduction is needed." Jamal smiled. "Harun, could you please brief us on the latest on *Veena*," and addressing Moni Cheng, he said, "This is the name of the trawler with the gold."

"The boat is hidden in a secret mangrove cove, actually not far from here, known only to a local group, part of the 'Aitinyos' tribe. They have been cooperating with us from the beginning. There is little chance that it could be sighted by plane or satellite. Unloading of the cargo is taking place as we speak. I can take you there, if you'd like to see the operation. What's important is that the gold be packed into small shipments that can easily be 'laundered' through the semi-official gold markets of India and Thailand. I assure you, we have the process under close control. And, by the way, the total load is worth nearly $1.5 billion!"

"Wow! That's more than I expected," was Jamal's nonchalant answer. "No, we don't need to see the unloading. It might just create confusion and unnecessary disruption. We are in touch by satellite phone and are now off to the city of *Timika*, the Gold Dust's strong-hold."

* * *

A few hours later and 200 km further east ...

Well before nightfall they landed at a tiny airstrip outside of *Timika*. The ride to the Grasberg Demise's small downtown office was uneventful—almost. The center square was replete with students and mine workers, who'd been protesting the abuses of the mine the entire day. Four laborers had died in a deep underground shaft due to safety negligence. They were crushed by a collapsing wall in a horizontal shaft. Not only did Gold Dust deny any wrongdoing, but they blamed the miners for the damage, so as to rebuff any claim for compensation. Not a week passed without demonstrations, often fraught with skirmishes and police interventions—and often ending in bloodshed.

City Hall, where the Mayor's Office was located, was just off the main square. The plaza looked like it had gone through a rough day of demonstrations and battles with police. The remaining people appeared unhappy, but not ready to disperse.

The air still carried the acrid smell of teargas. When the car slowed down, a student who must have recognized Jamal and Ramona broke loose from the group and approached the vehicle. Jamal stopped and lowered the window. The young man was outraged. "The police took away eight of our colleagues in handcuffs. Two were dragged by the police's horses; they were bloody and unconscious when they were finally stuffed into a car. We were peaceful. All we wanted was to ask the company to account for the accident. We were appealing to the city government. To no avail. The mayor didn't even show up. Instead we were suddenly confronted with a contingent of 50 armed policemen. We can't let that go. If we do, Gold Dust will just continue. It will get worse."

Jamal got out of the car and motioned his companions and the student to follow him. "Let's go to see the mayor right now." They pushed through the crowd and across the square, straight to townhall, an old flat brick building, a leftover from Dutch colonial times.

The mayor was a dubious person, always friendly toward the members of Grasberg Demise, but hardly to be trusted. He was most likely on Gold Dust's payroll, as were the police and military. "I am sure he would not discourage police intervention," Jamal said, "no matter what human rights abuses are at stake."

The mayor was not available, according to his secretary. But Jamal didn't pay any attention and rushed straight to the padded door, swung it open, and surprised the mayor at the head of a small conference table, in what looked like a heated discussion with five city government members. They stopped cold in their debate. Jamal addressed the mayor: "Mr. Sukarato, I want a word with you alone."

The mayor agreed, signaling with his hand to the government members that it would only take a few minutes; that they should not leave. He steered Jamal and his friends to a side door and into a small but cozy office with a comfortable sofa and a couple of puffy fauteuils. The room had a small corner bar with glass shelves on the wall behind it, filled with all sorts of liquors. Moni Cheng was wondering what sort of 'private' sessions might go on in these quarters.

Jamal didn't leave much time to reflect. Immediately to the point, he demanded, "Mr. Mayor, I want the eight students who were apprehended this afternoon released immediately. There was no reason, other than pleasing Gold Dust, the Grasberg monster, to put them behind bars. They demonstrated peacefully. The mining corporation is the criminal in this affair and you should call them to account."

The mayor uttered a few words on how the police told a different story, but it was obvious he knew Jamal was right. He agreed to release them in the morning and to call for a meeting with the CEO of Gold Dust.

Jamal grew impatient: "Not tomorrow, but tonight, right now.—And, we would like to be present at the meeting with Grasberg's management." This was a demand, not a request.

The mayor looked at him, not sure what to say. It was obvious; Grasberg Demise commanded a lot of respect. They had the full support of the people, the same people on which a great portion of Indonesia's economy depended. He was visibly embarrassed to be called to task by a group of revolutionaries in front of other visitors, notably one of the 'riot students', as he liked to call them. He said nothing, but took his mobile from a shirt pocket and dialed ... "Tarana, I want you to release the eight demonstrators immediately ... no, not tomorrow, I will explain later—right away ... thanks."—To Jamal he said, "They are free. Tomorrow first thing I will call the head of Gold Dust; and of course, I want you to be present."

It occurred to Jamal that his presence at the meeting would be to the mayor's advantage. For anything unpopular he had to say, he could blame Jamal's organization. Worse, Moffot, Gold Dust's Chief Executive Officer, would most likely want to talk about the hijacked gold cargo. Grasberg Demise was suspected of being behind the caper. He would have to pretend convincingly that he knew nothing about it. Not an easy deed.

Jamal got up, the others too, walked towards the door, "Thank you Sir. Call me as soon as you have an appointment. I'll be here in no time."

As they walked through the central square, where students and demonstrators started to disperse, he observed with certain anger: "The mine is expected to be exhausted, emptied and looted of its precious treasure, by 2040—leaving a projected waste of 6 billion tons behind. We must stop this criminal insanity long before!"

* * *

The meeting that was supposedly taking place at 9 a.m. was suddenly rescheduled to 4 o'clock in the afternoon. Moffot and the mayor were already drinking whiskey, when Jamal, Ramona and Moni Cheng entered the mayor's office five minutes early.

Strange, that they were already talking. Also unusual were the half a dozen special police guarding the mayor's office. Something was brewing. Obviously Moffot and the mayor had concocted a strategy for dealing with the rebels. Moffot immediately rose to shake hands and introduced himself to Moni Cheng. Before Jamal could speak about the mine accident and the compensation due to the families, the CEO bombarded the trio with questions and accusations about the stolen gold.

Jamal displayed his typically relaxed demeanor. "May we sit down?"

"Of course, of course," muttered the mayor apologetically. "We are here to talk about as many mutual concerns as we can cram into the hour at our disposal, taking advantage of the presence of an international representative." The mayor nodded towards Moni Cheng. "We would like to get some global exposure," he added. It was not clear whether this was sheer sarcasm, or whether indeed this was part of Moffot's agenda.

"I didn't know that we had to *cram* all our issues into a one-hour session, but we will do our best. Let me start then, with the accident that killed four miners—negligence of the company which so far has refused to admit fault. We know this is to escape compensation payments to the victims' families. Let's start there," Jamal said.

Moffot was prepared. "Before we talk compensation, I want to discuss your group's role in the disappearance of the fish cutter. You know," and he looked intently at Jamal, "even AsiaLink-TV already reported that Grasberg Demise—what a name! It says it all—was behind the capture of the boat. I am convinced they are right. We want the entire cargo back, before we discuss releasing the eight students arrested during yesterday's riots, or compensation, or any other subject for that matter."

Jamal glanced at his companions, then got up and literally yelled at the Mayor: "You promised last night that the students would be freed. I heard you speak to the police chief. You changed your mind, or *somebody* must have changed your mind." He looked at Moffot, but continued, "I find this outrageous. No integrity. No trustworthiness. If it weren't for your Grasberg cronies, the people of the city would have thrown you from your office long ago.—Let's go." He waved to his friends, and they followed him to the door.

"Not so fast!" Moffot shouted. He motioned to the guard to open the door, which he did, followed by six policemen storming in. They handcuffed the three and dragged them to a waiting four-wheel drive. The car sped away.

Neither Jamal nor Ramona imagined that this meeting would conclude with them ending up in the fangs of Gold Dust. No doubt, this kidnapping had been planned earlier. No matter what the result of their meeting with the Mayor and Moffot, short of returning the gold shipment, their fate had been sealed before they entered the Mayor's office.

There were seven people crammed into the car. Moni, Jamal and Ramona, three policemen and the driver. Escaping would not be easy. But Jamal had foreseen this. They had special rescue calls for such occasions. Members of the Grasberg Demise would always let the Operations Office know of their whereabouts. They had a special button with GPS features on their cell phones. Pressing it would emit a soundless and unique S.O.S. signal that would be received in the Operations Office and in the Security Officer's quarters, indicating the sender and his location.

Now Jamal quietly used this device, looking out of the window into the darkness that had fallen with tropical speed. They were racing over a bumpy road through a largely destroyed forest, presumably towards

Gold Dust's headquarters, about an hour away from the city. Jamal and Ramona knew that they had a dungeon-like prison there, where *misbehaving*, protesting miners were held and tortured for days. He desperately hoped rescue would come before they reached Grasberg's headquarters.

* * *

The car hummed along the winding road, with most of the passengers dozing off—except Jamal who was fully alert—when a sudden crash about 100 meters ahead awoke them. A huge tree smashed onto the road in front of them. The driver tried to turn the vehicle around, when another trunk collapsed onto the street just behind them. There was nowhere to go. Five hooded men with machine guns emerged from the remaining underbrush, surrounded the car and demanded the release of the three captives. The doors were pulled open. Moni Cheng, Ramona and Jamal jumped out. They ran behind the tree barrier behind the vehicle, while the gunmen slowly retreated, keeping the driver and the three policemen in their sights. The darkness of the jungle at night swallowed the three fugitives and left the four-wheel drive and its crew trapped between the gigantic tree trunks.

Rescue from Grasberg Demise was close behind, bringing them back to their *Timika* headquarters. Jamal called the Mayor: "You better release the eight students at once, or else you will face serious problems with our organization." He hung up without waiting for response from the mayor.

"It's time to move on, friends," Jamal said, smiling at Moni Cheng, "What is the fastest way to Freedom Ranch?"

* * *

Back at Freedom Ranch ...

The conversation that evening, initiated by Ramona, focused on the massive environmental and social destruction brought about by the Gold Dust company's exploiting of the Grasberg gold mine in *Irian Jaya*.

Sitting at a round table on the huge veranda with a group of friends from all over the world, including PJ, Ramona recounted their recent adventure in Papua. She started out by giving some background, explaining that Gold Dust, the American led, New Orleans-based mining conglomerate had dumped billions of tons of soot-colored mine waste into a jungle river in one of the world's last untouched landscapes; that they were shamelessly exploiting one of the world's largest gold reserves, in an area protected for its bio-diversity and indigenous societies; that their 18,000 employees worked under slave-like conditions, in total disrespect of human rights. She said the natives were enticed into the workforce with alcohol and other drugs, compelling them to labor deep underground under the most inhumane circumstances. They were paid a pittance, from which rent for miserable barracks living quarters and company supplied foods were deducted.

"How come the Indonesian government lets this happen? Why has this mining disaster never made major world news?" PJ, somewhat naively, wanted to know.

"Simple. There are several reasons. First, your World Bank ..."

"Sorry, please do not call it my bank, as I've disassociated myself from this institution," PJ interjected.

Ramona smiled. "OK, the World Bank and the IMF, under a 'reform' treaty with Indonesia, loaned the government hundreds of millions of dollars. In turn, the government has to promote the private sector in all walks of industry and public services. In other words, an 'enabling environment'—what a jargon they use, these neocons!—has to be created, in which, of course, standards for ecological protection and international labor laws have no place. There is virtually no control of what happens with the money, as long as the 'free market' flourishes.

"Second, Gold Dust, of course, pays off high-level government officials and decision-makers to keep them silent and to guard the company from the media. And third, within the last six years or so, Gold Dust has bribed the Indonesian military, which is 'advised' by American armed forces, with at least $5 million, to protect the mine from sabotage and from social disturbances and riots. You must also know that any American company, when they feel their investments are threatened, may call upon the U.S. military to defend them. It is better, of course, and less visible, if the local defense services and police do the job."

She paused, taking a sip from her *Masato*. Then she continued, "The pace of exploitation has progressed enormously in the last three years, well exceeding 100 tons of gold last year, a world record for any mine anywhere."

PJ was learning fast. He interjected, "Curious, in Peru, the *Yanacocha* gold mine in the Cajamarca Province is also exploited, without any regard for environmental protection and no consideration for the workers or the inhabitants of the surrounding villages. Behind this is also an American company. But no wonder, the gold price is rapidly inching towards $750 per Troy Ounce—and who knows how far it will increase. It always booms when there is insecurity in the world, wars, and threats of wars ... and perhaps in the United States the collapse of the dollar is looming in this heavily stretched and indebted economy."

*　　*　　*　　*　　*

22

REASSIGNMENT TO SUDAN'S DARFUR REGION

Back in the Andes ...

After returning from Indonesia, Moni Cheng, Jamal and Ramona spent a night in Lima. The following morning Moni Cheng put her friends on a plane to Tarapoto. She told them she had to settle an urgent affair in Bolivia and would see them shortly at the Freedom Ranch. She also called Enrique to make sure her two friends from Grasberg Demise were being picked up at the airport. Then she boarded the next flight to La Paz.

Back from the meeting with Evo Morales, to Raul's big surprise he found Moni Cheng in the World Bank's waiting room. She stretched out her hand, no kissing, and greeted him with a big smile. Before he could say anything, she said, "I have heard about your mission to change the government's mind on nationalizing their natural resources. I thought I wanted to catch up with you and see how successful you were going to be. And here you are. They told me you had an important meeting. With whom?"

He was dumbfounded, partly because of the unexpected sight of Moni Cheng, and also because he didn't know how much he should reveal, how much of all this should remain secret. Finally he said, "I just saw the President and his Finance Minister. We agreed that renegotiating the contracts was a good idea, something he intended to do all along. But the international media like the inflammatory term of 'nationalization'. It makes headlines. They associate it with 'expropriation'—which, of course it isn't. 'Nationalization' points to another Marxist government that tries to resist the ruling market economy. Even if Morales resists the capitalist free market theories, he is just seeking a more just distribution of profits."

"And what if renegotiating doesn't work?" Moni Cheng asked.

"Funny, that you should ask this question. Because you know the answer. First, I would say, let's cross that bridge when we get to it. Six months is a long time to start and carry on negotiations. And who knows, if progress is in sight, maybe the deadline can be extended. In any case, if negotiations fail with all or with some of the oil corporations, there is still the Chavez option of buying out the unwilling corporations at a 'fair price'. But how do you know about my mission?"

"You know I have my contacts," she answered curtly.

She didn't want to tell him that Jaime Rodriguez, the rebel fighter for the *Aymara,* was a friend of Hernan's, that she knew about the death threats and that she already knew about Melissa's murder. She wanted to wait and see how much of this information Raul was willing to share with her.

She added, "But I am glad that you and President Morales agree on Bolivia's decision to take more control of their natural resources. That would make you either a renegade World Banker or an outcast. Neither position is good to hold in the current ambiance of the World Bank, where the neocons strive to help the corporate empire take over the world's natural resources."

"Well, I certainly don't consider myself a turncoat. My mission was to talk sense to the government, with the aim of preserving the dialogue between the national authorities and the investors of the gas and oil industry and, ultimately, avoiding riots and possible bloodshed. I hope they appreciate this in Washington.—But, tell me, where is PJ? It seems as if he disappeared from the world."

Moni Cheng was quick with her advice. "You better check back with Washington, whether they approve of your actions and, indeed, whether you still have a job. As for PJ, I have no idea. Perhaps he simply had enough of these unethical activities of his employer. Maybe he needed a break and went to Spain to visit his daughter."

"Oh, I didn't know he had a daughter in Spain. Where in Spain?"

"He was, or possibly still is your colleague. And you don't know the essentials of his life? I don't know the details. Let's stick to our Bolivia agenda. What are you going to do next? What will the World Bank do?—Stop all their loans to Bolivia? Help to strangle them? Use the usual tactics of the capitalists if they don't get what they want?"

He'd never heard her talk like this before. She was now showing her true colors—which was good. At least his suspicion had been confirmed: it was best to separate. They wouldn't see eye to eye in the long run. He was wondering what she really wanted from him. "Moni Cheng, please tell me, why are you here?"

"I am seriously interested in knowing firsthand what is going on here, how the country is going to be influenced—or not—by outside forces. Peru has a new President. And, as you well know, ownership of exploitation rights, royalties of natural resources, gas and oil, and in addition, the destruction of the pristine Amazon rain forest by these irresponsible and inconsiderate oil giants, are also a big issue in my country. Actions taken in Bolivia may have an impact on the future of Peru. These are my reasons for being here: observing and learning."

He looked puzzled. So, she continued. "My intentions are not to stop you from doing what you are doing. You are doing your job, with which I may or may not agree. That is immaterial. I am trying to pursue my self-imposed mission, which is primarily to help the indigenous populations of the Andean countries take better control of their land and resources, so that they can improve their livelihood. And, my second objective is to help other organizations who have similar goals for their own people in their endeavors. I also believe environmental consciousness and protection which is an integral part of human well-being, is a good media, an appropriate vehicle, if you will, to lead the fight for these social causes. That is why I am here, Raul."

Again, wow! He thought. This woman has inner strength and conviction. That gives her the power she exerts. "I got you. Let me call Washington and find out what their latest position is. Maybe they won't even talk to me anymore. It is entirely possible. I am surprised at nothing. Oh yeah, and by the way, a young woman in Santa Cruz has been assassinated somehow in connection with this gas and petrol fiasco."

"Yes, I know. I was wondering whether you would tell me. But you did. I am glad."

He seemed to have gained back some of her confidence and was quick to add, "Worse, Melissa told me last night that the Americans may 'incapacitate' President Morales, if he doesn't respect the contracts signed between the previous government and the oil corporations. I just conveyed that message to *El Presidente*. As we wound up our meeting, the news of her murder reached us. The President immediately launched an investigation by his secret police."

He pointed to an empty office where he intended to call Washington. He smiled through the glass pane, as he closed the door behind him.

His face was grim when he came out. The conversation had been brief. He'd spoken to Vidali. Moni Cheng's face was questioning. He answered, "They didn't seem to appreciate my work. Though I wasn't told in so many words, but my boss was ice cold, ordering me back to Washington at once. I'd better check out the flights to Lima, pick up a few things and take one of tomorrow's flights north. What are you going to do?—I know, I know—none of my business. But tell me anyway. Perhaps I can help."

"I doubt you can help anymore than you have already helped—by warning the President. I am sure he was grateful. As for me ... well, I'll see whether I can help Jaime investigate Melissa's murder. She was one of us; a mole so to speak; working in the oil companies as a spy. They must have suspected it. When they found out that she wanted to meet with you in the evening—that was her death knell, I suppose."

"How do you know her name?" Raul asked.

"I told you already, I have my sources. To be truthful, Jaime and Hernan are friends, though their interests do not necessarily coincide on all fronts. This is how I know what is going on."

She went on, "As you may know, Hernan is part of the independence movement of the two departments of Santa Cruz and Tarija. This initiative is led by the business elite which are afraid that the government may seize the gas installations, nationalize the oil companies and perhaps even expropriate their investments. Together Santa Cruz and Tarija exports of hydrocarbon produce about a third of Bolivia's revenues or close to 10 percent of GDP. Both Departments are also rich in agricultural output and attract most of Bolivia's foreign investments."

He was listening intently to what she said. "The *cruceños* (inhabitants of Santa Cruz) prosperous entrepreneurs and oil tycoons are demanding more financial autonomy and control over their gas riches. But the Bolivian nationalists counter that after 40 years of heavily subsidizing these formerly poor Departments, it is now time that they contribute their share to the national treasury. Hernan is a moderate. He sees the advantages of being part of the Bolivian state, as long as the government doesn't go to extremes, meaning, expropriating the gas industry that has brought them a better standard of living. So far, Evo Morales has no such intentions."

Raul nodded absentmindedly. After the phone call, the worrier in him took over again. He had difficulties concentrating on Moni Cheng's story. His main preoccupation was how he would get the suitcase left behind in the Hotel Alameda in Santa Cruz, catch the next plane to Lima and then organize his trip back to Washington. Somehow he had the impression he wouldn't be back in this part of the world for a while.

Preoccupied with his own future, he wished Moni Cheng good luck, to take good care, and to not get lost, then he hugged her and said good-bye. He didn't even look up the Resident Representative any more, even though he still wore his jacket and tie. He grabbed his briefcase, rushed to the elevators and was gone.

* * *

In Lima, Raul didn't go to the office. He went straight home to his lovely apartment with the breathtaking view overlooking the Pacific Ocean with the *Costa Verde* and the *Rosa Nautica*—two first class, though touristy restaurants—down on the beach under the green cliff. It is now irrigated to look good for the well-to-do, who used to spend summer weekends at the beach, before it was polluted. Lost in thought, he stood on the balcony for a moment, with a premonition that this might be the last time he would enjoy this marvelous view from his apartment. Then he remembered the suitcase he had left behind in Santa Cruz and called the hotel. The receptionist told him that a certain *Señor Hernan* had already picked it up. He would forward it to the La Paz office of the World Bank. He phoned the La Paz office, telling the Representative's assistant to please forward the suitcase to Washington. She said, no problem, but that he should send back the borrowed coat and tie. He promised he would do it right away. This meant returning to the Lima office after all, something he'd wanted to avoid. He gathered his most essential belongings, clothes and documents, let his eyes wander a last time around the place and locked the door behind him.

* * *

In Washington, Vidali didn't even receive Raul. He was apparently away from the office, but his assistant refused to tell him where. To his surprise he was called by the Vice President for Latin America, a middle aged lady by the name of Patricia Redfox. Everybody called her the World Bank's Thatcher lady. He feared the worst.

She sat in her expansive corner office, like a queen on her throne, an artificial smile lodged between her cheekbones, "Please come in." He took a seat in front of her desk. "I understand you met with the oil company execs and with Evo Morales. What did you achieve?"

"My two prime objectives were to convince the managers of the *petroleros* to accept the President's invitation to renegotiate the contracts, rather than staunchly insist on the terms signed during the earlier administrations. This was to avoid social unrest and bloodshed, as well as to show goodwill and flexibility. After all they are guests in Bolivia. The second aim was to assure that the government would not nationalize or expropriate the investments. That was the focus of my meeting with Morales and his Finance Minister."

He looked at her, waiting for approval, which didn't come. So he continued. "On the first score—no success. Both Werter and Fox, the two CEOs, insisted that the government's proposal to renegotiate was illegal and that the existing contracts had to be honored. Besides, they would seek protection from the U.S. military."

He looked again into a humorless, bland face. He went on, "On the other hand, Evo Morales assured me that he had no intentions of expropriating the oil companies. He just wanted a fairer sharing of the profits, which is why he invited them all to the negotiating table. I think this is reasonable."

Now he wanted to test the Thatcher lady's emotions. "However, there are two additional points you should know, if you haven't already heard about them. Werter's assistant, Melissa, wanted to tell me something. She asked me to meet with her in the evening. The message was that she overheard a phone conversation between Werter and the U.S. State Department, from which it was clear that the plan was to 'neutralize' Morales, in case he nationalized the oil companies. She wanted me to warn Evo Morales"

"Did you?" The stony face asked.

"Yes, I did, and the President was grateful. As my meeting with *El Presidente* wound up, his distraught secretary barged into his office. She told him that Melissa's body had been found in the early morning, murdered."

This emotionless woman didn't even react to murder. "Did you consider it right to meet with Melissa and to be the courier for the warning message?"

He hesitated a moment. "Yes, I did. I think it is not only in the interest of the World Bank to be an intermediary, but it would have been unethical not to pass on a death threat message."

The cold face gave him her final verdict. "Hmmm, well Raul, you have certainly done your job. You have been very helpful with the World Bank's operations in the Latin America Region. It is time to move on. As of Monday, you will be working in the Africa Region. You will receive a short training on Sudan operations. Within a couple of months you should be ready for a field posting in Khartoum. You will be looking after Bank operations in Darfur and generate new ones. Eventually you may be posted to *Nyala*, the capital of South Darfur, where the oil and gas fields are."

She didn't wait for any reaction, but moved right on. "Once the civil war is over and Darfur gains independence, they will badly need support from the World Bank. You are good at preparing and process-ing budget support operations. There is no risk of default. As you know, Darfur has vast oil reserves. This will be a challenging job. I am sure you will enjoy it. I discussed the move in detail with my colleague Nestor Pattur, the Vice-President for Africa. We are all in agreement. Good luck to you!"—The Thatcher lady stretched out her hand and accompanied him to the door.

He went for a coffee to reflect on his next moves. Too bad PJ wasn't around. He would have loved to discuss this case with him. He was horrified to be condemned to godforsaken Darfur. But in reality, he expected to be taken off Latin America. That's what he was afraid of, when he was so suddenly called back to Washington. For the rest of the day, he just cleaned up his office, threw away most of his files. But he kept one book PJ had given him a few months ago, *Conquering the World—One Country at a Time.—The U.S. Quest for Dominance of the Planet's Resources.* He never thought he would read such radical literature. Maybe it wasn't that radical after all.

*   *   *   *   *

23

Turning Point

10 *flight hours south....*

The Freedom Ranch bustled with activity. People were arriving from all over the world to absorb knowledge and to contribute their own experiences on matters of social injustice and environmental destruction. What from the outset looked like a confused, messy congregation of people, was in fact a well-organized and disciplined camp of several hundred similar-minded associates. They organized and contributed to many seminars, workshops, discussion groups, and lectures; they quietly studied and prepared presentation papers in the Ranch's ample and richly stocked library. Wireless internet access was available every where. All of them were preparing for the big event, the week-long *Vision for a New World* workshop.

At the same time, and unnoticed by most, Moni Cheng's close circle, a small group of highly skilled permanent Ranch members, were monitoring events around the world—social upheavals, environmental disasters, demonstrations, skirmishes and brawls for human rights, labor disputes, and obscure civil wars. Many of them went unnoticed by the international main stream media.

It had been several weeks since PJ's arrival at the Ranch. He enjoyed every minute of it. He made friends from all corners of the earth, of different creeds, cultures and colors. The Freedom Ranch was a kaleidoscope of human species, spirit and intellect.

He learned from Ahmed, alias Mokhtar, the head of the health charity and freedom fighter in southern Sudan, about the 21 year-long civil war in South Sudan. The conflict was between Sudan's People's Liberation Movement (SPLM) in the south and government forces commandeered by Khartoum. The war began in 1983, when the Muslim-dominated Sudanese government declared *Sharia* law, the law of Islam, over the non-Muslim south. The conflict killed more than 2 million people and displaced and left at least another 4 million homeless. Most of them fled to Kenya, Uganda, and Ethiopia, countries which can't claim the cleanest human rights record themselves, thereby leaving the refugees vulnerable to abuse and exploitation. A so-called Comprehensive Peace Agreement (CPA) was signed on January 9, 2005, to be implemented over a six-year period. The partners to the CPA, the European Union, the United States and a number of individual European countries promised to finance a development plan of $ 4.5 billion coinciding with the CPA implementation period. But the plan was seriously imperiled, because the fighting started again.

Ahmed told him also about the ruthless assassination, disguised as an airplane accident—of South Sudan's first President. He was seeking more autonomy over oil fields in the South. This happened only six months after the signing of the peace accord. Yet, other than sending messages of condolences to his nemesis' family, the President of Sudan and the rest of the western world sat quiet, not demanding any investigation of the 'accident', thus, hoping for easier access to the black gold.

For example, the United States, which has officially decried the Khartoum regime for the genocide in Darfur and has maintained official trade sanctions against Sudan for years, has been quietly cooperating through the CIA with the Sudanese government on matters of so-called 'anti-terrorism'. Yet, officially Sudan is still on the State Department's black list of countries that sponsor terrorism. Simultaneously and unknown to the public at large, the United States has poured billions of dollars into the south through USAID—money to be used ostensibly to reconstruct the war-devastated infrastructure, but clandestinely to foment civil unrest with arms and propaganda.

As so many others throughout the world, this conflict is all about oil. Reserves are currently estimated at 563 million barrels, worth more than $45 billion at $80 per barrel. China, Malaysia and India are the main shareholders of an oil exploitation consortium, with China owning the largest share of 40 percent, followed by Malaysia (30%) and India (25%). Clearly, US oil giants would like to get their share, which largely explains USAID generosity. On the other hand, the oil fields require protection. So, China has supplied the Sudanese military with weapons which, in turn, have been used to scorn the CPA. According to some accounts, up to 80 percent of China's payments for oil flow right back to Beijing to buy military hardware. War is lucrative. The faltering peace agreement has been an obvious result of the profitability of hostilities.

Ahmed knew his stuff. He was no doubt prepared for a broad discussion, seminar-style, on the relationship between natural resources, weapons trade and civil war, as well as the consequences, the ensuing poverty and environmental devastation.

As leader of the South Sudan Independence Movement, Ahmed assembled a small audience around a group table in the large cafeteria hall. This place was never empty. At any time of day, clusters of people could be found in dialogues and discussions, watching slide shows or Power Point presentations on laptops—always concentrating on topics of world interest.

Ahmed continued. "Then, there is Darfur, the western portion of Sudan. It is sectioned into three parts, the northern Shamal Darfur, western Gharb Darfur and the southern Janub Darfur. Amazingly, the background of this conflict dates back to the 13th Century. It concerns two diverse groups of people populating the Darfur area: several non-Arab black tribes against different Arab tribes, Muslims, collectively called the 'Baggara'. At that time the confrontation of the two groups focused mostly on their different economic needs. The Arabs were mostly nomadic herdsmen, while the non-Arab tribes were sedentary agriculturalists, leading to clashes over water and land use. To this day, these remain the origins of the conflict. Of course, today this age old quarrel over land and water is exploited for more mundane purposes: the vast petroleum reserves.

According to Ahmed, the reality is that, despite threats of trade embargoes and other sanctions, neither Khartoum nor the Western World are seriously interested in peace in Sudan. "While everyday life is agony, the weapons' manufacturers enjoy their bonanza," says Ahmed quite convincingly.

In the course of his stay at the Ranch, PJ was brought up-to-date by Moni Cheng's friends, who slowly trickled in for the *Vision* meeting. By the time Moni Cheng arrived, he had a good understanding of the big picture, but didn't know all the gory details.

* * *

The arrival of Moni Cheng at the Freedom Ranch, a few weeks later than expected, came as no surprise. No announcement. She just dropped in. Her two friends Ramona and Jamal from Grasberg Demise, told him about her turning up soon.

She hit the ground running. After an impromptu welcome reception, Moni Cheng set out to organize the next few weeks, maybe months at the Ranch. In a general briefing session in the big Freedom Hall, Moni Cheng and her main partners and colleagues at the Ranch brought the several hundred members of the *Save the Amazon* alliance up to date on recent events, like the wars over water, oil and gas in Paraguay, Bolivia and Peru, the environmental disasters in the Peruvian Amazon caused by '*CAMISEA*' and by the Grasberg gold mine in remote Papua. She also talked about likely future conflicts and possible cataclysms man may bring about around the globe.

One message stuck out before all: No time was to be lost. Corporate imperialism was advancing in fast strides, looting countries' and entire regions' resources around the globe, destroying people's social fabric, their livelihoods and environment. The World Bank and IMF, were in full swing, promoting disaster capitalism. *Save the Amazon* members had to use their full brain power to stop this brutal onslaught.

The aim of the next few weeks for the *'Vision'* forum at the Ranch was two-fold: preparing counter-measures strategies, but foremost, discussing and designing an alternative economic system to replace the growth and greed-oriented free-for-all capitalism. Seminar-style group sessions, colloquia, simulated focus groups would be the mechanism form which the *'Vision'* would emerge. The results with action and protection agendas would then be disseminated to the world, and especially to the troubled regions and countries. Since none of these topics would gain the interest of the corporate mainstream media, STA had already contracted Telesur, Al-Jazeera, AsiaLink-TV and TelAfrica, to carry the forum's messages around the globe.

The main subjects on the agenda were:

The **pilferage of hydrocarbon** rich countries was merely to satisfy the boundless appetite of the industrialized world. The United States was using a third of the world's energy with less than 5 percent of the population. This resulted in social inequity, Global Warming ...

Iran was an equally intricate case. The United States' plans to attack the country with arguably the world's greatest gas reserves had been sealed long before the antagonism over nuclear energy vs. atomic bombs arose. Such an assault would be catastrophic for the people of the region and the world. In addition to the senseless and enormous loss of life and suffering that would ensue, hydrocarbon prices might soar to astronomical levels, unaffordable for many economies, causing their collapse—a domino scenario hard to imagine.

The risk of such aggression had, of course, nothing to do with a nuclear threat. Indeed Iran was no threat to the people of the United States of America, no matter how one churned and promoted the 'atomic risk' factor. It was a good pretext to intimidate the American public and to a lesser extent the rest of the world, and justify an attack on Iran.

A more likely reason for subjugating Iran was the fact that Iran intended to denominate the **price of oil and gas in Euros**, abandoning the dollar as a hydrocarbon base currency. So far the dollar has been the choice tender of OPEC and the reserve currency around the world. Iran's wider plans were to set up a Hydrocarbon Exchange in Euros, the *Iranian Oil Bourse* (IOB). Any oil producer could sell its petroleum products at the Teheran IOB in Euros.

Currently, the two major oil bourses are located in New York and London. Both are under United States ownership and both trade hydrocarbon in dollars, even the one in London. This is considered a key reason for the UK not adopting the Euro, for which the standards of the European Central Bank would apply. It is unlikely that the ECB would tolerate within its Euro area trading of this magnitude in a non-Euro currency.

Iran's sale of hydrocarbons in Euros might be a real risk to the U.S. economy. It could lead to a rush in sales of dollars for Euros around the globe. But how much are those who harbor huge dollar reserves, like China and Japan, willing to lose with a rapid decline of the Greenback?

Ecuador was yet in another league. Of its 14 million inhabitants, about two-thirds survive on less than $ 2 per day, the notorious World Bank poverty indicator. Poverty makes a country vulnerable. In 2000, under pressure from the U.S. Government, the World Bank and the IMF, Ecuador replaced its local currency, the *Sucre*, with the U.S. dollar. In the same year, Argentina's economy was in shambles, as a result of a similar move nine years earlier—the peso/dollar parity—also forced by the usual financial villain.

In Ecuador, six years on, the dollar has already left its disastrous footprints in the country. Poverty is rapidly increasing as dollar-priced goods are becoming unaffordable for the average money earner, leading to a widening gap between the haves and the have-nots—and to rampant unemployment. Local enterprises collapse under the pressure of dollar-based imports and are gobbled up by mostly U.S. corporations at a pittance. These mergers discard labor in masses. The former Ecuadorian President had announced nationalization of Ecuador's oil fields and expelled the U.S. oil giant, Occidental Petroleum, from the country for ruthless environmental degradation and abuse of indigenous people.

How will Ecuador's new President approach 'globalization' as understood by corporate power? His initial statements would indicate a cold shoulder towards the pressures of the neo-liberal interests, and towards the two Washingtonian financial Ivory Towers.—What's next remains to be seen.

The ruthless gold mining at **Grasberg, Indonesia and Yanacocha, Peru**, has brought about and is still causing enormous social and environmental annihilation—and that in the light of a rapid rise in the price of gold.—How will the new gold prominence impact the world economy?—More importantly, how can these corporate crimes be stopped and culprits be brought to justice in a world court of law with global visibility?

The financial instruments of 'blank check operations' of the **International Monetary Fund and the World Bank**, as well as its cousin, the **Inter-American Development Bank** are increasingly leaving a disastrous debt legacy behind.—How can these organizations be reigned in?

Latin America's largest **IMF** borrowers—Brazil, Argentina and Venezuela—have paid back their debts. They are freeing themselves from the fangs of the Bretton Woods Institutions, from restructuring their economies. Other countries may follow suit. Income from loans no longer covers the IMF's expenses and is projected to further decline over the coming years. A leaner and less opulent, but not less powerful, IMF may emerge.—Might IMF's new role return to the one it was originally intended for—to monitor and police monetary rules and adherence to a new Gold Standard around the world?

As for the **World Bank** and the **Inter-American Development Bank**, traditional project lending is no longer fashionable. It has become too cumbersome. Adherence to fiduciary and environmental regulations is too closely watched by the Bank's nemesis, the community of non-government organizations. These rules engendered high transaction costs and slow disbursements. It is more profitable to lend huge sums as simple monetary transfers for structural adjustment, policy lending, budget support-type operations—euphemisms for handing out blank checks to cover poor countries' current account shortfalls. These instruments, incentives for corruption, are also better suited for buying or bullying leaders of developing countries into consenting to privatize their public sector—and natural resources.—How can these development finance organizations be de-linked from the neoconservative bandwagon?

Global arms trade is second only to the drugs trade. It is highly profitable, to the tune of a trillion-plus dollars a year, and is also dominated by U.S. weapons manufacturers. They account for more than 60 percent of all weapons sales in the world, more than the rest of the globe's arms traders combined. Weapons are often sold clandestinely to warring factions within a country, fomenting endless civil wars, more often than not in developing countries with natural resources.—With the high profitability of this killer trade, who would be interested in peace?—How can peace be turned into an economic incentive, outstripping the weapons trade?

The all encompassing topic was, however, the conceiving and designing of a **new world economic model**. The current unfettered capitalism with its all-invasive globalization, corporate take-over of the world's resources, destruction of social fabrics and environment around the globe—and the wars it engenders—is a human disaster. It is bound to collapse. The longer it lasts, however, the more people will die and suffer from wars, inequity, discrimination, diseases and famine. Change is urgent. The challenge before the participants of the *Vision* forum was how to turn the values and incentive systems away from the current growth coefficients of material goods and production, towards peace and social equity. How could positive and negative coefficients be devised, for example for environmental protection or destruction, the exhaustion or conservation of natural resources. What methods could be used to measure progress towards improved public health, education, and reduction of famine? Would it be possible to design wellbeing indicators—measuring a society's state of happiness? Was the human race ready for the emergence of an economy based on **Eudemonism** (Greek *Eudaimonism*, a philosophy anchored on a concept of human ethics, developed by Aristotle—*Note 14*).

Moni Cheng counted on the brilliant brains of the STA members to come up with possible scenarios and solutions.

* * *

The Freedom Ranch was alive in a buzz of intellectual discourse by hundreds of participants from around the world. The place took the aura of a gigantic library, with hushing voices, solemn conversations and individuals walking calmly like on silenced soles from one meeting room to another, stopping at refreshment stands, taking breaks on the shady ample veranda of the Ranch. In the eye of an uninformed outsider, the scene must have looked like a mystery nest of scurrying ants, all with a purpose, known only to their queen.

Over the course of the weeks at the Ranch, PJ and Moni Cheng grew closer. Their friendship evolved into one of mutual respect, bordering on romance. They had picked up where they'd left off, in their sporadic meetings and telephone conversations, solidifying their common interest: stopping the corporate takeover of the world.

Now, at two in the morning, they were cuddling on a sofa at a candle-lit table on Moni Cheng's straw-thatched second floor balcony, listening to the tropical murmur of insects, birds, parrots, frogs, the occasional howl of a panther, and sipping *Masato*. They were lost in thought, when Moni's hand pressed firmly on PJ's. "Hear that?" she asked. He shook his head. "Listen carefully." There it was again. A soft brief whining song, repeated every few seconds. It came in series of three.

"What is it?" he asked.

"It is the love song of a Condor, descending from the heights of the *Cordilleras* (the Andean mountain chain). The male looking for his female companion. When he finds her, they mate. According to the native Shamans, the off-spring carry the spirits of deceased tribesmen. With the help of *ayahuasca,* a hallucinogenic drink administered during spiritual ceremonies, the shamans explore the seas and the continents of the world and bring their knowledge back to their descendents. Amazon Indians, who have never left their village, have been known to describe, for example, with minute accuracy ships on high seas.

He turned his head towards her, magnetized by her dark and sparkling eyes. All he could say was "amazing." He moved closer until he felt her lips on his. The soft kiss evolved rapidly into a fiery passion. Their hands ripped off each other's clothes—until the obstacles were gone. Then he felt her burning skin, their bodies embraced so tightly only an explosion could separate their skins.—And a carnal explosion it was.

Covered only by a white sheet, they lay on Moni Cheng's king-size bed, conversing into the wee hours. PJ chatted about his childhood and how his faint North African features had earned him more than one racist remark in the conservative south of France. He also talked about his marriage and divorce from Cynthia; then about his second wife for three years, Rosalind, who'd disappeared without a trace, leaving only a brief note, saying good-bye and wishing him well. She'd promised to be in touch some time in the future, when she would tell him all. But this day—it had been more than five years—hadn't come yet. He had no news from her, didn't know where she was. And frankly he no longer cared. There was just a hint of curiosity remaining in a remote corner of his brain. But this was fading too.

Mostly he spoke of his daughter, Primavera. She was going on nineteen. He hadn't seen her since last summer. She lived with her mother in the south of Spain, in Sevilla, the capital of Andalucía. Fortunately there was e-mail and SMS. They wrote regularly and exchanged occasional instant messages over their cell phones. She was about to make a crucial decision for her future—what and where to study. She was also a ballerina. With an iron discipline she kept up with dancing, since the age of four. Marked with devotion to music and dance, a couple of years ago she started taking Flamenco classes. He was very proud of her. But he also knew that in the big scheme of things, this was not important. Good grades, youthful stamina and discipline were helpful in academia and in society at large. But the social order on the totem pole of humanity that one attained was subject to other dimensions. Some called them fate, some coincidence, or simply the good fortune of being at the right place at the right time.

Moni Cheng smiled as she listened to his parental affection. She asked him for an anecdote or two that had stolen his heart or made him laugh—that stayed fondly in his memory. PJ reflected for a moment. A smile lit up his face, as he remembered an episode on the day of his wedding to Rosalind.

"On the day of the wedding, I got up at seven, drove to my ex-wife's place to pick up Primavera, then 12-years old, and drove her to school. She was pleasantly surprised. I had never done this before. She asked me why, and I said it was good luck for everybody. She topped this, by saying, if I find two shiny one-penny pieces, I should put one each in my and Rosalind's shoe for today and for good luck. It was a most beautiful fall day, cloudless, cool, the sun reflecting on the car's windshield. I reassured her that I loved her and that I always would. The marriage wouldn't change anything—ever. She smiled, looked at me and said, 'Dad, I love you too—and I think I like Rosalind. She is nice.'

"Then she changed the subject. 'Are you going to pick me up at Mom's at 1:45?'—I said 'yes', gave her a kiss, and off she went, disappearing with a flock of other kids behind the school's gate.

"I went for a car wash, bought gas, and set off to a bookstore to buy three Bob Dylan CDs and the book "The Universe in a Nutshell," by Stephen Hawking. I wrote a dedication for Primavera inside the cover, for her to excel in physics and as a souvenir of today's day—and put it under her pillow.

"Later, I read the newspaper, listened to Bob Dylan, picked up Preemie and was waiting—waiting for 3:30 to come, when our knot was to be tied.

"Three-thirty came and went. The five of us—Rosalind, her 20 year old son and her sister, Primavera and me—were waiting in a small austere room with a few rows of benches, a little stand-up pulpit in front, a table with a huge register-book next to the wall, a window looking out onto a courtyard. The late fall sun spreading bright light and long shadows in our little 'sanctuary'. A middle-aged jolly lady (the well-nourished kind) entered with a friendly smile, asked a few questions and went right on with the ceremonial reading, all the way up to … 'as long as you both shall live.'

"Afterwards, Primavera took me by the arm and whispered in my ear with a sly smile 'Dad, you must have spoken this sentence before … and you are still alive….' This crowned my day. I hugged her with a big kiss and thought, 'Preemie—you are so right. What a relief!' But I was still hoping that one day the sentence would be true.

"We were the last couple out of there, on the last day before Thanksgiving."

After a brief silence, Moni Cheng smiled. "Cute story. I am sure you're a good dad. The way you tell the anecdote hardly disguises that you miss your daughter. Maybe you should try to see her more often. Especially now that she's about to cross a major threshold in her life, becoming independent, leaving the nest, going to a university, being away from parental protection. She needs your advice. Maybe she would like you to guide her in this important decision, but she doesn't dare to ask. You are so far away."

PJ lay partially covered by crumpled sheets, resting his head on Moni Cheng's tummy, staring at the slowly rotating ceiling fan. "You are right; I should spend more time with my daughter. She said she may want to study in Geneva. I could meet her there."

"Do that. Take time off. You always know where to find me, us, your friends of the Freedom Ranch. I'll be around. Just don't get lost." She said it with a mischievous smile, tousling his hair.

After a pause, perhaps reflecting whether the question would be appropriate, she asked, "Tell me, whatever happened with Rosalind? How long did this '… as long as you both shall live …' last? This clever daughter of yours seems to have had a good sense of clairvoyance about you, hoping for your sake that she may be wrong."

After a pause and ignoring her question, he said, "I have another daughter, Sybil. She is 25. She is an artist, an excellent painter and photographer.

Although he couldn't see her face in the darkness of night, he sensed her questioning eyes.

"Well, it's a long story. I'll tell you some other time." And yet he continued, "She lives in Finland. She has found her home in the art scene of Helsinki and seems to like it very much there. She must like the cold climate, and must find the quiet introspection of the Fins inspiring. I have never visited her there. Maybe I could, if I go to Geneva …" His thoughts trailed off. He stopped talking.

Moni Cheng lay still. She didn't say a word, but kissed him softly and stroked his hair. As he rested, his head between her breasts, he noticed from her regular breathing that she had fallen asleep. He couldn't sleep and had the nagging feeling that something was about to happen. He wanted to go back to his room.

* * * * *

24

THE EMPEROR'S MASTER PLAN—THE COLLAPSING TRUST IN THE WORLD'S MAIN RESERVE CURRENCY

At 8 in the morning at the Freedom Ranch, 9 in Washington D.C....

The cafeteria was only sparsely populated at this time of day. But the large TV screens were always on, humming with news stories from around the globe.

On the way to his room, PJ caught some bits of the news.

The President of the United States was on. He was delivering a foreign policy speech. It must be important, PJ thought, if the Emperor speaks at such an early hour. But at first sight there didn't seem to be anything new in what he was sharing with the world.

The Iraq war, it needed to continue. Contrary to media reports, there was no civil war—only some isolated fights between Sunnis and Shiites fighting, but all was under control. The continuation, the perseverance of U.S. troops was necessary. In fact, Congress had just approved a boost of an additional 20,000 to 30,000 men. The new Secretary of Defense had revealed his plans: almost doubling the troops during a short time would crush insurgencies and local factional fighting. He trusted his Secretary, who had considerable experience from his previous jobs, with the CIA, the State Department, his involvement in Central America, when, according to this dimwit of a President, the communists threatened to take over and infiltrate the United States.

On another topic he talked about the security of Israel, that the United States supported wholeheartedly the construction of a wall between Israel and the Palestinian territories. At the same time it was necessary that the President of Palestine could be persuaded to hold new elections, thereby nullifying the previous elections, which had brought to power what he viewed as a terrorist group that could not be tolerated by the "free world." It was only under a different and friendly leadership that the free world could resume supporting the Palestine interim government with financial and technical assistance. PJ wondered where he got the arrogance to call the U.S.A. a *free country*.

PJ thought, 'What about democracy? According to international observers, the elections in Palestine had been properly held, fraud was not involved, and there was no destruction or disappearance of votes. It was different in the case of Mexico, where innumerable ballot boxes from poor neighborhoods were destroyed—or, indeed, in the United States, where both the 2000 and the 2004 Presidential elections were a fraud, stolen by the Republican party through manipulation of voting machines, through preventing hundreds of thousands of poor people from voting under false pretenses, and where 3 million votes were never counted—all from poor districts and from soldiers abroad, soldiers from modest and poor backgrounds, as most of them are. They were fighting for their country and being killed for the elite, for their greed, yet, they would not even be allowed a basic civil right—to vote.

PJ merely shook his head. Unbelievable! Whatever came out of this President's mouth was sheer farce.

The speech continued.

Iran was a nuclear threat to the world, but especially to the Middle East. Unless they immediately ceased enriching uranium and the pursuit of nuclear weapons, sanctions would have to be imposed by the United Nations, failing that, the United States would have to act alone for its national security. Their intelligence knew the location of the radioactive 'hot spots' which could be easily eliminated with a few air strikes. It had been suggested by his allies that the United States of

America should sit down with the Iranian leadership and negotiate a way out of the nuclear debacle. He said: "Make no mistake, my Government does not sit at the same table with a tyrant, who openly wants Israel to disappear from the face or the map."

PJ thought about the arrogance of a country that is armed to the teeth and has stockpiles of nuclear weapons to destroy the world many times over, to prohibit another country to even produce nuclear energy. But, what was even worse was that the international community just played along with the American power. It was sad.

Although, for some reason PJ had an urge to go to his room—a subconscious inquietude—he stayed glued to the screen.

The President continued, "On Globalization—we would like to reassure the world that we will carry on with the quest of a global free market economy which will bring uncountable economic and social benefits to our partners. We invite them to join WTO, the forum for free trade, and failing this, we stand ready to negotiate bilateral Free Trade Agreements with our friends. These treaties will open borders for exchange of goods, eliminate tariffs and allow the dynamic spirit of private enterprise to flourish, where so far outdated, inflexible and bureaucratic government rules have brought about stagnant economies and growth-impairing state subsidies.

"To help this process of liberalization, the two sister organizations, the World Bank and the IMF, will stand ready to help with loans and policy guidance for free market economies to take hold. They have done wonderful work in South Africa, after this country became a Democracy in 1994. They have helped refinance inefficient government-run water supply and electric grids and helped the government negotiate contracts with international private concessionaries. Other examples of relieving rigid state bureaucracies by introducing private entrepreneurship and good governance abound around the world. They will continue. I have been assured by the leadership of these fine institutions."

PJ shook his head ruefully. 'What a travesty!'—How could he, PJ, have contributed for so long and so blindly to this contrivance? Could this guy, the talking head on the screen, actually believe what he was saying? Or does he just hope the world will maintain its faith in the word of the United States?—How can this man be so far removed from reality? Does he really not know how disastrous an impact the interventions of the IMF and the World Bank had in South Africa? Privatization of the water supply drove drinking water prices to unaffordable levels for people living in the ghetto-like *townships*, the mostly underdeveloped residential urban areas. The inhabitants resorted to polluted open streams and child mortality and intestinal diseases in adults soared—health indicators sank. When South Africans expected finally to rise out of poverty and into the realm of western well-being, poverty increased.

But who knows? Maybe this man who calls himself the President of the United States of America actually believes in what he is saying, because he himself is only a puppet—a puppet leader put there by Big Business.

The joker wouldn't stop. He was now on what looked an almost unstoppable binge about the glory and divine goodness of the United States and all those who followed its free market doctrine.

He talked about the war on terror which was being led by the U.S., but was being fought by all its allies. And it would go on as long as it took to eviscerate 'this cancer'.

PJ knew this translated into fear-mongering, justifying 'preventive wars' and oppression of civil liberties.

"Last but not least," the President pounded on, "let me reassure those who consider the increasing debt of the United States as a danger to world economy. Do not worry; we have the resources to back up our financial obligations many times over. As you know we have physical oil reserves in and outside the United States worth several trillions of dollars. Plus, our corporations control the world's second largest oil fields. The Iraqi Government is about to sign a law, a big step towards a free market economy, under which our oil companies, and of course those of other countries, may sign concessions, oil exploitation contracts, for 30 to 40 years' duration, to assure the world ample supply of energy."

He abruptly stopped. The door opened behind the President, and the Secretary of State, Ms. Contessa, displayed her split upper front teeth in a nervous smile: "Mr. President, all news channels are full of reports that the world perceives as appalling, disastrous ... calls, electronic messages are coming in from all over the world. Our communications system is breaking down ..."

The President stood there dumbfounded, his face the speechless expression of a primate.

"Mr. President, you haven't heard yet ... there was information leaked from unknown sources, that the IMF will soon announce the return to the Gold Standard ..."

The screen went black.

PJ was surprised, but pleased that an unexpected event might bend the world's rules on who rules. He turned around, and, indeed, the other giant screens showed panicky reporting on this piece of news that obviously nobody had predicted and was able or willing to interpret on the spur of the moment.

The black screen in front of him revived. A reporter said, "This is TeleSur, stay tuned, we will keep you updated as information emerges on the leaked story of the new Gold Standard. In the meantime in other news—the President of Brazil declared today in a move of solidarity with the president of Bolivia, Evo Morales, that Brazil would stop buying gas from the provinces of Santa Cruz and Tarija if they persisted in pursuing secession.

"The struggle is further fomented by private Brazilian business men and corporations, largely suspected to be funded by the CIA or other obscure U.S. sources. It is well known that the United States seeks to destabilize the government of Evo Morales by any means necessary. Brazil is currently buying about two-thirds of Bolivia's gas from these two provinces. This statement, which was released earlier today by the Brazilian President himself, is expected to bring to a halt the independence movement of the embattled region."

The TeleSur newscaster continued providing the listeners with some background. "These two territories were among the poorest of the nation until ten to fifteen years ago, when gas and oil were discovered. Until then, they had received plenty of subsidies from the central government. The President of Bolivia has long held the position that the time has come for Santa Cruz and Tarija to share their wealth with the rest of the country. This sounds like a sound premise which apparently Bolivia's western neighbor supports.

"Let us now return to the Breaking Story of the new Gold Standard …"

'Later', PJ thought—and pursued his earlier urge to return to his room.

$$* \quad * \quad * \quad * \quad *$$

25

THE EMPIRE STRIKES BACK

It was about 8:30 in the morning, when he opened the door to his room. PJ found a yellow envelope on the floor, his name scribbled on it. He slammed the door shut with his heel, sat on the bed and ripped the envelope open. It contained a white sheet with a simple typewritten phrase "they know where you are" and a CD. He put the disk in his computer and suddenly saw himself at the airport of Trujillo, talking into his cell phone, talking to an old man, who was sitting on the floor, his back against the wall. Then he was shocked to see a picture of himself with Moni Cheng on the Ranch's veranda, sipping tea. It was yesterday afternoon. Somebody in Washington had found his trail and somebody at the Ranch knew about it and wanted to warn him.

But then he wondered how someone could get a hold of a CD with photographs of him? Unless, of course, the pursuer and the warning 'friend' were the same. He or she wanted to observe his reaction, whom he would contact, and where he might try to escape. He had no clue who at the Ranch could be the perpetrator. The faces of friends and colleagues he'd met during the last few weeks passed before him. Nobody seemed suspicious. But that was, indeed, the art of spying: be invisible and inconspicuous.

He had to inform Moni Cheng. But going back to her room would not be wise. The cell phone was not secure. Writing an e-mail?—Perhaps. But when would she read it? He sent her a text message instead, suggesting she meet him for breakfast in the big cafeteria hall no later than nine. His time was limited. If she didn't show up, he would wait on the veranda for about half an hour. The veranda was always busy, reducing his vulnerability.

He left the room, connected a thin white, almost invisible thread between door and frame on top and went straight to the canteen. He saw Veronica and Enrique bent over a small table for two, talking intensely. At the periphery of her vision, Veronica perceived PJ and waved him over without looking. He pulled up a chair and joined the duo. They stopped talking, smiled at him, and said, "Good morning."

Without ado, Enrique cut to the chase. "You found the envelope with the CD?" PJ was flabbergasted. How would they know?

Enrique continued, "I put it there. It's complicated. We will explain. But be aware, you are not safe here. We just discussed a plan on how to get you out of here when you walked in. We expected you to show up here sooner or later.

"Does Moni Cheng know about all this?" PJ interrupted.

"Probably not," ventured Enrique. "We haven't talked to her yet. This developed during the night. Here is what happened.

"A stranger approached Veronica about 11 last night, as she walked from a little chat with friends from the veranda to her apartment. He introduced himself as Oscar, a Latino. Judging from the accent, he could be Colombian. He claimed to be representing the State Department of the United States. He had the mandate to look for you, a renegade from the World Bank. Not to be trusted. Besides, you hold secrets of high value to the U.S. He offered a lot of money to Veronica, to be used by the Freedom Ranch, for handing you over."

"How much?" PJ blurted out the question. He wondered how much he was worth.

"I won't say, but a lot. Money, the center could well use. She acted interested and invited Oscar to her apartment. Not to be alone with a stranger, she called me. We also have a clandestine way of communicating with each other, those who run the Ranch. And since I smelled a rat, I brought Lucho along, the leader of the MRC."

Now Veronica continued. "While I prepared a drink, Enrique and Lucho overwhelmed the agent. We locked him into a basement room, where he's still 'resting' as we speak. We are sure he did not come alone. A back-up, maybe two, must still be on the premises. It would be too naïve to leave this task to a lone ranger. But we have no idea who the others are. For all we know, they may be observing us and wondering what happened to Oscar. But we don't believe they know what took place last night. As proof that he knew more than we, Oscar showed me the CD with the three pictures of you, those that by now you must have seen. We thought the best way to alert you about the seriousness of the affair was to give you the disc with a note. You see, they have been following you for a while. Your life is in danger."

She paused. Enrique intervened again, "We have to get you out of here as quickly and quietly as possible. When you are safe, we will release Oscar and make sure he understands that his safety depends on getting out of here and not coming back."

PJ thought for a moment. Then he said, "Releasing him might not be smart. The U.S. military is stationed in Peru, many of them in the area of the coca growers. They may attack the Ranch and destroy it, kill people out of vengeance. These brutes, they kill people at the drop of a hat. They are animals. They may do anything, simply to demonstrate that the Empire is not to be contradicted. It is clear to me that Vidali, my boss—eh, I mean ex-boss—has helped put the undercover agents on my trail. How they found me is a mystery. I may never know."

"Not so complicated," said Enrique. "Once they knew you were at Trujillo airport, they checked the surveillance cameras filming the check-in counters. By the way, the surveillance gear is also compliments of the United States of America. They then compared the pictures in the video with faces they knew and—'bingo!' The rest is history."

"How would they know that I was at Trujillo airport?"

"You didn't use a cell phone?" Of course, thought PJ. But shut up.

"So what do you have in store for me?" Was PJ's curious question.

"As soon as we finish breakfast we'll see to it that you get safely back to your room, pick up your essentials and we'll come by with a pickup, you jump into the back. There will be a tarp to cover you. We will get you to Tarapoto airport. From there take a flight to Quito. We understand from Moni Cheng you have a daughter in southern Spain, whom you haven't seen for a while. Perhaps you would like to go and visit her for a few days, a couple of weeks. We will stay in touch. If you are interested in continuing with our group, we will have an assignment for you. One that deals with what you know best—the international financial institutions and their evil doings." He smiled. "Have something to eat. It may be a while before your next meal."

"One question," PJ said. "Will I see Moni Cheng before departing?"

"Probably not, not now anyway," Enrique replied. "But she will know where you are and communicating nowadays is easy from practically everywhere."

* * *

Back in his room, PJ rummaged through his things that were strewn all over the place. The mess was his doing. Nobody had entered the room. The little seal at the door was not broken. It didn't take long to push his few belongings, including his small laptop case, into a duffel bag. He waited by the door until he heard the rumbling diesel pickup stop in front of his door. He ran out, glanced left and right before tossing the bag into the back, then climbed in and immediately hid under the heavy canvas. The truck sped off.

It grew unbearably hot under the tarp. But PJ had no choice. He lifted a corner of the cover for some air. He laid back and tried to relax.

But his brain was relentlessly at work. Was it a good idea to go to Spain? Vidali knew about his daughter. This would be a logical place to look for him, especially after he escaped the jackals. Seeing his daughter, Primavera, was undoubtedly an attractive idea. But perhaps not in Seville. Maybe in France, or better in Switzerland, in Geneva. Just before he nodded off, he was sure that he wouldn't go to Spain. But he would figure out an alternative plan, at the latest on the flight to Quito.

* * *

Wet from sweat he awoke from his doze when the truck came to a screeching halt. He had no idea how long he'd been asleep. Maybe only minutes, perhaps hours. Hardly hours, because the airport was no more than an hour away from the Freedom Ranch. He heard voices. It was dark outside but not night. He didn't dare lift the tarp, until a familiar voice called, "PJ where are you?" He was elated, as he instantly recognized Moni Cheng's voice.

He jumped from the truck. They were at the edge of a narrow jungle clearing, which explained the semi-darkness. They embraced, and then moved out of sight of the others, Enrique and Veronica, as well as Jaime Rodriguez, the *Aymara* leader from Bolivia, who'd accompanied Moni Cheng to the meeting.

They sat on a tree trunk. "What a pleasant surprise," PJ said. "I was sad that I wouldn't see you for who knows how long."

"Well, when Enrique told me about Oscar's nasty undercover mission and your emergency 'evacuation' so to speak, I insisted on seeing you, even if only for a few moments. I also wanted to give you this." She handed him an artifact, hard to make out in the darkness, and explained, "This is a GPS satellite cell phone. Several of us from the ranch have these. We can stay in touch from wherever we are on the globe. And I didn't want to lose track of you ..." She kissed him on the neck. "... And I was hoping it may be the same for you."

He felt a warm surge of happiness grow in his chest, spreading fast to his groin and giving him a delirious head. He just smiled and then embraced her with a passionate kiss. "But when will I see you again?"

She lifted her shoulders, "I don't really know, but certainly within a few months." Seeing his disappointed look, she quickly added, "I will make sure we do."

She said as an afterthought, "Apropos the GPS phone, you can also send text messages; and not to worry, the messages, both text and voice are automatically scrambled and decoded at the receiving end. The code was developed by the *Machiguenga* indios. It will take a while before even the CIA figures that one out. So, use the phone freely and as often as you like, or feel like ..." She paused with a playful smile.

"I will" he said.

"Are you planning to visit your daughter in Spain?"

He told her why it might not be smart to go to Spain. He would like to meet with Primavera somewhere else, possibly in Geneva. He hadn't spoken to her yet.

"But after that, what?" He asked rhetorically. "I have given it some thoughts. I would like to play an active role in the activities of the STA. From what I have seen happening at the Ranch, I believe we have a strong potential to change the course of current events, perhaps event to derail the Empire." He contemplated for a moment. "Maybe this is more like a dream, a day dream, at this stage."

"You are right." Moni Cheng's brain worked fast. "I have an idea. Your familiarity with the Washington-based financial institutions, which all follow the same neo-liberal politics, could be put to good use with the European Union, which I call a spineless lot. They bend over backwards to please the U.S ... No guts. No *cojones*, as we say in Spanish. Although this is a very *macho* term, it certainly applies to the EU, almost all member countries are led by males."

"To some extent, they may also be uninformed," said PJ.

She ignored his observation and continued: "There is also the World Trade Organization, the Geneva-based WTO, the third of the world's three most despised organizations. Maybe we could mobilize a few trade union leaders, farmers and intellectuals from Latin America, take them to Geneva," she fantasized, "and organize a forum for discussion at the university. The topics could be around the so-called 'free trade democracy,' the WTO treaties and, of course, the bilateral Free Trade Agreements between the United States and poor, but resource-rich countries. The forum would be followed by an internationally televised press conference. What do you think?"

"Brilliant!" said PJ, though he felt this idea was more a fantasy than a reality. How could he enlist the University of Geneva to host such a forum? He had no contacts. But not wanting to diminish her enthusiasm, he replied, "That is a good reason to go to Geneva. Count me in, especially if we can do this together."

"I am afraid," Moni Cheng said, suddenly changing the subject, "we have to say *hasta mas tarde*—see you later. You are nowhere near the airport. We are actually about an hour from the Ranch in the opposite direction of the airport. A ruse. It is more than likely that Oscar's partners in crime are observing and following any movement to and from the Ranch compound. Enrique believes he had been trailed by a motorcycle, but escaped the bike by a few hide-and-return tricks on unknown jungle tracks. Send me a signal when you are in a place where you feel comfortable."

They embraced. PJ hid under his tarp and the two vehicles sped through the underbrush in opposite directions.

* * *

The smoking gun becomes a smoking bomb ...

Approaching the Ranch, a plume of black smoke became visible above the trees. As they got closer to the compound, Moni Cheng observed other signs of abnormality. About half a dozen unfamiliar camouflaged vehicles, U.S. army style, stood scattered under the trees surrounding the large plaza in front of the Ranch's wrap-around veranda. Then the melee. About three dozen Ranch members were tying up some ten American servicemen. Strange, they must have been armed but didn't shoot.

At the outskirts of the compound, Moni was met by Santiago, who had so far escaped the skirmishes with his girlfriend, Gabriela. He reported that the U.S. militia threw a smoke bomb into the compound, for scare and attention. Then they stormed into the farm complex, allegedly to get an 'envoy from the State Department,' who disappeared. The man was obviously Oscar. Since none of the STA members knew about the U.S. undercover operation, much less the name of the chief perpetrator, they suspected it was the military's way of gaining a foothold in the Ranch. Instead of letting that happen, they overwhelmed the soldiers, tied them up with the intent to deport them to the city of Tarapoto, where they would let them loose.

Moni Cheng didn't think this was a good idea. She convinced the soldiers that there was no American envoy, that they better look elsewhere. She proved her point by liberating the soldiers in a bout of utmost trust. One of them introduced himself as lieutenant something or other, gave her a cell phone number and asked to call if this strange emissary should show up. She nodded and politely said, "We would like you to leave now."

Once they had left, she knew instinctively this wasn't the end of it. This was just the beginning. A serious attack on the Ranch was imminent. She needed urgently to organize an evacuation. She also remembered the stolen aerial photos of the Freedom Ranch, her ransacked room at Uncle Gustavo's house.

She entered the Ranch through the veranda, approaching the big hall, or what they called the 'Aula of the Gran Amazon'. There was a little unrest of a different kind under-way. A few dozen attendees, relieved over the harmless ending of the confrontation with the gringos, were now screaming and yelling at a huge TV screen. She first thought they were watching a soccer match, a common entertainment at the Ranch. But it wasn't soccer. It was a most unusual broadcast. The prelude to a worldwide televised presentation of the U.S. Government's NSS—the National Security Strategy for the 21st Century.

The letters 'SS' immediately brought to Moni Cheng's mind Nazi-Germany's terrorist police force. In the Third Reich 'SS' stood for *Schutzstaffel*, a paramilitary organization that terrorized the German population, especially the Jews, from 1934 to 1945. Interestingly, the double 'S' appeared now again in a right wing edict, the instrument to implement *Pax Americana*, the neo-liberals' plan in the making for the last quarter century on taking over the world, especially the world's natural resources. *Pax Americana* was patterned after the legendary *Pax Romana* which guided the Romans partly under Augustus Caesar through about 200 years of their 500 year Empire. From *Pax Americana* emerged *Project for a New America in the 21st Century*.

The STA crowd in the 'Aula of the Gran Amazon' was actually laughing and moaning at the reporter's comments in anticipation of the much awaited announcement of the strategy, which was, for those who hadn't noticed yet, already in full execution. The people at the Ranch, this laboratory of activists, were not prey to the manipulative and cunning methods of the American President and his companions in crime to brainwash the people with lies and distortions.

What followed, however, even surprised this alert group of people. The scene was a panel debate straight from the Capitol, from the Senate aula. The panelists consisted of the President himself, in the middle of the five member board, with Ms. Contessa, Secretary of State, and Ron Rommel, former Secretary of Defense (probably on his last public appearance); and the heads of the two major financial institutions, the World Bank and the International Monetary Fund.

The seats on both sides of the aisle of the Senate were filled with journalists from all over the world and people from the streets of small American towns. Cameras and microphones were strategically placed throughout the Senate floor. What was not known to the masses was that the audience was pre-screened, and had gone through lengthy identity and ideology checks by the CIA and FBI before the fake panel discussion.

The entire scenario appeared like an episode from a political fairy tale. Or was it simply, Moni Cheng thought, to divert the world's attention from the earlier Breaking News—the rumors of a new Gold Standard? Or was it a rehash of the earlier Presidential Foreign Policy speech, this time in the form of an international media event to bestow it with a 'participatory' note?

"Good evening, World." The President of the Free World opened the conference. "We are all gathered here as one world. I would like to present to you *Pax Americana* and the strategy on how we plan to implement this fine plan to bring about freedom and democracy to the most remote corners of the world.

"First, let me share with you what *Pax Americana* is. It is a dream of every one of our seven billion world citizens. A dream that encompasses one set of ethics, of moral values, and a singular faith in One Almighty, the one whose son died at the cross for our collective and cumulative sins 2000 years ago. Under this dream-come-true we will all live in unity, harmony, equality and under one big and lasting democratic system.

"This is our dream. *We* will have to realize it. It requires hard work and some sacrifices. It requires every one of you to give. What you will get in return will far outweigh the occasional suffering you may endure. Many of you will prosper right away. For others, prosperity will come later. But prosperity and democracy will engulf us all in the end.

"We the United States of America, with other free nations in Europe and Asia will take the lead in helping realize this dream. Our strategy is based on an axis of three principles—full globalization by opening borders for free transfer of labor and capital; free trade to allow each country to produce and export according to its comparative advantage; and a universally uniform monetary system, based on the American dollar, that follows strict rules of solvency and fiscal responsibility.

"I will elaborate on each of these points:

"_Globalization_ entails for our corporations, the embodiment and engines of the world economy, the freedom to extract, convert, use and distribute Mother Earth's resources as they see fit and best suited for the populations' particular needs. In the process, employment and wealth will be created for the benefit of all. Workers and capital can be transferred from one country to another according to the most efficient need of our corporations. No obstacles should be in their way. We will help governments to abolish any barriers. If necessary, we can assist them with our military. I repeat, corporations must be free to move and act however and wherever they deem is best for the economy. Remember, they are the motor of our economy. We are striving for a globalized and, eventually, borderless democratic world."

Even though she had other urgent matters to attend to, Moni Cheng was glued to this flagrant nonsense flickering across the giant screens. She couldn't help wondering how far this self proclaimed leader of the 'Free World' would go. And he continued:

"_Free trade_ is the first step to abolish poverty. It means that each country is given a fair chance to produce what it is best at and export its goods and produce at competitive prices. Competitiveness is the key to prosperity. But for competitiveness to succeed, countries have to abandon tariffs and import restrictions. In a border and barrier-free world those who produce at least cost and best quality will prevail. Others will be marginalized and eventually disappear. Each country will find its niche, its comparative advantage in goods and services.

Again, countries which encounter difficulties in coping with potential internal resistance, can count on assistance from America and its allies. Our military are ready to intervene when necessary. And it goes without saying, the two prominent international financial institutions stand ready to help you with budget support, and with funds to help you implement market liberalization policies." And he bowed his head towards the rulers of the World Bank and the IMF.

"A *uniform monetary system* requires one and the same currency worldwide, the same fiscal and monetary accountability universally and strict solvency rules, as well as trade that is in balance. How do we get there?—The United States dollar will gradually become the currency of choice. We expect that each and every country will have made the transition within five years. In fact, many of our friends already use the dollar, if not nominally then by inference, as their currency is closely tied to the U.S. dollar by trade. For example, countries in Latin America are already linked to the U.S. economy. External trade of many South American countries is to a high degree connected to the market of the United States. The price of our most coveted source of energy, hydrocarbons, is nominated in U.S. dollars. The American dollar is the dominant reserve currency for countries around the globe.

"To facilitate the transition and to assure fairness and equity in assessing the values of different economies in the process of conversion, the International Monetary Fund will announce today the return to the Gold Standard. Naturally, many poor countries will not be ready right away to meet 'solvency' rules. Specific ratios of money in circulation, debt and GDP will apply. The IMF will assist with implementing and monitoring these guidelines." He gestured to the left, "Mr. Haviland Gersten, the IMF's Managing Director, will be glad to answer questions and explain the new arrangements in more detail." Haviland smiled and nodded reverently.

"Many poor countries will not be able to convert to the dollar immediately, lest they become even poorer. Their economies are too weak and too dependent on outside assistance. The World Bank stands ready to help these countries reform their inefficient financial systems and grant them low interest or interest free loans, and in some cases even grants. These loans would not be subject to complex development projects which are governed by cumbersome environmental and fiduciary rules. Instead, they would consist of mere transfers from the World Bank to the treasuries of the countries in question, once economic and reform criteria have been agreed on." Dick Dingo displayed a sly smile, when the President nodded towards him.

Moni Cheng couldn't believe her eyes and ears. Does this half-wit actually believe that his 'Gold Standard' will fly? That countries, especially the Europeans with their strong Euro, will fall for it? Did he already forget the riots around the world, when earlier today the information of the return to the Gold Standard was leaked? Whom is he trying to fool?—Indeed, as she was turning her head towards other wide screens in the aula, the ongoing angry debate elsewhere in the world was not about how to adopt and adhere to the gold gauge, but rather how to fight it.

But Mr. President pressed on:

"Ladies and gentlemen, citizens of the world, these are the three principles which we like to call the 'Axis of Reform on the Way to Freedom and Democracy.' The floor is now open for questions and comments. Our able panelists will be happy to answer them."

Moni Cheng now firmly decided she couldn't take this anymore. While turning towards the control board of the giant monitors in the aula, she decided this hall was just the right place to discuss and organize the evacuation of the Ranch.

While the uneasy gut feeling of an imminent attack on the Ranch took over her brainwaves, she heard ever so faintly in the background how the Senate hall resounded with what must have been ear-shattering applause. TV cameras pointed to the audience on the Senate floor, showing an almost unilateral standing ovation. Here and there a benign sign of protest, a cardboard decrying the new paradigm as a farce *Corporate Greed No More*, and a T-shirt displayed above the heads of the crowd shouted *Muerte al Imperialismo! Viva Democeacia!*.

All to no avail. In fact, police in riot gear, standing guard at the various entrances to the aula, descended immediately, handcuffed and removed the 'rebels.' With all the prescreening that went on, it was unlikely that they were for real. More probably they were deliberately planted in the audience, not only to demonstrate that different views existed, but to show at the same time what would happen in the future to opinions that differed from those of the reigning Empire.

Moni Cheng turned all screens off, took the mike and addressed the aula: "Friends, most of you know that our center was almost attacked by U.S. forces. Under a ruse we were able to divert the immediate danger. But I am sure they will soon discover the ploy and then come back. When they do, they will be ferocious, as usual—no guns on hold. We have to evacuate fast. Within 15 minutes all members and visitors currently at the center need to be assembled here. Please fetch your colleagues at once."

She also pressed a button that triggered an emergency alarm, signaling everybody to appear in the aula.

* * *

... 20 minutes later ...

The aula was packed. Moni Cheng stood on a table in front of the cafeteria.

"Friends, I am sorry and sad beyond imagination, but the moment for evacuating has come. The enemy—alias U.S. troops—has discovered our refuge. A couple of hours ago, they have launched a scare attack, a few smoke bombs, attempting to capture one of our colleagues, who thanks to an early warning, was by then already on his way to safety. The militia men left to look elsewhere. But they will be back before long. We have an underground safety location a few miles away from here, underground and well camouflaged in the midst of the jungle. In 15 minutes you assemble in front of your respective housing blocks, A, B, C, D and so on, with your belongings to the extent you can carry them.

"Several truck convoys managed by the Ranch's core group will take you over different paths, fanning away from the Ranch in disguise, to the new location. There we will reassemble. I will brief you on the next steps. We may hold out there for a while until it is safe. Then, those of you who would like to continue with the STA movement, will be taken to another remote place about halfway around the globe, where we established long ago, in anticipation of what appears to be happening now, a parallel Freedom Ranch. It is ready to be occupied. Our work can continue almost immediately. Those of you, who prefer to go back to your respective countries and organizations, may of course also do so … and we will stay in touch. A set-back doesn't mean defeat. We will continue our drive, mobilizing people to stand up for their rights. And by doing so in ever growing masses, we will bring the Empire to its knees.—Please go now. I will see you later today."—With a sweeping wave of both her arms, she dismissed the meeting, jumped from the table and rushed to the door.

* * *

The last convoys were still being loaded, when a handful of helicopter gunships descended over the Ranch, dropping bombs, indiscriminately blowing up buildings and gunning down whatever was on the move. At first there was no telling how many STA members were killed and injured in this latest ruthless attack by the American army on unarmed people.

*   *   *   *   *

26

THE NEW WORLD

In Quito PJ called his daughter in Sevilla. It was at the end of the day in Spain. She just finished her Flamenco class and sounded surprised to hear from him. "Hi Dad, what are you up to? Haven't spoken with you for ages, I was afraid you may have disappeared somewhere in the jungle of your beloved South America." Her tone was slightly sardonic. "How have you been? Seriously. There is so much going on in the world, and I always suspect you are in the midst of it. You are always traveling to these places with revolutions. But hey, I don't really know. Andalucía is so quiet. The world could collapse around us and we'd hardly notice." She paused.

"You know, Preemie, the phone is a two-way street," he said.

She immediately countered, "I know, I know, Dad. I knew you would say that. I am sorry I didn't call. But please tell me, how are you? Are you OK? I really miss you. Even if you don't believe me, I do. When do I see you next? Soon I hope."

"Well, Sweetie, the reason for my call—would you like to meet me in Geneva?"

"That would be so cool. When?"

"How quickly can you be there? Tomorrow? The day after tomorrow?"

"Wow!—So soon! I have to talk to mom and to the headmaster of my school. But I think in two days would be fine. In fact, the idea is perfect. Since I'm interested in studying in Geneva in the fall, we could explore the city together for a few days."

"So, you seem to have made up your mind. Sounds perfect," PJ exclaimed. "When we meet I'll tell you what happened over the last couple of months in my neck of the world." After a brief hesitation, he added, "And why I am now a free agent ..."

As he expected, she wanted to know, of course, what that meant. But all he said was that she would be surprised. A bit of suspense could never hurt, he thought. They agreed on flights which would bring them to Geneva about the same time. He could hardly wait to be with Preemie and explore the lovely city by the lake with her. How long had it been since he'd been there? The picturesque Old Town and the multi-denominational cathedral on the hill.

After he hung up, he smiled, remembering that Geneva in the summer was also dubbed 'Riyadh by the Lake,' because in July and August white-robed, extremely rich Arabs swarmed the place. Now he understood the reason. In a manner of speaking, Geneva's banking system served as Saudi Arabia's Treasury, and the ruling sheiks deposited trillions of oil dollars there, immediately converting them into Euros and other hard currencies to escape the risk of a declining dollar, in which not even the Emperor's friends and allies bequeathed much trust any longer.

* * *

Geneva was at its pre-summer best: sunny, warm, outdoor cafés bustling with people. The early morning tang of the lake hung in the air; the Mont Blanc Bridge was decked out with Swiss cantonal flags.

Young girls in fashionable attire caught PJ's attention. Their friendly smiles seemed everywhere—in buses and streetcars, at street crossings, in sidewalk cafés, department stores. It had been a long time since his eyes were caressed by so much beauty and charm. Freedom was in the air. It didn't need to be imposed with a sledgehammer; no need for assertively repeating the mantra of Freedom in every political rally or speech, flashing it on TV; or the drip-by-drip indoctrination on the radio—all that was not necessary. Freedom had a scent. One could smell it. It was just there.

It was also a busy time in Geneva, the venue of myriad international conferences. Geneva police were well trained and prepared to handle the many dignitaries, their arrivals and departures. They did it most discreetly. Police sirens were rare. What a difference with Washington, D.C., where hardly a minute went by without deafening police sirens racing through the streets. Whether necessary or not, they were omnipresent. The citizenry were constantly put on high guard, made to fear the terror that might lurk around the corner. At the same time, people had to be lulled into a false sense of security: 'We are protecting you— just don't step out of line ...'

PJ felt good meandering through the streets with Primavera, sipping coffee, meeting her future professors at the university. Yes, she decided, that was where she wanted to start her studies. Later on, she might spend a year abroad. Who knew where. She realized it was a bold decision. She didn't know anyone, had to learn French and had to make her own life. It would be the first time away from her mother, who, she had to admit, had guarded and protected her like a chick in a nest egg. But she had enough character and perseverance to make it on her own. She sensed it was time to step out into the world.

They talked about her future studies in social sciences, the prospects this might bear, the direction she may embark on. PJ reminded her about the "Road less Traveled," Robert Frost's poem. She liked it. She sealed her page of the Baccalaureate's Year Book with it. She also learned with fear and respect about her dad's adventures of the past few months. What would he do next? Would he meet this Andean woman, Moni Cheng, again? Would he go back to South America? Maybe even to Washington? 'Into the hornets nest?'—'Or as you call it: the Belly of the Beast?'—She asked.

"Unlikely, highly unlikely!" he said, lost in thoughts.

None of these questions had immediate answers. And he certainly didn't tell her that he was still being chased, that some agent from the State Department or the CIA may be out there with a 'capture dead or alive' order. He sure wouldn't want to scare her.

They talked to the event organizers at the university, raising Moni Cheng's parting idea of a conference with farmers, intellectuals and trade union leaders to talk about themes around WTO, free trade, globalization and democracy. To their surprise they were very much interested, referring to their associated school, the *Institut des Hautes Etudes*, the champions in foreign relations studies. The organizers would get back to PJ with dates and more concrete proposals.

He was happy about this little achievement, a reason—a real reason, not just his romantic lusting—to call or maybe write to Moni Cheng.

PJ and Preemie walked along *Plain Palais*, when they were suddenly engulfed by a mob of African demonstrators, shouting, "Stop the arms trade," and waving placards with gory photographs of slaughtered children, cartoons showing little girls being raped and sexually abused by soldiers.

PJ was told by the leader of the demonstration that President Bongo of Kilimanda, the landlocked country bordering on South Sudan, was attending the three-day Human Rights Conference which had just begun at the United Nations, the *Palais des Nations*. The demonstrators were representing an opposition group consisting mostly of Kilimanda kids studying in Europe. Bongo's repressive government was one of the biggest human rights abuser in modern times, the leader of the mob, a black student clad in a red Mao T-shirt, explained to PJ.

According to the head of the demonstration, "Bongo's army supported an independent militia in the north that killed about 2 million children in the last twenty years."

"Why?" PJ wanted to know.

"They seek revenge against a Kilimanda rebel group in the oil-rich north of the country for seeking independence. The secession movement was supported by the quasi-government of South Sudan. Bongo was a murderer," the demonstrator said. "He should not be allowed to attend the conference, let alone to talk." The students wanted to boycott his speech which was to take place by noon.

Listening to the leader of the students, PJ and Preemie became increasingly interested in their cause. PJ thought the theme fitted nicely into the realm of social science, a textbook case in action. PJ also remembered that Bongo was the World Bank's model child, accepting structural adjustment loans for agreeing to 'reform' its government apparatus, privatizing water, electricity—even roads. The main road connecting Kilimanda's capital to the port of Mombassa was under a concession by a European operator. All for profit by transnational corporations.

Bongo was touted by the IMF and the World Bank as *the* African Reformer, the one who saw the light. Strangely, neither the World Bank nor the IMF later reported on the disaster this reform entailed: massive dismissal of government employees; rapidly rising unemployment, poverty and as a consequence crime; deteriorating health, because the water supply became unaffordable for the poor; and, ultimately, a stagnant economy. The same syndromes were apparent as in South Africa—as everywhere, where the bulldozers of the neocon monsters were running berserk.

They decided to wander towards the *Palais des Nations* and watch events unfold.

A tumultuous crowd was already assembled on the plaza in front of the entrance to the *Palais*. The 'Broken Chair' monument for the victims of landmines was looming impressively skyward. Next to it, in the center of the plaza, four gigantic screens were erected in the form of a cube. Each one telecast an ongoing event from inside the *Palais* or news from around the world.

On one of the screens, Bongo appeared. He was briefly introduced, then stepped up to the podium. On each side behind the podium were two wide screens, so that the speakers could be video-cast to distant spectators in the conference hall. Suddenly, as Bongo started to address the audience, the student leader who an hour earlier had spoken to PJ and Primavera appeared on the two side-screens. First, it was not clear from where he was speaking. Then PJ recognized him on the plaza, standing on a table, an improvised podium, with a microphone, being filmed. Somehow the students were able to botch the system and connect the inside screens with the outside speaker. Surely, they must have had helpers from within.

Their student friend's voice drowned out Bongo's. It was almost funny to watch. Bongo was furiously gesticulating and screaming, albeit soundlessly, for no one to hear. Eventually he raced down from the podium, disappearing from the screen, while the student leader presented in an articulate manner his case of human rights abuse to which Bongo was privy.

He talked about the slaughter of children, because they belonged to a tribe which sought independence for its oil-rich territory from Kilimanda. To mask Bongo's association with the atrocities committed in the north, his army would support a militia group in the north; supply them with weapons and money to fight on behalf of Bongo's dictatorship. Many of them belonged to the same tribe as the children they were torturing and killing. Then he expanded his case to the mostly illicit and often clandestine weapons trade.

"Arms trade," he said, "is not only a major cause of suffering, it is also one of the most lucrative businesses in the world. It benefits from globalization. Lacking sales in the weapons manufacturers' domestic markets must be compensated by new international markets. New conflicts, civil wars have to be fomented and maintained. Killing people around the globe is an extraordinary business for arms producing corporations.

"Global military expenditures and arms trade constitute the world's largest spending, topping a trillion U.S. dollars in 2005, about as lucrative as drug deals around the world. The U.S. supplied about two-thirds of the market. Seventy percent of this market consisted of civil or trans-border conflicts of developing countries. These figures do not even include arms deals by Mafia-type organizations, like those that bloomed after the fall of the Soviet Union."

"Ladies and gentlemen!" He exclaimed in a final call for attention. "Of course, the G8 and other nuclear powers want to avoid an atomic war, because they could risk their own lives. But keeping conflicts and civil unrest lingering in our poor countries is big business. The mass killings in northern Kilimanda, to name just one example among the worst humanitarian calamities, are not a mere windfall for the arms producers. In fact, these conflicts are much more than that. They help weaken the resistance levels of countries, preparing the terrain for international corporations to suck their lands dry of natural resources.

"Please friends, colleagues, fellow human beings—help stop this heinous trade and human rights abuse!"

He took a brief bow and stepped from the table. The spectators in the plaza cheered. The screen flickered, until a breaking news story from Iraq captured the attention of the open-air audience ...

"Just in—***Three horrendous car bombs exploded simultaneously in Baghdad's Green Zone***, destroying a large section of the U.S. Military Headquarters. The mess is enormous. Blood, severed limbs, fire and smoke is everywhere. No one is able to assess the damage, let alone the number of casualties. Hundreds, possibly thousands, have died. Stay tuned ... this is Al Jazeera reporting ..."

* * *

In the evening, PJ and Preemie had a farewell dinner. Still dazed by the news of the day, they sat quietly, both saddened that tomorrow they would separate again. For how long? They didn't know. They promised one another to communicate more often and to see each other again before the semester started in the fall. Yes, that they would do. That was only a few months away. In the morning, leaving again at about the same time, they hugged in front of the security gates at the airport—misty eyes, waving—and struck off in opposite directions: Primavera to Sevilla, PJ to London. When she asked him: "Where are you actually going, Dad?"

He just said, "I'll call you when I get there." She knew that would have to be good enough.

* * * * *

27

The Implosion

The car bomb in front of the New Society University in Buenos Aires left the meeting room and its two dozen 'Globalization' workshop attendants unscathed. After an initial shock, and assessing the damage by peering through the windows, they decided not to be deterred and to continue their brainstorming seminar on how to bring the Europeans to face their civil responsibilities.

After ten hours of heated debate, the workshop concluded on two principles; one: that *people power* is what needed to be promoted, liberated and unleashed; and two: that a *new world economic system* needs to be developed and promoted, one that would turn away from the destructive capitalist growth model, but instead would emphasize social values, peace, environmental protection, conservation of natural resources, health, equity—in brief, overall human wellbeing, Such a model, say *Eudemonism,* the workshop recognized though, could not be introduced over night. It would have to be nurtured and promoted through the world's education systems to become ripe for gradual implementation after one or two generations. Europe, the EU, could perhaps be persuaded to pioneer the model.

The findings of the New Society University workshop coincided with the outcome of the *'Vision for a new World'* seminar which the members of the *Save the Amazon* carried out in an abridged version at their security shelter after barely escaping the bombing of the Freedom Ranch. Both events proposed promoting and disseminating these principles—people power and *eudemonism*—through national education systems, the release of a relentless stream of information by non-corporate electronic and printed media. Four world channels were already rapidly gaining prominence: Al Jazeera, TeleSur, TelAfrica and AsiaTV-Link. International newspapers, like *The Guardian, The Independent, El Pays and La Libération* could capitalize on their tradition of truth seeking news. They would flourish as world leaders in reporting facts.

Both events also concluded, **People power** meant that with the massive spread of truth information people would come to recognize how the mainstream media kept them ignorant, usurping their trust by feeding them falsified news, and by a Hollywood entertainment industry addressing the lowest common denominator. They would start perceiving the systematic deprivation of social infrastructure, the descending spiral of social well-being. Eventually they would revolt; crying out in protest with work stoppages and other acts of civil disobedience, ignoring laws that were made by the rich for the rich. They would collectively stop paying taxes, which financed war machines instead of social services. They would no longer accept their hitherto muted suffering.

* * *

One year later ...

Amazingly, these conclusions were now rapidly gaining ground and coming to fruition in the real world. People spoke up. Traditional institutions were breaking down. People organizations became stronger than bureaucracies. It was a reminder of the smaller-scale uprising in the 1990s in Argentina, when workers took over manufacturing plants abandoned by their former owners for lack of profit. Against the traditional laws of ownership, they turned the machines back on, created labor, income and goods for the local markets. Similarly, people from all over the world started defying laws made for the elite, their corporations and the bureaucracies built around them for protection.

They stepped onto podiums and displaced despots.

Police and military united with the demonstrators they were supposed to fight, recognizing that they were in the same boat of misery left behind by a hegemonic corporatocracy.

Solidarity of farmers and workers were being forged across borders, striking against trade agreements—no harvest—no trade; no production—no trade.

Staffers of the World Bank had gotten rid of Dick Dingo, only to be replaced by another dogmatic neoliberal defender of a 'free for all' world open market—the former U.S. Trade Czar. They laughed at his new edict of '*Sustainable Globalization*' with which he was now trying to indoctrinate the developing world. Together with their colleagues from the IMF they refused to bend to the neoliberal doctrines, as they saw the devastating poverty they'd created.

And finally, *people the world over* became aware and woke up to elect their own leaders, those who defended *their* interests, their *common* interests. The *Me-Me-Me Concept* turned into a *We Vision*. They were no longer fooled by the propaganda launched by United States puppets. The trend had started in Latin America and was rapidly gaining momentum throughout the world. The groundswell for a new economic system was well under way.

* * *

The *Place des Nations* in Geneva had become a testimony for change to come. The huge cube of television screens in its center was broadcasting day-in, day-out astonishing, hair-raising, tradition breaking events—a messenger of revolution in the making.

The square evolved into an international meeting place. More and more people crowded into it, occupying street space and hindering traffic. The Municipality of Geneva decided diverting traffic and expanding the public arena. They built a protective canvas cover over the screen cube and the *Place des Nations* to shield the spectators from the moods of the weather. Thousands of people paid tribute to the world's transformation, watching events day and night. The square itself became an international news item.

No doubt, these events and actions throughout the globe were in part consciously provoked and promoted by Moni Cheng and her friends and allies. But perhaps to even a greater extent, they were prompted by neoliberals themselves, by their shameless, ruthless and relentless drive to implement their agenda of greed. The results were now playing out in the world theatre.

Initially, only the four corporate-free world broadcast channels were flooding the globe with a steady stream of news flashes signifying a systems change in coming. Later, when overwhelmed with the public's awakening, the corporate media felt compelled—for business interests, of course—to follow the trails of honesty. To no avail. Nobody paid attention to them anymore.

* * *

News Flashes ...

>>> **Leaders from Africa and South America** have announced an economic alliance in a summit in Lagos, Nigeria. The purpose, they say, is to stem the growing dominance of western nations over their economies. They want to break free from high interest loans and draconian social conditions imposed by the World Bank and the IMF. The President of Venezuela, Hugo Chavez, said that a Latino-African Development Bank, headquartered in Caracas and funded by oil producing countries in Africa and Latin America, would start its operations in 3 months. He said the institution will respect the sovereignty of nations and that borrowing from the Latino-African Development Bank may allow countries to pay back their debt to the World Bank and the IMF ...

>>> **The return to the Gold Standard with gradual conversion into a dollar-based one-currency world economy**—announced by the United States and the IMF was rejected by the world. Banks and stock markets around the globe were in upheaval, prompting a drastic flight into alternative currencies, the Euro, Yuan and Yen. The English Pound was shunned because of its association with the United States. The collapse of the monetary system, as we knew it, was imminent ...

>>> **In major cities of developing countries** throughout Africa, South America and Asia, notably **the G-77** alliance: Millions of people were requesting the dismantling and restructuring of the two financial Ivory Towers, bring them back to the Charter of the United Nations under which they were created, so they would fund people's real needs, promoting their capacity to help themselves, freeing them from their dependence on the U.S. Empire and its corporatocracy ...

>>> **Washington**—a million people marched on the capital protesting against privatization of their Social Security. They wanted the multi-billion dollar lobbying industry outlawed; and there were more

street clashes against the wars.—In *Foggy Bottom* (the Washington DC area where the State Department, World Bank and IMF were located): other massive protests erupted against the World Bank and IMF. Demonstrators demanded the two organizations be separated from the G8 capital and run like the rest of the UN system—one country, one vote. Eggs, tomatoes and an occasional Molotov cocktail were thrown against their Ivory Tower office buildings; police retreated, overwhelmed. No help could be expected from their brethren in other cities. They were all struggling to contain street fighting at home. The military was spread too thin already, engaged overseas ... the Capital of the Free World was plunging into chaos....

>>> **Middle East—***Iraq*: A devastating, all destructive civil war was blending in with the scenario of total unrest of a *Middle East* in flames; *Beirut, Gaza*: Bombarded by Israeli rockets—in *Tel Aviv, Haifa, Jerusalem* and other major Israeli cities, escalating suicide attacks, bringing bloodshed and a seemingly unstoppable rising death toll ... A million-plus Israelis were walking the streets, occupying government buildings in demand of peace, of a halt to their leaders' aggression on Palestine, and requesting the outright resignation of their government.—The formation of a strong alliance between *Syria, the new Hezbollah government of Lebanon and Iran*, was fomenting massive demonstrations against U.S. forces in the region, fearlessly attacking U.S. Embassies and other U.S. held installations, corporate offices of oil companies, a movement that made Al Qaeda look like Kindergarten ... the beginning of the crumbling of the *House of Saud* became apparent, as U.S. support for their corrupt and inhuman government was dwindling ... in preparation of the White House's last attempt to secure at least a portion of the region's hydrocarbons by perhaps invading Saudi Arabia ...

>>> **Indonesia, Banda and throughout Aceh** (*Note 12*)—Inhabitants of this oil-rich northern territory of Sumatra island and the Indonesian

military, after years of fighting each other, finally were uniting, combining their strength to oppose the American military support of their oppressive and colonialist central government, the looting by U.S. corporations of their hydrocarbon treasures. A general of this reformed Indonesian military declared: "We have come to recognize how our country's elite has been usurping the riches of our land for their own and for corporate profits. We understand how they were using us [the Indonesian military] and the support of the U.S. war machine to meet their ends ..."

>>> **Oaxaca, Mexico**—A reporter speaks with a trembling voice: "Hundreds of thousands of demonstrators, coming from all over Mexico to express their solidarity with the people of Oaxaca, marched the streets to take back the town hall seized over a year ago by police and military using bulldozers, water canons and tear gas. At least a dozen people were killed, including local and international journalists, since the disturbances began. The Governor, who had full backing from the new Central Government, said repeatedly he would not resign. Truckloads full of heavily armed military are expected to arrive in this once picturesque capital city of Oaxaca. The predictable outcome may be that hundreds of unarmed peasant demonstrators and students will be shot dead ... but a miracle seemed to be happening ...

"The armed forces and police arrived as planned and confronted the gigantic crowd of peaceful demonstrators. Although they were shouting and throwing an occasional rock, they were unarmed, carrying signs asking for a new State Government, free elections ... There was a deadlock. Nobody was moving; just a few shouts and screams from the protesters amidst burning cars and tires. The police weren't shooting."

The camera focuses in on one elderly peasant demonstrator near the frontline. He stretched up his fists, shouting, "Why do you want to kill us? You are part of us. You are peasants like we. Can't you see we just want justice ..."

And then the miracle: The police chief turned around in front of the rows of soldiers and policemen, ordering them to move back, motioning with his arms to retreat. Now he was coming forward, reached his hand out to the farmer—and looking around the masses of people, he called out: "Peace, *amigos*, peace. We will go. This is your city, your state."

Deafening cheers rose from the crowds, as the camera followed the police captain turning back and signaling the troops to withdraw.

The reporter returned, "Not since the Zapata Revolution has Mexico seen a scene like this. The officer and his troops must have realized that a bloodbath would ensue and that it would serve no one, certainly not the country, not democracy and not them. We will have more on the peoples' triumph later ..."

>>> **New Orleans**—The poor and destitute, mostly black and brown hard-working people were taking over City Hall. They rebuffed the capitalists' appropriation of their Hurricane Katrina devastated homes, which were to be rebuilt as expensive profit yielding housing for the rich, leaving them nowhere to go, relegating them to the margins, to shantytowns spreading throughout Louisiana ...

>>> **London**—Anti-government demonstrations: Three million people in major cities across the country were fed up with their government's seemingly blind alliance with the United States. They demanded the resignation of the entire government, asking for new elections. The government seemed to yield: The Chancellor of the Exchequer issued a media statement saying that the demand of the people was being heard, that the government resigned; that effective immediately he, the treasurer, would assume leadership and form an interim government. New elections would be announced within a month. People in the streets were cheering for joy.

>>> **London and New York**—As the oil price hit US$180 per barrel, and SUV sales slumped to an all-time low, U.S. car manufacturers, those who had survived so far, declared bankruptcy. Hundreds of thousands of workers would lose their jobs. People the world over, including throughout the United States, were boycotting the astronomically obscene profits of ExxonMobile and other oil corporations for weeks by using bikes and public transportation, leaving cars at home and airlines stranded.

>>> **Nigeria**—The numerous explosions of oil pipelines were no longer mere 'accidents,' caused by petrol stealing thugs. They were deliberate attempts at shutting down American and British oil usurpers, Chavelin Oil, XXION Oil&Gas, UK-Petrol—the oil monsters who in pursuit of appropriating the country's riches had committed heinous crimes on Nigerian workers, indigenous people, the environment in the Gulf of Guinea. Millions of people were in the streets of Lagos, thousands were besieging the headquarters of these corporations, demanding an immediate shut-down of their operations. Oil production has almost come to a standstill. No end to the unrest is in sight ...

>>> **Miami**—Pensioners were venting their anger against the pharmaceutical and health insurance companies, whose interest it is to keep the sick and elderly alive as long as possible, but not healed, so they'll spend their last pennies on medical expenses with little quality of life in return. Instead they are plunging ever deeper into dependency on the pharma-medical charlatans and thieves. The demonstrators were waving placards saying *The American Health Care System is a Sick Care System*. Cursing and jeering against the profiteering pharmaceuticals and their buddies, the insurance industry, they were putting their lives in peril, and surrounding shops of major pharmacy chains ...

>>> **Chicago and New York**—Workers of all segments of society were taking to the streets in protest of an unlivable minimum wage, cuts in their pensions and health benefits. Medical personnel were protesting against ever longer work hours, low salaries, increasing carelessness and neglect of the profit-hungry medical system >>> A fourth day of strike by New York City transit workers whose pension and health benefits have been cut for the third time in two years. The metro workers say the work stoppage will not end until the city's multi-billionaire mayor resigned. He's been the instigator of the continuous downgrading of the workers' social benefits ...

>>> **Peru**—Protests in Lima, Cusco, Arequipa, Chiclayo, Chimbote and even in remote Iquitos, in the middle of the Amazon—millions of Peruvians demanded the closure of *CAMISEA*, the heinously destructive hydrocarbon wells in the Amazon. Demonstrators also expressed their anger about the creeping U.S. military invasion under the false pretense of fighting drugs. They demanded the immediate withdrawal of the American soldiers.—Protesters also rejected the devastating and poverty invoking *Free Trade Agreement* with the United States. They rebelled against their President who defrauded their country already in the 1980s and now was at the bidding of the Empire and against the interests of the people ...

>>> **In other news from Peru**—After a lengthy investigation, the Government denied its cooperation with the CIA in an attempt to kidnap a Peruvian citizen at the G-77 conference in Bangladesh. However, one of the potential capturers—the camera focused on a blurry picture of a hooded man—who obviously did not want his identity disclosed, confessed to having been trapped, along with two other students, by three Latino-American agents who said they worked for the Government of Peru ...

>>> **Brussels, Belgium**—The European Union announced that its Euro-currency members were to withdraw their support of the World Bank and the IMF. They were no longer contributing to the replenishment of the World Bank's soft arm, the International Development Association. Instead they would bolster their own development agency, the European Bank for Reconstruction and Development, expanding its range of operation to developing countries throughout the world with an agenda of primarily supporting social sectors ...

>>> **In other news from Brussels**—In a press conference, the European Union announced the gradual introduction of *Eudemonism*, a new economic model based on general wellbeing. The system would replace the constant capitalist urge for tangible growth. Instead, values like environmental protection, social equity, public health, equitable and healthy nutrition, would be assessed and constitute a country's wealth. Surplus values created by production would no longer end up as profit and paid out to shareholders as dividends. They would be used to finance new social and environmental infrastructure at home and abroad, in poor countries which had a long way to catch up with social justice. In fact the profit concept, as we know it, would disappear.

The newsflash went on saying the EU recognized that the new system could not be introduced at once and by all EU members, that it required long-term education to reorient people's thinking from individual consumerism to collective wellbeing. Spain had agreed to pioneer the new *eudemonist* economic order. As progress took hold, the concept would be adopted by other EU members.

>>> **Washington, DC and Iquitos, Peru**—On a funny note, TeleSur reported on a group of World Bank staffers, who were accompanying their new illustrious President on one of his famous 'free market' junkets, trying to convince developing country governments that for *sus-*

tainable globalization they all had to open up their borders and abandon trade barriers. Sensing that their boss needed a thorough brain reform, they abducted him in the middle of the night from his hotel room in Iquitos, where he was supposed to meet the following day with executive officers of newly established American petrol giants. His mission companions dragged him through the underground garage and drove him to *Nauta*, a small town some 90 kilometers west of Iquitos on the Amazon River. There, they loaded him onto a small fishing boat and took him four hours into the jungle, where they had arranged an *Ayahuasca* session for the former U.S. Trade Czar with a local shaman—compliments of Moni Cheng.

Ayahuasca is a hallucigenous liana of the Amazon rain forest, used as a concoction in native ceremonies to heal people from all kinds of maladies, including mental disorders. It is said to make people 'fly' out of their bodies and let them experience visions that would help guide them in their future lives.

"Observers say," the TeleSur correspondent reported tongue in cheek, "the new World Bank President emerged from the shaman's hut as a reformed man, ready to embark on a true mission of development, actually siding with the poor rather than the interests of the G8. Stay tuned ..."

>>> **Teheran, Iran**—trust in the dollar was further collapsing with Teheran's announcement of the opening the Iranian Oil Bourse which will be trading in Euros. This exacerbated the rush by treasuries around the globe into Euros ... a shift prompted by the earlier unpopular announcement of the U.S. Government and the IMF that the world's monetary system would return to the Gold Standard. The world's monetary system was being jeopardized. Countries may actually have to live according to their assets and domestic production capacity ... a new economic paradigm may emerge ...

>>> In other news from Teheran—the dozens of American warships stationed in the Persian Gulf which stood ready to attack Iran, retreated, as China announced it would not hold back from retaliating against any aggression on Iran, one of its chief gas and oil suppliers ...

* * *

The state of the world was decaying day by day. Public squares like the *Place des Nations* in Geneva were re-created the world over. They assembled millions of people in Paris, London Frankfurt, Madrid, Bangkok, Hong Kong, Singapore, Shanghai, Tokyo, Buenos Aires, Santiago, Caracas, La Paz, Mexico City ...

They broadcasted events and demonstrations for peace all over the globe—protests hurled at the United States supremacy, their hegemony, oppression of civil rights at home, utterly dismissing human rights abroad—thousands of people dying every day in wars and conflicts for the ruthless exploitation of natural resources, the filthily, soaring profits by mostly, but not exclusively U.S. corporations and their executives—and displayed slogans everywhere *"No Blood for the Elite!"*—*"Leave Oil, Gold and Diamonds in the Ground."*—*"Death to the Killer Corporations!"*—*"War Criminals to the Gallows!"*—*"Nuremberg for the Neocons!"*—And the always and persistent chant ... *"Fight terrorism with Justice not with Bullets ..."*

News from Iraq compounded the tragedy of the Western World:

>>> Iraq—moving into a full-fledged civil war
—Hundreds of Iraqis killed every day ...
—U.S. death toll reaching more than 500 per week ...

>>> In the United States

—Americans in the streets—millions of people in all major U.S. cities, demanding withdrawal from Iraq—the Middle East …
—The U.S. President declares a State of Emergency … sends the army and National Guard—what's left of it—into major U.S. cities in a hopeless effort to stem the anti-government movements …
—In a last ditch for power, the President announces from his hideout cancellation of the next Presidential elections …
—Demonstrations continue—police and military clash with marchers—violence, bloodshed ensues …
—Populace requests the resignation of the President and his cronies—he refuses bunkered down who knows where, probably in his elaborate underground foxhole beneath the White House …
—Police and lower ranking military personnel begin to associate with the people—defending rather than attacking them …
—President loses grip on country …
—Major media stations are taken over by the people …
—The White House.…

* * * * *

Final Chapter—Epilogue

PJ awoke slowly—mid morning—in a remote desert area in the Australian Outback. Still halfway dozing, he was able to discern the quiet hum of the ceiling fan in his room—the smell of fresh coffee meandering through the open door. Then the affectionate voice of a woman calling, "Breakfast is ready, darling!" pulled him ever so softly into the world of the living. His head was churning. Confused he stumbled into the bright sunny kitchen and sat at the table.

He told Moni Cheng: "I had this dream—it was like real …"

"What was it all about?"

"It started with flashbacks … the return of the Gold Standard, my former colleagues demonstrating in the streets of Washington … The World Bank breaking apart … the world was like a flat plane. I was racing towards its edge. I am not sure whether I was escaping from somewhere or running towards … what?—An abyss?

"When I got to the chasm at the end of the world, I just saw the falling and disappearing bodies of four white men and a black woman. They were all desperately looking towards me, arms outstretched, screaming, falling faster and faster until swallowed by darkness."

Moni Cheng couldn't help asking: "Did you recognize any of the five …?"

He smiled slyly, "No, not really …" and after a few moments, "But at the end, when I gradually woke up to the hushed rotation of the fan, I had a gut feeling that the world was no longer how we knew it, that we were moving towards a new politico-economic system … it was all so real …"

Moni Cheng laughed. "Well—let's turn on the TV.…"

PJ walked towards the tellie, when his cell phone rang with a calypso melody that identified his daughter, who was now studying in Geneva. When he last saw her, knowing about his plans of disappearing for a while, he'd given her a 'Worldstar' satellite phone with an Everywhere Power Pack, so that they could be in touch at any time. He answered at once: "Hi Preemie—what's up?"

"Dad! Dad!" An all excited girlish voice came over the phone. He put her on speaker for the benefit of Moni Cheng.

"Dad, have you been watching the news?"

"No, Sweetie, not lately. Why?"

"Oh, my God! Oh, my God!—Dad! You are so lost in no-man's-land, in the middle of nowhere; so uninformed, I can't believe it. The UN General Assembly just declared unanimously in a special emergency meeting that they would move their world Headquarters to Geneva. The world is upside-down. Totally! The United States is …" and her voice trailed off—started to fade. A crackling noise was taking over. There was a word he couldn't quite make out, sounded like '… *disintegrating* …', but the disturbance in the connection fractured the sound. It could also have been 'disengaging' …, 'disconnecting' … or maybe 'disappearing'?—No, no—can't be.

They smiled at each other. "Let's turn on the TV." The sun crept towards its zenith and warmly brightened the large veranda with the open glass doors. Together they rushed towards the widescreen plasma set.

THE END

Author's Notes

(Note 1)

Yanacocha is a gold mine in the Andean highlands of central Peru, some 18 km north of *Cajamarca*. This 251 square kilometer open pit, reaching altitudes of more than 4,000 m, is considered one of the most profitable gold mines in the world. It has produced more than $ 7 billion worth of gold to date. In 2004 it produced 3 million Troy Ounces of gold, about $ 2 billion worth, at December 2006 gold prices. It is so profitable that the World Bank's private sector development arm, the IFC, has taken a 5% equity share in the mine. Newmont Mining (U.S.) holds 51.35% and Minas Buenaventura (Peru) has a 43.65% share.

In 1994, the mine was co-owned by Buenaventura, a Peruvian mining company, and the Denver-based Newmont Mining Corporation, the world's largest mining company, which also operates it. The mine has been fraught with a history of disputed ownership and corruption, involving also French and Australian mining companies. In a political move that favors Newmont, the United States influenced Peruvian courts with promises of support in a border dispute with Ecuador. The decision came down to the advantage of Newmont which won controlling interests in the mine. Under other deals negotiated with the former Peruvian government, Newmont may expatriate all profits tax free.

Furthermore, *Yanacocha* is also an environmental calamity. The name *Yanacocha* means `*black lake*' in Quechua, the language of the local Indians. But the lake has long ago vanished as the result of ecological degradation due to the mining operations. The mine uses large quantities of cyanide in the gold extraction process. The heavy poison has polluted waterways, leading to the disappearance of fish, wildlife and fauna. In 2004, the planned expansion of *Yanacocha* to '*Cerro Quilish*', the source of water supply to Cajamarca, was stopped by popular uprising. Water contamination, environmental damage and poisoning of close to 1,000 people in and around the town of *Choropampa*, caused by a 151 kg cyanide spill, is also the subject of a lawsuit in the courts of Denver. (*Main source: Wikipedia.com*)

In December 2007, the President of Peru gave the green light to expand *Yanacocha's* operations to the sacred mountain, *Cerro Quilish*.

*   *   *   *   *

(Note 2)

CAMISEA's gas deposits are located in the lower *Urubamba* Valley, in *San Martin* and *Cashiriari* of the Department (now called Region) of Cuzco, Peru, bordering on the Region of *Madre de Dios*, one of the world's richest areas in bio-diversity. The gas fields were discovered in 1984 by Royal Dutch/Shell. Proven reserves were indicated with 8.7 trillion cubic feet of natural gas (NG) and 545 million barrels of liquid gas (NGL) reserves. More recent estimates put these figures at 13 trillion and 600 million respectively. The value of these reserves could be as high as US$ 450 billion at current prices. A 40-year concession has been awarded in 2000 to two overlapping international consortia, one for gas production, another for gas transportation and distribution.

The cost of this project's <u>First Phase</u> is estimated at US$ 1.6 billion, of which the Inter-American Development Bank (IDB) finances a mere US$ 75 million, but by doing so is leveraging other funding from *Corporación Andina de Fomento* (CAF), the US ExIm Bank, SACE, the Italian export financing institution, BNDES, the Brazilian Development ment Bank and Peruvian commercial banks. The First Phase has three components. (1) The *Upstream Component*: gas exploration and exploitation, a gas processing plant in Las Malvinas, a gas liquefaction plant and marine loading terminal in *Paracas*. The *Upstream Consortium* consists of U.S. Texas-based Harbinger Oil, Pluspetrol (Argentina), SK Corporation (South Korea), and Tecpetrol, owned by Techint (Argentina). (2) The *Downstream Component*: Pipelines to *Lurin*, near the port of *Callao* and Lima (715 km) and to the marine terminal in *Paracas* (540 km). The *Downstream Consortium* comprises Tecgas (Argentina 23.4%), Harbinger Oil (22.2%), Pluspetrol (22.2%), SK Corporation (11.1%), Sonatrach (Algeria 11.1%), Tractebel (Belgium 8%) and Graña y Montero (Peru 2%). Construction of the gas processing plant for natural gas liquids in *Paracas* is contracted to Kellogg, Brown and Root, a subsidiary of Halliburton. (3) The *Distribution Component* of NG in Lima and Callao was awarded to Tractebel.

CAMISEA II—A <u>Second Phase</u> is under preparation to exploit new, adjacent gas fields. It would add another $1 to $2 billion to the cost.

About 50 % of the gas is expected to be exported to the US, but deals with Chile, Mexico and Argentina are also being discussed.

The project is said to add about 1% per year to Peru's GDP. This does not take into account the environmental and social damage caused by the project. During the five years of exploration by Shell in the 1980s, about half of the *Nahua* people died from infections contracted from the workers. The Nahua tribe lived isolated from civilization. The massive deforestation needed for the exploitation and the pipeline construction also caused uncountable damage. The displacement of native people and the continuous gas spills jeopardized their livelihood. Between mid-2004 and the end of 2005, at least four liquid gas leaks occurred. One of the more recent gas spills of liquid gas happened in the *Machiguenga* Communal Reserve, in a pristine tropical rain forest. At particular risk is the upper Urubamba basin, where the *Machiguenga* tribe lives. This part of the Amazon rainforest is renowned for one of the world's richest areas of bio-diversity. River contamination kills fish by the thousands. At peril are entire species, but foremost is the livelihood of indigenous people.

Initial royalties are said to be about 8% of the value of extracted hydrocarbons.

According to IDB loan conditions, the government agreed to set a small percentage of the royalties aside for mitigating damage incurred by indigenous people. Instead, in 2005 it channeled 40% of royalties into a special fund to buy weapons for the military and police. The IDB as well as the U.S. Government ignored this breach of contract. It will likely boost U.S. arms sales to Peru.

In November 2007, the President of Peru has given green light to go ahead with *CAMISEA II*.

In December 2007 the Free Trade Agreement between the United States and Peru was ratified. As a last minute give-away, the Peruvian Government allowed about a half a dozen U.S. Oil giants to establish their bases in the Peruvian Amazon to explore and exploit the region's vast hydrocarbon resources—and further destroy its pristine biodiversity.

*   *   *   *   *

(Note 3)

The World Bank and the International Monetary Fund (IMF) are also called the *Bretton Woods Institutions*. They were created under the charter of the United Nations, in July 1944, when delegates of 45 Allied Nations met at the Mount Washington Hotel in Bretton Woods, New Hampshire. The conference established the International Monetary Fund (IMF) and the International Bank for Reconstruction and Development (IBRD), later called the World Bank. The World Bank Group comprises five agencies: the IBRD, International Finance Corporation (IFC), International Development Association (IDA), Multilateral Investment Guarantee Agency (MIGA), and the International Centre for Settlement Disputes (ICSID).

The two international organizations became effective in 1946. The IMF was to regulate and monitor the international monetary system, based on the *'Gold Standard'*—the convertibility of industrialized nations' currencies at a fixed exchange rate to gold—1 Troy Ounce (31.1 grams) = US$ 35. This was the official inter-country exchange rate, even though the market price for industrial uses of gold was much higher. When in 1970 the U.S. ran a huge balance of payment deficit due to the Vietnam War, Nixon unilaterally canceled the Gold Standard and the Bretton Woods agreements at large, liberating huge sums of reserve gold to be sold on the open market, raising the price rapidly above US$ 300 per oz. This occurred on August 15, 1971.

The World Bank was to help finance reconstruction of post-war Europe.

The **International Trade Organization (ITO)**, also proposed at the Bretton Woods Conference, and later agreed to at the UN Conference on Trade and Development, held in Havana, Cuba, in March 1948, failed to be established, since it was not ratified by the U.S. Senate.

At the 1995 Uruguay Round of GATT (General Agreement on Tariffs and Trade), the **World Trade Organization (WTO)** came into existence.

The World Bank, IMF and WTO representing neo-classical economics complement each other and emerged at once as the three most controversial agencies under the UN Charter.

The World Bank and the IMF, though UN affiliates, with 184 members each (December 2006), are basically run by the U.S. and dominated by the world's eight richest nations, the G8 (Britain, Canada, France, Germany, Italy, Japan, Russia and the United States). Unlike in the UN proper, where one country has one vote, in these two institutions, the richer a country the higher its voting right. The United States' share in the World Bank is 16.4%, followed by the UK and France with 4.3% each. Key decisions require an 85% majority, meaning the U.S. can block any motion they don't like.

The 1961 reformed **OECD (Organization for Economic Cooperation and Development)** was created by 20 industrialized member states (30 members in 2006) to help administer the Marshall Plan ($ 13 billion—in today's terms $130 billion). The funds, destined to rebuild war-torn Europe, were channeled through the World Bank.

OECD countries account for about two-thirds of all the World Bank's shares. Developing countries hold a mere token of representation.

The two international bodies, World Bank and IMF, wield enormous influence in the world's economies. They have become convenient instruments in manipulating capital flows according to the interests of the rich, and since the mid-1990s, they've pursued a U.S. neo-conservative agenda. According to many critics, they help indebt the poor but resource-rich countries to such a degree that they have no choice but to sell their resources for a pittance to be able to service their debt. The World Bank's favored, albeit controversial, lending instrument consists of *structural adjustment* and different kinds of *budget support* loans (*Development Policy Loans—DPL; Sector Wide Approach Projects—SWAP*), euphemisms for no-questions-asked 'blank check' transfers. They are similar to IMF loans.

By 2002, these loans exceeded 50% of the World Bank's annual loan portfolio. Today they fluctuate between 35% and 45% per year. Under this scheme the World Bank transfers billions of dollars to developing countries' treasuries, no strings attached, no transparency of spending, no serious accountability, and no procurement rules imposed. These transactions, pleasing the elite, have no tangible economic or social benefit for the countries who receive them, but they add to a mounting debt burden and foster corruption. Moreover, by conveying with these loans to the international financial world at large a false trust in the integrity of corrupt governments, the World Bank's and the IMF's blanket transfers may leverage billions of additional funds from private banks.

The proportion of *project lending* activities, socioeconomic development and basic infrastructure have drastically declined in the World Bank's portfolio. These activities, better suited for economic development, are closely supervised by World Bank staff, including the application of strict procurement rules. With the ascent of the Washington Consensus of neo-liberal '*laissez faire*' economics, these traditional operations serve merely as a 'poverty alleviation' publicity stunt, a veneer for the public-at-large to disguise the disastrous '*blank check*' operations.

*   *   *   *   *

(Note 4)

Buenos Aires Water Utility, Argentina: >>> *"Privatize or perish,"* is a slogan touted by the World Bank in the 1990s and was taken over by President Menem of Argentina.

In 1993, the government privatized the Buenos Aires water utility under heavy pressure from the World Bank, the IMF, and the U.S. Government. The alleged reason: private firms would be better at bringing water and sewage connections to poor areas. Privatization as a concept, together with the dollarization of the nation's economy, could help save Argentina from an economic crisis that had produced hyper-inflation of almost 5,000 % in 1989.

The government granted a 30-year concession to *'Aguas Argentinas,'* a consortium controlled by two French corporate giants, *'Compagnie Générale des Eaux'* (now *Veolia Environment*) and *'Lyonnaise des Eaux'* (now *Suez*). The consortium promised to reduce water rates and to improve and expand water and sewage services to poor neighborhoods. The World Bank declared the Buenos Aires privatization an over-whelming success, made it a model for privatization of water that followed with similar schemes in the Philippines, Indonesia, and South Africa.

In reality, the Buenos Aires water privatization was a disaster. Tariffs increased and service expansion to the poor did not meet contractual agreements. The move enriched a group of union leaders, crony capitalists and officials in the government of former President Carlos Menem. The economic crisis and the related peso devaluation put pressure on *'Aguas Argentinas,'* which obtained at least 75 percent of the money it invested from the World Bank and allied international financial institutions.

In March 2006, *'Aguas Argentinas'* was renationalized and is called *'Aguas y Saneamientos Argentinos'*.

*   *   *   *   *

(Note 5)

Privatizing of water supply in Cochabamba, Bolivia—At the insistence of the World Bank to reduce subsidies, *Cochabamba* privatized its municipal water supply services in 2000—*'Aguas de Tunari'*—by concession contract to International Waters Limited (IWL), a UK subsidiary of Bechtel Corporation of California. *'Aguas de Tunari'* under foreign management, imposed large tariff increases, amounting to an average monthly bill of US$ 20—as compared to an average wage of less than US$ 70/month. In addition, IWL demanded that peasants pay for rainwater collected from their roofs.

In mid-January 2000, Cochabamba residents shut down the city for four days in a general strike, led by an alliance of labor, human rights and community leaders. The Government relented in agreeing to roll back prices. Details were to be worked out within two weeks. In early February 2000, during a peaceful demonstration pressing for settlement, Dictator Hugo Banzer used violent repression, tear gas, and shooting—6 people died, 175 injured. But the people did not back down. They insisted that IWL/Bechtel must leave. They closed down the city again starting April 4, 2000.

The Government declared martial law. The police took over the streets. They shot and killed a 17-year old boy. On April 10, the Government finally conceded, agreeing to every demand the people made. IWL/Bechtel left, now suing the state of Bolivia before the 'International Centre for Settlement of Investment Disputes' (ICSID), a court which is part of the World Bank Group.

*   *   *   *   *

(Note 6)

The Group of 77 (G-77) was established in 1964, at the end of the first session of the United Nations Conference on Trade and Development (UNCTAD) in Geneva by 77 developing countries. They were the signatories of the "Joint Declaration of the Seventy-Seven Countries." The first Ministerial Meeting of the G-77 was held in Algiers in 1967. It adopted the Charter of Algiers, a permanent institutional structure, gradually leading to the creation of Chapters of the Group of 77 in Rome (FAO), Vienna (UNIDO), Paris (UNESCO), Nairobi (UNEP) and the Group of 24 in Washington, D.C. (IMF and World Bank). The membership has since increased to 133 countries, but the original name was retained, because of it historic significance.

The purpose of this largest Third World coalition is to articulate and promote collective economic interests, enhance its joint negotiating power in the UN system and promote economic and technical cooperation among developing countries (ECDC/TCDC).

Activities of the G-77 are coordinated by a chairman who rotates on a regional basis between Africa, Asia, and Latin America and the Caribbean. Ministerial Meetings, the highest decision making body of the G-77, are convened annually at the beginning of the UN General Assembly in New York. They also assemble periodically in preparation for the UNCTAD sessions and the general conferences of UNIDO and UNESCO.

Member states and other developing countries finance the G-77 activities. They include joint declarations, action programs and agreements on specific topics, such as the Arusha Program for Self-Reliance (1979); Agreement on a Global System of Trade Preferences among Developing Countries (1988); the San Jose Declaration and Plan of Action on South-South Trade, Investment and Finance (1997), and more. Their actions, negotiations, and pronouncements are carried out under the aegis of the United Nations.
(*Main sources: Wikipedia.com, and G77.org*)

*　　　*　　　*　　　*　　　*

(Note 7)

The Washington Consensus is a set of policies promulgated by neoliberal economists to promote economic growth, initially in many parts of Latin America, later throughout the world, by introducing various market-oriented economic reforms to make the target economy look like the United States. It was first presented in 1989 by
John Williamson, an economist from the Institute for International Economics, an international economic think-tank based in
Washington, D.C.. It attempts to summarize the commonly-shared themes among policy advice by Washington-based institutions, such as the International Monetary Fund, World Bank, and U.S. Treasury Department, which were believed to be necessary for the recovery of Latin America from the financial crises of the 1980s.
The dogma of the so-called '*Reforms*' were initiated in 1989 and gradually adopted by the two Bretton Woods organizations. The World Bank summarizes them in its year 2000 Poverty Report. They are still—and increasingly so—the ongoing policy of these institutions:
> *Fiscal policy* discipline

> Redirection of _public spending_ toward education, health and infra-structure _investment_.
> _Tax reform_—Flattening the tax curve: Lowering the tax rates on pro-portionally high tax brackets (typically above median income), and raising the tax rates on the proportionally low tax brackets (typically below median income); lowering the marginal tax rate.
> _Interest rates_ that are market determined and positive (but moderate) in real terms.
> Competitive _exchange rates_.
> Trade _liberalization_—replacement of quantitative restrictions with low and uniform _tariffs_.
> Openness to _foreign direct investment_.
> _Privatization_ of state enterprises.
> _Deregulation_—abolition of regulations that impede entry or restrict competition, except for those justified on safety, environmental and consumer protection grounds, and prudent oversight of _financial institutions_.
> Legal security for _property rights_.
(Quote from Wikipedia.com)

*   *   *   *   *

(Note 8)

The US Military Base in _Manta_, Ecuador—is the subject of a ten-year lease agreement between the United States and Ecuador. The U.S. says the base is there to help the people of _Manta_. According to an anti-U.S military base group called _'Movimiento Tohalli,'_ "_Manta_ is part of a broader U.S. imperialist strategy aimed at exploiting the con-tinent's natural resources, suppressing popular movements, and ulti-mately invading neighboring Colombia. The base in Ecuador is an integral part of the U.S. counterinsurgency strategy in Colombia.

Ecuadorians worry that the U.S. could pull their country into conflict. The base is also used to block mass emigration from Ecuador to the U.S.

Officially, U.S. activities at the base are to be limited to counter-narcotics surveillance flights. Ecuadorian citizens are not happy with the base or the way the US has abused it. In Colombia, the U.S. is intervening through private corporations. Most of the military operations and spraying of biochemical agents are contracted out to private firms and private armies. DynCorp, one of the private American defense contractors, runs the military base in *Manta*. The Pentagon's decision for DynCorp to run the base indicates that the U.S. has more than drug interdiction in mind when it set up shop in *Manta*. DynCorp was awarded a $600 million contract to carry out aerial spraying to eliminate coca crops which also contaminates maize, yucca and plantain-staple foods of the population; children and adults develop skin rashes. The chemical, the foundation for the herbicide Roundup, is sprayed in Ecuador in a manner that would be illegal in the United States.
(*Sources: Project Censured, www.projectcensured.org/censored 2006/ index.htm#17; Michael Flynn, Bulletin of the Atomic Scientist, Jan/Feb 2005; Sohan Sharma and Surinder Kumar, 'Z Magazine', December 29, 2004*)

The new Government of Ecuador has declared it will not renew the lease contract when it expires in 2009, unless the U.S. Government allows Ecuador to set up a base in Florida.

*   *   *   *   *

(Note 9)

Comparative Advantages of US Corporations

—First, <u>US corporations dominate the United States political process.</u> In the two-party system, Republicans and Democrats, both are right-wing parties (one a little more than the other), they are both paid by the same corporations, and both are committed to facilitating expansion of US corporate power, something that is not imaginable in the multi-party democracies of Europe.

—Second, <u>only about 10% of the private sector labor force belongs to trade unions</u>—and these 10% depend totally on the two parties. There is no socialist or left political challenge to the decision-making process governing social issues (unlike in Europe). U.S. trade union leaders are often working with corporate officials, reducing benefits, forcing new technologies, and new job classifications. They are helping to out-source secondary services. The U.S. corporate workers are at the mercy of corporate profit-maximizing principles; their union leaders are hostages to 'job security'.

—Third, <u>U.S. corporate taxes are the lowest of the industrialized world</u>, accounting only for 10% of federal revenues. Income taxes on wages amount to almost 50%. US corporations have the highest percentage of workers without health coverage of any industrialized and semi-industrialized country, all factors leading to greater profits, greater potential to buy out competition around the world.

—Fourth, <u>the US Treasury prints money freely and indiscriminately</u> to finance the nation's huge and increasing debt. No other industrialized/OECD country does the same. Because the US dollar is still the official reserve currency for most of the world, the debt burden is distributed around the world by Treasury Bonds (*total estimated debt US$ 8.6 trillion (late 2006), increasing daily by about 3 to 4 billion*)—to protect their economies, owners of the debt have no interest in an abrupt collapse of the US economy.

—Fifth, <u>the U.S. Treasury officials are the most influential members of the Board and staff of the World Bank and IMF</u>, dictating economic policies through 'reform' mechanisms, facilitating privatization of public services and natural resources, and finally U.S. corporate takeovers.

—**Sixth**, <u>the U.S. imperial state exerts power and influence throughout the world</u>, through its many agencies (Pentagon, CIA, Commerce, Treasury, its stronghold on NATO in Europe), aiding and facilitating the seizing of foreign assets by U.S. corporations.

—**And finally**—<u>nowhere else in the world exists as strong a corporate amalgamation</u> through mutual funds—currently at the rate of about $7 trillion, about half the US corporate capital—geared to maximize quarterly profits for the benefits of the 'shareholders' (and the companies CEOs!), an incentive and drive to infiltrate (mostly poor) foreign countries to exploit their natural resources and labor forces. This happens mostly in total disrespect of human rights and environmental protection around the world.

*   *   *   *   *

(Note 10)

Size of world's largest banks based on core capital

(shareholder's equity or *'tier 1 capital'*)—Figures in billions of U.S. dollars (2005)

1. Citigroup (U.S.)	79
2. HSBC (Hong Kong)	75
3. Bank of America (U.S.)	73
4. JP Morgan Chase (U.S.)	72
5. Mitsubishi UFJ Financial Group (Japan)	64
6. Crédit Agricole Group (France)	60
7. Royal Bank of Scotland (U.K.)	48
8. Sumitomo Mitsui Financial Group (Japan)	40

9. Mizuho Financial Group (Japan)   39

10. Santander Central Hispano (Spain)   38

... World Bank (International Organization)   32

(Sources: Wikipedia.com; WB Annual Report 2006)

*   *   *   *   *

(Note 11)

The current Darfur conflict started in February 2003, when two non-Arab groups, the Justice and Equality Movement (JEM) and the Sudan Liberation Movement (SLM) accused the Khartoum Government of discriminating against non-Arabs and attacked government forces. An armed militia composed of Arab rebels from neighboring Chad and western Sudan (Darfur), the *Janjaweed* ('armed men on horseback', or 'outlaws') have been in existence since 1988. They are primarily pursuing control over land and water. They are fighting the non-Muslim blacks of Darfur. The similarity in skin color and faith (Muslims are on both sides) of the two factions exacerbates the problem. It is often difficult to distinguish who is fighting whom. As a result, distrust of the population is everywhere.

The '*Janjaweed*' are armed and supported by the Sudanese government and became Khartoum's *de facto* counter-insurgency force, although government officials vehemently deny it. What started as a local civil war of competing farmers and cattle-herders in Sudan's arid western province of Darfur, escalated into a brutal political and ethnic genocide, claiming more than 200,000 lives and displacing in excess of 2.5 million people from their homes. Many of them have become refugees in Chad; a country itself now plunged into brutal civil war. Interestingly enough, both Darfur and Chad are rich in hydrocarbons.

With the failed 2004 'Humanitarian Ceasefire Agreement' on Darfur, a new peace agreement was reached in April 2006. While fighting continues, ruling sheiks of the region are skeptical that a truce might take hold, because the accord was signed only by small belligerent nomadic tribes. Under the new peace agreement, the United Nations is to replace the 7,000 African Union troops, who had the narrow mandate to monitor, not to enforce, the 2004 ceasefire—a daunting challenge in a territory as large as France. But the Sudanese government doesn't want the U.N. controlling its territory. There is logic behind it. All too often the U.N. has been a door-opener for U.S. troops to invade a country. The allusion to the two recent cases of Iraq and Afghanistan is unmistakable. The former, rich with hydrocarbons, was trampled to the ground during 10 years of U.S.—imposed U.N. sanctions and has become an easy prey for invasion. The other was the link to gigantic oil reserves in Central Asia, which needed to be connected by pipeline to the Indian Ocean. Even if one disagreed with the Sudanese position, the argument was undeniably valid.
(*Main source: Wikipedia.com*)

* * * * *

(Note12)

Synopsis of Indonesia's 'hot spots'—Indonesia consists of 17,500 islands within a space of 1.9 million km^2. Since independence from Dutch colonial rule in 1949, the government struggled against various secessionist conflicts and independence wars to keep the island state together. The strongest movements took and are taking place in regions that abound in natural resources.

Papua—is Indonesia's easternmost province (formerly Irian Jaya), with the capital of *Jayapura*, on the northwestern coast of Papua. The province covers a surface of about 422,000 km2 with a population of about 2.8 million (2005 est.), divided into a dozen ethnic groups. Up to 700 indigenous languages are spoken. About 75 percent of the population is Christian and 25 percent Moslem.

While colonized by the Dutch in 1848, Papua gained self-rule on December 1, 1961. Under the aegis of the UN the Papuans were told to decide within six years whether to stay independent or be incorporated into Indonesia. Instead, in 1963 Indonesia annexed Papua and called it Irian Jaya. Since then the province has been involved in constant secessionist skirmishes, killing thousands of Papuans in the last four decades. The Free Papua Movement (Indonesian acronym OPM) was created in 1965 and is as of this day struggling for Papua's independence.

Under a UN-sponsored referendum in 1969, the 'Act of Free Choice', Papuans voted for integration with Indonesia—though many Papuans and foreign observers claimed the vote was rigged.

The fight for independence and increased control over its resources was exacerbated with the gold mining operations of Grasberg, owned and managed by the U.S. conglomerate Freeport-McMoRan and the ensuing horrendous environmental devastation and human rights abuses. In 2002, the province achieved Special Autonomy and adopted the name of *Papua*.

Aceh province (capital *Banda Aceh*) at the northeastern tip of Sumatra (pop. 4 million) also waged a bitter independence war for close to 30 years. It killed about 15,000 *Acehnese*. The Free Aceh Movement (GAM) was born in 1976. Its main objective is to gain full sovereignty of the province—which is to be seen in the context of the 1971 discovery of huge gas reserves (according to some estimates among the largest in the world). They are ruthlessly exploited by ExxonMobil with the support of the Indonesian and United States military. A 2005 peace agreement aims at ending the conflict. But mistrust and lingering clashes continue, as the issue of an equitable distribution of the hydrocarbon revenues remains unresolved.

East Timor—colonized by Portugal in the 16th Century became in 2002 the first new country in the 21st Century. The Republic (surface 14,600 km2; population 950,000—2005 estimate), capital city *Dili*, is predominantly Catholic and one of the world's poorest countries with a GDP of $400 (Purchasing Power Parity—PPP—adjusted). Literally abandoned by Portugal, on November 28, 1975, East Timor declared itself independent, but was invaded nine days later by the infamous Indonesian military, which received the overt support of the United States. In a meeting with then Indonesian President Suharto, U.S. President Ford and Secretary of State Henry Kissinger gave their 'green light' to the invasion and supplied virtually all the arms to the Indonesian military which was known for torture, mass killings and other abject human rights abuses. In fact, Kissinger noted in his meeting with Suharto that this take-over better be quick, lest the U.S.-made arms [which the world may discover] could cause problems. The U.S. support was but an act of solidarity with an invaluable, oil rich Asian ally who was also a major client of the U.S. mammoth weapons' industry. Arms sales to Indonesia continued throughout the Clinton Administration. Amnesty International estimated the death toll during the Indonesian occupation of East Timor at 200,000.

Under a UN sponsored self-determination referendum, East Timor decided in 1999 for independence. But skirmishes with the Indonesian military and pro-Indonesia Timorese militia continued many bloody battles until a UN-brokered peace agreement gave East Timor inde-

pendence status (on May 20, 2002) and made it the 192nd member of the UN in September of the same year.
(*Main source: Wikipedia.com*)

The main causes for conflicts over control of East Timor are hydrocarbon resources. The recently discovered off-shore *Greater Sunrise Gas Field*, conservatively estimated at a value of $ 40 billion, located 170 km southeast of East Timor, continues to be a source of disagreement and international court cases between Australia and East Timor. Australian oil extracting companies offered a miserly 18% royalty to East Timor, walking away with 82% of the benefits, reminiscent of Bolivia before Evo Morales. Ongoing negotiations would split the benefits equally between Australia and East Timor.

*   *   *   *   *

(Note13)

Grasberg is known to be the largest gold and third largest copper mine in the world. It is located on the 4,884 meter high *Mount Jaya* in the *Sudirman* Mountains of Papua (former Irian Jaya) the easternmost province of Indonesia. The mountain is considered sacred by the local population.

The mine was built in 1988 near *Timika* by Freeport, at a cost of $ 3 billion. Today it is owned and operated by Freeport McMoRan, the largest U.S. mining conglomerate. The mining operations, one of the country's richest assets, are shrouded in secrecy. Indonesian military and police generals were said to be paid about $ 5 million in three years (NY Times) to protect the mine from environmental activists and journalists. Such payments are illegal under Indonesia law, but the government turns a blind eye to these and other acts of corruption.

The mine's treasures are estimated at 46 million ounces of gold (at current prices about $35 billion), plus about 18 million tons of copper (about $ 120 billion). 2005 production:
—700,000 tons of copper
—2.9 million ounces of gold
Total 2005 earnings of $ 4.1 billion of which less than 2% go to the central government. Yet it is said to be Indonesia's largest single source of income.

The mine has a crater of about 2 km in diameter, with a pit almost 1,000 m deep. It is socially and environmentally highly controversial, producing daily 700,000 tons of toxic tailings (mine waste) which are dumped into *Lake Wanagon* and the *Ajkwa River*, destroying an entire ecosystem of wetlands (230 km2) and tropical rain forest (130 km2).

The mine employs about 18,000 workers and has controversial human rights record, blemished by abuses of all kinds, murder and torture. It is therefore regularly involved in skirmishes with activist groups.
(*Main sources: New York Times, Wikipedia.com*)

*   *   *   *   *

(Note 14)

Eudemonism—The Greek philosopher Aristotle (384 BC—322 BC), student of Plato's, developed a concept of ethics (*Eudaimonism*) that centers on human happiness and wellbeing. Though it focuses first on the individual (inner happiness), Plato later extended the theory to the whole society by applying 'the correct social rules', behaving in ways that do not contradict inner happiness, one's own conscience. This state of wellbeing is not linked to material goods, but rather to 'good deeds' one accomplishes—or in the extended form, actions a society carries out for the common good, doing no harm to individuals or segments of society.

One of the more recent applications of the concept of *Eudemonism* stems from the liberal Australian political theorist, *Clive Hamilton*. In his book about economics and politics, *"Growth Fetish"* (2002), he argues that unfettered capitalism which made its rapid ascent after the Second World War, has largely failed. Despite the overall increases in personal wealth, people are not happier today than 50 years ago. To the contrary, he argues, the pursuit of growth has become a fetish that instead of curing all of society's ills, it has produced high costs in terms of environmental destruction, erosion of democracy, as well as the degradation of social values as a whole. He proposes a system in which societies who live reasonably well would divert their economic 'surplus' (growth) to create the social and physical infrastructure in poor nations that have not yet reached the level of wealth required for 'comfortable living'. Under this theory, *Eudemonism* becomes an economic concept in which the yardstick of general wellbeing would replace GDP.

*   *   *   *   *

978-0-595-45349-8
0-595-45349-X